The Education of Ruby Loonfoot

The Education of Ruby Loonfoot

Paxton Riddle

Five Star • Waterville, Maine

The characters in this book are fictional. Any relation to real people, living or dead, is purely coincidental. To protect the sacredness of the biijiinag bakaanigeng oshkiniigikwe, the ceremony described herein is not the Ojibwe ceremony. It is the puberty ceremony outlined by Black Elk in The Sacred Pipe (University of Oklahoma Press, Joseph Epes Brown, recorder and editor). According to an Ojibwe elder who performs this ceremony, the two ceremonies are similar.

First edition, second printing.

Published in 2003 in conjunction with Paxton W. Riddle.

Set in 11 pt. Plantin by Al Chase.

Printed in the United States on permanent paper.

Library of Congress Cataloging-in-Publication Data

Riddle, Paxton.
The education of Ruby Loonfoot / Paxton Riddle.
p. cm.—(Five Star first edition women's fiction series)
ISBN 0-7862-4437-2 (hc : alk. paper)
1. Indians of North America—Fiction. 2. Conflict of generations—Fiction. 3. Mothers and daughters—Fiction. 4. Boarding schools—Fiction. 5. Catholic schools—Fiction. 6. Ojibwa women—Fiction. I. Title. II. Series.
PS3568.I3584 E34 2002
813′.54—dc21 2002026613

For Beth and Courtney

Acknowledgments

Special thanks to honored Ojibwe elder Eddie Benton Benai (*Bau-dway-Widun*), grand chief of the *Midewiwin* lodge. Your advice and assistance was valued greatly, along with your permission to use material from *The Mishnomis Book: The Voice of the Ojibway* and other material. I must also thank my friends and colleagues with Shelton Working Writers who faithfully read every chapter and made valuable comments. Thanks for remaining Ruby's biggest fans.

Also, many thanks to my Indian-sensitive editor Russell Davis, who helped bring Ruby to life via the graces of Five Star Press.

Foreword

The incidents of physical and mental abuse in this book are very real. They are the testimony of Native residential school students in Canada and the United States. At the time of this writing, court cases are still on the dockets in Canada, and as we go to press, the American media are rife with stories about priest pedophiles.

St. Nicholas School represents a composite of Native boarding schools in these two countries, though most were co-educational. Likewise, Ruby Loonfoot represents a kind of "everyman"—a composite of male and female experiences. In fairness, various religions operated residential schools where Native children had positive and rewarding experiences. But many did not. Soon after Native people were exiled to reservations,* missionaries flocked to the rescue. The reason for boarding schools, as opposed to reservation "day schools" was that you could not "wash out the Indian" in children if they were allowed to return home each day. Overenthusiastic churchmen and women, who seldom tried to understand Native spirituality, told Indian children that they were pagans and would burn in hell if they did not convert to Christianity and cease their practice of tribal ceremonies and traditions. Few ecclesiastics searched for commonalities.

Non-Native people often wonder how Indian parents and tribal officials allowed this to happen. As one Ojibwe elder put it: "In those days the Church was God in Indian country. People were scared to death of them." Thanks to the government, from the establishment of the reservation system and into the mid-twentieth century, tribal councils lay in shambles amid malaise and poverty. The federal government was firmly in charge of tribal activities. In the early days, at least in the United States, the government appointed chiefs. Once open tribal elections were allowed, the government maintained control of the electoral process and held sway over the council via an official from the Bureau of Indian Affairs (BIA), who usually sat in at council meetings.

Native people who stayed on "the rez" found themselves to be not unlike prisoners of war—dependent on the fickle goodwill of their subjugators. Suffice it to say that those of us who didn't experience reservation life between 1840 and 1970 will never truly grasp the situation.

And so boarding school students learned first to be ashamed of themselves, then of their parents and grandparents, some of whom remained traditional Indians back home. This book is for them.

One important postscript. Due to the sacredness of the Ojibwe puberty ceremony depicted in this book, I have used instead the puberty ceremony outlined by Black Elk in *The Sacred Pipe* (University of Oklahoma Press, Joseph Epes Brown, recorder and editor). However, according to an Ojibwe elder who performs this ceremony, the two rituals are similar.

By 1957, the time period used for this story, these schools had for the most part "cleaned up their act" in the United States, and many tribes were sending their children to local public schools under the Johnson-O'Malley Act and Public Law 874. But in Canada, physical and sexual abuse at residential schools continued into the 1970s. Over twenty years later, many who had been abused as students finally came forward to give testimony.

* It is telling that the Ojibwe word for reservation is *shkonigun*, meaning “left over.”

Dear Reader,

Though I've taken "literary license" this is my story, my recreation of 1957, a year that culminated my girlhood and transformed me into womanhood, and later, into a teacher. I've not spoken to those outside my family about these things until now. It took that long for the healing.

I was one of the lucky ones. Though we had our troubles, I had a loving family, a home to escape to over the summer. So, unlike many of my Indian brothers and sisters who came home troubled or broken from boarding schools, I managed to survive with my spirit intact. Much of this must be attributed to my grandmother's love, strength and teachings, which stands as testimony to the importance of family and cultural roots. It is to her, and all elders like her—to the wisdom-keepers, the faith-keepers, the spirit-tenders—that I dedicate this book. And to my fellow boarding-school survivors, who find themselves unable to read this story because of the memories it brings; I reach out to you with my spirit. You are in my thoughts and my prayers. The healing will come.

Ruby Loonfoot
Bineshee Ogichidaw

P.S. For non-Ojibwe readers, I've included a glossary of terms at the end of the book.

PART I

St. Nic's

"Now I will no longer have to hide my tears in the rain."
—Suicide note of Cyril Paul,
Indian boarding-school graduate.

"Let all that is Indian within you die. You cannot become truly American citizens—industrious, intelligent, cultured, civilized—until the Indian within you is dead."
—Principal's commencement address,
Carlisle Indian School, 1893

Chapter One

A cold, spare December dawn crept over Loon Lake, momentarily stirring Cecelia Pitwoniquot. The grating caws of a murder of crows brought her to wakefulness. She groped for and found her eyeglasses on the shelf next to the bed, then squinted at the dented oversized alarm clock. She hadn't been able to afford a new eyeglass prescription in eight years, and one of the clock's legs had broken off so that it sat lopsided, making it trickier to decipher.

Hazy light filtering through the window hinted that it was well past dawn. It was a good thing no one was around to see her still in bed so late, yet she dreaded leaving her warm cocoon. Judging by how icy the tip of her nose was, and by the frigid air against her face, she knew the house was cold as a grave. Still, the sooner she got up, the sooner she could get the small propane furnace going before her old friend Marvin Big Shield showed up. Marvin did his best to check on his fellow reservation elders, especially during winter. Sometimes the tribal chairman, Luther White Bear, did the checking if Marvin was ill or at a ceremony.

Cecelia grunted as she tossed aside the blankets and extricated herself from the old army sleeping bag her nephew had given her. After prolonged rest, her bones protested any movement. Her bursitis seemed to be getting worse. Maybe she'd ask Marvin to doctor her again. If that didn't work, perhaps she'd ask him to drive her to the clinic for some of those pills the *chimook* doctor gave out, though she didn't have much confidence in him, or the pills. Gingerly, she donned her "eyes", being careful with the taped earpieces. After starting up the tiny furnace, she bundled up in her old sweater, coat and galoshes, gritted her teeth and opened the front door. A frozen wind swept over her, chilling her to the bone. She made it to the outhouse and back in record time, thankful she didn't have to visit the cistern and pour hot water down the pump to thaw it. She had left some fresh water standing in the sink before she went to bed. Breaking a thin layer of ice, she dipped her hands in the water, rinsed her face, then removed her dentures from the narrow window ledge. "Hooo." She shivered with the insertion of her chilled "chompers". After clacking her teeth together a couple of times to set them, she ambled into the front room.

By tradition, the front door faced east so she could welcome the morning sun. At the front window, she pushed aside frayed curtains and squinted at the heatless orb, still low in a lupine-blue sky. Picking up her turtle shell, its inner surface charred from years of use, she lit the partially burned braid of sweet grass that lay within it. She added a pinch of tobacco. Then, wafting the sweet smoke over her face and head, she chanted her morning prayers.

They were the old prayers, the *nagamoon* passed on to her from her parents, who had passed them on from their parents. Cecelia didn't know how old they were, but she knew they went back at least five generations, maybe more. That's why they were such good songs, why they had power. She thanked Grandfather, *Gitche-Manitou,* for the warmth and light of *Geesis,* for the blueness of the sky, for the trees, the birds, the animals, for the air she breathed. She thanked Him for all the good things in life, for her family, and for the *Anishinabeg,* the Ojibwe people. Last, she asked Him to watch over her daughter, Theresa, and "her girls"—Ruby and Susan; especially her little warrior, Ruby.

"Watch over her, Grandfather. Protect her. Keep her safe and happy, Grandfather. Keep her strong."

Her morning prayers finished, Cecelia started the coffee. Her attention drifted to the shelf on the wall crowded with family pictures. She homed in on Ruby's, touched it gently with her finger. How she missed her, worried about her, wondered what she was doing this very moment. She worried about what lay under those inked-out lines in Ruby's infrequent letters. Even so, she had saved them, tied them in a neat bundle with a piece of red yarn and kept them in a special drawer. She read them over and over, though it was hard, what with her eyes and having little education. Sometimes she'd have Marvin or Theresa help her.

Be strong, Little Warrior.

Little Warrior, *Bineshee Ogichidaw,* was Ruby's Indian name. Cecelia smiled, remembering chiding Theresa when she once worried that Ruby might not be big enough to defend herself against Betty Potter, a local bully. "Theresa," Cecelia laughed, "that girl would fight a buzzsaw with a willow switch. Be proud, my daughter. Ruby is Martin clan!"

Cecelia was pleased that Ruby had inherited her tenacity, coupled with the deep inward spirit of her grandfather, a man Ruby never got to know since he passed over when she was only three. Ruby didn't yet realize what she'd inherited from her grandfather, but she'd know when she came home this summer. It was time her Ojibwe education went to the next level. It was time she came into full Ojibwe womanhood, with all its power and mysteries. Once she had this knowledge, her spirit would be fortified. She would be prepared to stare life fully in the face and to respect and know the Creator the

Anishinabe way. Most of all, she would be protected from the Robes.

Cecelia felt a twinge of sadness as she thought about how she had failed to accomplish this task with Theresa. Theresa had never shown much interest in the old ways, and she returned from boarding school an ardent Catholic. "I'm finished with that old-fashioned stuff," she had announced.

But Cecelia would not fail Ruby. This thing had to be done now, Cecelia decided, before the white priests washed out the Indian in her. Besides, there was the looming onus of the Ojibwe prophecy, spelled out in the sacred *wee'gwas* scrolls, of the Sixth Fire: "Those deceived by this promise will take their children away from the teachings of the elders. Grandsons and granddaughters will turn against the elders. In this way, the elders will lose their reason for living, their purpose in life. At this time a new sickness will come among the people," the prophecy foretold. The cup of life might well become the cup of grief. Well, the prophecy might indeed be in progress, as some of her fellow elders lamented, but she would be heard.

There was a knock at the door. Cecelia opened it, allowing into the front room a frigid draft and a blue-lipped Marvin Big Shield. He was a tall man, in his early seventies, slightly stooped. He had a lean, angular body honed down by years of hardship. Most of the time his face presented a detached impassivity. It wasn't that he was without emotion. He was old-school, raised by his grandfather in the old ways, where one didn't wear his feelings on his face, but stowed them carefully. But like most of Cecelia's fellows, his stoicism was really a mask for deep shyness around outsiders.

"Ahneen," he piped.

"Ahneen. Beendigin," Cecelia replied, closing the door behind him.

Marvin continued in Ojibwe. "How you feeling this morning, Cecelia?"

"Pretty good, just my bursitis a little." She hurried over to the stove and started making coffee for Marvin, Ojibwe tea for herself. "You?"

"Can't complain," he said as he removed his hat, coat and gloves. Tiny crystals of ice sparkled in his white, braided hair. "Except for this cold snap coming. Fifteen below." He shivered, looking about the room. "It's almost as cold in here as outside."

Cecelia remained busy with her beverage makings.

"Now Cecelia, you can't turn that old furnace off at night," he scolded. "That gas might leak into the house."

She waved him off. "Eh! What's so bad about that? I'd be with my ancestors. No need for gas up there." She peered at him over the rim of her glasses, a slight smile on her lips. "And it'd be better than looking at your wrinkled old face so early in the morning, *eya?*"

Marvin mumbled something to himself as he checked the furnace switch.

Cecelia turned and watched him. "What can I say? I prayed for more propane. It didn't come. You got more influence with Him," she said, pointing her finger toward the ceiling, "than I do. You should pray for me."

While her husband had been a third-degree *Mide* priest, Marvin was a fourth-degree. Though no one respected the holy man more, Cecelia liked to tease.

"In fact," she went on, "I've been thinking the Lodge should come up with a gas ceremony. Now there's something useful the *Midewiwin* could do for us old people, *eya?*"

Satisfied the furnace was lit, Marvin took his usual place on the worn and faded couch under the front window. He cupped his hands and blew on them as one white eyebrow rose in thoughtful expression. "I'm all for that. I'll bring it up next meeting."

He was still handsome, she thought. He reminded her of her Calvin, or maybe it was just because Marvin and Calvin had been friends and colleagues, both respected holy men for all those years. Both were quiet, deeply spiritual, displaying a dry wit with close friends or family. What was within them was carefully retained, never spilled away. Cecelia liked that in a man, an inner peace that bespoke self-assuredness and wisdom, yet was tempered with a good sense of humor. But most of all, she respected Marvin's spiritual powers—his wealth of understanding of the *Midewiwin,* his keeping of the old ways.

"So, how is your young nephew coming along?" She was referring to the young man who Marvin hoped would be following in his footsteps.

Marvin's frown accentuated the deeply carved lines in his weathered face. Each line split into many tributaries, some deep and others shallow, like the knowing rivers and streams that had flowed through Ojibwe country for countless centuries. "I think we will lose him. Like the other young ones, he sees no use in the old ways. He doesn't want to work that hard, wants to drink and run around on his wife."

Cecelia felt a sudden sadness. She brought the coffee, tea and a plate of corn muffins she'd made yesterday to the rickety card table, and sat next to Marvin, who now was blowing warm breaths on his fingers. "It is a shame." She sipped her tea thoughtfully. "Isn't there someone? Someone you can teach?"

"It's too late for Luther." He was referring to Loon Lake tribal chairman Luther White Bear, Marvin's nephew. Marvin pursed his lips and shrugged. "Maybe Lester Mink, but I'm not sure."

Cecelia sighed. "We got to shake up these young people. They come back from these schools and disrespect their parents and elders. Don't want to speak their language any more. Don't believe in our ways."

Marvin studied his coffee cup and shrugged. "What can you do?" He made a half-smile. "I remember my father saying the same thing when we were kids."

Cecelia's gaze drifted back to the window. The sun shone brightly now, peeking through the tops of yellow birches. She knew she was preaching to the choir, but she hated to see Marvin so dispirited. She took on a more upbeat tone. "Maybe you should talk about this at the next council meeting, *eya?* Maybe it's time we had our own school. An *Anishinabe* school—with *Anishinabe* teachers!"

Marvin gazed into her eyes with interest.

Cecelia felt a surge of excitement. She had been thinking and praying about this school for some time and was enthusiastic about sharing the idea with Marvin. "A place where we could teach our language and traditions to our young. Get them early on, I say, before them blackrobes get them. Fill them full of *Anishinabe* pride, *eya?*"

Marvin made a dry laugh. "All you have to do is pray away the church and the BIA."

She waved away his remark. "We could teach regular school, too. We have to get our children out of those Robe schools, where they are ruined."

"It is a good thought," he said, and took a slug of coffee. He stared at the cup wistfully. "A good dream."

Chapter Two

I stood at the end of my metal dormitory bed, a pair of barely soiled panties pulled down over my head, the stain directly over my nose. Sister Margaret, obese, fiftyish, with piercing green eyes, her ruddy cheeks cobwebbed with broken blood vessels, tapped her foot and glared at me.

"Cleanliness is next to godliness, Miss Loonfoot." Her fisted left hand rested on an ample hip. Her other hand poked at my side with a polished pine paddle. "Do you understand me?"

I clenched my own fist, my arms braced at my sides, squeezing my left hand tight against the quarter-sized piece of polished agate Gram had found in the creek of the Little People near her house. It was the only special thing I managed to rescue from my school-confiscated medicine pouch, now packed away in my trunk in the school basement.

The dorm floor was dead quiet save for the hollow *tock-tock* of the ancient grandfather clock at the north end of the floor. I could feel the stares of my dormmates, standing by their beds, mute as trees. I couldn't believe I'd been caught. Underwear inspections were usually on laundry day, tomorrow. For reasons known only to the Blessed Mary, Fatlips—better known as Sister Margaret—was on a tear that morning and pulled a surprise inspection.

Fatlips gritted her teeth. "You've learned nothing in the four years you've been here. You're still a little savage." She raised the paddle. I waited for the stiff rustle of her starched habit, then heard the whoosh of air. I held my breath and braced for the sting.

WHAP!

I'd learned how to flex my thigh muscle to lessen the pain, but the blow knocked me off-balance for a moment and I staggered right. It still hurt like hell.

"Now answer me!"

I could just make out her thick dry lips, like the gila monster's I saw in the Encyclopedia. *Makade majii-manitou,* I thought, but said, "Yes, Sister."

Sister Margaret's eyes slitted in disdain. "It is disgusting. You'll wear them for the remainder of the morning, sitting outside my office. Perhaps that will cure you of your filthy habits, not to mention your disrespectful attitude. Now repeat after me: 'O Heavenly Father . . .' "

I parroted the words, thinking of the mechanical man Doris Labeau told me about in a book she read.

"Help me and guide me . . ."

I pitched my voice low, as defiantly monotone as I dared. "Help me and guide me."

"Bring me out of darkness . . ."

I parroted the rest of the degrading prayer that inferred I was unclean physically and spiritually. I used to believe it, but now, at thirteen, and after four years at St. Nicholas, I rejected it, rejected everything Catholic, except I hadn't made up my mind about Christianity on the whole yet. That scared me a bit. I mean, what if Purgatory and those burning fires of hell were true?

Fatlips glared at the other girls. "Well? Don't just stand there like a bunch of ninnies. You can rehearse your hymn for Friday morning's Mass." Her eyes darted back to me. "It's certainly appropriate in Miss Loonfoot's case."

I mentally cringed as she raked me with an accusing eye. But anger boiled up inside me when I heard the reedy tweet of her pitch pipe. Everyone sang:

> *"Our hearts were black and savage,*
> *until we opened them to the gift of our Lord, Jesus Christ.*
> *And now our hearts are red and bright, because we've seen the light.*
> *The darkness of our skin reminds us of our heathen past,*
> *but the acceptance of our Lord takes us to a place of light and love that will last . . ."*

The bell rang, thank God, signaling breakfast. Fatlips turned back to me. "I'll see you in the office," she said and waddled out the door.

I waited as the girls hurried after her, and I reflected that many of them had bought into the whole catechism. They knew little of their people's histories. Maybe they didn't have a Gram like mine who'd planted fertile seeds of Indian pride deep within them.

Of course Gram had to do it in secret; Mom didn't approve of "Indian religion."

God, how I ached to see them—Gram, Mom, and Sue. In a few days I'd be home for Christmas.

Breakfast was humiliating. At least Sister Greta, this morning's cafeteria monitor, allowed me to roll the panties up on top of my head like an obscene hat while I ate. After breakfast, the panties back in place, I groped my way to the office and slumped in the polished oak chair that sits in the alcove between Fatlips' and Principal Blewett's office. The alcove reeked of Murphy's Oil Soap.

In a moment of fury, I yanked the panties off my head and

stuffed them into the outer office waste can, burying them under the trash. I decided that whatever punishment was exacted would be better than walking around with them on my head. I was too old for that crap.

I started thinking that I'd spent too many long hours in this chair. I didn't mind sitting across from President Eisenhower's photo, but the stern, probing eyes of Pope Pius XII eyeing me from above and behind, spooked me. He watched, evaluated, judged.

I shook away the thought and looked again at Eisenhower's visage. Never had a man looked less like a war chief. All the pictures of Ojibwe warriors I'd seen in family albums and in the tribal office at the Loon Lake reservation were strong, sober faces that reflected strength and fierceness. I thought about our tribal chairman, Luther White Bear. Now there was a warrior—tall, muscular, his handsome face assuming either ferocity or calm benevolence as the situation required.

The principal's door opened. Father Quentin Xavier Blewett's lipless mouth creased into a sad, thin line as he shook his head. "Ruby, Ruby. What am I going to do with you?"

I eyed the gaunt, dog-faced principal blankly, then looked past him, glimpsing a glaring Sister Margaret sitting half-turned in a chair in front of Father Blewett's desk.

Father Blewett checked his watch and sighed, "All right, child. Come in, come in."

I followed his flowing black cassock and sat in the remaining chair that faced his huge wooden desk. I avoided Fatlips' stare by focusing on a large painting of St. Nicholas that hung on the wall behind the principal's desk. The saint was surrounded by worshipful children, none of whom looked like us.

Father Blewett groaned into his seat and looked at me with faded gray eyes. His glasses had bottle-thick lenses that magnified his cloudy pupils. Wispy white hair, combed forward from the back of his head, struggled in vain to hide his baldness. His hand palsied badly as he selected a cigarette from a wooden humidor and lit it. After a deep drag, he blew smoke from his nose, followed by a phlegmy cough, then looked at Fatlips with a bored expression. "So, what is it this time, Sister?"

Sister Margaret straightened in her chair, her voice bristling with denunciation. "As we have discussed so many times before, Father, this child not only ignores our rules but continues to influence the other children with her disrespectful attitude. Our usual methods of discipline seem to have no effect."

Father Blewett exhaled noisily. "Is this true, Ruby?"

I opened my mouth to answer, but Sister Margaret interrupted. "If you want my opinion, Father, she's one of the incorrigible ones." She added with a sniff, "She still doesn't know her catechism."

"I see." He removed his glasses and tiredly pinched the bridge of his nose. "Well, Ruby, what do you say to all this?"

I glared at Sister Margaret. She had no right to say that, the witch. I switched back to Father Blewett. "I try, Father, but Sister Margaret ain't—isn't—mad about my catechism. She . . ." I felt my face warming. "She made me wear my underwear over my head."

Her eyes shot knives at me. "And where are those panties, young lady?"

Father Blewett cocked his head and winced as if he'd bit into something sour. "Not another underwear incident, Sister. Is it really necessary?"

Fatlips stiffened. "Cleanliness is part of learning to be a

proper lady. If we let these children make their own rules they'd be running amok like their ancestors."

Principal Blewett drummed his fingers on the desk. "It's just, well—so—distasteful. Don't you think you could—"

Sister Margaret intercepted him, straightening her shoulders and taking on an air of righteous indignation. "Father, you selected me as assistant principal. You said I was to be in charge of discipline."

He started to arrange pencils jutting from a Loyola College mug. "Yes, yes, I know, but . . ."

"I know these children," she went on. "If we don't maintain discipline, they'll revert to their pagan way of life, a life of alcohol and depravity, as you well know."

Pagan. Sister Margaret's favorite word. "We aren't alcoholics!" I snapped.

Sister Margaret's jaw muscle twitched. "You see? You see how she sasses?"

I scowled at the floor, so angry I wanted to heave Father Blewett's heavy glass ashtray at her bulbous nose.

Blewett's chair squeaked a complaint as he fidgeted. "Very well, Sister," he sighed. "Continue with the Lord's work, then." He added, "But, ah—try to be a bit more sensitive, all right?" His voice dropped in pitch as he watched her with apprehension, as if he feared he might've angered her. "Perhaps," he hedged, "you could, well, find ways that are a little—shall we say—more uplifting to the soul."

Fatlips' jaw muscle worked away.

Father Blewett attempted a smile. "All right, Ruby. Run along to class."

Gladly! I got up and headed for the door.

"And do try to follow the rules, child."

I turned toward him. His eyes pleaded with me. I nodded and left the room.

As I trudged to class, I brooded over Blewett's looming retirement, rumored to be as early as next year. I tried my best to respect him, but he had the backbone of an eel. Still, though he was bullied by Sister Margaret, he sometimes managed to temper the old witch.

Actually, I had been raised to respect elders and holy people. Gram always said, "Do not laugh at old people, but give them the driest log in your bundle." But at St. Nic's it was hard, very hard. Holy people at St. Nicholas were nothing like our holy people at Loon Lake. Like Mr. Big Shield, for example. He was introspective and soft-spoken and was always nice to me.

My thoughts returned to Father Blewett. When he retired, what kind of man would replace him? Priests and nuns who couldn't make it in white churches—those who made trouble or chased congregants' wives or who drank—were never fired, just reassigned. Often to Indian schools. We got the castoffs. Everyone in Indian country knew it.

In the dim, cavernous hallways, doing my best to ignore the snickering and mean comments of my fellow students, I thought about Mom. Surely she had her own bad experiences at boarding school. But she had always talked about how "nice" it was at St. Paul's. Others, like Mom's friend Irene Dubois, never broached the topic, avoided it like a coiled copperhead—like something *manitouwaadizi*. Once I walked by the kitchen when Mom and some other ladies were snapping peas, discussing their school days. They went stone silent when I came in. Grownups seldom discussed things that happened at "the schools," especially in front of kids. Now, after four years at St. Nic's, I knew why.

The thought angered me. If only Mom had prepared me, told me what to watch out for. Daddy attended a BIA school; perhaps that was different, but surely they both knew bad things happened to some of the kids. And suppose I had known what to expect? Would anything have been different? I was, after all, just another Indian kid, and the Church and the BIA ruled Ojibwe country.

On my way to class, I realized the answer to my question was no.

Chapter Three

Oatmeal again.

At least that's what they called it. I glowered at the Melmac bowl in front of me. That's all they ever served for breakfast except on special holidays or when visitors came. But my stomach felt empty as a dried gourd. After floating a bit of skim milk upon the gluey gruel, I added sugar and wolfed it down, along with the one piece of cold toast allowed us. I never thought I'd get used to skim milk, but constant hunger overpowered even the most finicky eaters.

"This bread's moldy," a new girl sitting to my left said with disgust.

I gave her a sharp look. "Keep your voice down," I hissed, then swiveled my head to look for Sister Greta, the dining hall supervisor. Seeing her a safe distance away, I gave the girl a sideward glance. "Just scrape it off."

"Uh-uhhh. I ain't eating this."

"I'll take it," Katie Red Star volunteered, stretching out her hand.

The new girl made a face and, using two fingers, gingerly handed the mold-speckled slice to Katie. Katie smiled, made a half-hearted effort to scrape off the fungus with the edge of her spoon, and gobbled down the toast. The rookie grimaced. Katie ignored her and plunged into her oatmeal with renewed vigor.

"Don't mind her," I quipped. "She's an orphan. She'll eat anything."

The new girl frowned at her bowl. "Is this all we get?"

" 'Fraid so," I said between mouthfuls. "Better eat up. You'll be starving by dinner as it is." I downed the last spoonful, then went to work on cleaning the bowl of every last speck. "Volunteer as much as you can for kitchen duty or clean-up," I said.

The girl's brow furrowed. "Why?"

"You can swipe extra food. You know, scraps, leftovers." I checked the location of the Robes again and whispered, "Kitchen duty is okay, but the best is working the staff dining room. They get all the good stuff: eggs, bacon, fruit, raisins, fried chicken."

The newcomer's eyes widened. "Jeez!"

"Keep your voice down!" I warned again.

"Yeah, but they don't get to play stretch," Katie said. "Watch this." Katie shoved her spoon into the oatmeal and pulled upward. The paste stretched almost four inches before giving way.

"Not bad," I retorted, then with grim determination dipped in my spoon and managed to stretch the stuff almost six inches.

Three other girls sitting around us joined the contest, tongues poking from their mouths in serious concentration.

"Better watch it," one frowning girl said. "You'll get a lickin' if Sister Greta sees that."

The new girl frowned, looked around, then whispered, "We don't have to put up with this. I'll go to the principal."

"You do and you'll bring Fatlips down on you like a momma grizzly," I said.

Her eyes crinkled into question marks.

"Sister Margaret, the assistant principal," I clarified. Not only was the girl new, but judging from her lighter complexion and brown hair, she was probably a quarter-blood, the minimum blood quantum allowed for tribal membership. Quarter-bloods and *wisikodewinini* had a tougher time at St. Nicholas, at first. The full-bloods gave them a hard time, especially if the girls didn't speak Indian. In time, however, she would find her life at St. Nicholas much easier because the staff favored the lighter-skinned girls. Their message was clear: the less Indian blood, the smarter the girl.

The greenhorn studied my face as if measuring my sincerity. A look of resignation formed in her eyes. "Steal food, huh? Well, I guess there's no point in being good if you gotta be hungry, too."

"Mum's the word," I warned, then looked at Katie who was cleaning her bowl with her finger. I looked back at the rookie. "I'm Ruby and this is Katie. What's your name?"

"Rose Captain."

"Ojib?"

"Uh huh."

"Which rez ya from?"

"Lac Courte Oreilles."

"Hmm. You're as far from home as I am," I said.

"Where's that?"

"Loon Lake."

Rose brightened. "We got relatives there, I think." She had bright, friendly brown eyes with glints of orange, like tiger's eyes.

"Yeah? I heard we had relations up in Canada, too—somewhere." I jerked my head toward Katie. "Katie's from Bad River."

Katie grinned between mouthfuls, her dimples in full bloom.

I leaned back toward Rose and whispered behind my hand. "She's part Sioux."

A sudden commotion at the next table interrupted our

conversation. Sister Greta was standing over a crying girl seated at the table. Eight-year-old Ellie Cedar had vomited in her plate. She had been feverish and sick all night. There were rumors she had measles, which scared everyone, since a lot of girls died from it a few years back.

"I don't feel so good, Sister."

"Think of all the starving children in China and Africa, God help them. Now eat that," Sister Greta snapped.

Ellie cried harder. The surrounding girls watched in gloomy silence as Ellie picked up her spoon with a trembling hand and dipped it into the mess in front of her. She lifted it to her mouth, then gagged. Sister Greta jumped backward with a grunt of disgust. Her face pinched in anger. "Stand up!"

Girls in the surrounding seats cringed and did their best to scrunch themselves into insignificance.

"Lean over!"

Ellie stood slowly, her body heaving with sobs as she leaned over her chair. Sister Greta produced "the strap"—a half-inch-thick piece of leather, three inches wide and three feet long with metal studs. She raised Ellie's dress over her back, revealing her panties, and swung the strap three times across Ellie's buttocks. Ellie cried out. Most of us in that room knew exactly how that strap felt. My body jerked sympathetically.

A merciful bell rang and the dining hall exploded into a din of scraping chairs and clanking metal trays as we hustled them to the cleanup window. Rose was wide-eyed with horror. "They can't do that! That poor girl was sick. You could see she was sick."

I gave Rose a sidelong glance as we returned our trays. "Welcome to St. Nic's."

After supper, I waltzed into the rec room, my reddened

hands wrinkled like prunes from washing dishes in the kitchen. Waving to Wanda and Evelyn at the checkers table, I plopped down on a rickety metal folding chair on the other side of the upright piano so that it obscured me from view. I reached into my dress pocket, pulled out a shiny red apple I had swiped from the faculty food locker, and bit into it hungrily. Now and then I peered around the piano to make sure no one was coming. I didn't feel like sharing tonight, and I didn't want to do any food swapping until I'd devoured my hard-won prize. Fruit was hard to come by. God, it tasted good. It might as well have been an Oh Henry! bar.

A minute later I heard Katie's cheerful banter with the other girls. Sure enough, her cherubic face peeked around the piano.

"Boo!" She relaxed her monster pose when she saw the apple. Her hands disappeared behind her back as she rocked back and forth on her heels as if expecting a reward.

"Hey, brat," I quipped as I reached into my skirt pocket and produced a banana.

A smile broke out on her face like a sunrise. "Oooh, *wewaagijeezid.*" She took the fruit, then peered warily around the piano. Satisfied that no one was watching her, she peeled it and chomped away like a starved wolf cub, her cheeks bulging like a chipmunk.

"Jeez. Take it easy, Katie, you'll choke yourself," I chided, inwardly pleased with her progress in learning Ojibwe. I had been secretly instructing her. Katie remembered a little from when she was two years old, before she ended up in an orphanage. Her father was a Sioux, but he died soon after she was born. Diabetes or TB, I forget which. The identity of her mother, an Ojibwe woman, was a mystery.

Katie's response was mangled in the mush in her mouth. "I don't care. I'm starving."

"Yeah, well you start choking and you'll bring a bunch o' Robes down on us." I peered around the piano and frowned. "Or one of their spies. Hide that banana," I hissed, glimpsing Agnes Knockwood stalking in our direction.

Katie's eyes widened as she stuffed the remainder of the banana into her mouth and shoved the peel into her pocket two seconds before Agnes and one of her pals appeared.

"Well, if it ain't Beanie and Cecil," Agnes said with a smirk, referring to the popular cartoon characters.

I glared at the two intruders. "Well, if it ain't Mutt and Jeff."

Agnes's mouth twisted into a grimace. "You're gonna get yours one day, Loonbutt, and real soon."

I made a show of rolling my eyes. "What do you want, Agnes?"

"You know what I want."

Agnes knew I had kitchen duty and assumed I had filled my pockets. I produced a partially eaten apple I had saved from the garbage in the staff dining room for just such a bribe, and plopped it into Agnes's outstretched hand. "That's all I got. Sister Greta was around."

Agnes glanced at the apple. "You're gonna have to do better than that, dearie, unless you want me to report you."

I sighed. It was easier and smarter to pay Agnes off than to fight her. Even if I won, I would face Fatlips' wrath for attacking her pet. "My mom's coming up on Friday. She'll have some gum."

Agnes mulled the bribe a moment. "You better or you and the squirt here will be warmin' the Sister's paddle." After glowering at Katie, who stood saucer-eyed, her banana-stuffed cheeks puffed out so far I could see veins, Agnes wheeled and strode away. Her cohort remained a moment, then jabbed her finger into Katie's left cheek. Banana mush oozed from Katie's pursed lips. The poking girl cackled.

I rocketed from my chair. "Don't you touch her!"

The poking girl looked surprised, then a cynical smile pulled at the corner of her mouth and she walked away.

Katie swallowed. "They wouldn't tell, would they? I mean, if they told, the Robes would fix it so nobody could swipe food."

I watched Agnes buzz around the room, gathering favors, making threats, laughing with her buddies. "Don't count on it. She'd figure some way to tell on us and still get food. I got a *nimisenh* back home just like her."

I looked toward the door and perked up immediately. "Hey, Sister Steph is here."

Sister Steph bounced into the room. "Good evening, girls, good evening." A gaggle of girls chorused cheery hellos and headed toward the piano. The fresh-faced nun chuckled as she pinched Katie's cheek and grinned at me. She whispered conspiratorially, "And how are my two favorites tonight?"

Katie and I grinned back. "Fine, Sister."

Pleasingly plump, as she referred to herself, and fresh out of the novitiate, Sister Steph always seemed on the verge of bursting into joyous laughter. She smelled wonderfully of a scented soap she said was called Irish Rose. Her blue-green eyes sparkling with gleeful enthusiasm, she was almost one of us. She was only eight years older than me, and her uncle had been the rector for the Rocky Boy Reservation, an Ojibwe-Cree reservation in northern Montana. Sister Steph had been raised around Indians. She understood the People, knew their ways and customs. She even spoke some Ojibwe.

We flocked around the piano as Sister Steph found her key, unlocked and opened the keyboard cover. "Well," she said. "What'll we sing first?"

There followed a chorus of shouts. Sister Steph pointed at

Sarah Kingfisher. "Ah, that's a good one, Sarah."

Sister Steph always began with a hymn. The piano sounded tinny and the two lowest keys emitted a wooden clack when struck, but I didn't care. This was the one time every week when I felt my spirit soar. Music, especially singing, made me feel so alive, so full of emotion, feelings common when I was at home and scarce as crow's teeth at St. Nic's.

Sister Steph played the opening chords and everyone sang:

"All things bright and beautiful
All creatures great and small
All things wise and wonderful
The Lord God made them all."

I sang the familiar lyrics with emotion, feeling that wonderful vibration in my chest and throat. I loved that particular hymn. It praised God for creating the animals, the flowers, the birds, the Earth—just like an Ojibwe prayer.

"Each little flower that opens
Each little bird that sings . . .
The pur-ple-head-ed moun-tain
The ri-ver run-ning by . . ."

We practiced four more hymns, then some fun songs like *Jimmy Crack Corn* and *Someone's in the Kitchen with Dinah*; and for the next hour laughter, fellowship, and the joy of song replaced loneliness and hunger.

After a while, Pat Boone lured a bunch of the girls to the radio at the opposite end of the rec room. Sister Steph broke into a Mozart minuet. I sat on the piano bench next to her and watched her delicate fingers. Like a doll's, I thought, each finger white and sculpted, each fingernail clear and smooth, not ragged and chewed like ours. They darted across the keys, alighting here and there with the airiness of butterflies. What I wouldn't give to be able to create such wondrous sounds, to caress beautiful melodies from the keyboard.

Now Sister Steph's eyes were closed in some inward bliss, and I imagined her spirit dancing with the *manitouog*. Why couldn't it be like this all the time?

On the last note, Sister Steph's eyes opened. "Oh." She smiled. "I guess I forgot myself."

"Do you feel closer to God when you play like that?" I wanted to know.

Sister Steph gave me a look of amused surprise. "Why, yes, Ruby." She shook her head in awe. "You are a precocious one."

That was a new word. "Percoshus?"

She laughed. "Smart." She winked and elbowed me. "Just like me." Giving the room a quick check, she cupped her hand to my ear and whispered, "The two of us—the smartest gals in the whole place."

Unused to compliments, I flushed and chuckled nervously. I brushed my fingers across the keys as if stroking a baby. "Sometimes, when you play like that, I see myself playing, and I close my eyes and see myself dancing with the spir—ah, with the saints."

"Why, Ruby. What a beautiful thought."

I felt the warm glow of her praise flow through me as I gazed into her guileless blue-green eyes, like a Wisconsin lake.

"Sister Steph, do you think I could learn to play like that?"

"Why, of course you could, Ruby. As quick as you are, you'd pick it up in no time." She looked thoughtful for a moment, then leaned closer. "Tell you what. If you're willing to give up your free time on Saturday nights, I'll teach you. How would that be?"

"*Really?* You would?"

Sister Steph laughed. "It's a deal, then." She patted my hand. "For now, how 'bout a little 'Chopsticks'?"

I bit my lip and smiled. "Could we play my favorite first?"

Sister Steph rolled her eyes. "Don't you ever get tired of *Heart and Soul*?"

I shook my head. "Uh-uh."

The corners of Sister Steph's eyes crinkled. "Oh, all right. Now remember: thumb on Middle C."

I placed my right thumb appropriately, my tongue protruding from the corner of my mouth in preparatory concentration. This time, I thought, *no wrong notes!*

Sister Steph bobbed her head, "And-a one and-a two and-a . . ."

Chapter Four

"Psst."

I swiveled and spotted Katie peeking out from under the staircase. She followed me around like a puppy, but I didn't mind. At eight, she was the same age as my sister, Sue. I had adopted Katie as a substitute little sister. I ducked under the staircase and wrinkled my nose. The space smelled of rotten apples. Someone had enjoyed a furtive snack, then tossed the core into the back corner. I craned my neck to peer around the corner and swept the hallway with squinted eyes, looking for lurking Robes. Seeing the coast was clear, I said, *"Boozh', nisheeme."*

Talking Indian was comforting, a remembrance of home and something the Robes couldn't take from us. But it was also dangerous. Getting caught meant a mouthful of soap, perhaps the paddle or strap, not to mention the loss of privileges.

"Ahneen," Katie said with hushed concern. She rested her hand on my arm, which was crooked to hold two text books and my hopeless sewing project. "It was crummy what Fatlips did to you yesterday," she said, referring to the panty-stain incident. "I was crying, weren't you? I mean, you wouldn't have got whacked if you would'a acted like you were sorry."

I frowned. I loved Katie, but the girl cried too easily. "Sorry, hell."

Katie's mouth rounded into a surprised O. "Ruby!" She

covered her mouth and snickered. "You're so bad."

"You gotta toughen up, Katie. Don't let the Robes scare you so easy." I checked the hall again. "*Waeginaen baebau-nindoyaek?* We'll be late for class."

"Oh, yeah," she chirped absentmindedly, "your mom is coming to visit on Wednesday. I overheard in the Witch's office."

I felt a lurch of apprehension. A phone call usually meant something bad had happened. "She's not supposed to pick me up until Friday." I felt a sudden burst of anger. "I'll bet Fatlips called her all the way in here just to gripe about my underwear."

Katie pouted. "At least you're going home for Christmas."

I bit my lip as I regarded my orphaned friend. She so reminded me of Sue, whom I missed terribly. Sue's Ojibwe name, *Nodinens,* fit her breezy and chatty personality. I missed her voice, her silliness, even her aggravation, now that she was at the peak of brathood. But any negative memories had dulled with time, and now I missed feeling her next to me at night, feeling her warmth as she spooned up against me, the comforting sounds of her breathing.

Sleeping alone was one of the things about boarding school that was hardest on the youngest ones and new arrivals, who felt most alone and homesick. I remembered when I, too, whimpered for that familiar warmth and reassurance on those long, cold Wisconsin nights, eventually falling into a sleep of unease. Suddenly, I was determined not to leave Katie by herself over the holidays. I grasped her hand. "You're goin' home with us. I'll fix it with my mom." The more I thought about it, the more enthused I became. "You'll love my sister, my whole family, and they'll really like you. I know it."

Katie brightened like a summer moon. Her hand flew to

her mouth. "Oh, Ruby. Do you really think so? I mean, you think your mom will say okay?"

I found myself stifling my own giddiness. "Of course, silly. Don't worry. I'll take care of it."

Katie's grin widened, forming deep dimples on either side of her mouth. Then she lifted her eyebrows in afterthought. "Are you gonna tell her about, you know, yesterday?"

My mood took a definite dip. "She doesn't like to hear about what goes on in here. She won't believe it, not about priests and nuns." I shrugged. "Besides, what can she do about it, anyway?"

Heavy footsteps echoed down the long arched hall. I peeked around the corner, glimpsed Father Slater, and pulled back quickly. *"Kokoko!"* I blurted in a panicky whisper.

The color drained from Katie's face. *"Naagaj apee."*

"After a while, crocodile."

We darted up the stairs on tiptoes and disappeared into our classrooms, beating the bell by two seconds. I settled into my desk and watched Sister Steph write on the blackboard. Now and then the chalk emitted an ear-grating squeak and a shiver ran up my spine, making me feel even colder than I was. Like the other girls, I wore two pairs of socks, a sweater, and a worn flannel jacket. The school never warmed enough in winter. From time to time the register under the frosted windows clanked or groaned as if it might come to life, but remained only lukewarm to the touch.

I heard whispers and turned around to see Agnes Knockwood huddled with one of her cronies. Agnes stopped whispering and shot me an icy glare. I turned around just as Sister Steph finished writing a compound sentence.

"Good morning, girls," she piped with her usual good humor.

Sister Steph was my favorite all the way around. I felt uplifted when with her, especially after her weekly music class, the highlight of my week.

"All right," she bubbled. "Who would like to come up and make a sentence skeleton for this sentence?"

Four apple-polishers frantically waved their arms. Sentence skeletons—what a bore. I glanced out the window. Pale light squeezed through thick clouds and tiny snowflakes scurried about like white fireflies.

I tried not to think about my growling belly.

Wednesday morning dragged like a dull plow. I found myself checking wall clocks wherever I went. Each time I checked it seemed only a few minutes had passed since the last time. Finally, dinnertime came . . . and went. No mom. Part of me didn't worry. Mom, like everyone else back home, was on "Indian time". Rez life was unrushed. If someone said they'd be somewhere at dinnertime, it meant they could arrive anywhere between ten in the morning and three in the afternoon. Besides, it was a long drive from Loon Lake, and Lord only knows what kind of vehicle she had borrowed. The few vehicles on the rez were traveling breakdowns waiting to happen.

It was almost two o'clock before the office sent for me. Tingling with apprehension, I sped down halls, into the office and through the anteroom door. Mom was peering distantly out the window, wearing her favorite, though faded, polka dot dress. Even in profile she looked tired and drawn, tiny crows'-feet clawing at the edges of her mouth and eyes.

Despite that, I thought her attractive, even at the old age of thirty-six. Her long, raven-colored hair was coiled tightly in a bun. I wished she would braid it and let it fall down her back, Indian-style. I loved to brush it, then braid it, just as she had done for me before St. Nic's chopped off my braid. "You look just like a princess, Momma," I used to say. She'd wave her hand. "Silly. There's no such thing as an Indian princess. The *last* thing we got is royalty." But she'd glow nonetheless.

Of Mom's living children, only I now attended school. James, my elder brother, died of measles when I was only two. Firstborn and the only son, he had left a great hole in Daddy's heart. So, Mom seemed to be holding on to Sue, but I knew not for much longer. Soon, Sue too would be sent to Catholic boarding school.

Mom was a product of the boarding-school system, though apparently a kinder one than mine, and did her best to be a good Catholic. And, despite on-and-off poverty, her depression since Daddy left and her unrealized dream of living in town, she tried her best to be a good mother.

"Momma!" I rushed into the anteroom and into her arms, basking in the warmth of her embrace, the familiar smell of rouge, a hint of laundry starch.

In a few moments she pulled back with a sad smile. "Look how much you've grown." She felt my ribs. "But you're getting too skinny. We're gonna have to fatten you up when you get home."

I grinned. "I can't wait. And to see Gram and Sue, and—"

I stopped mid-sentence when I saw the sad look on her face. "What's wrong, Mom? Did somethin' happen? Is Gram all right?"

Mom shook her head and took my hand. "Everybody's fine, honey. It's just, well, I kinda got some other bad news."

I braced myself. Bad news seemed to chase us through life.

She patted the seat next to hers. "Here. Sit down by Momma."

I sat warily, dread creeping into me like a winter draft. Oh, God. Somebody died.

"I—I can't pick you up Friday, honey. Your daddy—well—"

I felt as though the four-foot pile of snow on the dorm roof fell on me.

"—he got hurt down in Aberdeen. He's okay, but—"

I grimaced. "Aberdeen!"

Mom nodded. "He was working. Drivin' that big truck for Schmidt Brothers, you know, on his way to Rapid City."

A tremble came into my voice. "Mom, we haven't seen Daddy in over a year. He walked out on us, remember?" I wasn't sure why he left. There had been trouble between him and Mom—arguments, angry words, then one day he was gone. So family finances were another main reason I was serving time at no-cost St. Nic's. Mom just couldn't afford to take care of herself, me, and Sue on what Daddy could send her when he was working, the pittance she earned picking berries in the summer and taking in laundry in the winter. But I also knew Mom wanted her girls to get a Catholic education, to be faithful followers of the Church. The closer I could get to being an Indian Virgin Mary, the better.

Across the hall in the kitchen, heavy twenty-gallon pots clanked, silverware clinked and Melmac dishes clacked as the kitchen crew prepared another starchy, tasteless supper.

I fidgeted in my chair and shot Mom a frustrated glare. "What about Daddy?" Then a thought struck and my frustration transformed into cautious hope. "He's coming home for Christmas?"

I wasn't sure how Mom would react, seeing Daddy home again, but the idea set me tingling. There could be no better Christmas present than having them together again.

Mom's shoulders slumped. "Daddy got beat up, honey. It was all a big mistake. They thought he was another man—from around there." She patted my knee. "I talked to him. He'll be okay."

I read through the code. "They hate Indians there. They beat him up 'cause he was Indian, didn't they?"

Mom stared at her lap. I wasn't surprised she would travel all the way to South Dakota. She'd hitchhike to the moon if she had to. She loved Daddy to distraction. I loved him, too, though I harbored a blizzard of bitter feelings about his sudden departure from our lives. Why didn't he say anything to Sue and me before he left? Why punish us?

"What about the cops?" I asked.

"Who do you think they'd believe?" She sighed. "Anyway, Daddy's in the hospital there." Recovering her composure, she continued, "I'll be gone three or four days, honey. I have to leave now, right away."

I perked with sudden inspiration. "Take me with you, Mom. I'll help with Daddy, and we can still be together for Christm—"

Mom was shaking her head again.

"Why not?" I pouted.

"Because I have to take the bus, and I can't afford tickets for all of us."

Disappointment struck me like a cold rain as I saw my plans washed away. The thought of spending Christmas at school, not seeing Gram or Sue, was unbearable. I felt tears welling.

"Don't leave me here, Mom, please. Please take me home."

Despite my efforts, tears leaked from my eyes as bitter words tumbled out in a torrent. I hated to cry. "Why haven't you done something, Mom? I told you about them locking Sadie Yellow Cloud in the basement for two days. And two days ago they made Ellie Cedar eat her own puke."

Her eyes shut tight, her mouth a tight seam, Mom shook her head violently as if to shut out the offending words. Her hands pushed deep into her lap, fisted around a dingy white hankie. The protruding edge, embroidered with tiny Ojibwe floral designs drooped wearily over her thumb. Like its owner, it was worn and frayed before its time.

"Stop shaking your head! Why don't you believe me?"

Mom grappled with her purse.

"Why don't you believe me, Mom? You never believe me!"

She wrestled with the clasp lock. "Now, Ruby. I—I don't want to hear such stories. It's not so bad. I went through it. Thousands of Ind'n kids have gone to boarding school." She searched the room like a cornered mouse. The clasp suddenly obeyed. The purse opened, spitting a balled-up Kleenex, three bobby pins, and a nickel into her lap. I smelled the familiar fragrances of face powder and Spearmint gum. She fished out her compact, flipped open the lid and examined her face in the mirror, then attempted a chuckle. "See?" she said, nervously patting her cheeks with the powder puff. The tiny compact was virtually devoid of face powder, it was so old. "You'll mess Mom's makeup." She dabbed the corners of her eyes with the hankie. "Now you be a good girl."

She took my hand, put three packs of school-forbidden gum into it, closed her own hands around mine, and smiled in a futile effort to cheer. "Sister Margaret says they're having a Christmas party for the girls that are stayin'. There'll be cookies, and presents, and a tree—"

Now I was the one shaking my head. I moaned, "Nooo, Mom, nooo. I promised Katie—"

Mom plowed on, naming off banal aspects of the party as she stroked my hand, but there was agony in her eyes. She hugged me hard, then produced a tiny box wrapped in green foil and tied with yellow ribbon. "Look; Momma brought your Christmas present. Now, don't you open it until

Christmas morning, okay?" She stood. "I'm sorry, hon. I'll make it up to you, I promise," she said and walked out the door. She looked back one last time. "Promise."

I sagged in the chair, held my face in my hands, and sobbed.

Chapter Five

Alone in his room, Father John Vincent Slater whistled the tune to *Holy, Holy, Holy* as he peered into his mirror and admired his beard. It was close to his face, perfectly manicured to ape the pictures he'd seen of the handsome Spanish priests of olde. He smiled. Of Christ, himself? Friday was his favorite day. It meant the start of the weekend and the mouth-watering aroma of fish—broiled, baked or fried, he didn't care. He liked them all. But beyond the food, an exhilaration accompanied Fridays; a feeling of freedom while much of the meddlesome staff escaped for the weekend. That's why he always volunteered for weekend duty. Someone had to do it, after all. Someone had to live up to the motto of St. Nicholas: *Sacra fide*—In Sacred Trust. And if he didn't work the weekend, he wouldn't hear confessions.

He checked to make sure his notepad was in his cassock pocket. In it were carefully recorded notes about the girls' confessions, specifically their delicious responses to his usual question, "And did you touch yourself inappropriately this week? Tell Father about it."

Through the power of the confessional, with just the right questions, it was amazing how much detail he could extract using his "guided confessions." Of course he'd had a good teacher, his own parish priest, Father Dugan, who had corrupted young Johnny Slater in his altar-boy years. But Dugan was to be despised. He was a homosexual, an unforgivable sin, the ultimate in depravity.

As he opened his room door he thought of Katie and felt a tingling sensation. Lord, how he loved that child. He was sure Katie loved him as well. All his children loved him. Whistling more jubilantly, he locked the door and strutted down the hall toward his Latin class. It looked like another glorious day.

I watched Sister Stephanie close her eyes and tighten her lips in frustration. "Katie, now how many times have we been through this?" She swept her eyes across the entire cast. "Girls, ready or not, this play opens on Christmas Eve, which, in case you've forgotten, is tomorrow night." She noised an airy sigh as she spotted six-year-old Christine Labeau crossing her legs and holding herself. "Crissy, tomorrow I would appreciate it if you would go to the lav before we start."

Crissy continued to writhe.

"All right; run along, but don't dillydally. We'll work around you."

Crissy made a beeline for the door. Giggles chased her out. Sister Stephanie clapped her hands for order, then frowned as she spotted Agnes Knockwood chewing her nails and staring out the window. It was frustrating when the girls didn't take the annual play seriously. "Mary," she critiqued, addressing Agnes by her stage name, "is that appropriate behavior for the mother of Jesus?"

Agnes turned with a dull expression and blinked. Sister Stephanie sighed again. "Character, ladies, character. You can't play a role if you fall out of character all the time." Then she noticed me. "Joseph, where's your staff?"

"I couldn't find it, Sister. It—" I shot a hostile glance at Agnes "—disappeared."

Agnes's jaw dropped, her hand flew to her chest as if she

were shocked by the accusation.

Sister Stephanie surveyed the cast. "Has anyone seen Joseph's staff?"

The cast looked at each other blankly; a few shrugged.

Sister Stephanie's fists perched on her hips. "We'd better find it by tomorrow."

I gave Agnes a scowl that would freeze water. I wanted everything to go well for Sister Steph's sake.

"All right, places everyone. Let's take it from the top."

Nine-year-old Pearl Akiwenzie raised her hand. Sister Stephanie nodded at the angel with crooked wings. "Yes, Gabriel, what is it?"

Pearl parked her hand on a jutted hip and looked annoyed. "Do I have to stand next to Doris?"

Doris pinched her face and stuck out her tongue.

"See what I mean?" Pearl whined.

"Yes, you must," Sister Steph said. "The three Wise Men stand together. Doris, kindly return your tongue to its proper place and stop annoying Pearl."

Doris *tsked* and rolled her eyes. "She touched me."

Pearl's eyes widened. "I did not!"

"Did too."

"Did not."

Sister Stephanie cut off the snippy cross-talk with three loud claps. "All right, places everyone, places!"

It was going to be a long rehearsal.

Chapter Six

Later, in the rec room, Katie and several other girls stood with me in awe before the eight-foot Christmas tree donated by a nearby tree farm. It seemed Jones's U-Cut donated a bigger one every year. We had finished decorating the room, and now the task of trimming the tree lay before us.

Along with some of the older girls, I took a nearby seat to watch the decorating. Rose Dubois looked at me in surprise. "Ruby? Aren't you gonna help decorate?"

"No, thanks," I said with a lopsided grin. "You go ahead, Rose," and opened my book of Emily Dickinson poems Sister Steph had given me, enjoying one of the few moments I had to myself.

Rose scrunched her face in puzzlement, then joined Sister Elizabeth.

Since Sister Elizabeth—we called her Sister E—seldom noticed anything not in her immediate purview, I dared to have the book with me. Sister Steph had warned me to keep it under wraps as some of the faculty would deem it blasphemous or prurient and confiscate it. I wasn't sure what "prurient" meant, but it sounded bad, so I heeded Sister Steph's advice. I kept it hidden along with the wonderful Marie Sandoz book about Crazy Horse she had loaned me. I loved Marie Sandoz. She had a way of making me feel at home, like I was right there with her on the Nebraska plains. And she liked Indians!

By default, Sister E always supervised the tree decoration because, over the years, the other nuns had become frustrated with her finicky correctness. Unlike Sister Margaret's brusque, choppy movements, or Sister Steph's warm, airy manner, Sister E moved with a quiet elegance, as if each movement had been thoughtfully planned. As others placed an ornament here or some tinsel there, Sister E would frown, then rearrange it. No one, it seemed, could do it just right.

Sister E had a system. "You can't just throw your decorations on the tree, helter-skelter," she always said. "If you go about it in an orderly fashion, you will have a beautiful tree."

Per Sister E's system, Katie and three of the youngest girls had arranged the ornament boxes by size and color. The lights had been checked and, as usual, some strings didn't light. The search for the errant bulbs took forty trying minutes. When they finished, Katie knitted her brow. "How can we put these away every year and they're working, and then, when we pull them out of the box the next year, they don't? It don't make sense."

"Only the shadow knows," I said, aping the low, ominous radio voice.

"Little *Chimook* gremlins," Lucy Otter whispered in Ojibwe, then snorted a laugh. The girls within hearing distance covered their mouths and giggled.

"That's *doesn't,* dear," Sister E corrected without moving her eyes from the neatly arranged ornament boxes. She mumbled absently to herself, "Now, we need the large ones first . . ." She looked up at the girls. "Shall we start with the blue or the gold ones?"

"Blue," Katie almost shouted.

Pearl chirped, "Let's start with the little ones first, Sister. Just to do it different this year."

I grimaced in expectation of an explosion.

Sister E looked annoyed. "Absolutely not. Start with the little ones? Why that's backwards, child."

Pearl sighed and plopped down on a chair. Decorating the tree had become a chore, another regulated activity with a set of rules. The older girls had drifted away to checkerboards, gossip groups, or to the radio, where Bing Crosby crooned *White Christmas*.

Sister E now had only two young helpers. She didn't seem to notice, her eyes sparkling and intent upon the globes as she placed each one with forethought and exactitude. I lost myself in Emily Dickinson's words. Actually, I understood few of her poems, finding most of them enigmatic. But the ones I did understand—their words and phrases melted into my soul.

Emily understood. I didn't know how—she was white, and most of her poems were a hundred years old—but she did understand. She contemplated all the things I contemplated, worried about the things I worried about. She understood loneliness, grief, God, sadness, even death.

A whimpering sound interrupted my thoughts. Little Crissy Labeau was scrunched in a far corner, crying. I went to her and squatted down. "What's wrong, Crissy?"

Her cheeks were shiny with tears. "I wanna go home. I want my mommy."

I sat next to her and put my arm around her. "I know, I know." I didn't know what else to say. Mommy will be here soon? A lie. I had overheard Sister Margaret and the visiting doctor talking last week. Crissy's mom was dying of TB. Her father was killed in Korea. No one knew much about the rest of her family.

"It'll be all right, Crissy. Tomorrow is Christmas Eve and the play, and then it'll be Christmas morning, and you'll get presents."

Crissy sniffed. "What kinda presents?"

"I don't know, but I bet it will be swell. Santa always brings good stuff, doesn't he?" I gave her a hug. She was so tiny, so afraid. She should be with her mom, her family, not in this cold, faraway place. "Now why don't you go over there and help Sister E? You're real good with colors, aren't you?"

She nodded.

I whispered, "Sister E is sorta color blind. I think she needs your help telling the blue ornaments from the gold." I blotted Crissy's eyes with my hankie. "All better?"

Crissy nodded again, a residue of sadness still on her face.

"C'mon," I said cheerily and took her to Sister E. "Crissy wants to help, Sister." I winked at the nun. "She's really good with colors, so I told her she can help you pick the right ornaments."

Sister E eyed Crissy. "Very well. Crissy, you can be in charge of the blue ones." She pointed to the ornament box. "There, you can hand me one of those big ones."

Crissy's homesickness made me suddenly sad and I plodded over to one of the big windows. I shivered at the chilly draft flowing from it. A haloed moon as bright as a spotlight hung in a frosty indigo sky and splashed its light across the stark countryside. Ice-crusted snow like smoothed white frosting glistened in the blanched light. Shadows of trees, their skeletal limbs waving in a sudden night wind, danced across the surface.

I thought of Gram, sitting in her cold shanty, bundled up in her coat and gloves. The little propane furnace was a poor match for the bone-chilling winters of northern Wisconsin. Why hadn't she answered my letters? She wouldn't just ignore me. It didn't make sense. God, I hoped Mom had made sure Gram had enough propane and food.

My breath fogged the frigid glass and I fingered letters in

it: R U B Y. I laid my book on the frigid, glazed-block sill and turned the pages. I found one of my favorites—a poem called "Hope." The first stanza was underlined:

"Hope" is the thing with feathers
That perches in the soul,
And sings the tune without the words,
And never stops, at all

Chapter Seven

"Shh. Shh."

Nervous girls tried to subdue their noisier castmates in the organized chaos behind the makeshift curtain. Four bedsheets had been pinned to a clothesline that stretched across the center of the rec room. A small pulley at one end enabled Joyce LaFrance to open and close the curtain.

At least that was the plan.

Sister Steph seemed to be in five places at once as she scurried here and there adjusting costumes—mostly old, dyed sheets fashioned into ancient robes—rearranging the set, calming nerves, answering questions. She spotted me. "Ah, Joseph. Glad to see you found your staff."

"Yes, ma'am. It just reappeared. Kinda like a miracle."

Sister Steph offered a dubious smile, then glimpsed Crissy playing with her cardboard-and-cotton sheep's tail. Sister Steph patted the first-grader's head. "You did remember to go to the lav, didn't you?"

"Yes, Sister."

The apprehensive director looked relieved. "All right, girls. You're going to do just swell. You're all wonderful actors." She made a fist, swished a right hook in the air. "Now let's go out there and knock 'em dead!" She turned to take her place in the front row, then had another thought. "Er, I mean 'break a leg!' "

Katie's eyes grew big as melons.

I was puzzled for a moment myself, then realized Sister Steph was just nervous. I told Katie, "Oh, she didn't mean it. She's probably nervous as a treed cat, the bishop being here and all."

"Bet she ain't as nervous as we are," Rose chimed in, panic building in her face. "My mind's gone blank."

I gave her a glare. "It better not be," I said, then I looked at my fellow cast members and in a stage whisper said, "Okay everybody, let's do this right for Sister Steph."

The audience, made up of faculty, staff and a few invited dignitaries from nearby Doanville, had milled in and taken their seats. All heads turned when the bishop flowed into the room with his grim procession of acolytes: Fathers Slater and Potts, Principal Blewett, the bishop's secretary, Father Flarety, and Sister Margaret. Everyone stood.

I peeked around the curtain. I'd seen the bishop only once before in my four years at St. Nic's. Tonight he was dressed in a black cassock piped with scarlet, a magnificent, tasseled red sash, and a silky red beanie cap. His face reminded me of a wrinkled basketball. The basketball sat upon a neckless body shaped like the sacristy wine cask on stubby legs. An imposing silver crucifix hung from his neck to the top of his protruding stomach. Several faculty members rushed over to kiss his ring. To us he seemed imperious and untouchable. I never saw him smile. No one knew his first name, if he even had one, and people whispered his last name as though they might be struck down by a bolt of lightning for even mentioning it.

Father Blewett, the school principal, hustled ahead of the bishop at the last moment and held the back of one of the two red velvet altar chairs brought in from the chapel. The prelate nodded regally and sat.

Sister Steph and the two narrators stood in front of the curtain. Sister Steph took a deep breath. "Your Excellency,

Father Blewett, and honored guests. On behalf of the children I would like to welcome you to St. Nicholas's first annual Nativity play. We have a wonderful cast this year, and the children have worked very hard to make it the best play ever. We hope you enjoy it." She took her seat in the front row and nodded at the narrators.

"This is the story of the first Christmas," said the first narrator, who then looked at her partner, the second narrator. "The Angel Gabriel visits Mary and tells her that she will soon have a baby."

The narrators turned to look at Joyce, the curtain puller. Joyce yanked the rope and the curtain parted halfway, revealing me, Mary, and Gabriel. Mary and I looked at Gabriel, awaiting her words. But Gabriel stared vacantly at the audience.

There was a strained pause. My teeth on edge, I whispered, "Say something."

Gabriel stood stiff as a broom handle.

I gave her robe a surreptitious yank.

"Oh," Gabriel croaked, then cleared her throat. "Mary, God has sent me to tell you that he has chosen you to be the mother of his son. Soon you will have a baby boy and you will call him Jesus."

The first narrator said, "One day the king tells everyone that they have to pay him tax money."

I said my lines in a loud voice, a bit overdramatic. "Mary, the king says that we have to pay our taxes. We have to go to Bethlehem to pay them."

"But Joseph, that is a long way away."

"Yes, Mary, it is. You will have to ride the ass."

Two girls stifled snorts and I cringed as I realized I had flubbed the line. I was supposed to say "donkey." I cursed my overconfidence.

The first narrator said, "So Mary and her husband Joseph go on the long journey to Bethlehem. The road is hard and dusty and they get very tired."

The second narrator droned, "When Mary and Joseph arrive in Bethlehem they . . ." Her voice trailed off, her face blanched.

Sister Steph stage whispered, "Crowded."

The narrator pinched her face in frustration as she looked at her prompter. "Huh?"

Sister Steph cupped her hands. "The town was crowded."

The narrator looked relieved. "Oh, yeah. And the town was too crowded."

The curtain parted another couple of feet to reveal a girl wearing a fake beard that hung slightly askew on her face. She was standing next to another girl whose hair had been streaked with gray. They stood in front of a piece of cardboard painted like an ancient inn. The play continued smoothly until it was time for the Wise Men to visit the Christ child. The curtain opened further to reveal the manger scene.

Crissy, on all fours by the manger, her hair full of cotton balls, her nose painted black, brayed "Baaahh." Another girl, covered with a sheet painted with brown and white spots, mooed.

The second Wise Man said, "Surely a king would be born in a king's palace? Let us go there."

Tall, spindly Harriet Sigwadja appeared, dressed in a flowing sheet dyed brown, a curly black beard and a tinfoil crown. She attempted a basso voice, which came out something like a croak. "I am King Herod. Welcome to my palace."

The third Wise Man said, "We are looking for a new baby king. We are following the star that told us that he has been born."

Herod replied that she knew nothing about a new baby king, that the wise men must find him and to "come back and tell me where he is so I can go and see him, too."

The first Wise Man bowed courteously, grabbing her crown as it slid precariously on her head. "Thank you, my lord king."

Herod said with a swagger, "Any time."

The Wise Men's eyes widened at Harriet's improvisation.

Rose Captain took up a pole from which dangled a large cardboard star wrapped in tinfoil. She suspended it above the Wise Men and led them to the manger. Along the way she tripped on her too-long robe, stumbled, and fell. The pole crashed against the inn backdrop, which keeled over on top of Mary and the manger.

"Ow, shoot!"

The audience guffawed. Sister Margaret and the bishop were tight-lipped. Sister Steph's hand flew to her mouth, her eyes wide. Then she scurried to help straighten the scenery and check on Mary and the star carrier. After some frantic straightening, the play continued.

The narrator shakily announced, "The three Wise Men follow the star again, and it leads them to Bethlehem. They find the baby Jesus and give him lots of gifts."

Wise Man One said, "I bring him gold because he is a king."

Wise Man Two added, "I bring him franks and sense because he is God's son."

Wise Man Three chimed in, "And I bring him burrs."

Wise Men One and Two, along with the audience, snickered. Wise Man Three frowned in puzzled annoyance.

On cue, at the final line of the play, Joyce tugged the curtain line. Nothing happened. She tried again, with no result. The cast rolled their eyes in her direction, set smiles more like macabre grins on their faces. Joyce, her face painted with grim determination, gave the recalcitrant line a mighty tug. Snap! The curtain collapsed, covering most of the inn cast, who squealed and groped around under the sheets. The audience roared, applauded and whistled while the staff and faculty looked to the bishop for a signal as to the appropriate response.

Sister Steph uttered an "Oh!" and ran to rescue the victims. Principal Blewett stood and faced the audience. "Well, that was—ah—wonderful, children." He nodded toward Sister Steph. "Let's give a nice hand to our own Sister Stephanie for all her fine work."

The audience applauded with gusto. Sister Steph blushed and made a tiny bow while still trying to extricate kids.

"And now," Blewett continued, "I believe our kitchen staff has prepared some refreshments in the dining room."

Still chuckling and talking animatedly, the audience filed out behind the bishop and moved toward the dining room.

I stalked over to Joyce. "That's just swell, Joyce. Way to go."

"Listen to you," Joyce scowled, "little-miss-ride-the-ass. And it ain't my fault we had a crummy curtain."

I felt like yanking out her hair. " 'Ass' is perfectly correct. It's the word they use in the Bible."

"Nice try, pet!" Joyce wheeled and walked away.

I saw red. Being called a teacher's pet was about the worst slur there was. I was about to clobber her when Sister Steph walked over. I immediately deflated. "Gosh, Sister, we did lousy. The play was ruined."

Sister Steph smiled. "Don't be silly, Ruby. Everyone did a swell job. Didn't you hear the applause?"

I remained unconvinced. It seemed like everything that could go wrong, did. "It ain't supposed to be a comedy."

She gave me a one-armed hug. "Oh, the audience knew that, and I'm sure they appreciated seeing the Nativity story so—uniquely played. As for the other things, well, that's the theater." Her hand moved comfortingly to my shoulder. "I know you did your best. Don't worry about it."

I looked into those forgiving blue eyes. She always knew what to say to make things better, but she couldn't completely hide her disappointment. I shook my head in disgust, thinking of Harriet's ad lib. When I speak to her later, I thought, I'll give her a piece of my mind. *Any time*—jeesh.

Chapter Eight

"Hark! the her-ald an-gels sing,
Glory to the new born King
Peace on earth, and mer-cy mild
God and sin-ners rec-on-ciled . . ."

Me and seven other girls crowded around the piano as Christmas Day drew to a close. A crackling fire warmed the rec room, and for the first time since—when?—Thanksgiving?—I actually felt full. Each of us had received a Christmas box containing a handful of peanuts and jawbreakers, a small bag of mixed candies, an orange, two apples, some religious cards, jacks, a jump rope, a small doll, a drawing book and a kaleidoscope. Besides the food, the kaleidoscopes had created the most excitement. We marveled at the magic palate of colors that swirled into twinkling geometric patterns as we peered through the pencil-sized holes. Oohs and ahhs accompanied the twisting of the sleeves as we passed our tubes to each other, shouting, "Look at this one! Look at mine!"

"Who's ready for some Christmas carols?" Sister Steph asked. Her pudgy cheeks blooming like two roses, Sister Steph opened the piano and with her usual verve began to pound out *Deck the Halls* on the very flat piano. I sang at the top of my voice, but by the end of *Away in a Manger* I was beginning to wonder about Katie, who had gone upstairs twenty minutes ago to retrieve a special gift she had made for me.

Now the party was almost over. Then again, it wasn't unusual for Katie to get sidetracked.

"Je-sus our Im-man-u-el.
Hark! the her-ald an-gels sing
Glo-ry to the newborn King.
Ahhhh-men."

Sister Steph looked up and called to Isabelle Sunigo and Millie Migwans, deep in quiet conversation at the far end of the room. "Isabelle. Millie. We need some sopranos over here."

Isabelle and Millie were two of the older girls, both sixteen. I hardly knew them. And, like Katie and me, they were inseparable and kept mostly to themselves. It was strange, though. They usually loved to sing.

"Coming, Sister Steph," Millie called.

At the other end of the piano, Norma Red Sky shrieked suddenly and fled the room, chased by a giggling Alice Nadjiwon, who dangled a rubber mouse from her fingertips. The girls laughed heartily. Sister Steph stifled a laugh, then clapped her hands for order. "Norma, you quit that." The girls dashed out of the room. "Norma Red Sky!" Sister Steph breathed a good-natured sigh and swished after the running pair.

I took that opportunity to slink out and take the stairs to the third floor. What would Katie have for me? Near the top of the stairwell I stopped short when I heard a man's voice. One of the heavy metal doors that opened onto the dorm floor was ajar. The lights were off.

Something in the back of my mind urged caution. I tiptoed to the half-open door and listened. I recognized the voice now; it was *Kokoko*'s. Then, a whimper—soft, barely audible.

A finger of fear traced up my spine. Oh, God. Not Katie.

My bed lay just inside the door and to the left. Katie's lay across the aisle and up three beds from mine. On hands and knees I crawled to the side of my bed, then slipped underneath and peered through the support bar. Katie was on her bed. *Kokoko* sat vulture-like on a chair he had pulled up next to her. Moonlight illuminated the pair through the high, narrow window. He was mumbling softly to her, stroking her hair, her face. He gazed at her the way a wolf eyes a rabbit. Katie lay stiff as a toy doll, her dress hiked up to her waist.

She looked so small next to him, so vulnerable.

His hand grabbed Katie's, pushed it down, his voice breathy. "Is this how you do it to yourself?" His voice became a whisper now, so I couldn't catch what else he said. Blisters of perspiration dotted his brow above his thick, bushy eyebrows. His jaw hung slack.

Katie's white cotton panties were exposed. *Kokoko*'s hand trembled with effort but easily overpowered her resistance. Under the elastic waistband now, her captive hand pushed lower until an obscene bulge tented between her legs. The priest leaned closer, still whispering.

Oh, God. He's touching her . . . rubbing her with her own hand.

Katie's face twisted in a mask of torment. "Please—no—Father, please." Stifled sobs broke her speech. "I don't—want—"

Kokoko's left hand cupped over her mouth. "Shhhh. Shhh," he hissed in her ear. "It's all right. Show Father how you do it to yourself."

I wanted to close my eyes, to suddenly be somewhere else, to make the odious scene go away, but I couldn't. The repulsive lump between Katie's legs kept pulsating. Katie squirmed and jerked, tried to scooch away, disengage somehow, but it was no use.

Frozen in place, I swallowed back a wave of nausea. A shout struggled to escape but froze in my throat. I had no idea what *Kokoko* might do if he discovered me, what he might do to both of us. My fingers ached as I gripped the iron bed support—tighter . . . tighter.

In my mind it was not the rail I was squeezing but the priest's hand. I squeezed harder, felt his hand wriggling in my fists like a trapped rodent.

HARDER.

I was mashing it, crushing it, felt the bones crack, watched his face contort in agony, saw him raise his mouth upward and SCREAM.

Across the aisle the horror scene played out: *Kokoko* whispering, panting; Katie sobbing, begging.

Anguish gushed through me. I'll jump out and scream. I'll run over and hit him. I'll gouge out his eyes! But I couldn't move, could do nothing but watch, frozen in place like a doe in a headlight.

Suddenly he stiffened, his face tipped upward, his mouth dropped open. He made an animal-like grunt as his body jerked.

The undulating lump between Katie's legs trembled, then stopped. She made muffled sobs while *Kokoko* closed his eyes and gulped air, his head drooping. The scene seared itself into my mind: the priest with bowed head, his hand on Katie, Katie swaddled in her dress and mussed bedding, like some perverted imitation of Joseph hunched over the Christ child.

Kokoko recovered the violating hand and looked around nervously, then he looked down at Katie. "There, there, now. We gave the devil a hard time, didn't we?"

Katie looked away, one finger in her mouth. She had stopped crying, strangely fixed on some point on the wall.

Kokoko shushed her again, stroked her forehead. She flinched and cringed away, curled into a ball and lay on her side. I felt the same, wanting to constrict myself into insignificance, wanting to be anywhere but there.

Slater pulled Katie's blanket up snugly over her shoulders and tucked it around her. "Why don't you go to bed early tonight, Katie?" He gave her a peck on the forehead. He leaned closer and whispered, "You are forgiven. Your secret is safe." Then, as if in afterthought, he said, "Remember—God loves you." He stood, adjusted his cassock, stole a quick look around and glided out the door.

When his footsteps faded away down the stairs, I rushed to Katie. "Katie, oh, Katie," was all I could say. I touched her shoulder. It was trembling violently. "I'm here, Katie, I'm here." But Katie remained tense as wire. When I gently touched her face, she flinched and shrank away.

Confused and heartsick, I sat by the bed, my thoughts snarled together like discarded threads from Gram's loom. If only I could sleep with her tonight, hold her like I did Sue when something bad had happened. But the night matron would soon be making her rounds.

Later that night, in the darkness, I heard Katie cry out in her sleep. And for the first time in a very long time, I cried myself to sleep. I cried for Katie, for my own cowardice and humiliation. But mostly, I cried because I sensed that something special, some fragile and sacred portion of our spirits, had died.

It was at recess two days later before I could prod Katie into conversation about the incident. I had tried several times, but she remained in a funk, her eyes continually cast downward. On our third loop around the playground, I could restrain myself no longer. "We've got to tell someone, Katie.

We got to." My breath, along with the open question, hung in the frosty air.

Katie shook her head adamantly. "I don't want to talk about it!"

"But Katie—"

"No!" Her eyes drilled into me and she suddenly seemed years older. "It didn't help the others, did it?" It was a clear statement. Suddenly, Katie was older than me. "It'll only make things worse. *Nobody's* to know, *nobody*. I couldn't bear it."

"But, Katie, you can't let *Kokoko* get away with it. I'll go with you to Blewett."

Tears suddenly sprouted, her eyes wide with fear. "No! If you're my friend, you won't tell!" She grabbed my arm with surprising ferocity, making me flinch. "Remember what happened to Dora. Promise me! You got to promise!"

I remembered all right. Two years ago, when it was discovered that Dora Swan was pregnant, she admitted she had been raped by a seminarian who had since returned to the seminary. Fatlips didn't believe her. Neither did we, for we guessed the true perpetrator. Then Fatlips locked Dora in the basement for three days and three nights for making up "sinful lies." A week later two girls found Dora dead in the shower room, crouched in a corner, sitting in a pool of her own blood. She had opened her veins with a kitchen knife.

But hers was hardly the first suicide in the proud history of St. Nicholas. Like everyone else, I had heard plenty of rumors about unmarked graves in the school's cemetery, about girls who had passed over from untreated illnesses, even malnutrition.

I felt that sick, helpless feeling in the pit of my stomach again. "Oh, God. I should've done something, Katie. I should've done something right then."

Was that the right thing to say? I wasn't sure. I wished I

knew the grown-up words, magic words that would mend the rip in Katie's soul. If only Gram were here, she would know what to say.

Katie didn't answer. She had that distant look again. That special sparkle she once had was gone, replaced by a frightening listlessness. "I'm a bad girl," she mumbled. "Bad."

I was startled. "No! How can you say that? It was him. That slimy—" I couldn't think of a bad enough word. I grabbed her hand. "You're one of the nicest kids in the world. You could never be bad."

For the thousandth time my mind swam through a torrent of conflicting thoughts. Maybe I should tell Sister Steph. No—too dangerous. Suppose she got angry and told off Father Slater or reported the incident to Fatlips? Fatlips might do something bad to Sister Steph. Worse, what if Sister Steph didn't believe me? I could destroy the one friendship I had with a teacher.

Maybe I should go directly to Father Blewett. That, too, seemed impractical. I'd be in more trouble than I could ever imagine for "cooking up such lies." Even if by some stretch of the imagination he listened to me and confronted Father Slater, Slater would only deny it, twist everything around.

I felt my shoulders sagging to match Katie's as I pictured both of us, alone in the basement, in the dark—a punishment far worse than the strap. It would be our word against a priest's. No one ever believed kids, anyway. Especially Indian kids.

The supper bell rang. I saw a chance to be upbeat. "Hey, c'mon. You don't wanna miss out on any food." But since the incident, Katie had seemed indifferent about eating and trudged, zombie-like, toward the dining hall.

Mom's letter arrived five days after Christmas. Sitting cross-legged on my bed, I stared with mixed emotions at the envelope lying next to me. I wanted to rip it open and find out how Daddy was, yet I also wanted to ignore it in revenge. I picked it up and studied it. The postmark was from Starke, the closest post office to Loon Lake, so I knew Momma was safely back home. With a sigh, I tore off the end and pulled out the one-page note:

Dear Ruby,

Well, I'm back home. Your daddy was releesed from the hospital on the 27th. He had a concussion but he's fine now. He sends his love. He's back to work for Schmidt Brothers. I'm sorry about Christmas, honey. Did you like your present? You always liked that loket your daddy gave me so I thought you'd like one of your own. I'm sure you liked Gram's present. I told her you wouldn't be able to wear it there but she insisted. As usual, she did a wonderful job of beeding. You can wear it at home, espescilly at the powwow this summer. The powwow comitee had its first meeting yesterday, I hear. Big plans in the making I guess. Ha. Gram is doing fine. Arnery as usual. I checked in on her this morning. She wanted to know all about you and how you are doing. I tried to get her to come and stay with us at least over the coldest months, but you know her. She won't give up her indipendence. Well, I have to get back to my chores. Sue says she misses you lots! Oh, and she wants to know if you know where her rag doll is? Write momma soon, ok?

All my love,
Momma

P.S. The dime taped to the letter is for stamps, not candy!

My fingers went to the tiny heart-shaped silver locket around my neck. Daddy gave it to me. Thank God he was okay and Gram was okay. Sue, it seemed, hadn't changed, still misplacing her toys.

Disappointment seeped into me. I wanted to read that Daddy had come home, that he and Mom had patched things up and were waiting to greet me, together. But it was not to be. Maybe this summer . . .

I thought of Sue again. How was she really doing without me? I felt a lump in my throat as I recalled one of my favorite Emily Dickinson poems I'd found in the book Sister Steph had given me. Titled "Sue," it was a perfect fit and I had memorized it:

> One sister have I in our house,
> And one, a hedge away.
> There's only one recorded,
> But both belong to me.
>
> One came the road that I came –
> And wore my last year's gown –
> The other, as a bird her nest,
> Builded our hearts among.
>
> Today is far from Childhood –
> But up and down the hills
> I held her hand the tighter –
> Which shortened all the miles –
>
> I spilt the dew –
> But took the morn –
> I chose this single star
> From out the wide night's numbers –
> "Sue"—forevermore!

* * * * *

Trunk day! It was our monthly visit to our personal trunks in the basement, a special time everyone looked forward to. We lined up and marched down to "the dungeon," located our trunks, and were given ten minutes alone. Opening the lid, I went first to the neat stack of banded letters from home and added Mom's recent letter to it. I often reread these old letters over and over. But today I needed something else. I smiled as I removed old tissues and touched the magic surface of my dance barrette. Gram had beaded it to match my dance outfit. The thick oval-cut leather was covered with precise rows of miniature white seed beads. In the center was a crimson rose, beaded in meticulous detail. Gram had used the smallest-sized beads available in order to get the rich detail she wanted. Its forest-green stem, complete with tiny thorns, blended into rich red rose petals on the verge of opening into full blossom.

I traced my finger over the rose, felt the love that went into every stitch as Gram struggled to find the microscopic hole of each bead with a needle the thickness of a hair. "*Manitou-min-esag*—little spirit seeds—that's what we call them. The old people said they were gifts from the *manitouog*. Each bead," Gram had said with her special smile, "carries a prayer for you."

I breathed a heavy sigh. I couldn't even try it on. St. Nicholas had cut my hair too short. I missed beading with Gram, sitting together at the kitchen table, surrounded by strips of cloth and deer hide and a dozen little tin containers filled with colored beads of various sizes as Gram softly hummed and chanted old Ojibwe songs. I missed that wonderful feeling of watching my own floral and geometric designs take shape like gifts from God. I had designed most of my own shawl-dance outfit. But the special rosette I wore around my neck at powwows, and now the barrette, were gifts from Gram, who, everyone agreed, was the finest beader on the rez. People were always asking her to bead something for them.

This summer, I thought with anticipation, Gram would teach me how to gourd stitch—the secret of beading on round things like pipe stems, rattle handles, eagle fan handles, and the like. Next to rosettes, they fascinated me the most.

Taking special care, I re-wrapped the barrette, hid it away in a sock, then gazed toward a high, filthy basement window that admitted feeble daylight. Summer seemed a century away.

Chapter Nine

It was a day I'll never forget, a particularly frigid day in February, around four in the afternoon. I had just walked by the school front entry on my way to kitchen duty. The door burst open and two policemen, followed by three local men I'd never seen before, tramped in. Father Blewett and Sister Margaret must've seen them pull up for they scurried to meet the men in the outer hallway. I flattened against the wall and peeked around the corner.

"We found your missing girls, Father," the first policeman said quietly. "I'm real sorry. If we hadn't had that storm yesterday, we might'a saved 'em."

Father Blewett's body sagged as he crossed himself. Sister Margaret's expression affected me the most. It was the only time I ever saw her look shocked and speechless.

"A real shame," the policeman said. "One of the saddest things I've ever seen. Their tracks show they just kept walking in tighter and tighter circles. Nobody could navigate in that white-out." I heard him sigh. "They had their arms around each other, froze stiff that way. Tryin' to keep each other warm, I guess."

I stiffened and shut my eyes. Like everyone else over the past two days, I'd been rooting for the two runaways, Isabelle and Millie, hoping against hope they'd make it home somehow. When it became obvious they had run away, the faculty panicked and turned the school into a prison camp.

Cops arrived, adding to the tumult. Everyone had to help search the building. The faculty and staff became stone-faced, eyed all of us with menacing looks of suspicion. It was as if they thought we had something to do with Isabelle and Millie's disappearance, as if we had used some kind of sorcery or something. We were lined up and hauled into the principal's office for angry interrogations. Lockers were searched and personal letters scrutinized for clues to the runaways' plans.

The day Isabelle and Millie ran away was unseasonably warm, and most of the snow had melted, but that night a storm hit, a blizzard that plunged temperatures to thirty below and whited-out the night. I pounded my fist against my thigh. Why didn't they wait for spring? Stupid, stupid! Why, *Gitche-Manitou?* Why do you let these things happen to us?

I thought of their families, pictured their weeping mothers and fathers, the stunned faces of sisters and brothers. How many kids had fled this place since 1880, I wondered? How many had made it home?

I searched my memory and the singing words floated into my mind, clear as Loon Lake—not the Our Father or the Twenty-Third Psalm, nor any other Christian devotion, which was fresher in my mind—but *Anishinabe* words, words that had comforted Ojibwe families and eased the *babamadiziwin* of Ojibwe dead into the Land of Souls for countless generations, words I had heard too many times at too many funerals back home.

N'daumaak, k'd'ninguzhimim
N'daumaak, k'maudjauh
N'daumaak, k'cheeby'im
N'daumaak, neewi-goon cheeby-meekunnuh
N'daumaak, waukweeng k'd'izhau

Our sisters, you leave us.
Our sisters, you are leaving.
Our sisters, your spirits.
Our sisters, four days on the Path of Souls.
Our sisters, to the Land of Souls you are bound.

After sewing class the following day, I took a pair of scissors and slid them into my skirt pocket. That night I decided to hold a mourning ceremony for Isabelle and Millie, the nuns be damned. A few brave souls, including Katie, joined me. Together we chanted the death song. A couple of the girls who had been friends with Isabelle and Millie softly wailed in the traditional way, the way they had learned from their mothers and grandmothers. Then I produced the scissors, handed them to Katie and sat on the bed. Katie solemnly took the shears and cut a half-inch off my already short school-shorn hair. Only this way could a woman properly show her grief.

Several other girls patiently waited their turns. I stood and faced them, shears in hand. I felt intensely Indian at that moment. There was a communal sense of pride and heritage, a sense of inner triumph over St. Nicholas and everything it represented.

"Who's next?" I said.

Then Agnes Knockwood, accompanied by two of her cronies, sauntered into the room. They went bug-eyed. "You must be crazy, Loonfoot." Agnes scrutinized the other girls surrounding me. "You bark eaters are dumber than you look. That old Ind'n stuff is gonesville. Don't you know that? You think the Sisters won't see what ya done, your hair all chopped like that?"

I glared at Agnes. Over time her tired Mohawk epithet for us Ojibwes had lost its bite. "We'll all look the same, Agnes, if you go along. Why don't you try being *Shinnob* for once?"

Agnes scoffed. "I'm through with that bull, and if you guys were smart, you'd be too. This is the twentieth century, in case you ain't noticed," she said, regurgitating Sister Greta's favorite exhortation.

I felt like slapping her ugly face. "Isab—" I caught myself, almost speaking the name of the dead. "Two of us are dead, Agnes. How can you be so . . . ignorant at a time like this?"

Agnes smirked. "Why don't you say their names, Ruby? Huh? Isabelle and Millie, Isabelle and Millie, Isabelle and Millie."

I was boiling now. Several of the girls gasped. Katie pushed her way forward and glared up angrily at Agnes. "You're mean and bad, Agnes. You'll get yours for saying the names of the dead."

Agnes looked down her nose at the diminutive girl. "Oh, yeah," she chuckled as she looked at her friends, "their spirits will haunt me now." The Knockwood contingent laughed.

"Make fun all you want, Mohawk," I growled. "But I wouldn't want to be near your bed at night."

Agnes seemed indifferent to the warning. Joyce LaFrance, one of Agnes's sidekicks, arched her eyebrows and raised her hands in the air claw-like. "Ooooo."

More laughter. I thought about twisting her fingers off.

Rose Captain moved to my side. She was a better match for Agnes, who stood an inch taller than me. But Agnes didn't scare me. I'd dealt with her type all my life.

"Why don't you buzz off, Agnes," Rose warned with half-lidded eyes. "If you don't want to go along with the hair cutting, then dry up and blow away."

Agnes sized up Rose with a scornful eye. "Well, if it ain't the white Indian. I don't see you cuttin' your hair."

Rose glanced at me, then back at Agnes. A look of determination painted her face. "Ruby?" Without taking her eyes from Agnes, she plopped on the bed among the hair cuttings. I gave Agnes a triumphant glare as I defiantly snipped the scissors twice for effect, then cut Rose's hair.

Chapter Ten

Theresa Loonfoot was in a funk as she waded empty-handed through calf-deep snow from her mailbox at the reservation general store. She felt empty. It had been two weeks, and yet another of her letters to Jim had gone unanswered. She had thought her appearance over Christmas at the Aberdeen jail to bail him out might've magically mended the chasm that had grown between them, that it would soften his angry feelings.

And it seemed to . . . for a couple of hours.

Theresa sighed. Her love for Jim Loonfoot had not dampened in the eighteen years she'd known him. It began like a match flaring in the night, but the flame remained bright and hot, never shrinking. Such was the reason his long absences as a truck driver, and now his scorn, gave her what her mother called soul-sickness. She wasn't made to be without him. When he was gone she felt anxious and off-center.

For a moment, Ruby's image nudged into her mind. Theresa recalled their meeting at St. Nicholas just before Christmas. Ruby's face had worn expectation like rouge, so excited about coming home for Christmas, about seeing her sister and her grandmother. It made Theresa heartsick to leave her. And Sue had moped around for a week when she learned her sister wasn't coming home.

Theresa looked at the picture of Jesus in the cracked glass frame that hung on a nail above their St. Vincent De Paul sofa, and her mind slipped back to Jim. Since he left, the days had stretched ahead like a hundred miles of bad road. Secretly, she had been glad of the Aberdeen incident—not of Jim's beating, but of his predicament. Perhaps it was one of the Lord's mysterious ways of bringing them together again, offering her a second chance at reclaiming her man.

In Aberdeen, South Dakota they had stayed at the Wigwam Lodge, a ramshackle collection of one-room huts on the fringes of town the owner called cottages. The proprietor, a fat, ruddy-faced man with a drooping beer belly and a coffee-stained undershirt, eyed them with contempt as he grudgingly handed them a key.

"You two married?"

"That's right," Jim replied.

"Well, don't be messin' up the place."

Good old South Dakota. Indian country.

Their key in hand, they drove to the IGA and bought sandwich makings, then splurged and bought two sixpacks of Pabst. Jim switched on the room radio and the soothing voice of Tony Bennett struggled through static.

"I've gone from rags to riches . . ."

"Aw, find some Christmas music, will ya, hon?" Theresa implored, sugar in her voice.

Jim twisted the dial. Gene Autry twanged out *Rudolph the Red Nosed Reindeer.*

"That's better," Theresa cooed.

Jim frowned as he sat on the bed and shucked his boots and socks. "I can't stand that singin'-cowboy shit."

Theresa jumped to soothe. "It'll be over in a minute, hon."

Jim mumbled something unintelligible, then "I'm gonna take a shower, T. Why don't you open us up a couple beers?" He took off his shirt and slid off his jeans.

Theresa brightened. It had been a long time since he had

called her T. "Sure," she said.

A threadbare towel thrown over his left shoulder, Jim disappeared into the bathroom. Her eyes slid down his smooth back, to the fleeting outline of hard, round buttocks beneath his shorts. Dare she hope? Maybe he'd finally forgiven her. They could start over, put the past behind them and go home together. She hummed along with Gene Autry as she used the bottle opener, screwed to the wall by the door, to open two bottles of beer. Using one of the beds as a table, she opened the packages of bread, mayonnaise, and bologna. Twin beds, she noted ruefully. That would make it harder. She turned and stared at the other bed, still on mental tiptoes. Should she turn it down? No, too obvious. She took a long sip of beer and wondered if she could still seduce Jim like she used to, if she could still work "that old black magic," as he used to put it. She felt suddenly warm as she remembered how she used to be able to get him so worked up, to really wind his clock. She returned to the sandwiches. She mustn't let herself get too hopeful, mustn't let herself in for another disappointment.

The bathroom door opened and Jim walked out in his under shorts, rubbing a towel vigorously against his gleaming, shoulder-length, black hair. "Got that beer?" he asked.

Big Jim. Six-four, broad shouldered. He still had a thirty-four-inch waist. "You bet, hon," Theresa replied as she darted to the dresser, retrieved the open bottle and shoved it into his hand.

He took a long slug.

Theresa said, "How 'bout a sandwich?"

"Sounds good."

Theresa turned to retrieve the sandwiches. When she turned back to Jim he was slipping on his jeans. She felt a dip of disappointment as she handed him the sandwich.

"How's my girls?" he wanted to know.

She didn't want to talk about the girls. She wanted to talk about them and their future together. "Ah, which one?"

He raised an eyebrow. "We still have two, don't we?"

"Well, Ruby's a little blue, you know, not being able to come home for Christmas and all, and Sue, she's bratty as usual, what with Ruby gone."

Jim nodded, sat on the bed and looked sad for several moments. Then he glanced at his watch. "I guess you're spendin' the night?"

She winced at the directness of the question. She wanted things to happen naturally tonight. "Well . . . I guess . . . I was kind of hoping . . ."

His brow creased. Theresa felt a rising tide of apprehension. Damn it, why was she such a coward? She hated herself for always feeling guilty. At boarding school she had learned there was always something to feel guilty about. She moved the sandwich makings aside and sat on the opposite bed, facing Jim. "Well, I was kind of hoping we could talk."

Jim finished off the beer. Theresa reached out for it. "Here, hon. I'll take that for ya. How about another?" she offered, already pulling out another bottle. She opened it, handed it to him. "I just wanted us to have a couple days together like we used to." This time she sat next to him on his bed. She combed her fingers through his damp hair. He stiffened.

"It's just that I miss you so much. I . . ." She trailed off, unsure how to phrase her feelings without using words like "forgive" or "trust," words that would remind him of why he left her in the first place.

He looked sharply at her. "How the hell do you think I feel? I miss my kids. I miss my house. I miss having a wife."

Theresa swallowed her pain and squeezed his arm. "But

you can have all that. It's what I want, what the girls want."

He made a hard, dry laugh and looked away. Theresa felt a gnawing feeling of desperation, which came out in a cloudburst of words. "You know I'm sorry, Jim. I made ONE mistake. In a way, I didn't—I mean—it was him more than me. I told you I kept saying no, no, no, but he just kept pushing and pushing, and I'd had too many beers, and you and me had that fight before you left, and you'd been gone so much with your job and all—"

Jim shook off her hand. "Bullshit!" He stood. "You screwed my own cousin in my own house. I was out bustin' my ass, trying to make a living for you and the girls, and you screwed me over." He chugged down the beer.

This was going all wrong; she had blown it again. Angry tears began to flow. "Jesus, Jim, haven't I paid for my sin a hundred times over? Earl raped me!"

Again the biting laugh. "That's not the way it looked when I walked in, babe." The way he emphasized "babe" made her insides shrivel, made her feel like she was a common tramp. But she wasn't a tramp. She was a virgin when she and Jim married and she had never even thought of straying. Sometimes she almost convinced herself that the Earl incident never happened, that it was a bad dream. She had always trusted Jim's cousin, let him console her that one lonely night, and somehow it had gotten out of hand and his strong hands were everywhere, knowing just where to touch, whispering in her ear words she desperately wanted to hear from Jim. He had taken advantage when she had been vulnerable, her mind swimming from the booze, and she kept telling him no, that it was wrong, but he wouldn't stop and she had been too weak, too intimidated to push him away and throw him out.

God, she was sick of feeling intimidated by men—by her

father, by her brothers, by priests, by her husband. Like an old record, her life spun in an endless, dreary circle, slowly wearing down the grooves. It seemed everyone except her controlled her life. She felt it, hated it, but felt powerless to change it. Her throat thickening, she let the argument die, as she always did, by hanging her head and crying.

Later, they went to a nearby café and had an uneasy dinner, their conversation sparse and insipid. That night they climbed into separate beds. After a while, her courage restored by the darkness of a moonless night and the distant strains of *Moonlight Serenade* from the cabin next door, she remembered how he used to kiss her neck while they danced close, that the radio was playing their song. She turned to tell him, but his back was to her, his breathing measured in the slow dance of sleep.

Chapter Eleven

Sister Margaret added the last column of figures, leaned back in her chair and frowned. She scanned the grocery invoices again. Something was out of whack but she couldn't pinpoint it. There was shrinkage taking place somewhere. Father Blewett had turned over food buying to her and she had done what she could with a budget of fifty-nine cents a day per student and $1.37 for the staff. After all, store-bought bread was sixteen cents a loaf, and milk was an outrageous eighty-eight cents a gallon.

The school had always used lard instead of butter in the student cafeteria. She wasn't about to serve lard to the staff. So she had started buying two-day-old bread, then stopped putting mayonnaise on student sandwiches. Government powdered eggs helped, as did surplus pork and flour. Finally, she'd had to substitute skim milk for whole. That, she was unhappy about. She always felt children should drink whole milk and plenty of it.

She knew the children were often hungry and were no doubt filching from the pantry.

She couldn't blame them. Next to the church, food was her favorite pastime. She sometimes worried about the sin of gluttony. But it was too painful to consider. The word "diet" was harsh as a sailor's curse in her ears. Besides, look what she had given up to work with these heathen children in the middle of nowhere. What other pleasure did she have in life?

She wouldn't investigate the shrinkage for now. And if the

diocese cut their food budget one more time, she'd go to the bishop personally. How do they expect children to learn if they're hungry?

Fools.

Men.

There was a shave-and-a-haircut knock at her door, and Father Milton J. Potts peeked in. "Busy, Sister?"

She nodded. "I just finished."

Potts came to St. Nicholas last summer after a stint in the Army. The "character code" in his personnel file was marked with a "D," denoting "lack of suitability." With a bit of detective work, Margaret had put the pieces together. The Army had ruled Chaplain Potts unfit for duty after he gave the post commander's nephew a severe whipping at a church retreat. He was given a choice: take a general discharge from the Army or join the Indian service. Since Sister Margaret controlled all files at St. Nicholas, Milton had become one of her best informants, grateful for her silence.

He closed the door and took a seat. "I'm afraid I don't have much on those two runaways except it seems they were planning their getaway for several weeks. They had cut themselves off from the other kids. Whispered together a lot. Their grades were lousy."

"What about others?"

Smiling, Potts shook his head. "I don't think we'll have any more runaways for a while after two Indian Popsicles."

Sister Margaret glowered at him.

Potts cleared his throat and leaned forward. "Get some heat from HQ, did you?"

Potts loved military jargon. He swaggered around like some misplaced top sergeant. Sister Margaret's eyes narrowed. "Nothing I can't handle." She allowed her stare to linger a while, then, "But Father Blewett looks like he's on the verge of a breakdown. He can't take that kind of pressure."

Potts nodded, his brow furrowing in a transparent attempt at solicitude.

Margaret stood and peered out her window, her hands behind her back. She tried not to look at him for very long. He was probably the ugliest man she'd ever seen. Turning back to him she said, "Still, I'm worried about more runaways come spring."

Potts shrugged. "They know if they're caught they'll get their heads shaved and a couple nights in the hole."

Margaret eyed the priest again, a touch of sarcasm creeping into her voice. "And you like to shave heads, don't you, Milton?"

His face colored slightly, but he recovered quickly, placing his hands on his paunch and interlocking his fingers in an attitude of studied indifference.

Margaret nibbled at her lower lip in concentrated thought. "Still, we'll have to do something to nip future runaways in the bud." She looked sternly at him, as if he alone held the key. "I don't want any more deaths on my conscience. Mother of mercy, we're here to make these children good Catholics and productive members of society, not kill them off." Potts's glazed-over eyes annoyed her. She removed her glasses and peered directly at him. "You're new here, so I'll give you our philosophy. These are children of a helpless race to be pitied and cared for. Our mission is to educate them as to the ways of the modern Christian world, which we've been doing successfully since 1880. We painstakingly remove the Indian in them, give them an education and some domestic skills, then send them home, where they continue our work. It is the going-back-home that is important here. They take these little seeds of knowledge and skills and spread them to others—the nonbelievers—back on the reservation. Our children show them the ignorance of their ways. The holdouts back on the reservation slowly become social outcasts until they either submit to reality or keep their opinions and pagan ceremonies to themselves."

Potts shot her a look of wide-eyed innocence, his hand covering his heart. "I couldn't agree more, Sister."

Margaret narrowed her eyes. "All right then. I'll bring up runaways at tomorrow's faculty meeting. In the meantime, see what you can come up with to ensure we have no runaways this spring."

Potts pursed his lips, then, "I'm sure I can come up with something."

Chapter Twelve

Finally, a letter from Daddy came. I had the same feelings about opening it as when Mom's letter came, but I opened it quickly, hoping for answers, hungering for his words.

Dear Ruby,

How's my best girl? I'm sorry I haven't written for a while. Schmidt Brothers have been keeping me reel busy. I been every where between Hayward and Seattle! I can't wait to see you in June! Honey, I know your mad about me and Mom and all but we love you both very much. I just wanted to tell you that what happened between Mom and I had nothing to do with you or Sue. These things are adult things. Ruby, your a big girl now so you need to know that sometimes adults cant work these things out. I'm not saying we won't, I just don't want you to get your hopes up too high.

Oh, yeah, almost forgot. A few weeks ago I happened to be near Anadarko and they were throwing a big powwow over there. I traded that beaded pouch I had for a really swell Canadian goose dance fan for you! You'll look great with it at the Loon Lake dance!

Well, I got to get this letter to the post office since I got to get back on the road early in the morning. I'm just outside of Boise right now and got to be in Portland early tomorrow. Sending hugs to my little warrior.

Love,
Daddy

I didn't completely believe him about things not being my fault, but I glowed from the assurance of his love. Did he mean it? God, if only I could be sure.

Later, in the cafeteria some thirty of us stood in line awaiting our turns at collation, the 4:15 snack.

"I hate these," Rose complained as she watched me and Katie munch hungrily away at our raw turnips.

"Suit yourself," I retorted between bites. "It's almost two hours till supper."

Rose looked sadly at the turnips. "Gosh, what I wouldn't give for a hamburger."

I rolled my eyes at her. "Don't even say it or you'll get us thinking about it, too."

Rose sighed and bit into the turnip. She made a face but kept chewing. "I'm sick of being hungry. Sick, sick, sick! I can see my ribs in the mirror."

I scanned the near vicinity. Seeing no Robes, I made a pious face and lowered my voice to sound like Father Blewett. "Welcome, my child, to St. Starving—uh—I mean St. Nicholas."

Katie snorted, "St. Starving!" and almost choked on her turnip.

"God, you sound just like him," Rose chuckled admiringly. "You're really good."

Katie piped up. "That's nothin'. She can do a bunch others even better."

Rose looked intrigued. "Yeah?"

Katie nodded with enthusiasm. "Do Fatlips, Ruby!"

Mildly embarrassed but inwardly pleased, I declined.

Katie looked pained. "Aw, c'mon. *Daga?*"

I didn't need much encouragement to show off. I scanned the area again, then furrowed my brow in mock sternness, put my hands on my hips and waddled penguin-like while saying in a raspy voice, "All right. Which little heathen did it? We'll stand here all day if we have to, but by Joseph, I'll know the truth before the day's out!"

My audience laughed, their hands flying to cover their mouths.

"I can't believe it—that's her!" Rose exclaimed.

I stopped grinning when I glimpsed the big wall clock. "Shoot, chores in four minutes. What you got today, Katie?"

"Mopping."

"Kitchen duty," Rose reported wearily.

I smiled. "I got the chapel."

"Luckee," Katie said.

"Hey, that reminds me," I said. "Have your confessions worked out for tonight. *Kokoko*'s doing confession again."

Katie's face fell.

Rose said, "So?"

I laid a consoling hand on Katie's shoulder, then looked at Rose. "You're still new to this, Rose. I'll tell you about it at supper." I switched my attention to Katie. "Now don't be getting all upset. We've gone over this. Just make up three innocent little sins and don't let him talk you into any others. Little white lies are always good, like, 'I lied to Rose Dubois when I told her her hair looked nice when it really didn't.' Just think three, three, three—'all I got is three sins.' Okay?"

Katie's expression grew distant, but she nodded.

"Why three?" Rose asked.

"Two's not enough," I said. "They never believe just two, but three makes 'em happy."

A bell rang and the halls filled with scampering girls, headed in every direction for chore time. I strolled down the hall and into the chapel, whistling *Heart and Soul.* I almost smashed Father Potts in the face with the door, though even if I had, it couldn't mar his face further. He had a puss like pounded steak, a mass of pits and scars.

"Oh, sorry, Father Potts."

He glowered at me. "Whistling in the chapel?"

I put on my best penitent look. Though he was different from *Kokoko,* there was something about him that gave me the willies.

"What are you doing in here, anyway?" he barked.

"Chores, Father."

Potts grunted.

I tried not to look at his tiny, pig-like eyes.

"Let me see your number." I reached under my collar and pulled out my school necklace. He tugged at the attached rosary bag, pulling it closer to see it better in the dusky chapel light. He eyed my student number on the affixed medallion. His breath reeked of wine.

"Well, enjoy the easy duty, B807. Next week you can have latrine duty—all week. That'll teach you to whistle in God's house."

He stalked past me and out the swinging doors. Anger and revulsion hit me. An unusually good day ruined. Like everybody else, I avoided lavatory duty like the plague. Smelly, backed-up toilets, grimy floors, hairy sinks—we were hardly a neat lot—and in the winter, freezing drafts and frosty-rimmed toilets. Now my entire weekend was ruined just thinking about it. Approaching the altar, I genuflected out of habit, then turned right into the sacristy. More smells of old wood and stale air, then a slight aroma of incense greeted my nose. I sneezed.

Incense—one of the reasons I hated High Mass. The priest swung that stupid smoker over and over until my eyes burned and my nose ran like Gram's pump. Why couldn't he just swing it once and be done with it? That gave me an idea. I began searching for the incense maker, opening cabinets, pulling out drawers. I finally found the smelly gadget in a lower cabinet and examined it in the sunlight that struggled in through a small, dark stained-glass window. It was rather pretty for such an offensive thing. The filigreed, polished silver gleamed. I lifted a small domed cover that revealed a round, charred plate, obviously the holder for the burning incense. Remembering the Nativity play, I wondered if it used frankincense.

Why didn't they use sweet grass or cedar like we did back home? The pleasing aromas of smoldering sweet grass or cedar smelled a whole lot better, and they didn't make me sneeze. Another of the great mysteries of the Church. I guessed all religions were full of mysteries and secrets. I sneezed again and cursed the thing in Ojibwe—a mild curse. Now, where to stash it?

My scheme was interrupted by a soft knock at the heavy door that led outdoors. Who could that be? I slid the heavy bolt aside and cracked the door. Billy Whitaker's pudgy mug looked at me in surprise, his cowlick fully aroused.

"Oh, it's you," he said.

"Who'd you expect, St. Catherine?" I retorted. Icy air swirled around the door. "Well, c'mon, you're lettin' in cold air."

He stepped through the door and I closed it behind him. "Father's not here if you're looking for him," I snipped, hoping that would send him on his way. I couldn't stomach this flabby, sneaky-eyed kid. Billy came from nearby Doanville to assist the priests for Saturday and Sunday Mass. Though we were the same age, he was smaller and stockier. His freckled cheeks were rosy from the cold wind. He wore a red-and-black plaid coat with a matching billed cap, which sported built-in earmuffs that flapped down over his ears.

Aside from being the only altar boy and Potts's toady servant, Billy had developed a reputation among us girls as a harmless panhandler and a general pest. He maintained a constant wide-eyed expression of innocence until he was up to something, then shifty eyes darted in every direction as he spoke. But he was a boy, a rarity at St. Nicholas, and therefore a curiosity to some and, as nauseating as the thought may be, interesting to a few. There was even a rumor that that *dedeens* Agnes saw him kiss Joyce LaFrance in this very room.

In spite of myself I felt suddenly—and irksomely—self-conscious about my appearance: my school skirt that was one size too small and cut into my waist, my blouse—two sizes too large and yellowed from months of starch. I felt like a gunnysack.

"I thought maybe Agnes'd be here," he said, never looking directly at me, his eyes alighting on the bulky oak wine cask at the far corner. It was Agnes who usually drew chapel duty, thanks to her suck-up relationship with Fatlips.

"Well, she ain't. I got chapel duty today. Now what do you want? I'm busy."

"Ah, well, ah—"

I tossed my head, sighed and folded my arms across my chest, looking as pained and impatient as possible.

Billy pulled off a mitten with his teeth, shoved his hand into his right coat pocket and produced a canning jar. "I'll give ya a nickel if ya fill 'dis up," he mumbled through still-clenched teeth.

"With what, holy water?" I answered incredulously.

He whipped the mitten out of his mouth with his other hand. "No, no." His hazel eyes darted around like tadpoles. "With wine," he whispered.

"You *are* crazy. Now get out of here," I said, starting for the door.

For a fleeting moment, Billy's eyes actually focused on me. "No, wait!" He groped his pocket and produced a coin. "Okay, I'll give ya a dime."

The dime screamed TAKE ME, but I ignored it with surprising will power and went for the door handle. Billy said, "Hey, they'll be havin' candy store day on Sunday. A dime could come in handy." He waggled his eyebrows.

Every Sunday after the second Mass, Sister Steph ran a "candy store" in the rec room, where we could buy a small amount of candy. A box of Dots danced in my mind, then a couple of sticks of red licorice. Who's to know? I thought. "Okay. Give me the jar." Billy grinned and handed it to me. I took it to the sink and filled it with water.

"Heyyyy," he complained.

"Hold your horses," I chided, pulling out the plug in the top of the cask. I peered into it, then poured in the water. Twisting the spigot, I filled the jar with wine and handed it to him. "That way," I said with aplomb, "nobody'll be the wiser."

Billy scrutinized the jar, then took a sip. "Well," he paused a moment, "I guess it tastes okay."

"Of course it does, silly. The barrel's almost full."

Billy's mouth formed a lopsided grin as he dropped the dime in my greedy palm. "Say, you're all right. What's your name?"

I opened the door. "Never mind. I prefer to remain monomonous," I said with my nose tilted slightly upward, pleased with myself for using a phrase Sister Steph had used in English class.

Billy's eyes flitted over my shoulder. "Somethin' wrong with that censer?"

I followed his gaze. "Is that what they call it?"

"Yeah. Didn't ya know that?"

I gave him a cold stare. "You never saw that censer, get me?"

Billy's eyebrows shot up in surprise.

"You didn't see the censer and I never touched that wine barrel, right?"

"Oh—sure," Billy winked, "I get ya."

I gestured toward the open door. "Now, out! It's freezing in here and I got work to do."

Billy shrugged and strutted out the door.

Closing the door, I examined the dime, smiled, and pocketed it. I turned and eyed the censer on the countertop. What to do with it? At first I had wanted to make off with it and bury it under the goop in one of the big kitchen garbage cans, but Billy had seen me with it. Also, I knew that when *Kokoko* discovered the censer was missing, the first people suspected would be those who recently had chapel duty. A thought struck like a church bell. Agnes Knockwood would be the first blamed, the sacristy being her usual domain. She would be back on duty tomorrow. I laughed out loud at the brilliance of it.

I finally found a niche in the back of a lonely cupboard that contained some old towels and glasses that obviously hadn't been used in years. I laid the censer down behind the towels. That should do it, I smiled to myself, and after finishing my chores, I headed triumphantly to the dorm for study hour.

Chapter Thirteen

Father John Vincent Slater sat at his desk polishing the last few lines of the evening's homily. He was on a roll. This evening's sermon would be the third in a series covering the seven deadly sins, a perfect tie-in for his "guided confessions." The central theme was "The Seventh Commandment and Sins of the Self." Last Sunday he had lectured on the insidiousness of self-abuse. This Sunday he would cover the inherent wrongs of self-importance, greed and selfishness. Finally, he would stress the value of self-denial.

With a flourish, he poked the last period onto the page. He would definitely have to send a copy of this to his cousin, Bishop Swazey, along with an outline of the entire "self" series. With any luck, Swazey was talking up Father Slater with his superiors. Another feather in John Vincent's cap, a complimentary memo in his file to aid his own ascendancy to bishop one day. Maybe archbishop?

He leaned back in his chair, closed his eyes and heard a disembodied voice: Ladies and Gentlemen, Archbishop John Vincent Slater. A brilliant E minor chord swells from an enormous pipe organ and reverberates throughout the stone-vaulted ceiling of a great cathedral. A hundred-voice choir lifts their voices in splendid euphony. His congregation rises to their feet as he flows majestically down thick, red-and-gold carpet, dressed in the crisp whiteness of an archbishop's robes and dual-peaked hat. Behind him march priests, deacons, subdeacons, and nuns, their hands peaked in an attitude of prayer. Now the priests arrive at the bishop's chair, a massive, high-backed throne with a tufted red velvet seat at the far end of a great marble altar.

That's how it will be, he thought. The vision had played across his mind in Cinemascope so many times. He knew every detail, every nuance of it.

Suddenly, he thought of his father, Philip, the man he dared not disappoint. Dad always managed to upset John Vincent's apple cart. "Son, the greatest day for your father will be seeing you in bishop's robes." Philip had wanted to be a priest, but *his* father would have none of it. After all, Philip was an only child, the last of the line to carry the Slater name. His task in life was to produce a son. Unfortunately for his grandfather, John Vincent had also been an only child. So the demise of the Slater name had only been delayed, and the promise of a doting relationship between grandfather and grandson collapsed in bitter disappointment. John Vincent's grandfather had not spoken to him since John Vincent announced he was entering the priesthood.

The proud priest frowned. He hated it when these thoughts poked their way into his mind and spoiled his day. His eyes fell oncc more on the text of his homily. He read it through again, basking in his gift for trenchant prose and witty turn of phrase. Thoughts of his father and grandfather evaporated like a mirage as John Vincent, whistling *Nearer My God to Thee*, left his room and strode off toward the chapel. Mustn't be late for confessions.

Chapter Fourteen

I stood in line staring at the curtained confessional in front of me. I was next, and was starting to feel the familiar dry mouth and clammy hands that always accompanied confession. Knowing I had to be strong for Katie, I turned and forced a smile toward her fearful face. "C'mon, you know what to do. It'll be over in a minute. Nothin' to it."

Katie eyed me doubtfully and fed on her fingernails. I squeezed her hand, then looked at Rose Captain, standing behind her. Rose's eyes were distant, as if she were concentrating on something. Probably getting her three sins straight.

The confessional curtain whipped aside, and Agnes Knockwood strode out. "You're next, Loonybird," she quipped as she sashayed by. "I left a surprise in there for ya," she sniggered. I frowned at Agnes's back, then glanced down at Katie, managed a wink of reassurance and entered the dark booth, thankful there was a wall, albeit thin, between me and *Kokoko*.

I almost gagged at the lingering odor and fanned the air. Agnes was definitely the most disgusting girl I'd ever met. *Smells like you look, Agnes*.

I crossed myself. "Bless me, Father, for I have sinned. It's been a week since my last confession." I always thought this statement was stupid. Of course he knew how long it had been. We went through this every Friday.

"Well, Miss Loonfoot, what have you to tell me tonight?"

His voice was beckoning, syrup-smooth.

"I lied three times this week, Father. Little white lies, though."

"I see. To whom?"

"Some other girls."

There was an expectant pause, then, "Surely there's more?"

"That's all, Father."

He was silent a moment, then, "Did you pay attention to what I said in last week's homily about self-abuse?"

My ears felt suddenly hot, and I shrank in my seat. "Ah— yes, Father."

"Did you understand what I was talking about?"

"Yes."

"Well, then, did you touch yourself this week?"

No matter how much I prepared for *Kokoko*'s confessions, it always felt like he jumped out of the dark and yelled "boo." The image of his hand tented under Katie's sheet popped into my mind like a buoy released.

"No, Father. Good girls don't do that," I embellished, hoping this would end his interrogation.

"You're so right. Very well, say three Hail Marys. Go, my child, and sin no more."

I flew from the booth, and in my rush to escape almost crashed into Katie. Katie's face paled and I cursed myself. For her sake I had planned to exit the confessional in a nonchalant manner, like it had been a snap. Then I spotted Sister Greta a short distance away, watching. I straightened and hurriedly crossed myself.

Well, Katie had to start toughening up if she was to survive St. Nicholas. I had certainly given "little sister" enough pep talks. I gave her a tight smile and a thumbs up. "Piece 'o cake," I whispered and bolted for the chapel doors.

Chapter Fifteen

John Vincent was delighted when the next girl slipped into the confessional. He could make out her features through the screen.

"Ble-bless me, Father, for I have sinned. It's been a week since my—"

"Ahh, my little Katie."

She had squeezed herself into the tiny corner, her head bent down in an obvious effort to not look at him. "I missed you today," he said. "I watched for you in the halls but I didn't see you."

Katie said nothing.

"Did you miss me?" he prompted.

"Uh—yes—Father." Her voice sounded like mouse squeaks.

"You sound frightened. Don't be frightened. You know Father loves you, don't you?"

"I—I guess." Barely audible.

"Good," he said, his voice soft and comforting. "I don't want you to be frightened of me. I want you to love me as much as I love you. It's our secret, Katie. Remember? It's because you're special. You're different from the rest."

"B-but why does it have to be a secret, Father?"

They always asked this sooner or later. His answer was practiced. "Because they wouldn't understand, Katie. They could never understand the kind of love we share. They would punish you if they knew. That's why we must be secretive, right?"

"Ye-yes, Father."

"Good. Now, what were those little sins you wanted to tell Father about tonight?"

"I told three white lies, Father"

There was a pause. "That sounds familiar. And you feel bad about that, don't you?"

"Yes, Father."

John Vincent paused. Perhaps she'd elaborate, but she said nothing more.

"And you want forgiveness."

"Ye-yes, Father."

"Did you touch yourself this week?"

He heard her suck in her breath.

"Oh—no, Father."

"That's good, Katie. You and I—we know the proper way to take care of that, don't we?"

Again he paused, then, "All right, say one Glory Be and two Hail Marys and I'll see you later."

"Yes, Father," she mumbled, then crossed herself in a blur of hand motions. The required words fountained from her. "Oh my God, I'm heartily sorry for having offended thee. I dread the loss of heaven . . . fear the pains of hell . . ." then she bolted from the confessional.

When the next girl entered the confessional, John Vincent squinted through the screen, trying to place her. After she spoke the opening words he recognized her. "You're the new girl."

"Yes, Father."

"Well, we'll have to get to know each other," he said with disinterest. She was too old, too plain. "Now, what do you have to tell me tonight?"

Even through the dark screen John Vincent could see her face scrunch up in anguished thought, as if she were trying hard to recall something. A memorized answer, no doubt.

"Well?"

She blurted, "Ah, I, ah . . . I . . . broke the sixth commandment, Father."

John Vincent was shocked. "YOU WHAT? YOU DARE MOCK ME?"

"Oh—oh, no, Father. I—I—"

Shock turned to anger. How dare this pipsqueak girl mock him? "ARE YOU AWARE OF THE SEVERITY OF MOCKING THE CONFESSIONAL? ARE YOU?"

Tears flooded down her cheeks. "I'm sor—sorry, Father. I got mixed up. I didn't mean—"

"You'd better be sorry, young lady. You'll say ten Our Fathers and the Apostles' Creed tonight and think about what you did. And I'd better NEVER hear this kind of mockery again or you'll wish I'd given you a hundred Apostles' Creeds. Do you understand me?"

"Yes, Father."

"NOW GO."

The impudent girl stumbled through the Act of Contrition and fled the confessional. Slater flung aside his curtain, stood, and watched her flee up the aisle and out through the chapel doors. He'd remember her, this Rose Captain.

I was startled when Rose burst through the chapel doors and into the outer hall where Katie and I were waiting. "What happened? We heard him yelling all the way out here."

Rose broke down in sobs. "I'm in big trouble. I messed up."

The poor girl was devastated. I touched her arm. "What do you mean, you messed up?"

"I-I don't know. I had it all worked out perfect—"

Our conversation halted when two other girls emerged through the doors. A girl with buckteeth said, "I only got three Hail Marys. Whad' you get?"

Her friend frowned and looked at the floor as they walked down the hall. "Three Our Fathers."

"Gosh," the long-faced girl with buckteeth exclaimed. "Those are sooo long."

When the girls had disappeared around a corner, Rose continued ruefully, "I was going to say I broke the commandment about coveting your neighbor's stuff. I thought it was the sixth commandment and—"

I bit my lip, trying not to laugh.

Rose stopped in mid-sentence, her brow furrowing. "What?"

"Rose, the sixth commandment is the one about adultery."

Rose's eyes widened to the size of saucers. "Oh, jeez!"

I covered my mouth to stifle a snort. I didn't want to laugh, Rose being so humiliated and all, but I couldn't help it. I guess my odd-sounding snigger served to jump-start Katie's comic giggle. Then we were all laughing, laughing harder than we had in a long time.

I squeezed myself between Rose and Katie, threw my arms around their shoulders and drew them close. "Hey," I whispered, "that's nothin'. Wait till he can't find the incense maker this Sunday."

Rose and Katie grinned at each other like two cats who'd shared a canary.

Chapter Sixteen

Billy Whitaker helped John Vincent don his alb for the second Mass of the morning. He lifted the heavy green-and-white chasuble and held it as Father Slater slipped in his arms. "All right, Billy, you can light the censer," he said as he kissed the embroidered stole. Billy opened the cabinet where he'd last placed the censer. Nothing but old glassware. He opened the adjacent cabinet. Nothing but some old albs and yellowed altar cloths.

Father Slater turned. "Problem?"

Billy's face scrunched in bewilderment. "Ah, well, the censer ain't where it's s'posed to be, Fadder."

John Vincent frowned, both at Billy's remark and at his irritating country-bumpkin accent. "Try down there," he suggested, pointing to a cabinet below.

Billy checked. "Not there eedder, Fadder."

Together, they began opening and closing cabinets. Suddenly, Billy's face lit up as if he remembered something. "Gosh, I just saw—" He stopped midstream, his face paling and eyes widening as he looked at the wine cask.

"What is it?"

"Ah, notin' Fadder. I was just surprised it wasn't where I put it, 'tsall."

John Vincent grunted and checked his watch—8:50. Mass started in ten minutes.

Five minutes later they had opened every cabinet. John

Vincent's eyes narrowed as he appraised his acolyte. "If this is some kind of prank, Billy . . ."

Billy's ears reddened. "Honest, Fadder! I put it right there, where I always do. I wouldn't never fool with sompin' like that. That would be a sin. Maybe Fadder Potts put it somewhere, you know, by accident or sompin'."

John Vincent eyed the boy skeptically.

Billy brightened again. "Maybe somebody was cleanin' it and put it away wrong."

The priest's skeptical expression transformed into a knowing frown. "Agnes," he thought aloud. "She's usually the one who cleans up in here." He checked his watch again. Three minutes. He watched Billy's prominent Adam's apple jerk up and down like a toad's, a trait of the boy's when he was nervous. John Vincent felt his stomach tighten. There was no precedent for this. Frustrated, he ground his teeth as he opened the door leading to the chapel and peeked out at the full pews. How can you conduct High Mass without incense?

Billy interrupted his thoughts. "Gosh. Whad'a we gonna do, Fadder?"

John Vincent felt like strangling this kid with the kinky red hair, freckles and protruding yellow-green teeth. "Do? There's nothing we can do. Now get out there and light the candles. We're two minutes late."

John Vincent seethed as he watched the boy light the altar candles. Though he disliked violence, he visualized a hard, flat paddle smacking against Agnes Knockwood's soft, round fanny.

Chapter Seventeen

After Mass, Katie, Rose and I pranced into the rec room, barely constraining our glee. "Did you see Slater's face?" Rose chuckled, her hand cupped over her mouth.

"He looked really mad," Katie giggled.

I bit my lower lip, then snorted a laugh. "Funny, I didn't sneeze once."

We all roared.

"Hey," Rose said. "Let's turn on the radio."

I went over to the Philco and turned it on. I was in a great mood. Both Masses were over and this afternoon was candy store day. The shiny new dime Billy gave me was burning a hole in my pocket.

While the radio warmed up, most of the other girls strolled into the rec room from the chapel, laughing and talking. The radio came to life with Patti Page.

"How much is that dog-gie in the win-dow?" she sang.

Katie and I made dog paws with our hands and stretched out our necks, "Arf! Arf!"

Rose laughed, then chimed in at the next refrain.

Patti Page finished up and Big Joe Turner jived-up the beat with *Shake, Rattle and Roll.*

Rose's face lit up and she grabbed my hand. "C'mon, let's dance."

Our hands joined and I felt the beat driving through me. I loved to jitterbug. We dipped, spun, and twirled each other, now and then whooping in delight at our own skill. Katie clapped while she studied our dizzying footwork. Several girls gathered around, laughing and clapping to the beat, then two other girls started to dance with each other. Rose and I were now in full swing, our faces flushed, shirttails pulled out and flapping, our bobbed hair bouncing.

No one paid attention to Agnes Knockwood as she sauntered by until her hand suddenly darted out and smacked the back of Katie's head. Katie let out a yelp and turned to glare at Agnes. "Quit it, bugle beak!"

I saw the blow from the corner of my eye. A burst of red-hot anger shot through me. "Leave her alone!" I shouted.

Agnes swiveled on her heel and faced me with slitted eyes. "Make me!"

I took two steps closer. "Don't think I won't."

Agnes planted her fists on her hips. "You and whose army?"

Rose stepped up next to me. "This one."

I continued to eye Agnes. "I don't need an army to whip a chicken that beats up on little kids."

Agnes moved to within breath-smell distance, her face screwing up into a sneer as she peered at Katie over my shoulder. "You mean Father Slater's little girlfriend?"

I heard Katie's sudden intake of breath. Rage detonated within me and I was on Agnes like a mother bobcat, landing a ringing slap on her right cheek. Agnes's eyes grew large as melons as she faltered back a step. But I was a tornado of swinging arms and with my left hand grabbed a fistful of Agnes's hair and yanked while pummeling away with my right. Agnes cried out in surprise but managed to get a fistful of my hair with her left hand and thrashed away at my side with her right. Agnes's best buddy, Joyce LaFrance, moved toward us, but Rose took a step forward, halting her midstride with a menacing glare. "Don't even think about it," I heard her say.

Joyce blinked and stepped back.

"Fight! Fight!" The girls in the rec room swarmed around Agnes and me, yelling and shouting, the two of us like entangled dervishes, pulling hair, slapping, yelling.

"WHAT'S GOING ON HERE?" Father Slater's voice cut through the din as he, Sister Margaret and two other nuns surged into the room. The crowd parted to make way, leaving Agnes and me, still going at each other in the center of the room like prizefighters in a ring. I landed one last blow before Sister Margaret's meaty arm pulled me off Agnes and Father Slater held Agnes's arms behind her back. "WHAT'S THE MEANING OF THIS? WHO STARTED IT?"

Agnes and I started talking at once.

Sister Margaret glowered at me. "QUIET!"

I shut up, eyeing the gleaming paddle in her right hand.

Sister Margaret glared at Agnes. "What's going on here?"

Panting, Agnes touched two fingers to her nostrils, then frowned at the streak of blood on them. She thrust an accusing finger at me. "She started it! I was just walkin' by, mindin' my own business."

"That's a lie!" Rose blurted.

"It is not! I saw the whole thing, Sister. Ruby started it all right," Joyce defended.

Sister Margaret glared at Rose. "You keep quiet! No one asked you." She looked at no one in particular. "Turn off that radio. I can't hear myself think."

Someone switched off the radio. Sister Margaret's face was livid with condemnation. "You're a troublemaker, Miss Loonfoot. And now, fighting. And just after Mass." She shook her head as if in disbelief.

Her lower lip trembling, Katie took a fearful step forward,

her voice barely audible. "Hon—honest, Sister. Ruby was just standin' up for—"

Fatlips shot Katie an angry glare. "I didn't ask for your opinion, Miss Red Star."

Katie's head drooped.

Turning back to me, Fatlips said, "You know the punishment for fighting."

I stiffened. Despite my anger, I mentally cringed at the thought of the paddle. Still, I managed to keep my face expressionless, refusing to give her the satisfaction of seeing my fear.

Fatlips looked at Joyce. "Pull that chair over here."

With a smirk, Joyce pulled a chair next to me.

"You know the position, Miss Loonfoot," Fatlips said.

I glared at the nun for several moments. I can only imagine the hatred in my eyes as Sister Margaret looked—for a second—taken aback. I grasped the back of the chair with my left hand, reached around and pulled up the back of my dress with my right. My breath started to come in quickening spurts as I tightened my butt muscles and braced for the pain.

Katie started to sob, panic in her voice. "But Sister—"

Fatlips pushed her aside, walked behind me and pulled down my panties. From the corner of my eye I could see *Kokoko,* still holding Agnes's arms, his eyes glued to my fanny, and an almost smothering feeling of humiliation overtook me, piling on top of the dread. Slater's eyes, my fellow students' eyes, all focusing on my exposure.

Smack!

Regardless of my preparation, the power and swiftness of the first blow caught me by surprise and I sucked in air. Just as I was feeling the sting, SMACK—the second blow, then the third, the pain building, throbbing, stinging like a hot iron against my skin until, finally, I cried out on the sixth blow.

The hated tears came. I bit my lip, hard, and squeezed shut my eyes.

Smack!

I bit down harder, hoping to switch the pain from my butt to my lip.

Smack!

Oh, God!

Smack!

Jesus, help me . . .

Smack!

My stomach wrenched; I tasted the sour warning of vomit.

Smack!

I cried out, almost a scream.

Fatlips stepped back, her shoulders drooping, breathing hard. "Let that be a lesson to all of you. We *do not* condone fighting."

I was sobbing so hard I could hardly catch my breath as I straightened and shakily pulled up my panties. All I could think of was that at least I didn't puke in front of everyone.

Rose and Katie ran to take my arms, Katie straightening the back of my dress, bawling, "I'm sorry, Ruby; I'm so sorry."

Rose's face was a mask of hatred as she glowered at Fatlips.

I glanced at Agnes. Her expression had changed from smugness to a kind of begrudging respect.

"Hold on to your paddle, Sister. We're not done yet," Father Slater announced.

Fatlips gave him a questioning look.

Slater's eyes narrowed at Agnes. "How many whacks do you think someone should get for stealing my censer?"

Fatlips' eyebrows arched as she thought aloud. "I thought something was missing from Mass this morning—of course, the incense." She frowned. "But Agnes? I doubt—"

Agnes's mouth dropped open as she apparently began to realize of what she was accused. "Not me, Father. I didn't—"

Slater cut her off, his dark, bushy eyebrows twitching like frenzied caterpillars. "Forget it, Agnes. You're the one who usually cleans the chapel. I know Billy didn't hide it."

Agnes paled. "But—"

"Save it, Agnes! Between now and next Sunday, you will replace the censer, and for penitence, after you've said thirty Our Fathers, you can clean the lavatories for the next month." Slater appeared to be enjoying the shock on Agnes's face. He obviously disliked the gawky, big-nosed girl.

Agnes looked beseechingly at her mentor, but Sister Margaret was now looking at her with disdain.

Slater looked back at Margaret. "Well? How many?"

Handing him the paddle, Fatlips muttered, "That's your decision, Father."

Slater looked surprised, as if her answer wasn't what he'd expected, as if he had expected Fatlips to do the paddling. We'd never seen him with the paddle. But all eyes were upon him now so he begrudgingly took it.

Agnes started to blubber, "But—Sister Margaret—you can't let him. I didn't do it!"

Slater pointed with the paddle to the chair. "Assume the position and raise your dress."

Trembling and sobbing, Agnes did as she was told, still protesting her innocence. "Why don't you believe me? I wouldn't never do anything like that!"

Slater cleared his throat. "Uh—Sister. If you'll—" He pointed the paddle at Agnes's underpants.

"Let's look into this first, Father," Fatlips said hesitantly. "It isn't like Agnes to—"

Slater gave her a withering glare. “Don’t argue with me, Sister.”

Sister Margaret sighed, then reluctantly pulled Agnes’s panties down just enough to expose the upper part of her bottom.

“Please, Father. I—I didn’t do nothing, honest.”

Yes! I thought. Give it to her! She may not have done this particular prank but she’d made so many of us miserable.

Slater flushed as he stared at her bare buttocks. Pinpricks of sweat beaded his brow. Finally he swung the paddle at half the force of Sister Margaret’s blows. Agnes squealed. He winced and swung again, somewhat lighter. Agnes screamed louder. He hesitated then swung again, and once morc, wincing at the horrible smacking sound, the piteous howling from Agnes. I was taken aback. He looked as if he didn’t really want to do this. He raised the paddle for the fifth blow, but the paddle hung suspended like a still shot. His face suddenly paled. For a moment I thought he might faint. Suddenly, he thrust out the paddle to Sister Margaret, wheeled around and fled the room.

A whimpering Agnes looked piteously at Sister Margaret, who sighed. She looked as if she might reach out a comforting touch, then pulled her hand back. “Shush now, child,” she said. “You can certainly suffer a little when you think of how much our Lord suffered for us.”

Chapter Eighteen

Completing their business at the smoke shop and general store, Cecelia and Marvin picked their way across the frozen mud and gravel road that separated the clinic and the tribal office. Parked in front of the tribal office was Luther's '48 green International pickup. Cecelia recalled that the tribe had presented it to him as an honor gift when he returned from Korea. Though it was bought used, it was an expensive gift for people who didn't have two nickels to rub together. But that was Ojibwes. Honor the veterans, the warriors.

She glanced at Marvin, remembering the ceremonies he had led, the special prayers, the sweats. And there was the gift of a ceremonial *opwagun,* and finally the special dance put on for the returning vets: Luther, Frank and Harley. Everyone came and everyone brought gifts. There were speeches by the council, testimonials from friends and family, a blanket dance that raised over $800, and to top it off, the pickup for Luther, who was the only returning vet without a vehicle.

The two elders trudged up the four wooden steps into the building that Luther said reminded him of his boot-camp barracks: gray clapboard with a green shingle roof. Weathered paint peeled sadly in several places.

"Well, *boozhoo,*" said a surprised Thelma Wemigwans, Luther's secretary. "Look who's here! Come on in and get warm."

"Who's that?" Luther asked as he walked in from his back

office. *"Ahneen, Ahneen,"* he said as he shook their hands. "How 'bout some coffee?"

"Sounds good," Marvin replied, then glanced at Cecelia. "Cecelia?"

She nodded as Luther helped her off with her coat and scarf, then held her arm as she eased onto a lumpy couch against the wall. "Make that three coffees, Thelma," Luther said as he took Cecelia's cane and propped it in the corner.

"Comin' right up," Thelma called from the doorway. "Got some good sweet rolls left, too."

Cecelia winked. "You know my sweet tooth."

Thelma sidled over to a small work area to pour coffee and picked out two sweet rolls. "Want a roll, Luther?"

"No, thanks, Thelma." He patted his belly. "Gotta start watching the waistline."

Thelma served Marvin and Cecelia their refreshments. "Oh," she said over her shoulder to Luther, "that letter you been waitin' on came."

"From BIA?" he asked over the too-loud religious music on her radio.

"Yep." She handed him the already opened envelope. Thelma was the first to know anything that happened on the rez, thanks to her position and her uncanny network of informers and gossips. But she was good-hearted and loyal to Luther. Last week, Cecelia heard, she had hustled Millie Shell out of the office for calling Luther a do-nothing.

"Same ol' crap," Thelma divulged. "Dear Chairman White Bear," she chanted, her head bobbing rhythmically with the words, "We're doing our best to serve the needs of all the tribes with very limited funds. Be assured that the funding your reservation receives is in line with other reservations of similar size, blah, blah, blah."

"Oh, bull—" Luther stopped midsentence and eyed

Cecelia. He never swore in front of women. "I know darn well that we're getting screwed. How the hell do those jerks in Washington expect us to run a tribe of 813 souls and 5,100 acres on the pittance they send us?" He shook his head and looked at Cecelia. "Nothing's changed in a hundred years. They interpret treaties to the benefit of the government."

"Eya," Cecelia agreed. She knew that, at Luther's request, the tribal finance committee had recently completed a yearlong study of past treaties versus monies received. Their efforts revealed that the Bureau of Indian Affairs owed the Loon Lake Tribe well over three million dollars, probably a lot more.

"They might as well let John Dillinger run the BIA disbursement office," Thelma added.

Luther grunted, then, "C'mon back to my office. I'll crank up the space heater for you."

Cecelia and Marvin followed him in.

Luther leaned down and turned on the space heater, then straightened and combed his fingers through his long black hair. "There's a bunch of money going in somebody's pocket, *Nokomis,* but it sure isn't going to the tribes. We've got elders freezing in winter, kids without shoes, homes without heat or water, no school, and no jobs other than the nineteen at the tribal fishery."

Thelma interrupted his thoughts by calling from his office doorway. "Hey, Chief. Did ya hear that?"

"Hear what?"

"On the radio," she said, blinking her eyes in astonishment. "They were talkin' about Stalin and said he died three years ago. I didn't know that."

Luther made a wry smile. "Don't you believe it, Thelma. He's alive and running the BIA."

Thelma *tsked* and waved him off.

Cecelia was wondering who Stalin was.

Luther paused at the large worktable in front of his desk and stared briefly at a pile of engineering drawings and reports. "Well, here it is, Cecelia. The Yellow Hill water project."

Yellow Hill was the oldest section of the reservation and home to many elders and traditional Ojibwes, including Cecelia. Luther had made a campaign promise to put running water in every Yellow Hill home. "Every time I manage to get some money put aside, another crisis sprouts up—like food or fuel. I'm ashamed that so many Loon Lake elders are without running water."

Marvin gave Luther's shoulder a fatherly grasp. "You're doing your best, Nephew. When it is meant to happen, it will. The Creator provides."

Luther sighed, walked around the desk and dropped into his government-surplus desk chair, which squeaked and dipped precariously to the right. "Here's something else you two will find interesting." He held up a letter. "This is from our good neighbor, the town of Starke. The gall of these people. The mayor is asking if I and a few of 'my people' would participate in next month's Treaty Day Celebration for the centennial of the 1857 treaty."

Cecelia knew the treaty very well. It forced the tribe to cede the bulk of their lands and move onto a reservation and was signed at the Starke courthouse. She followed Luther's eyes to the large portrait on the opposite wall of Maengun, The Wolf, chief of the Loon Lake Tribe during treaty times. It was a wonderful rendering, inked by a man named George Catlin, Luther had told her, during his travels through Indian country in the 1830s. The Wolf was in his twenties then. His uncle was chief at the time. Maengun's reputation was that of a natural leader, a man who could not be plied by alcohol, money or gifts, a man of fairness and extraordinary inner strength. It pleased her that Luther had chosen him as his moral compass.

"Thelma?" Luther called toward the door.

"Yeah, Chief."

"Call the mayor's secretary and tell her we're tied up."

"You got it."

Once everyone was resettled in Luther's office, they conversed about the weather: a frigid winter, the lack of propane money, the death of an elderly couple who had frozen to death in their home in January.

Marvin shook his head sadly and switched to English. "Every winter we lose elders. It ain't right."

Cecelia watched Luther's shoulders slump. "Now, don't you go blaming yourself, Luther. It is not your fault. Everyone in Indian Country knows the BIA owes us money, them," she said, her English colored by Ojibwe grammatical rules.

Luther nodded.

Marvin's eyes drifted to the pile of engineering drawings on a worktable beside Luther's desk. "Sure wish we could get that water going."

Luther wistfully eyed the drawings. "We're trying, Uncle, we're trying."

"We been trying to get that water project funded for ten years. Folks out at Yellow Hill are still using outhouses and cisterns, them." Marvin grumbled,

"I know, Uncle. We'll get it done one way or another."

Marvin set his coffee cup on the table and produced a pack of Camels from his shirt pocket, offering one to Luther. He knew Cecelia didn't smoke. Luther accepted.

Marvin sat back, took a long introspective puff, and cleared his throat.

The time has arrived, Cecelia thought.

The holy man nodded his head in her direction. "You know, Cecelia's granddaughter goes down there at that school, her."

Luther frowned in thought.

"You remember my *noozis* Ruby, Theresa's daughter," Cecelia prompted, slipping back into Ojibwe. "The fancy dancer," Cecelia added.

"Sure—Ruby, Theresa's daughter. She gonna compete again at the powwow this year? How's she doing?"

Marvin said, "Cecelia don't know."

Luther looked at Cecelia. "Doesn't know?"

"She's still at that school," Luther added.

"Which one?" Luther asked.

"St. Nicholas," Cecelia said flatly.

"Well, what's Theresa say?" Luther asked. "Doesn't she hear from her?"

Cecelia shook her head. "She doesn't hear much. Besides, that girl's got a lot of her own problems to work out, her." She felt a momentary brush of sadness.

Luther asked, "Isn't Ruby writing to you and her mom?"

"She writes," Cecelia shrugged, "but she don't say much. They mark out a lot of her words."

Marvin knocked ashes off his Camel into a heavy glass ashtray. "They look like some of them letters we used to get from you boys after the Army finished with them."

Luther nodded in understanding. "Censors." His brow creased in annoyance. "Never understood what a school needs with censors."

"They been doing it for years, them," Marvin said. "I hear a lot of strange things happen up there."

Luther said, "Well, those stories are about the old days. This is 1957. I know those nuns can get a little tough now and then, but . . ." His face lit up. "Tell ya what. Why don't we call them up right now, *Nokomis,* and you can talk to Ruby."

Thelma's voice came from the doorway. "Forget it, Chief. They don't let those kids talk on the phone."

Luther turned toward her with a look of irritation. She was leaning against the doorframe, arms folded. "Thelma, haven't you got something to do out there?"

Thelma shrugged, stepped from the doorway and closed the door.

Marvin leaned forward again, his eyes drilling into Luther's as he spoke. "Nephew, you're a good chief, but you're young. You were gone for four years in the Army. Then you came back here and got elected chief. Before all that, you went to that public school over in Hayward. You don't know about these other schools because most folks don't talk about it. Your father, for instance."

Surprise painted Luther's face. "My dad?"

Marvin nodded. "I'll bet he didn't talk about his schooling, *eya?*"

"He was a man of few words as you remember, Uncle," Luther said, still looking puzzled.

"Notice he didn't send you or your brothers to them schools, him."

Luther and his brothers, Cecelia knew, had lived with an uncle in Hayward so they could attend public schools. They had come home every weekend and during the summers.

Luther nodded. *"Geget."*

"You ever see those scars on his back?" Marvin asked.

Luther blew out smoke in a quick stream and eyed Marvin with an I-know-you're-working-toward-something look. "Sure, they were from a farm accident."

Marvin often made his point via a story or a reference to a person or a place, just like her Calvin, Cecelia reflected.

Marvin Big Shield was not an educated man, but he was the wisest man on the rez, and Luther knew it.

Marvin's eyes turned grave as he shook his head. "*Gaawiin gwayak*. Them were belt-buckle scars." He leaned forward in his chair. "Nephew, what we need is our own school."

Chapter Nineteen

Saturday morning I stared out the dorm window at a cold, damp, blustery day. I hated March, the broken-snowshoe-month, when winter should be over but wasn't. It was too wet and soggy to go outdoors. Worst of all, Lent was coming, the time of sackcloth, ashes and self-denial. Right down *Kokoko*'s alley, I thought. I wondered what he would give up for Lent. For me and the other kids, it would be sweets. When given a choice, everybody picked something easy to forgo, like gum, which we could only chew in the rec room on candy day, so Sister Margaret had decided to cancel Candy Store Day for a month. Actually, it wasn't bad. It reminded me of our fasting tradition, those times when Ojibwes fasted, sometimes for three or four days in preparation of special ceremonies or for spiritual cleansing. They did it a lot in the old days. Nowadays, mostly just the boys do it during their *bawajigaywin*. Gram, though, says fasting is good for the body and spirit.

I heard a metal pail clank against the floor and turned to see that Agnes Knockwood had just run out of the lavatory, a handkerchief pushed against her mouth and nose. She was cleaning the toilets. Thanks to ancient plumbing and poor maintenance, toilets often stuffed up or wouldn't flush, so one held her breath, flushed, ran out, sucked in fresh air, ran back in, scrubbed a bowl, ran back outside, breathed, and then started over with the next toilet—hold, flush, run, breathe, scrub, hold, and so on. Sometimes they overflowed and then you had a *real* mess to clean up. No one paid her any mind. Not even her friends offered to help, not for lav duty.

A hint of shame crept over me again. Still smarting from the pain and humiliation of my paddling, I had witnessed the first whack on Agnes's fanny with intense satisfaction. I wanted her to hurt, to pay for her cruelty, to feel the humiliation of baring herself in public. But the third smack made me wince with empathy. And on the fourth blow a sudden surge of guilt rushed through me, that sour taste lapping again at the back of my throat. Watching the sobbing and cowering Agnes, surrounded by her friends, who had moved away from her, I found myself glad her beating was brief. I wished I'd never seen that damn censer.

I sneaked into the sacristy the day after her paddling and put the censer in plain sight on a countertop. Should Billy Whitaker ever think to mention he saw me and the censer together that one day, Agnes would surely get her revenge. But I had that covered. Should Agnes come swinging at me, I'd threaten to tell *Kokoko* that Agnes was selling wine (and Lord knows what else) to Billy. No wonder she was always flush with candy money.

Such was the delicate system of checks and balances that worked so well at good ol' St. Nic's.

I jumped when Rose Captain appeared as if from nowhere and touched my arm. "Criminy, Rose! You scared me."

"Sorry," Rose said, eyeing a group of girls close by. She leaned close to my ear. "You up for a kitchen raid tonight?"

That perked me up. "Hey, you're catchin' on fast!"

"I heard the staff had apple pie and chocolate chip cookies last night. There oughta be some leftovers, don't ya think?" Rose winked.

"You bet," I said, my mouth already watering at the thought.

Katie walked up and pulled on my sleeve.

I gave her a playful poke. "What's up, brat?"

She looked miserable as she rose up on tiptoes and whispered in my ear. She had wet her bed again, the fourth time in the past two weeks. So much for a raid tonight. I gave her a frustrated glare. Katie flushed and stared at the floor. I didn't want to hurt her feelings, but the bed-wetting was getting old fast. Each time she had an accident, we had to strip the bed, wipe down the mattress, sneak the smelly sheets down to the laundry, and swipe fresh ones. All this to protect her from the strap.

"Katie, this has gotta stop."

It came out harsher than I intended.

Katie sniffed, turned on her heel and ran to her bed.

I sighed in exasperation. The bed-wetting had started out of the blue this year.

Heavy footsteps sounded in the stairwell, then the tap-tap of a yardstick against the metal door. "All right, ladies," Sister Margaret announced. "By your beds. Surprise inspection."

I gasped and my eyes met Katie's across the room. There was a communal groan as we made our way to the feet of our beds. Fatlips started on Katie's side of the room. Katie's bed, third from the door, was still unmade. Fatlips started to inspect the first bed and surrounding area when she spied Katie's rumpled bed. She quick-stepped to it and eyed Katie. "What's this?"

Katie studied the floor, trembling.

"What's that I smell?" Fatlips sniffed, leaned over and felt the damp sheet. She made a sound of disgust and turned to Katie. "You should be ashamed of yourself!" The edge of the yardstick came down with a thud on the top of Katie's head. Katie yelped and covered her head with her hands. The yardstick whipped through the air again—SMACK—striking the top of Katie's hands, and she cried out again.

I clamped shut my eyes and willed Katie to be tough, to remember our innumerable conversations about being an *ogichidaw*. But Katie's reply was always a woeful, "I can't help it."

"Get that sheet off the bed!" Fatlips demanded.

One hand still protecting her head, Katie tugged off the sheet.

"Put it over your head!"

Katie slowly pulled the sheet over her head.

Fatlips turned angry eyes toward me. "Miss Loonfoot. Come over here."

I knew what was coming.

The whites of Fatlips' eyes were cold as lard. When I stood next to Katie, Fatlips lectured on. "Since you're her guardian angel, I'm putting you in charge of making sure Miss Red Star keeps this sheet on all day. Get some string and tie it so she can walk."

This was the standard punishment for bed-wetting. I didn't answer; I wished Fatlips would eat rat poison and die. Public humiliation was the last thing Katie needed. Was Fatlips blind to what Katie and some of the other girls were going through with *Kokoko?* Or didn't she care?

Fatlips' glare returned to Katie. "It's for your own good, young lady. Maybe this will embarrass you enough that you'll not repeat this infantile behavior." She shook her head. "A girl your age."

It was the longest Saturday in history. I had to lead Katie by the hand everywhere, and while many of the girls kept their silence, others snickered and whispered behind their hands. Katie grew more silent, her hand growing colder, her grip on me tighter.

At supper the sheet of shame was finally removed, and we went our separate ways for chores and homework. Later, I went to the rec room. Near the radio several girls, led by Rose, were mooning over Frankie Laine as he sang a throaty "I be-lieve that love is the answer. I be-lieve that love will find a way."

Katie was drooped in a chair in a far corner, alone. "Katie?" I called. She just stared at the floor. Her entire body was trembling. I filled with dread. She had been out of sight for three hours. I kneeled beside her, rested my hand on her knee. My mouth felt dust-dry. "Did *Kokoko . . . ?*" I decided to rephrase the question. "Were you with Father Slater again?"

Katie studied the floor another moment, then lifted glistening eyes to me. Her voice was almost a whisper. "He l-loves me, ya know."

Chapter Twenty

In his room, John Vincent gave Lucy Otter absolution and a soft caress on the behind, then showed her to the door. He adored her—but not as much as Katie. Katie was special. He loved all his children, and they loved him. Why shouldn't they? He was their good shepherd. He gave them what they wanted, what their sinful young bodies craved, then gave them absolution for it. A perfect symbiotic relationship, all kept within the sanctity and purity of the church. Immaculate sin, he termed it. Since children were naturally prone to sin, their urges could be satisfied through a son of the church, thereby obviating the child's need to transgress outside the confines of the church. The urge, the act, then absolution—all within his personal trinity: Jesus Christ, himself as intermediary, and the child.

He looked at his watch. Student supper hour—perfect. He left his room and stole up the green-painted stairs to the dorm floor, where the air was redolent with girl smells. Tonight he decided to start his tour at Katie's bed, going first to her stand-alone metal closet. He opened the door and smiled as he swept his eyes across her hangered white school blouses, her extra plaid school skirt, a faded yellow jumper, a frayed flowered sundress.

He pulled the jumper close to his face and inhaled deeply, relishing the prepubescent girl smell. One by one he fingered the blouses, sniffed one or two. With exquisite expectation he slid out her underwear drawer and with an almost religious reverence, gently selected one of the white cotton panties. He touched it to his cheek and closed his eyes, feeling it, no, sensing it against his skin, luxuriating in the tactile sensations on his fingers, careful not to rush.

He thought of the treasured novel secreted away under his mattress, and Nabokov's words flooded his mind. "Ah, my Lolita. So shy, so teasingly demure, so close to perfection if it were not for her natural predilection toward sin."

Closing his eyes, her image floated across the backs of his eyelids like a movie: wide onyx eyes, soft pouty mouth, silky black hair, softly downed tawny skin. Now he was tenderly pulling her closer, his hands—barely touching her—moving down her sides, then to the gentle curve of her lower back. He swayed, almost losing his balance in his languor. Only Nabokov understood his feelings, his guilt—

Lolita. Light of my life; fire of my loins.
My sin, my soul. Lo-li-ta.

A bell rang, shattering his fantasy. Still, it took a few seconds for him to return to reality. Lately, it seemed his urges were growing more powerful, taking over, sapping his will. Perhaps it was because reality never equaled fantasy, and so he kept trying, kept secretly aching for that one sublime feeling of ecstasy his Lolitas never produced; secretly because personal gratification was not supposed to be his goal. That was Lucifer intruding, he knew, that corrupt side he must continually guard against, else fall inexorably away from the light and toward darkness, destined to prowl schoolyards and carnivals like some depraved heathen. No—he was, after all, only carrying out his mission, his holy purpose of cleanser and helper. Those other feelings, those black fantasies conjured by Lucifer, were God's way of testing his faith, his vows.

John Vincent looked self-consciously around. He was still alone. Like a lover long deprived he brushed his fingers across the blouses before he shut the closet door. On his way to the dorm door, he hovered near Ruby's bed. Now there was a titillating but troubling little temptress. So confident, so brash. And so intimidating, that nymphet with the moody mouth and wary eyes. She was the kind that could not be confirmed into his holy trinity.

With a quick glance toward the stairway, he picked up her pillow and sniffed. She was there—her scent more mature but still girlish. He once had her picked out for his trinity, but even then she had been so . . . emasculating. Those precocious, shrewd eyes warned him away, hinted at something feral inside, which three years ago had almost driven him mad with unholy desire. He had wanted to break that rock-hard barrier, wanted to soften that threatening glare of hers, tame her wildness, bring her "into the fold." His jaw tightened in frustration. In the end, foreboding had supplanted want. Instinct told him she was dangerous.

Laughter and girl talk echoed from the stairwell. He sighed, straightened his collar and combed his fingers through his thick brown hair. His mind shifted to his class tomorrow morning and his mood took an upswing. Katie would be there.

Chapter Twenty-One

My fingers moved hesitantly over the piano keys as I struggled to hit the correct notes for the melody, maintain middle C position, and, with my left hand, coordinate the bass line. There was so much to think about in preparing each finger move, but for the last eight measures it all worked gloriously. My fingers fell under my command, spidering across glossy keys, and the simple melody sounded like a symphony in my ears. I was actually doing it—making music! It was magic—as if I and the piano were one, drifting and floating across the rec room ceiling. I held down the final G-major chord, and it hung in the air like Momma's sweet perfume.

"Excellent job, Ruby!" Sister Steph praised. "You're catching on fast." Sister Steph looked at her watch. "Gracious. I'd best be off for Bible study. Now, for next week," she turned the page in the étude book, "work on the next étude. Be careful. This one starts in the G position."

I touched her arm. It had taken me all week to summon the courage; it was now or never. Someone had to be told about Katie, and Sister Steph was the only one I trusted.

"Sister Steph, can I talk to you a minute?"

She smiled. "For you, I always have a minute."

I scanned the room. We were alone for the moment. "I'm—I'm worried about Katie."

Sister Steph raised an eyebrow. "Katie Red Star?"

"Yes, ma'am. You see, well . . ." God, what was the right

way to say it? "I have to tell someone, and—"

Sister Steph's brow furrowed slightly. "What is it, Ruby?"

I felt my confidence ebbing now that she sat facing me. "It's—it's about Father Slater."

"Father Slater? I thought it was about Katie."

"Well, yes, ma'am, it's about, uh, them both."

She looked puzzled. "Go on."

I felt my throat closing up. "Father Slater has been, well, touching her."

Her brow pinched ominously. "Whatever are you talking about?"

I sucked in a breath. "He's been touching her . . . in a sinful way."

Sister Steph's face paled. "Ruby, do you have any idea what you are saying?" She crossed herself and looked around the room, her face flushing. Her voice became a tense whisper. "How could you say something like that?"

I bit my lip. Her tone of voice and accusing eyes made my stomach start to hurt. I couldn't bear to lose her friendship and trust. "I'm not making it up. Honest."

She started to get up, her voice cold, almost accusing. "I won't hear this. I won't. I can't believe you'd say such a thing."

I grasped her sleeve. "I saw it happen."

Sister Steph's frown deepened as she slowly settled back down onto the piano bench. "Saw what happen?"

I recounted the night in the dorm when I had hid under her bed and watched *Kokoko* and Katie. Then I told about Katie's bed-wetting, her morose behavior, and finally, Katie's insistence that Slater loved her.

She looked like she'd seen Satan appear.

I blurted on, "I'm sure Katie ain't the only one."

"Jesus, Joseph and Mary." Her eyes became distant,

peering somewhere over my shoulder. "I can't believe it. I just can't." She rose, her eyes already searching out the doorway. "I—I have to go. I need time to think, I . . ." Her voice trailed off. She looked flustered and frightened. "We'll talk about this later."

Then she hurried from the room.

Chapter Twenty-Two

Sister Stephanie drifted down the hall in a daze. How could she not know something like this was going on? "And Katie's not the only one," Ruby had said. Good Lord, how could this be?

She shook her head and silently prayed. Oh, Heavenly Father, let this be a misunderstanding—perhaps Ruby had misinterpreted what she saw. She was at that age when hormones were beginning to surge. It wasn't unusual for a girl to fantasize about an older man, especially one as handsome as Father Slater. After all, it was only seven years ago that she was Ruby's age.

That had to be it. No priest in her experience had been anything but devout and caring, starting with her Uncle Mark, who had ministered to the Indians at Rocky Boy. A more gentle and considerate man never existed. And Father Slater—well, he was the epitome of a priest destined for higher office—and the Bishop's cousin. No, the idea of a molesting priest was just too preposterous, too sickening to contemplate. Such a reality would shake the foundation of her devotion to the Church.

A flurry of conflicting emotions swirled within her. What was Ruby trying to do? An elder brother often teased Stephanie about being idealistic and naïve, that she should go and experience what life was really about before taking her vows. But this was too much. Could she have so misjudged Ruby? Had Ruby's charming behavior and her concern for

Katie all been a pretense? Did Ruby in reality despise the Church so much that she would make all this up? In hopes of what? Causing trouble for Father Slater? Ruining St. Nicholas?

She couldn't believe that, no matter how naïve she might be. Her head ached. She was sure she knew Ruby, this bright and honest diamond in the rough. Or *had* she been duped?

This would take some time and a great deal of prayer to sort out. In her current dark mood she didn't want to confront Ruby again, not until she had calmed down and prayed for guidance. The Blessed Virgin always came through for her in times like these. *She* would lead Stephanie in the right direction.

Chapter Twenty-Three

Shoulders slumped, I trudged to the dorm. I couldn't forget the expressions on Sister Steph's face: horror, disbelief, then . . . anger? I fell on my bed and buried my face in my hands. Obviously I had made a horrible mistake in telling her about *Kokoko*. The whole thing had backfired, and now Sister Steph was angry with me. Worse, she apparently thought I was a liar. Didn't she realize how special our relationship was, that I would never lie to her?

A familiar veil of loneliness draped over me, the return of an evil presence I thought I had exorcised long ago. I peered out the drafty dorm window. A late April snow flurry fell, blanketing the trees and ground in a sheer white robe. Eddies swirled around the window. The Earth still sleeps, Gram always said.

A three-story maple, my favorite, stood budding against the greening landscape, its great limbs reaching toward a murky light above. I was suddenly flooded with memories of home: ice fishing with Dad, watching Gram stirring bubbling pots of sap, the luscious taste of fresh maple syrup. Before boarding school, when I was little, it was on days like this when we gathered at Gram's house for *manomen,* blueberry pie and stories—Ojibwe stories. I searched my mind and remembered two or three, but like old photos, they had faded with passing years. I sighed, fighting a rising tide of melancholy, but it continued to accumulate, piling on me like wet snow.

A flicker of movement outside caught my attention. A lone cardinal, flame red, perched on a branch. I touched a finger to the frosty glass. *Misko-binesheenh, have you brought me a message?* The cardinal looked at me and cocked its head as if listening, then flitted away. Spring is coming soon. Gram would say that's what the cardinal's early appearance foretold.

I went to my footlocker and retrieved the Emily Dickinson book. Lately it seemed I looked at it only when I felt lonely or homesick. I opened to the poem "Loneliness." The first and last stanzas hit home.

> The Loneliness One dare not sound,
> And would as soon surmise
> As in its Grave go plumbing
> To ascertain the size,
>
> I fear me this—is Loneliness,
> The Maker of the soul
> Its Caverns and its Corridors
> Illuminate—or seal

A thought poked into my mind. Gram had once cautioned, "When there's trouble, *Bineshee Ogichidaw,* people side with their own kind." Sister Steph would side with her own. It seemed it was me and Katie against the world.

Chapter Twenty-Four

Two weeks later a gentle rain pattered against the school windows. Sister Stephanie sighed deeply as she held a sobbing Katie, her own cheeks shiny with tears. She had left Katie for last, not wanting Katie's story to influence her thinking during the other interviews.

Mother of God—five little girls. She knew now what she must do, and it would be the most difficult, the most wrenching thing she would ever have to do.

Katie's sobs subsided into a string of ragged, halting sighs as Stephanie wiped the child's tears and nose with a handkerchief. Katie's glistening dark eyes peered piteously into Stephanie's, expecting . . . what? What could she possibly say to assuage a child's shattered soul? What rationalization could she make about a monster priest; about a system, of which she was a part, that remained aloof while evil festered within? She wanted to rage at Father Slater: WHAT ARE YOU DOING HERE, YOU TRAITOR TO GOD, YOU PERVERTED BEAST? Her ears warmed in shame for the half-spoken curse, and she said a silent Hail Mary.

Katie pleaded, "He s-said he l-loved me, like G-God loves me. But I think God hates me."

Stephanie rocked her gently back and forth. "Oh, little one, God does love you. He loves you more than anything in the world. It's Father Slater, darlin'," she consoled, slipping into her Irish grandmother's soothing brogue. "He's been . . .

mixed-up," was all she could think to say. "Something has made his soul sick."

"Throw-up kinda sick?"

"No, darlin'," Stephanie said, touching her finger to Katie's forehead. "Sick in here."

Katie searched Stephanie's eyes, then nodded. "He said he loves me." She paused. "But then he hurts me."

Stephanie tightened her lips and swallowed a sob. This hadn't gotten any easier, even after four similar gut-wrenching interviews, and she fought the urge to run, to flee to the warmth and safety of home and family, never to see St. Nicholas again. "I know he did, darlin'. But that's all over now. Sister Steph is going to take care of this. In the meantime make sure you are never alone. Always be with a friend. If Father Slater tells you to come to his office or some other place by yourself, you tell him you can't because you're on an errand for me. Understand?"

Katie nodded.

"Okay, now," Stephanie said with a tentative smile. "You just leave this to Sister Steph. Father Slater won't hurt you anymore. I have to go monitor Sister Elizabeth's exam now. She's ill today. You can stay here in my office for a bit if you like. I've written a pass for you. When you're feeling better, go on to your next class, okay?"

"Okay, Sister."

A sense of despair fell over Stephanie as she made her way to Sister Elizabeth's class. Her stomach dipped as she recalled last night's dream where she was drowning in an inky sea. There had been a radiant-white lifeboat glowing not ten yards from her. It was full of clerics, among them Sister Margaret and Father Slater. But they merely looked on dispassionately as she sank below the roiling surface.

After class, Stephanie hurried to her room without

speaking to anyone. Since she had discovered the truth about Slater she felt suddenly isolated. Who else knew the obscene secret? Was there a conspiracy of silence?

She had decided not to speak to Sister Margaret about the molestations. In some ways she feared the imperious keeper of the files as much as she now did Father Slater. Besides disbelief, Stephanie felt the elder nun's first reaction would be to protect her school and the Church.

As for Father Blewett, he hibernated in his office. Stephanie had no rapport with him whatsoever. No, someone outside St. Nicholas had to be made aware of these outrages, someone with the power to do something about it quickly. But what would be the repercussions for her, barely out of the novitiate, for being the messenger of such unspeakable news? That unanswered question shook her to the core. The Church, the Sisterhood, were her life.

She decided to write the most important letter of her career. The letter would be anonymous, though it made her feel small inside. Then, she would face Ruby and beg her forgiveness for doubting her. With pen in hand she began her letter to Bishop Swazey.

Chapter Twenty-Five

I trudged to English class, my mood sagging with each step of the stairs. I used to look forward to Sister Steph's class, but she seemed distant since I told her about *Kokoko*. In the hallways she averted her eyes from me. And though I had waited for her, she hadn't shown up for my Saturday-night piano lesson for two weeks. My sadness transformed into bitterness. Why should I feel guilty about telling the truth? And how could Sister Steph betray me so by making me feel guilty?

As always, Sister Steph stood at her classroom door, greeting each girl, her habit sleeves waving like raven wings. I looked at the floor and started to rush by, but she touched my shoulder. "Wait here a moment, Ruby," she said quietly.

I discerned the old softness in her voice, and stood aside as the last two girls filed in. The young nun clasped my shoulder and we moved away from the doorway. She leaned down and whispered, "You were right, Ruby. I'm so, so sorry. Will you meet me in front of the rec room tonight?"

The remainder of the day passed with the speed of a slug. Finally, suppertime arrived, and after a pasty repast of macaroni and cheese, the third time that week, and after chore time, I raced expectantly to the rec room. Thanks to Sister Greta, who had made me scrub the entryway grout with a toothbrush, I was twenty minutes late. Just as I had feared, Sister Steph was not there. I'd missed her. I struck the wall with the heel of my hand, then slumped against it. Now what would Sister Steph think of me?

"I thought I saw you," Katie said, peeking around the doorway. Her face screwed up into a frown. "What's the matter, you sick or something?"

"Naw," I muttered.

Her face anxious, Katie grabbed my hand. "C'mon. Elvis is on the radio."

I allowed myself to be pulled into the rec room. Four girls were holding their Christmas kaleidoscopes like microphones and harmonizing along with *Love Me Tender*, while a flock of others sat cross-legged or slouched in chairs around them, eyes closed and swaying with dreamy looks on their faces. The St. Nic's backup singers were pretty good, but Katie, who usually chimed in, only watched. I looked on with mild interest. However, watching Katie's less-than-enthusiastic participation gave me an idea, and after the song I pulled her to a far corner of the room. "Katie, did Sister Steph talk to you about *Kokoko?*"

Katie's face fell. "You promised you wouldn't tell."

I sighed. "I'm sorry, but Sister Steph was the only one we could trust to do something about it and you know it."

There were squeals and laughter from a nearby group of girls playing Hearts. Someone had been slipped the queen of spades.

Katie plopped down in a chair and sulked. "I don't want to talk about it. You're ruining our whole night."

"All right, no more questions." From the corner of my eye I glimpsed Sister Steph standing at the doorway. I patted Katie's shoulder. "I forgot something in the kitchen. I'll be back."

When I reached the doorway Sister Steph said, "We have to talk. C'mon, the chapel's empty."

Besides being the coldest place in the school, the chapel

always felt eerie to me when it was empty and graveyard quiet. I sensed troubled spirits there, spirits of students who had long since passed over to the other world. I had often sensed these restive spirits in other parts of the school, but they seemed most concentrated in the chapel and the basement.

We sat in the back pew. Sister Steph took my hand in hers. "Ruby, I—I owe you an apology. I did some investigating and you were right." Her hand tightened around mine. "I hope you can find it in your heart to forgive me. I must've hurt you very much, I know. Can you forgive a silly, stubborn nun?"

I felt the weight of a boulder lift from my shoulders and a sudden resurgence of my feelings of admiration for my friend and teacher. "Sure, I forgive you, Sister, and you're not stubborn!"

Sister Steph's hand flew to her mouth with an Oh!, then she pulled me to her in a fierce embrace. I felt like I did after a glassful of piping Ojibwe tea. Hugs were scarce as hen's teeth at St. Nicholas. In fact, this was the only one I could remember in all my time there.

When we broke the embrace, Sister Steph dabbed at her moist eyes and sniffed. She chuckled as she saw I was teary-eyed as well and fished a Kleenex out of her robe pocket for me.

"You talked to Katie, didn't you?" I asked while wiping my eyes.

Sister Steph nodded. "And several others. I swore all of them to absolute secrecy."

I nodded. That explained Katie's evasion of the subject. "What are you gonna do?"

She nibbled her lower lip, then, "I wrote the bishop."

I was simultaneously surprised, fearful and excited. "Are you going to tell Sister Margaret? I guess you'll have to."

"Of course that was my first thought, but now—well, I think I made the right decision."

Sister Steph's azure eyes belied the confidence in her voice. "But it's my responsibility, Ruby. I want you to say nothing further about this to anyone, understand?" She peered into my eyes. "I mean it. Absolute secrecy."

I crossed myself, wanting to please her and to assure her of my sincerity. "Yes, ma'am."

She took my hands in hers. "Good."

I had never before seen such deep worry and sadness in Sister Steph's youthful face. St. Nicholas had claimed yet another free and happy spirit.

Chapter Twenty-Six

After several false starts spring finally matured in earnest. Tulips, planted in front of the school, bloomed like promises of good things to come, and crocuses bordered the walkway from the circular gravel drive to the portico. The rich green lawns smelled fresh and sweet.

At recess, I bolted outside and inhaled deeply. I love being outdoors. Only there do I feel truly close to God. I've never felt the least bit spiritual when under a roof, certainly not in the chapel. There were too many bad memories there, not to mention the troubled spirits. And besides, I worried that God couldn't see me for the roof, that our prayers merely bounced off it.

The good memories came from the painted forests of home, from a startling blue sky, from the ferned and mossy creek near Gram's house. I loped over to the towering maple I admired every day from my dorm window and threw my arms around it. "Happy spring, Grandfather Tree." I held my ear against the rough bark, hoping to feel some vibration or sound that would reveal the spirit Gram said lived within. "Just like you, all God's things have a spirit," Gram had taught. "Trees, water, animals, the Earth."

"Even rocks?" I had asked when I was six.

Gram had smiled and answered in Ojibwe. "If *Gitche-Manitou* took the time to create it, it has a purpose and a spirit."

I had picked up a rock and said, "Rock spirit, are you in there?" I held it to my ear and listened, then looked at Gram. "He doesn't answer."

"That's because you and me don't speak Rock, *eya?*"

"Can anybody speak Rock?"

Gram eased herself down on a tree stump and plopped down her basket, piled high with plump wild blackberries. "In the old days there were some who could. Some holy people could speak Rock, some could speak Tree. And in the oldest days, when the Ojibwe people were first made, all the animals talked."

I remembered being exhilarated by such an idea. "Really, Gram? What did they say?"

"Ho! They said a lot of smart things in them days. Animals taught us a lot, them." She took out a handkerchief and mopped her brow. "Still do."

"Like the ravens you told me about?"

Gram winked. "Oh, them ravens are plenty smart."

Katie skipped up with two of her young friends in tow and broke my reverie.

"*Ahneen,*" she chirped, her old self momentarily revived. Her mood swings had become confusing. One minute she'd be her usual bouncy self, the next, silent and morose.

"Hey, guys. What'cha doin'?" I asked.

Katie shrugged. "Nothin'. We wanted to play hopscotch, but Pearl Akiwenzie and her friends are hoggin' the court." She made a little sneer when mentioning Pearl.

I had an idea. I hadn't told a story in a long time. Gram always said storytelling was very important, that in the old days people who knew lots of stories were highly respected within the tribe. She said it was important that I practice my stories as part of my preparation for motherhood.

I grinned down at the girls. "Wanna hear an Ojib story?"

"Yeah!" they chorused.

"All right," I said, delighted to have an audience. "We can sit right here under Grandfather Tree.

The girls sat cross-legged in a half-moon around me, and I began:

"There once was a man who enjoyed watching the ravens fly around, play, squawk, and chatter. He enjoyed them so much he would climb trees just to be near them. One day, an older raven, flying far above, dropped a walnut right on the man's head. It was done on purpose and all the ravens almost fell off their branches laughing so hard the way they do. One raven was flying and was laughing so hard he had to crash-land right in front of the man.

"The man was hurt by being made fun of, so he asked the raven in front of him, 'Why are you all picking on me?'

"The raven stopped laughing and became very serious. 'We thought you understood us. If you did you would know that we are not mocking you—well maybe a bit—but it's done in fun. It is not to be taken seriously. You should know us better.'

"Over time, a few more practical jokes were played on the man, and he in turn pulled a few good ones on the birds. A good time was had by all, and the man became even closer to the ravens.

"One day a young raven swooped out of the sky and pecked the man on the head. Then another young raven swooped down and did the same thing. The man ran across the field and into the woods, but the ravens kept chasing him and bothering him. Finally the two crows stopped and started to yell mean words, fighting words, at the man.

"Again the man did not understand, but he knew the two ravens were very mad at him, so he decided to leave and let the ravens be. The man went away for many months. As he did his duties in his tribal village, he told all the people about his adventures and what he learned about the ravens.

"Some listened to him, others just thought the man was a fool to study the ravens so. The villagers gave the man a new name of Black Feather because of his close relationship to the birds, but the man objected and said, 'I am no longer close to the raven people.'

"From above there was a squawking sound of a single raven. People looked up and were surprised they could understand the raven. Others just looked around because they could hear nothing but squawking. The raven was speaking to the man and said, 'It is true, you are closer to us than any *Anishinabe* before you. You are close, but you still don't understand us fully. I invite you to return to us. Many miss you.'

"Black Feather followed the raven but then stopped at the edge of the village. He looked around to make sure no other *Anishinabe* could hear, then asked the raven, 'Why do you ask me back when those two ravens were fighting with me and were mean?'

"The raven landed at Black Feather's feet and said, 'See how little you understand us? The two young ravens did not fight with you because you are *Anishinabe,* it was because they accepted you as a member of the raven people. We fight among ourselves, too. It is a part of our way of life. Instead of sulking and leaving, you should have fought back.'

"Black Feather stood in silence, then said, 'There is much about ravens I don't understand. Maybe we are too different to ever understand each other. I should return to my people in the village.'

"The raven again shook his head and told Black Feather, 'That is your choice, but again I tell you that you have come closer to us raven people than any other *Anishinabe*. Would you throw this all away just because you cannot understand us yet?'

"Black Feather responded, 'It's useless. How can I ever understand you? I can't even fly!' A thousand bursts of laughter were heard from the surrounding trees.

" 'Of course you can't fly. You are *Anishinabe* and we are ravens. But we accept you as one of us. We play with you. We fight with you. We love you and want you back. But don't try to fly in order to be like us, because then, you would not be *Anishinabe,* nor a raven, but something else. We like you as an *Anishinabe* that understands us as ravens. Join us or not, the decision is yours.'

"Black Feather returned to the *Anishinabe* village and bade everyone farewell. He had decided to live with the raven people. All the *Anishinabe* people were there to see him off, and high overhead were a thousand ravens.

"From high above, one of the older ravens dropped a walnut shell and again, with remarkable aim, plunked Black Feather right on the head. All the ravens laughed, and all the *Anishinabe* laughed, too. Black Feather laughed, looked up at the old raven, and said, 'Good shot!' "

Katie and her friends giggled. "I like that one," a girl named Bonnie said.

"Me, too," Katie echoed, then peered longingly at the sky. "I wish I had a raven friend."

Everyone looked skyward, but no ravens appeared, only two robins perched high in the maple.

"Maybe you will one day," I said.

Sally, the third girl, who was so skinny she was merely a smile on a stick, went slack-jawed with a sudden brainstorm. "Heyyy. Maybe the Robes are the ravens and we're like that *Anishinabe* man. I mean, think about it. They all wear black and we can understand them 'cause we learned their language. And now we live with them."

Now it was Katie's turn to look as if a bell had gone off in her head. "Gee, maybe she's right. Only instead of dropping walnuts on us, they hit us with paddles."

"Yeah!" offered Bonnie. "Like in the story, maybe we just don't really understand them yet, and when we do they'll be nice to us and we'll all be happy together."

I stared at their intent faces and felt suddenly old. Had I once been so innocent?

The bell rang. Everyone groaned and filed into the stark building. The rest of the day wasn't half bad, though. English and history were somewhat interesting. After supper I reported for kitchen duty. The kitchen air was humid and thick with cooking smells. I went right to the gaping sinks and began filling them with soap powder and hot water when Mrs. Olsen, the cook, accompanied by three other girls, ambled over. A drooping finger of gray hair escaped the tight, braided bun under her bobby-pinned hair net.

"You won't be doing dishes tonight, Ruby. I need you to work with these girls on making sack lunches for the field trip tomorrow."

Shoot! I had been so preoccupied with Sister Steph that I had forgotten tomorrow was Decoration Day and the annual field trip to Oak Hill Cemetery. Normally, any trip outside St. Nic's would be a treat, but I had learned to despise this one.

We accompanied Mrs. Olsen to a worktable piled with loaves of bread. There was a large container of sliced bologna, a bushel of turnips and a neat stack of folded lunch sacks.

"All right, girls. I want one bologna sandwich and a turnip in each bag. We'll leave everything in the refrigerator for tonight and hand them out as everyone boards the bus in the morning." She continued, "Now just one slice of bologna per sandwich, then cut it in half, like so, and wrap it in this waxed paper. Got it?"

I said, "Can we have some lard or somethin' on them this time, Mrs. Olsen? They get awful dry and then the bread gets stuck in your mouth." Then I thought I might as well go for broke. "Maybe even something sweet?"

Mrs. Olsen shook her head. "Sorry. Sister Margaret says we got to economize."

Three decrepit school buses rumbled in at eleven o'clock under iron-gray skies. Ellie Cedar, Sister E and I handed each student a lunch bag and an orange drink as they boarded. Agnes took hers between pinched fingers, held it away from her body. "I hope you didn't put your cooties on it."

"Nope, just horseradish," I quipped without skipping a beat. I wanted to say rat turds, but Sister E was too close by.

"Hardee har har," Agnes deadpanned and moved on, but the old bitterness in her voice seemed diminished. Now that I thought of it, Agnes had taken a lower profile since her paddling in the rec room, and she had apparently leashed-in her wolf pack regarding the harassment of Katie. Our old relationship of wolf to wolverine had moderated into an uneasy truce, a begrudging respect of territory.

Five girls later, Katie trudged by. I could tell she was having another of her blue days. "Save me a seat," I said, trying to sound cheery. Katie nodded drearily, took her lunch bag and boarded the bus. My own mood matched hers—the annual cemetery trip would sour a clown. I wished Rose was coming, but she and two other girls were down with the flu. Lucky, I thought.

"Well, Ruby. You're doing a splendid job." *Kokoko*'s voice interrupted my cheerless thoughts. I swallowed the dark feelings that flooded me whenever he was near and nodded. I hadn't expected him to go on the field trip. It wasn't his kind of thing.

His smile transformed his face from leering wolf to altar-boy wholesomeness as he clasped his hands behind his back and whistled his way toward the bus. I could see why some girls melted at that smile, the dimples at the corners of his mouth, the handsome square jaw. I tried to picture him when he was my age in his red-and-white altar boy outfit. The image wouldn't form, and my mood turned from dreary to bleak. God, don't let him sit next to Katie.

After the last girl retrieved her lunch bag I stepped up onto one of the table chairs to see into the high bus windows. *Kokoko* boarded last, and after exchanging pleasantries with Sisters Margaret and Elizabeth at the front of the bus, stopped at Katie's seat, said something to her and sat. With some fast footwork and only a little elbowing I scrambled aboard the bus ahead of the other serving girls. Sister Steph was sitting at the rear. For a brief moment her eyes met mine, flicked to Slater and Katie, then back to mine in a silent message that she, too, was watching. I claimed a seat behind Katie and Slater. It would be a longer hour than usual to reach the cemetery.

But the ride turned out to be uneventful. *Kokoko* was the epitome of propriety, and I found myself daydreaming about home. In only two weeks—*two weeks*—I'd be home for summer! My mind swam with images of Gram, Mom, Sue, cousins and friends. Maybe I'd even get to see Daddy.

When we stepped off the bus, Sister Elizabeth handed each of us several miniature American flags on sticks; then we lined up along War Memorial Drive to watch the parade. This was the only part of the trip I enjoyed. There were two marching bands, four homemade floats, marching troops of

Boy Scouts, and of course, soldiers. The best was always saved for last: three shiny, red fire engines, lights flashing, sirens wailing. I joined the crowd and waved. There was nothing like a parade to lift my spirits.

Afterward, we followed the crowd to the bandstand in the adjacent park and listened to the same old dreary speeches. The mayor droned on about sacrifice and patriotism. It sounded exactly like last year's speech. The American Legion commander followed, and then some man with the baffling title of Most Puissant Grand Master Mason, but I had stopped listening by then. My thoughts were again at home. I wondered if Gram was beading today, wondered what mischief my little sister was up to. I even dared to fantasize a bit about Dad coming home.

After the speeches, we walked over to our picnic tables—set off a respectable distance from the townsfolk, who didn't want to be too close to the Indians—and devoured turnips and dry bologna sandwiches, watching with hungry eyes the faculty as they champed away on fried chicken, noodle salad and apple pie.

When I finished eating, I headed for the restrooms, a forest-green concrete building in the center of the park. Inside, I pretended to wash my hands while a plump, matronly woman in a garish flowered dress with matching hat freshened her fire engine-red lipstick and straightened her girdle. She beamed down at me, clasping her purse close to her body. "Oh, what a cute little Indian girl. How nice to see you children here today, all cleaned up and dressed nice, and with your little flags."

I managed a sickly smile. Apparently satisfied, the woman left. I immediately threw all but three of my flags into the trash barrel next to the sink and left. While ditching the flags was delicious revenge, part of me felt guilty. I was raised to hold patriotism and veterans in the highest esteem, which I did—except for those now moldering in their graves at the north end of Oak Hill Cemetery. For them I held only contempt.

Two White girls my age walked into the bathroom as I left. I overheard one whisper, "Don't use the one she used."

I arrived back at the picnic table to witness a small commotion.

"Have you seen Father Slater or Lucy?" an annoyed-looking Sister Margaret asked.

"No, ma'am. Not since on the bus." I caught Sister Steph's glance, our mutual alarm suspended in the air between us.

Fatlips checked her watch and made an impatient sigh. "Where on Earth could they be? We're going to be late for the grave decorating." She turned to Sisters E and Stephanie. "All right. Sister Elizabeth, you go that way. Sister Stephanie, you go that way. I'll go this way. They've got to be close by."

"There they are!" shouted a pointing girl.

Kokoko led Lucy by the hand as they wound their way through the tree-shaded park, the shepherding priest whistling a happy tune.

"We were just about to send out a search party," Sister Margaret said with a frown.

The priest gave a nonchalant chuckle. "No need. I took Lucy to the lavatory and we got a little turned around." He squeezed Lucy's hand and grinned down at her. "Didn't we, Lucy?"

I was just at the lavatory, and there had been no sign of Lucy or Slater.

Lucy nodded blankly.

Sister Margaret eyed them for several moments, then clapped her hands. "All right, ladies. Has everyone used the lavatory?" Heads nodded and voices murmured assent. "Very well, single file now."

Following the meandering crowd of townspeople, we walked—the little ones skipped—across the street and into the cemetery.

"Agnes, would you please demonstrate to the others how to decorate a gravesite?"

Agnes walked over to a grave marked with a brass medallion and planted the tiny flag in the ground next to it.

"Very good, Agnes." Sister Margaret turned to the girls. "Now you may spread out and place your flags at any grave that has a brass veteran's marker. Remember to save a flag for the ceremony at the Third Cavalry site. And remember," she added sternly, "never walk on the graves." She turned to Agnes. "Agnes, I'm putting you in charge. Please have the girls gather at the Third Cavalry plot in twenty minutes."

I gritted my teeth. Wouldn't they ever forget about the stinking Third Cavalry?

I hooked up with Katie, and we wandered around the rolling hills, planting her flags and admiring the surrounding spring-lush forest, splashed with sundry shades of green, and the perfumey aroma of fresh flowers that decorated the graves. I asked Katie, "Is *Kokoko* behaving himself?"

Katie nodded as she placed a flag next to a medallion. "I guess."

"Make sure you sit with me on the way back, okay?"

"Okay," she replied listlessly.

I was just beginning to enjoy being outdoors when I heard Agnes's grating voice, calling us in.

"Oh, crap. It's time," I groaned, feeling the anger and tension building within me.

In a few minutes we stood around a rusty iron fence that encircled the twelve graves of the Third Wisconsin Cavalry.

"Pre-sent, arms!" The honor guard from the Legion post snapped to attention and saluted, while another man in uniform played taps. I felt a slight push as *Kokoko* inserted himself between Katie and me. He caressed the side of Katie's face with his right hand, like a father with a beloved daughter. I picked up my right foot and put my entire ninety-five pounds on the toe of his left shoe.

"Oww," Slater yelped and jumped back.

Several townspeople and Sister Margaret gave him dirty looks. I donned a mask of concern and embarrassment. "Oh, I'm so sorry, Father," I whispered. "I didn't see you." I looped my arm through Katie's, blocking *Kokoko*'s access.

He glowered at me but could say nothing, the solemn graveside ceremony still in progress.

"Or-der, arms!"

The rusty gate, whining in protest, was opened.

"Agnes," Sister Margaret said matter-of-factly, "show them what to do, please."

Agnes stepped through the gate, walked around to the far grave—that of Captain Nathan Starke—and planted her flag. I clenched my fists as I watched *Kokoko* and the nuns place their hands over their hearts, watched my fellow students plant their little flags. Every year it was the same humiliating ceremony.

"Where's your flag, Ruby?" Sister E wanted to know.

"I used them all up, Sister. Guess I forgot."

Sister Elizabeth's lips tightened into a disapproving grimace, but she said nothing. Too many townsfolk looking on, I guessed with barely repressed gratification.

As we sauntered back to the bus, *Kokoko* appeared at my side. He grabbed my arm in a bone-crushing squeeze, and I cried out. "That was intentional." He spoke out of the side of his mouth as we walked, his voice harsh as a rasp.

"Leave me alone!" I hissed, and then an approaching Sister Steph rescued me, and he released my arm.

On the bus ride home, the others talked animatedly and made funny faces at each other, but I was reflective as I massaged my bruised arm. At least this year I had made my protest, however small. I had kept *Kokoko* away from Katie and managed not to tread into the Third Cavalry plot. I could tell Gram I didn't shame myself or our people, for it was Starke and his men who, at dawn on February 6, 1857, massacred eighty-seven starving women, children and elders of the Loon Lake Ojibwe tribe, including my great-grandfather. Now they lay in a mass grave under a farmer's field on land that was once reservation land, land Ojibwes now had to ask permission to visit. No honor guard played taps over Great Grampa's grave. There were no parades, no tiny flags for a veteran of many battles. My heart ached as I remembered that every year, after each plowing, rotting shreds of tanned hide, broken pieces of Indian jewelry, and bits of bone were gouged from the earth and lay naked in the sun.

Chapter Twenty-Seven

"Father?"

Father Blewett jerked awake at his desk.

"It's the phone—the bishop—for you," his secretary announced.

He hadn't heard the phone. The last thing he remembered was going over the budget spread out on his desk in front of him, then . . . Good grief, he'd dozed off again. With a sigh, he glanced at his desk calendar, something he seemed to do a hundred times a day lately. In just six months he'd be retired and sitting on his boat, bass fishing his days away in his boyhood home—exactly what he had been dreaming about.

He straightened in his chair. "Very well, Joyce. Put him through." He picked up the phone. "Good afternoon, Bishop. Always good to hear from you."

"I wish I could say this was a pleasant call, Quentin."

"Oh?" Blewett replied, his reverie fading.

"This morning I received a repulsive letter, apparently from someone who works at your school."

Blewett pulled at his clerical collar. "Letter?"

"An anonymous letter." Anger crept into the bishop's voice. "This—person accuses Father Slater of molesting *your* students."

Blewett stiffened. Father Slater? The bishop's cousin? Good Lord! "That's outrageous! Bishop, I can assure you—"

"There's no need, Quentin," the voice interrupted. "It is

obvious someone at St. Nicholas is trying to defame the school and the Church. There are plenty of anti-papists out there, and you've apparently hired one."

Blewett stood. His mouth felt chalk-dry, a symptom often manifested when the bishop called. "Bishop, I—I'm horrified by this—this character assassination of one of our finest priests."

"I'm going to mail this letter to you marked 'Urgent and Confidential.' I want you to find out who this person is and release them! We can't have some disgruntled employee flailing away at us from within."

"I agree." He had never heard the bishop so angry. "Ah—perhaps it's a test of our faith, our strength as God's servants," Blewett prattled on, not knowing what else to say.

The bishop went on. "I want this woman discovered and gone before the summer break."

Blewett was taken aback. "Woman?"

"Definitely a mature feminine script."

"Of course, Bishop. I'll take care of this personally."

"See that you do, Quentin. And quickly."

Quentin Blewett paced his office three days later, his hands locked behind his back while he awaited the mailman. "We've got to root out this person as soon as possible," he said to Sister Margaret as she sat in one of the Queen Anne chairs in front of his desk. "I want this cleared up quickly," he swiveled to face her, "and quietly. If the diocese rumor mill gets hold of this, my reputation will be ruined."

The assistant principal's face was stony. "I couldn't agree more, Father."

He continued to pace, mumbling to himself. "Only six months left before my retirement, and I'll be dam—" He looked slightly embarrassed, then, "I refuse to leave under a cloud." He shot Margaret a reproachful glare. "All of our reputations are at stake here, Sister."

Margaret checked her watch. "The mail should arrive soon. If the letter is from one of our faculty, I'll recognize it."

There was a knock at the door. Blewett started. "Yes, come in."

His secretary walked in. "Your mail, Father."

The principal snatched the stack from her hands and began shuffling through it. "Thank you. That'll be all, Joyce."

Margaret sat on the edge of her chair. "Well? Is it there?"

Blewett pulled an envelope from the stack. "Here it is." He opened it, then read the contents silently. "My God," he groaned as he handed the letter to Margaret.

Margaret's expression darkened as she read. When she finished she studied the script closely.

"Well?" Blewett demanded.

Margaret's voice was almost a whisper as recognition dawned in her face. "It can't be." She looked up at her superior. "I want to check something in my office to be sure."

In her office, Margaret went to a drawer, pulled out a file and laid the calumnious letter next to a hand-written memo. In a moment she slumped back in her chair. "I can't believe it."

Blewett looked as if he might explode from frustration. "What? Who is it?"

Margaret looked slowly up at him. "It's Sister Stephanie's writing."

Blewett stiffened, then everything came into focus—the young nun who had become overly attached to her students. "Of course!"

Chapter Twenty-Eight

"All set, Mom?" Theresa called from Cecelia's front room at six o'clock. *Eya,* I'm ready," Cecelia called from her bedroom. She shuffled toward the front door. Though broken nearly two years ago, her hip still pained her from time to time, but today excitement dulled any discomfort. Today they would pick up Ruby.

Theresa stepped inside and found Cecelia's cane leaning next to the door. Cecelia squeezed her daughter's arm as she took the cane and waved it toward the door. *"Ombay, ombay!"*

Theresa sighed. "I wish you'd speak English, Mom."

Cecelia moved carefully down the two steps. "English is for the English. Ojibwe is for Ojibwes. Now get this old truck started and head south. My granddaughter's waiting."

They climbed into the pickup and headed east on Route 1, admiring the blooming lupines along the roads.

"Nice of Luther to loan us his truck," Cecelia remarked. She gave her daughter a speculative look. "A shame Jim is not here to pick up his own daughter."

Theresa's expression soured. "He'll be home soon. We just have to work some things out."

Cecelia gazed out the side window. "Look. There's Millie." Cecelia waved as they passed the dilapidated wood-and-tarpaper house of Millie and Charlie Shigwadja. "It's a shame about Charlie," she went on, trying to rekindle more pleasant conversation. "Diabetes took his leg last year, you know." She clicked her tongue and shook her head. "Now their place needs a new roof, and their son is a hopeless drunk, him."

"Yes, I know."

"It's not all your fault, you know," Cecelia said.

Theresa gave her mother a quick glance, then swept her eyes back to the road. "What's that, Mom?"

"Jim. He has a family waiting for him. It is time he stopped feeling sorry for himself and came home, him."

Theresa didn't answer, so Cecelia continued. "Especially with Ruby being home for the summer. The girls need their father, *eya?* It's not right, him punishing them this way."

"You're preachin' to the choir, Mom. I don't know what more I can do. He don't answer my letters."

Cecelia frowned. She was angry with Jim, but it was Theresa who'd made a terrible mistake, a mistake that had brought shame upon her within the community and made it hard for Jim to return home with his pride intact. There were few secrets at Loon Lake, especially sordid secrets like affairs, not to mention lying with a relative—even if Earl was Jim's cousin, not Theresa's.

Cecelia spotted a tear forming in Theresa's eye. She reached over and patted her daughter's leg. "It will work out." She watched Theresa's pretty face and felt a creeping sadness. Theresa tried hard. In her heart, where it counted, she was a good and honest woman, but she had always been weak when it came to men. Both men she had dated before Jim had been hard-drinking and domineering. One even knocked her around a few times, but Cecelia had put a stop to that. She had Marvin and his son "talk" to the young man.

Then Jim came into Theresa's life. He, too, was a strong man, but in all the right ways. He obviously loved Theresa, and, though it was sporadic, he had a job, something few men on the rez had, what with most unable to find work. And he had turned out to be a good father, until he left. *Geget,* Theresa had had a hard life. Who hadn't? But she had more than paid the price, and Cecelia ached for her.

Mother and daughter rode down Route 53 in silence until they approached the junction with Route 70.

"Isn't that the road to the St. Croix?" Cecelia asked.

Theresa nodded.

"I wish we had time to stop in and see cousin Mae. It's been so long."

"I know, Mom, but St. Nic's is almost to Eau Claire. It'll take us ten hours to get there and back. I wanna be home by dark."

Using her right hand Theresa fished a cigarette from her purse, stuck it between her lips, and pressed the dash lighter. Cecelia regarded her a moment. "You know, Marvin and I talked to Luther about us building our own school."

Theresa made a wry smile. "Sure. And the money will fall from heaven."

"Maybe," Cecelia said, squinting through the bug-splattered windshield at the sky. "But just in case, we got some ideas of our own."

Theresa replied, "Even if the government let us build a school how we gonna get good teachers, Mom? Advertise? I can see it now: 'Come to beautiful Loon Lake Indian Reservation and teach in our new, modern school. No running water, no housing, bring your own books, wages paid in fish and firewood.' "

Cecelia slowly shook her head. "Is there no more *Shinnob* left in you, *Nindaan?*"

"Look, Mom. Ruby is getting the best education an Indian kid can get these days. And it's free."

Cecelia scoffed. "It is free because those *anama'ewikweg*

want to wash the *Shinnob* out of her."

Cecelia watched her daughter's jaw tense, her knuckles whiten as she gripped the steering wheel. She didn't want to anger her, but the conversation needed to run its course. "Remember, back in the old days, what that old chief said to that Indian agent after all the Indian boys came back to the rez useless from them white schools? 'Why not send us some of *your* boys,' he said, 'and we will make men of them.' " Cecelia stifled a chuckle. She loved that quote.

Theresa rolled her eyes. "Mom, I don't want to go through this again. What kind of life would Ruby have if she didn't get an education? I'll tell you what she'd have—nothing. She'd be another dumb Indian girl hanging around the rez on relief. She'd be married and have a kid by the time she was sixteen."

Cecelia looked at Theresa and sadly shook her head. "You have so little faith in your daughter?" She looked thoughtful a moment, then, "*Eya,* Ruby should go to school. It is the way of the world today." Frustration crept into her voice. "You know why I do not like our children going to the Robe schools, where they teach them that our ways of worship, our ceremonies, our stories, are bad—to a place where they hit them." Or worse, she thought. "We do not tell their children that their churches are bad, that they should believe only in the *Shinnob* way, *eya?*" She threw up an exasperated hand. "Each to his own. That's the way *Gitche-Manitou* wants it."

"Mom, will you stop with the *Gitche-Manitou?* White people run the world today, and if Ruby and Sue are going to make it, they're gonna have to fit in, they're gonna have to get an education, get off the rez and get a good job."

Cecelia gave Theresa a hard look. "Leave their home? Leave the graves of their grandfathers? You're saying you want them to stop being *Shinnob,* to be white people."

Theresa jammed out her cigarette in the ashtray. "That's

what it boils down to, Mom. Nobody knows anything about Indians. They never see us unless they're driving through on vacation and wanna buy a pair of moccasins or a rubber tomahawk for the kids. Look at old Joe Wolf, dressing up in buckskins and that big war bonnet, standing by the road, taking money from tourists. 'How,' they say when they talk to him. 'Look at the Indian, Johnny,' they say. 'Shake hands with the big chief, Mary.' Jesus, Mom. Nobody gives a damn. Nobody gives a damn if we sit out our lives on the rez until we fade away. Well, my girls ain't gonna fade away. They're gonna get something out of life besides heartbreak, powdered eggs and babies."

Cecelia's eyes narrowed. "And be good Catholics, *eya?*"

Theresa stiffened and cocked her head with belligerent pride. "The least I can do is save their souls."

Old memories gushed into Cecelia and she tensed with anger. "Do not ever forget, *Nindaan,* they came and *stole* you away from us." Her voice shook with bitter emotion. "They came with their robes, your soul-savers, and with that agent, and they pulled you from my arms, and they took you away!"

Theresa held up a trembling hand, then in a sharp downward movement, chopped off the discussion like a sharp ax. Cecelia watched the dotted lines in the center of the road disappear under the front bumper as she caught her breath. It had been a long time since she had been this angry, especially with her own child. She wasn't against the new ways as much as she was for the old. Of course times had changed. People had to make a living and support their families. And, yes, they lived in a white world, but that didn't mean one stopped honoring the old ways. If anyone was expert at adapting—at surviving—it was Indians. What scared Cecelia most was the thought of people leaving the reservation. If everyone abandoned the rez, she knew, the *Anishinabeg* would cease to exist.

The language, the elders, the stories, the dances, the songs—all would be lost. The *Anishinabe* prophets warned of such catastrophes.

Her thoughts swung back to Theresa. She thought of the happy days before the Robe school, when she and Theresa were as one, when they used to laugh together and talk Ojibwe, when Theresa helped her with the *manomen* and berry gathering and went ice fishing with her father.

When Theresa was Ojibwe.

Cecelia closed her eyes. She didn't want to dwell on such depressing thoughts. Not today. She settled into the seat and softly chanted an old Ojibwe song her mother used to sing. Ruby's beaming face swam into view. One thing was for sure. She'd not lose Ruby, too. *Gaawesa!*

Chapter Twenty-Nine

St. Nicholas Indian School
Rural Route 2
Doanville, Wisconsin

ANNUAL REPORT TO HIS EXCELLENCY..........Page 15

CONCLUDING REMARKS:
The Indian is not and never will be a denominational asset of any great value, yet Indian work gets a firm grip on you, and with all their faults we develop a strange fondness for them. Three years ago, you may recall, we had two Indian groundskeepers and, for Indians, they were not half-bad. We just have to remember that they have limitations, which are in the main those usually associated with the Indian character.

On another note, I hope you can find us a quick replacement for Sister Stephanie. Per our discussion, I will be advising her today of her transfer. I hope that, after prayer and reflection, she will apply herself anew. I am sure she'll do better at a non-Indian school. She is rather clever and fairly good in a classroom, but useless to us otherwise, perhaps because she was raised in too close proximity to the Indians and has taken on too much of their nature.

Yours in Christ,
Rev. Quentin Xavier Blewett
Principal

Chapter Thirty

I hugged Katie, then Rose, as Rose's father finished loading their things into the car. "I'm so glad you're going to spend the summer with Rose. You're gonna have a ball, I know."

Katie grinned and nodded. "Rose has her own horse, and I'm gonna ride it."

"Luckee," I pined with mock jealousy.

Katie beamed with satisfaction at Rose, who smiled down at her, then gave me a wink.

Apparently worried about my feelings, Katie added, "Maybe I can go home with you over Christmas."

"You bet, kid," I replied, recalling how mad and embarrassed I was when Mom said it was too much to handle three girls for the summer, forcing me to let Katie down.

"Okay, girls. Ready to go?" Rose's dad said as he joined them. He smiled. "Nice meeting you, Ruby. Rose tells us lots of good things about you in her letters."

I saw where Rose got her light skin and brown hair. Her dad was white and her mom was a half-breed. I felt my face flush as I smiled back at him. I didn't know what to say.

"Well, we're off," he said. "Have a good summer, Ruby."

Katie scrambled into the car, followed by Rose, who then leaned out the window. "Write to us, Ruby. We'll write back."

"Okay," I called, waving as the sedan pulled away.

Katie poked her head out the window. "See ya next year!"

After the car turned onto the hard road, I inhaled the warm, sweet June air. There was a brilliant sun, and wispy clouds, like shreds of pulled cotton, floated lazily across a pale-blue sky. The front drive was filled with all manner of cars and trucks and the bustle of chattering, laughing girls and family members. It was almost noon and my excitement rose as I watched the far end of the road. I felt a hand on my shoulder and turned to look into Sister Steph's smiling face.

"Have a wonderful summer, Ruby. I'll miss you." She glanced around then hugged me. "I hope we'll have everything straightened out here by next fall. So you just have a good time and don't think about it, okay?"

I nodded, then remembered something. "Oh—Sister Steph. Can you wait here with me a little while? I'm expecting my mom any time now and I want her to meet you."

Sister Steph grinned. "Sure. I have a few—"

A stern-looking Sister Margaret descended the steps. "Sister Stephanie. Principal Blewett would like to see you in his office right away."

"Of course, Sister." She turned to me. "This shouldn't take long, Ruby. I'll be back in a wink."

I smiled halfheartedly, then gave Fatlips a glare. She always found some way to ruin things. I watched the two nuns disappear inside, then turned my attention back to the road. A minute later an old pickup turned off the hard road and into the long drive. I recognized Mr. White Bear's pickup, and giddy excitement spurted through me. I jumped up and down, waving and shouting, and as the truck loomed closer I saw Gram waving. I couldn't believe my eyes. I jumped and yelled all the louder. The pickup lurched to a dusty stop. I flung open the door and was in Gram's arms before she could get out of the truck. "Gram! Gram!"

Gram whooped and laughed as she patted my back. "My *Bineshee Ogichidaw.*"

Mom popped out and came around to my side. "Mom!" I shouted, turning and rushing into her arms.

She laughed and hugged me tight. "I missed you so much, sweetheart."

"Me too, Mom, me too. And thanks for bringing Gram. It was the best surprise ever!"

"Well isn't anybody going to help an old woman out of this thing?" Gram called in Ojibwe. "If I don't move these old bones around soon, you won't be able to get me out with a pry bar."

I rushed to help her from the cab. Gram grunted when her feet hit the ground and retrieved her cane, then looked around at the hubbub. Three squealing girls raced between us, causing her to stumble back a step. She laughed. "Busy place."

"Hey, watch it!" I shouted after them. "Don't ya know how to respect your elders?" I looked at Gram apologetically. "Some of these girls didn't get raised right, Gram. Some of 'em got taken from their families before they were old enough to learn *Shinnob* manners."

Gram looked pensively after them; then she smiled and touched my face. "They're just excited to be free, them." She looked apprehensively about the grounds, then at the stark, towering edifice of the school. She rubbed her arms as if suddenly chilled. "Come. Let's put your things in the truck. I want to get away from this place."

"Okay, Gram, but I was hoping Sister Steph would be back. I wanted you and Mom to meet her. She's really swell. She's only eight years older than me." I eyed the front door for a moment. "Wait here. I'll go get her."

"Hurry up, Ruby. I want to get home before dark," Mom called.

I bolted into the building and ran down the hall to Father Blewett's office. Two nuns were already waiting there. "Excuse me, Sister E. Would you know how much longer Sister Steph will be?"

Sister Elizabeth gave me a grim look. "It could be a while. You'd best run along home."

Darn! I hated to leave without at least saying good-bye, but two short horn beeps called to me. Torn, I looked at Sister Elizabeth. "Could you tell Sister Steph that I said good-bye and that I'll write her as soon as I get home?"

Sister Elizabeth nodded. "I'll tell her."

I hurried back to the truck and, with a few more shouted farewells, hopped in next to Gram. As we sped off, I held Gram's hand and let the wind fly through my hair. I didn't look back.

Chapter Thirty-One

In the sacristy the following Saturday morning, John Vincent walked in to find Father Potts and Billy Whitaker. The oversized boy was sitting on the floor looking dazed. Spotting John Vincent, Billy groaned and got back on his feet. He wiped away a tear with the back of his hand before he turned to look at Potts, now looming above him, his boxing-gloved hands on his hips.

"You got too rough again, Fadder," Billy said in a barely audible voice. "You promised you wouldn't be so rough no more."

Potts sneered at John Vincent. "Christ. Everything is a promise with these kids. Be with you in a minute."

John Vincent frowned. *How could this foul-mouthed Sergeant Rock be a priest?*

Potts eyed the boy. "Life is sometimes painful, Billy," he said, removing his gloves. "You gotta learn how to defend yourself sooner or later. You gotta be a trooper."

Billy didn't answer.

"Well, don't you?"

Billy eyed the floor and shrugged.

Potts ran his hand over his face, then rubbed his temples as he recalled one of Margaret's favorite platitudes: "Think of the pain as penance. Think of the agony our Lord suffered on the cross for your sins. Think of that crown of thorns pressed on his head, those nails hammered through his flesh." He glared at the sniveling boy. "Run along now. I got work to do."

Billy took on a hangdog expression. "I—I kinda thought we could play catch or sompin'." His brow creased with hopefulness. "I brought my glove."

Potts stood. "I'm not your old man, kid."

John Vincent had heard that the boy's father died five years ago, and now he seemed to want Potts to fill the role.

"I said I got work to do!"

Billy winced as he gingerly touched his sore jaw.

Potts eyed the clock on the sacristy wall.

The corners of Billy's mouth bowed downward, his face puckered as if in pain as he tucked in his shirt. John Vincent thought the boy might start crying at any minute. Suddenly, he was filled with sympathy for the blubbering youngster. His own face at age twelve superimposed itself over Billy's. For a moment, young Johnny Slater was in the rectory, and Father Dugan's hand was slipping inside Johnny's pants.

Potts broke John Vincent's reverie when he shot from the chair and grabbed Billy's new Sears denim jacket from the back of it. "Here."

Billy's shoulders slumped as Potts hurried him into the coat. With a hand prodding at the boy's back, Potts ushered him out the door. "See you next week. And say your prayers."

Potts closed the door and fiddled with his thinning hair in an effort to cover the bald spot. He looked sharply at Slater. "I keep asking myself what the hell I'm doing in this God-forsaken place."

"You liked the Army better?"

"Damn right. I was a chaplain—and a damned good one." His eyes lost their focus for a moment, as if he were somewhere else. "There, we had the camaraderie of men, of soldiers. We had honor and duty. And there were the bivouacs, the parades." His eyes refocused on Slater. "Most of all I had respect. Here, I'm nothing more than a go-fer for an old fat nun and a gutless wonder for a boss. Jesus, the humiliation of it!"

John Vincent was taken aback. For a moment he worried that Potts might attack him. The man was obviously unbalanced.

Potts sighed—a long, frustrated expulsion of air. "I'll tell you, John, the Church couldn't have punished me worse than sending me to this den of nosy nuns and Indian brats. Why don't they face it? Nobody cares about Indians anymore. They've become irrelevant. As for kids, well, they ought to be sent away somewhere until they're adults, when at least they're good for something."

"Uh-huh," was all John Vincent could muster as he eyed the door, hoping for an early opportunity to flee the room. He could come back later to pick out his vestments.

"And that dyke Margaret is no different," Potts rambled on, his face coloring again. "She might be shrewd and tough like a man, but she's arrogant and condescending." He made a sound of disgust. " 'Behave or else' was the message she gave *me*." Now he made a derisive laugh. " 'Do her bidding' was what she meant. Typical female! They get their kicks deballing men. Their greatest joy is getting a man's nuts in their fists and s-q-u-e-e-z-i-n-g."

John Vincent backed off, Potts's fist now thrusting out toward him in a gesture of squeezing.

Calming now, Potts continued, "The only other man in this place is Jake Muller."

"Jake? The custodian and maintenance man?"

"He might be an ignorant bumpkin, but at least he served his country as a Seabee."

John Vincent knew Potts and Jake sometimes played poker and drank beer down in Jake's basement office, but he had had no idea Potts actually respected the man. Personally, he couldn't stand being anywhere near the odiferous janitor.

Potts communed with his watch. "Speaking of Jake, I gotta run down to see him about something." He smirked. "A little mission for her highness, Queen Margaret."

John Vincent made a show of checking his own watch. "Gosh, look at the time!"

Potts smiled. "You got plenty of time. Come down with me to Jake's. I'm beginning to see how things work around here. I might need a witness."

"A witness! For what?"

Potts took his arm in a comradely manner. "You'll see. You might even find it interesting," and he led John Vincent through the door. At the end of the echoing and empty halls, Potts opened the heavy metal door. They trotted down two flights of steel stairs and negotiated a narrow hallway forested with asbestos-wrapped pipes and naked lightbulbs that dangled from ancient wires. The original 1880 brick walls had never seen a coat of paint, and the basement retained a perpetual musty odor. They turned the corner and sauntered into Jake's warren, which reeked of stale sweat, turpentine, and machine oil.

Jake raised his gaunt, stubbled face from his task at a worktable where he was tinkering with some kind of valve. His short, dirty-brown hair stuck out in every direction like a kid who'd tried to give himself a haircut. "Hey there," Jake said, looking up from his task. "Bit early for cards, ain't it?" Then he noticed John Vincent and his eyes darted back to Potts.

"Father Slater's here with me, Jake, and we're not here for cards. Got an interesting project for us to work on."

The custodian's eyebrows lifted. "Yeah?" He stubbed out his Chesterfield in an ashtray that looked like it hadn't been emptied since Truman left the White House.

"Yeah," Potts continued. "Something Sister Margaret needs. How are you at electrical stuff?"

Jake scratched his chin whiskers. "I can do basic wirin'. Why?"

Potts opened the rusty icebox Jake had rescued from a junk pile and fixed up. He grabbed three beers, handed one to the maintenance man and one to John Vincent.

"Er, no, thanks. I'm not much of a beer man myself."

Potts's eyes narrowed, then he nodded. "Guess I shouldn't be surprised." He set the beer bottle down on Jake's worktable. To Jake he said, "You better hope the old witch doesn't check out this fridge. Where's the church key?"

Jake pulled out a drawer and handed him a bottle opener, then opened his own beer and took a slug. "Ha!" he scoffed. "She never comes down here. Always sends one of the kids to get me if she needs me." He offered Potts the Chesterfields.

Potts accepted one and gave it three solid taps on the table. "Speaking of the good Sister, she wants to make sure there's no more runaways. She wants me to come up with some ideas."

"Yeah?" said Jake, his cigarette dangling precariously between his lips. He clinked open his Zippo and lit Potts's cigarette, then leaned back against the workbench, squinting one eye against the curling smoke.

Potts opened his beer and plopped down on one of the two rickety wooden chairs around a paint-stained card table, then shot Jake a just-between-us-guys look. "Think you could rig up some kind of . . . electric chair?"

John Vincent blurted, *"What?"*

Jake's cigarette almost fell from his mouth.

PART II

Loon Lake

"We do not want churches because they will teach us to quarrel about God as Catholics and Protestants do. We do not want to learn that. We may quarrel with men sometimes about things on this Earth. But we never quarrel about God."

—Chief Joseph, Nez Perce

I do not believe you
The things you say,
Maybe I will not tell you
That is my way.
Maybe you think I believe you
That thing you say,
But always my thoughts stay with me
My own way.

—Student poem from *The Colored Land: A Navajo Indian Book*, Rose Brandt, ed.

Chapter Thirty-Two

Summer was in full bloom at Loon Lake. Sitting under a lofty spruce near the lakeshore, I spotted a trio of stately Sand Hill cranes strutting among the cattails. Puffy loon hatchlings rode their mothers' backs, while proud fathers with their long, tapered beaks and black-and-white checkerboard plumage, preened nearby. Pale pink bog laurel dotted the marsh at the water's edge, along with white calla lily and the soft purples of blue flag. The world seemed to be singing, renewing itself. And I was home.

As I watched the pageant before me I remembered the things Gram had taught me about each of these creatures, about the lake, the plants, the wildflowers. From the red eyes of the loon to the call of the catbird, each had a story and a purpose. And each had earned a special place in my heart.

These first two weeks back home had floated by with the dreamy pace of a mallard swimming across the lake, and St. Nicholas seemed as distant as *neebageesis*. There had been joyful reunions with pals, family members and neighbors. Sue was bursting with kids' gossip and a thousand questions about St. Nic's. I had listened raptly to the gossip and had answered the school questions without embellishment. There was no reason for her to know everything about St. Nicholas. I hoped to dissuade Mom from sending her to boarding school, *especially* to St. Nicholas. Then again, maybe it would be safer to say nothing, hoping Mom would wait another year.

I didn't want to think about it. I flung a pebble into the sun-sequined lake and watched the circles ripple outward and fade.

"Gotcha!"

I jumped as Sue grabbed me from behind. "Brat!" I yelled as she lost her balance and the two of us rolled on the ground. Sue half-screamed, half-giggled when my fingers found her vulnerable underarm. As if struck by a jolt of electricity, she stiffened and her arms fell away from my neck to protect her most ticklish spot. She laughed wildly as I maneuvered to straddle her chest, my fingers digging away like octopus tentacles.

"Stop! Stop! Okay, uncle!"

Satisfied with my revenge, I let up and sat back.

Sue lay on her back, still chuckling. "Some Indian you are," she gloated between breaths. "I walked right up behind you and you didn't hear me."

"I heard ya. I just pretended not to."

She adopted a dubious grin. "Sure."

Two squirrels that had stopped their play on a nearby tree trunk to watch the commotion flicked their tails in agitated interest, then chased up the tree. Sue plopped down next to me as I threw another pebble into the lake. Together, we watched the fading circles.

"Don't ya wonder where all those rings go?" Sue asked.

I laughed and shook my head. "I bet Gram has a story about them."

Sue pulled her knees to her chest. "Yeah, probably about some secret place in the lake that stores up zillions of water rings."

"Yeah, and the little people use them for some secret ceremony that makes sure the lake always has fish or somethin' like that."

We studied the lake in silence, listening to the jays and killdeers, watching terns spear the surface.

Nearby, a pair of ospreys were repairing a nest in a dead tree, stopping from time to time to eye a family of black terns hawking in the lake for insects.

Sue turned to me. "Is it true they whip you at school?"

There was a squeezing sensation in my chest. Sue's toughest questions always popped up when least expected. "Well—sometimes—if you're real bad."

"Do they do it very hard?"

I stared out over the lake. "Yeah, it hurts." I looked back at Sue. "But if you do what you're s'posed to, you don't get hit."

Sue reached down and plucked a blue flag, put it to her nose. "They'll cut my hair, won't they?"

I gazed regretfully at her Indian-black hair that spilled over her shoulders and down her back, still bent and tangled after being freed from braiding, just like mine before St. Nicholas. "Yeah, they'll cut it."

Sue looked belligerent. "I won't let them."

"I like your spirit, Sis, but that'll only earn you a lickin'. And," I added with a sigh, "they'll still cut your hair." I gave her a reassuring smile. "It grows back."

Sue's brow knitted. "Why do they have to cut it, anyway? What's wrong with our hair like it is?"

"Head lice, they say."

"Head lice?"

"Tiny bugs."

"I don't have no bugs!"

I stood and extended a hand-up to her. "I know. They say some girls do when they first come in. But I think it's just an excuse."

"Whad'ya mean?" She brushed at her overalls and drifted toward the wood line.

I frowned and shrugged. "Something to do with all of us looking the same—looking more white. That's what we think."

The interest in Sue's face disappeared like a light gone out. "I'm hungry," she announced. "Let's see what Gram's got to eat."

I grinned. "Race ya!"

Sue squealed with delight and sprinted toward Gram's with me close behind. It felt wonderful to run through the woods again. We dodged around maples and black ashes. Yellow pines towered over a patchwork carpet of soft pine needles and crunchy leaves, now dappled with a silky-white tapestry of trillium. The woods gave way to a wide meadow, and we raced through tall goldenrod, pussytoe, and buttercups, ducking maize-and-brown swallow-tailed butterflies that floated airily above the wildflowers, laughing at the armies of grasshoppers that took sudden flight before our flying feet. There was no place like home, I thought. For us, this was heaven.

Then, suddenly, with Gram's house coming into view, I felt a warm stickiness between my legs. Ahead, I could see Gram, smoking her clay pipe, weeding her herb garden. She glanced up as she heard us laughing.

Sue bolted into the yard, her chest heaving. "I win! I win!"

Gram grinned then looked toward me, but I had stopped, bent over, frightened, trying to figure out what was the sticky liquid between my legs.

"Looks like you beat your sister again," I heard Gram chuckle to Sue in Ojibwe. "Guess she's getting old, *eya?*"

Sue giggled between breaths, then cupped her hands and shouted back at me. "C'mon, slowpoke!"

I walked the last hundred yards back to the house, beaming. I now knew what had happened.

Sue's hands flew to her hips. "Gosh, you couldn't even make it to the house. Gram says you're getting old." Her chortle was cut short by what must have been the strange expression on my face.

"My moon time has come, Gram."

Sue grimaced worriedly at the trace of blood on my fingers, but a wide grin lit up Gram's face and she rushed to me and gathered me into her arms.

I soared to the top of the world. I'd seen many of my classmates get their moon time and had prayed my time would come at home, not at school, where the nuns hushed it up and hid it away like a dirty secret. More than anything I wanted to be grown up—a woman—to go though the *biijiinag bakaanigeng oshkiniigikwe.*

"It's a great day, little *ogichidaw,* a great day," she crooned. She stepped back and stared out toward the meadow in anxious contemplation. "Much to do, much to do."

I winked at Sue. Gram was preparing to go into action.

Three days later and back home, Sue asked with obvious disappointment, "But why can't Gram do the ceremony? She's a clan grandmother. She's done it lots o' times."

"Because," I said with impatience, "you have to go by the *odo-iday-miwan.* Our clan is Daddy's clan, so Gram will have to ask Grandma Shade to do it." I used the proper honorific for Mrs. Shade's position and stature. "She's the *wabizhashti* clan grandmother."

Sue's frown deepened. "Well, it seems dumb to go to somebody who ain't even family when your own Gram can do it."

I sighed. "It has to be done by your clan grandmother."

Sue shrugged and went back to her beading, bobbing her head in time to Pat Boone, who was making a feeble attempt at *Tutti Fruiti* on the radio. I touched her arm and leaned in close. "Just remember, don't say nothin' to Mom about it yet, okay? Wait 'till Gram talks to her first."

"I know, I know," Sue retorted. "I'm not a little kid, ya know."

I finished my stitch, then looked at my sister. "One day, it will be your turn."

Sue made a face. "Yech. No thanks." Her lips tightened in annoyance, and she turned and tried to smooth a piece of poking plastic that had come loose from the taped-up back of the kitchen chair.

I laughed and jabbed her with an elbow. "Just remember not to say anything about it within earshot of the *dedeens*, 'cause you know he's a gossip and a tattletale."

Sue grinned.

"It's our secret for now—just between us and Gram, okay?"

"Okay."

"And what are you two plotting this time?" Mom asked as she walked in from the front room and folded her arms, her face painted with good-humored suspicion.

I looked up from my sewing with my best wide-eyed-innocence look. "Nothin', Mom. Just girl talk."

"I'll bet," she said as she automatically turned down the radio, leaned down and planted kisses on our cheeks. She cradled my face in her hands. "It's so good to have you home."

"It's good to be home, Mom." I was dying to tell her about my moon time, but I had agreed to let Gram handle it. Darn, it would be so much easier if Mom didn't act so white sometimes.

I spied the mail clutched in her hand. "Have you heard from Daddy?" I risked, banking on her good mood.

Mom turned away and headed for the sink. "Any day now, I expect. Daddy's been real busy lately—you know, driving day and night."

I heard the fib in her voice as she pretended to busy herself, straightening items on the counter that didn't need straightening. She pushed a faded curtain aside that covered the dish cabinet and inspected our six dishes. "Why don't you send Daddy a nice letter?" she suggested. "You could tell him you're home and how much you miss him."

Sure, I thought. Why should he answer this one when he only answered a couple over six months. But I said, "Sure, Mom, okay."

"Good." Mom pulled the curtain back into place, turned, leaned back against the counter and smiled. Late-afternoon sunlight drenched her back and arms as it streamed through the window over the sink.

Without looking up from her beading, Sue said, "How come Daddy's mad at us, anyway?"

Yeah, why, Mom?

Mom looked away. "Daddy ain't mad at us. I told you, he's just working a lot of overtime 'sall."

Sue frowned and looked at Mom. "But he never comes home. Why's he like work more than us?"

I knew there was more to it than his work. Like an iceberg, much more lay below the surface. But although I knew Daddy was mad at Mom for some secret reason, part of me couldn't help sharing Sue's anguish that he was punishing us as well.

Aside from the fact that I hated writing letters—I could never think of anything to say—it was because of my anger that I hadn't written him much during the school year, hoping he would write and tell me what was going on between him and Mom. Then again, I mysteriously feared knowing. I worried it might be about me, that perhaps Sue or I had done something to cause the rift.

All I wanted was for him to say he loved me and missed me so much that he was coming back home, that everything would be like it used to be. Now the day seemed ruined as my mood turned gloomy. I wished Sue had never brought up the subject.

There was a polite knock on the front screen door. "Anybody home?"

"I'll get it!" Sue yelled and she dashed to the door. From the front room she hollered, "Momma, it's Mr. White Bear."

Mom smoothed her apron and fluffed her bobbed hair. "Oh, and look at me!"

I liked and respected Mr. White Bear. He reminded me of Dad. They were about the same age, and both were tall and dark and muscular.

Luther White Bear ducked into the kitchen. "Well, how's the best-looking girls on the rez today?"

"Morning, Mr. White Bear," I chirped.

He eyed our handiwork on the table. "Well, I can sure tell you two are Cecelia's granddaughters. That's some really fine beadwork."

Sue beamed and showed him the barrette she was working on. "It's a wild lily."

He leaned over and studied the barrette. "I see. Beautiful job." He looked over at my shawl that was partially spread on the table. The crimson cloth matched my dance dress. On the center back of the shawl I was sewing yellow, black, and silver sequins into a pretty realistic swallowtail butterfly. Smaller butterflies of varying colors decorated each corner.

"Always remember the Creator as you work," Gram had

taught. "If you say the right prayers, your work will go easy and come out right. But don't try to make it perfect," she had warned. "Only *Gitche-Manitou* can make perfect things, *eya?*"

When I was little Gram told us that butterflies should be called upon to join in our play. Outside, Sue and I would run about calling *"Me-e-memgwe, me-e-memgwe."* Believe it or not, they came to us.

"Ruby, that's the prettiest swallowtail I've ever seen. I got a feeling you're going to be tough to beat this year," Luther observed.

My mood brightened. He was referring to the shawl-dance contest at the Loon Lake *Wee-Gitche-Neme-Dim* powwow in August. "Thanks."

Mr. White Bear would be in charge of judging this year, and more than anything I wanted that first-place ribbon. Last year I'd come within three points of first place, taking second to Paula Gunhouse, who had won the past three years. If I was lucky, Paula might be dancing somewhere else this year, now that she was seventeen and competing all over Wisconsin. In fact, I might even have a shot at Powwow Princess—an honor Paula also always seemed to win, depending on which of the other older girls would be around this summer. For me, it was a long shot at age thirteen, but butterflies could dream, couldn't they?

"Can I get you some coffee, Luther?" Mom asked.

"Sure, if it ain't too much trouble."

Mom hustled toward the stove. "No trouble at all."

Luther sat at the table. "I could patch that torn screen of yours. Mosquitoes are likely to be bad this summer," he said to Mom, then turned his attention to Sue and me. "You girls going to the social tonight?"

I nodded. "Sure am."

"Me, too," Sue piped.

He was referring to one of the summer socials put on at the powwow grounds, potluck get-togethers sponsored by one family or another. Somebody would bring a drum and there would be singing and dancing and socializing. They were our summer entertainment, not to mention good practice for the Big Dance in August.

"That's the Brave Rock's social, ain't it, Luther?" Mom asked as she brought two cups of coffee to the table.

"Yep." Luther took a sip. "I heard Sammy's home from school." He shot Mom a wink.

Sammy Brave Rock was a dreamy fifteen-year-old I had known since we were kids and had always harbored a secret crush on. Sammy attended an Episcopal boarding school that got out later than St. Nicholas. I heard he got home yesterday. I felt my ears get hot and returned to my sewing.

"Sammy Brave Rock?" Sue complained. "That ain't no reason to go to a social." She glanced at Luther. "Are you going, Mr. White Bear?"

"If I get back in time from a meeting over to Hayward."

"Is that about the water project?" Mom asked.

"Yeah. We're going to get that money this time if I got to drive to Washington to do it."

Mom looked at him admiringly. "Oh, it'd be a godsend if you could. It'd be wonderful for Mom and them other folks out there to get running water. I worry about her all winter, out there in the snow, pouring hot water down that frozen old cistern pump."

Luther nodded, a determined look in his eye. "It would mean a lot to all the Yellow Hill people. All I have to do is convince our 'common uncle'."

Sue's face scrunched up. "What uncle?"

I sniggered. "Yeah, if Gram gets running water we won't

have to worry about Sue getting her tongue froze on the pump."

Sue slapped her barrette down on the tabletop. "Why you gotta keep bringing that up every year? Everybody's tired of that old story."

The rest of us chuckled.

"See?" I taunted. "No, they're not. It still gets a laugh."

Around five o'clock Sue and I made the three-mile walk to the social. As we neared the powwow grounds we were greeted with the sweet scent of new-mown grass. The men had obviously worked hard all day, mowing and scything down tall grass and weeds. Some were setting up the old, bent-up folding tables stored in the shed at the south end of the grounds. Women chattered while they spread patched sheets and tablecloths over the tables, while teens carried covered pots and dishes from parked cars and pickups. A gaggle of smaller children scampered about, playing tag.

"Ahneen!" called Mr. and Mrs. Mink.

"Boozhoo!" we answered. We returned several other friendly waves, then jumped in and helped the older ladies set out food items, joining in the chitchat.

Nearby, Mr. Brave Rock, Sammy and a few other men were setting up the Brave Rock Singers' big drum. It was a huge drum with thick hide heads that, when suspended from four rope loops attached to a wooden stand, hung about two feet from the ground. Ten men on folding chairs could sit around it knee to knee. I saw Sammy sprinkle a bit of tobacco on the drumhead and mutter a brief prayer. I liked this tradition—blessing the drum as a gift to The People, as a living spirit in itself. It felt that way whenever the drum sounded, setting my feet to moving.

If a drum was playing, I was dancing.

I was proud of Sammy, too. He had been learning to sing since he was big enough to hold a beater. This year, I had heard, he would sing "second" to his dad, the lead singer. The group consisted of fourteen members of the Brave Rock extended family, and they were my favorite Drum. They had something special—a deep, driving beat, ten beaters striking the drum in perfect synchrony, the men's powerful voices sliding easily from normal pitch to thrilling high falsettos. A women's quartet stood behind them, embellishing the song with a nasal harmony that made the crowning difference between Drum groups. From my view, a Drum wasn't a Drum without a women's chorus.

One mystery always remained, however. How could grown men with such low, manly voices sing such high notes? Sammy had told me that it was a men's secret, taught to him by his father and uncle, who knew the "way of the drum."

Soon, several of my friends and cousins arrived. The teens began to gather at a small set of weatherworn, homemade bleachers a few yards behind the drum. When I finished helping the ladies I meandered over to them. "Hi, Sammy."

Sammy turned and smiled weakly. "Oh, hi, Ruby. How's it goin'?"

"Okay." My heart fluttered at his good looks and new height. He must've grown another two inches, I thought as I stared up into his kind, dark eyes. I also noted some sparse hair on his upper lip. Would he notice my new maturity, now that I had become a woman? I certainly felt womanly tonight.

He glanced at Sue. "Hey, Sue, how'ya doin'?"

"Fine," Sue twittered, grinning back and forth at us like a kid awaiting a treat.

I scowled at her. "Why don't you go play with your friends?"

She made a face and trudged off.

I rolled my eyes. "Little sisters."

He chuckled. "Can't be any worse than little brothers."

I chatted with the other kids a few moments, then turned back to Sammy and asked absently, "So, how's St. Paul's?"

He shrugged. "The same—shitty." He shoved his hands into his pockets. "How's St. Nic's?"

I was a bit surprised at his profanity. I didn't remember him cussing last year. "Don't ask," I droned. "You gonna sing later?"

"Yeah. We'll probably start up after supper."

I grinned. "Gonna do any Forty-niners?" I was talking about the group singalongs that took place after powwows, when the dancers and singers relaxed, socialized and sang whimsical English lyrics to Indian tunes.

"Probably." He smiled. "Picked up some new ones last summer."

I said dreamily, "Wish I could travel all summer, go to all those powwows."

"Yeah," Sammy said, "and get paid for it, too."

"Heck, I'd do it for free!"

"Well, you'd at least get day money." He was referring to the couple of dollars dancers were paid at the end of a dance if enough was left after paying the drums and other expenses. "But hell, Ruby, you're good enough now. You could make good money at some of them competition dances."

I felt my ears warm at the compliment. I'd heard about these new kinds of powwows, where dancers competed for money. "Oh, I ain't that good yet. Besides, my mom wouldn't let me to do that on my own."

Sammy shrugged. "You're too modest. You're one of the best fancy dancers I've seen."

"You really think so? I mean, do you really think I could win outside of Loon Lake?"

"Man, there's no doubt in my mind. A lotta girls have quit dancin', you know—" His upper lip curled into a slight sneer, "—bein' good Christians."

"Ha!" I declared. "The day I stop dancing will be the day I die."

Sammy grunted. "Yeah, and they'll never make me quit the drum, neither."

"Food!" somebody yelled.

At the tables, Marvin Big Shield bowed his head and prayed in Ojibwe. "Grandfather, *Gitche-Manitou,* we thank you for the warm breeze and the clear blue sky today. We are thankful for all that you've given us, Grandfather—for Mother Earth who sustains us, for the rains that quench our thirst, for the sun that warms our faces. We thank you for this good food, for the blessings you've bestowed upon us. We thank You for our friends and our families, Grandfather, and for the good times we will have together tonight. *Aho.*"

"Aho!" everyone chorused.

By tradition, the kids waited for the elders and then the adults to fill their plates. I saw Grandma Shade sitting nearby, a tattered shawl bunched around her hunched shoulders. The venerable granddaughter of Chief Maengun was eighty-five now. Her leathery face, framed by two long white braids, bore the imprints of a hundred deep lines, a near century of hardship and *Anishinabe* history. I filled a plate and set it in front of her. She smiled and nodded. A few of the other kids filled plates for elders who were chair-bound.

The food was delicious. Like an inmate released from prison, I stuffed down two bowls of deer-meat stew, a healthy portion of bean casserole, and two pieces of corn bread soaked in real butter. I even managed a heaping tablespoon of coleslaw, a piece of sweet potato pie, and a mound of fluffy *manomen.* The only time we ate like this was at a social, when folks could pool their resources. Stuffed, I leaned back and sadly eyed fresh rabbit, fish chowder, and all sorts of berry pies. I'd get to them later.

After supper, me and the other girls started helping Mrs. Brave Rock and the other ladies clean up. Mrs. Brave Rock took a pile of dirty paper plates from me with a good-natured grin. "Never you mind, Ruby," she said in Ojibwe, her hand whisk-brooming us away. "You kids go and have fun. We'll take care of the mess."

I heard the drummers start. Mr. Brave Rock settled into an easy beat, setting the pace for the first song. His eyes closed, his hand cupped to his ear, he trilled out the lead verse in a high falsetto. The drumbeats vibrated in my chest and worked their way down my legs and into my feet. I was glad everyone wore regular clothes to socials since my new outfit wasn't ready, but out of respect and tradition, ladies always wore some kind of covering over their shoulders when dancing. I donned my old shawl, my back straightening to the proud posture of a shawl dancer, and then my feet flew into motion as if I had danced yesterday instead of months ago.

Other shawl dancers twirled by, and then a grinning Sue bounced past, hands on hips as she hopped and bounced the dance of a jingle-dress dancer. I was impressed. Despite her fooling around, Sue had really improved. She had all the makings of a champion.

I danced around the drum, passing several women dancing the slow, stately movements of traditional dancers. They moved together in groups of twos and threes, laughing and chatting as they toe-heeled six inches at a step around the circle. Mr. Brave Rock picked up the tempo on the next song, a wild, driving pace that set my blood to rushing and tested my stamina and the agility of my footwork. The boys and several of the men showed their appreciation of the lightning pace by letting out whoops and yells in the old way as they crouched and bobbed around the dance circle.

From time to time I glimpsed Sammy, his eyes sometimes closed in deep concentration. I saw him raise his beater high and pound out the honor beats at the appropriate time and with the appropriate rhythm. He was doing a grand job as the second.

After a few more songs, the drummers took a break and I joined Sammy at the big water container near the drum. Sharing the tin ladle, we gulped down three or four ladlefuls each. “Wanna take a walk?” Sammy asked. He nodded in the direction of a woman about Mom’s age. “My Aunt Sally and her friend will go with us.”

“Sure,” I replied, thrilled at the suggestion.

At our age, being together required a chaperone. We sauntered across the field under a bright full moon, our chaperones tagging behind at a polite distance. A million stars, like glimmering bits of creek mica, crystaled an indigo sky.

“You’re doing great on the drum tonight,” I said. “But I wish we had more powwow songs in Ojibwe.”

“Oh, you’ll start hearing more of them. Dad’s been bringing a lot of the old Ojib songs back. And he’s starting to compose some new ones. Wait till *Wee-Gitche-Neme-Dim* and you’ll hear some of ’em.”

“Neat!”

“Yeah,” Sammy said with pride in his voice, “then they’ll be Brave Rock family property, and other Drums will have to get our permission to sing ’em.”

We walked along in silence for a while, then sat on the bleachers that faced the powwow arena. Our chaperones sat at the opposite end. June bugs whirred through the night air, their hard brown bodies thudding against the light pole above us. Sammy poked at the ground with a stick he'd picked up in the field. Out of the blue he said, "Ever think about running away from school?"

"Sure, lots of times." I felt a twinge of sadness as I thought of Isabelle and Millie. "Two girls tried this winter at St. Nic's." My voice dropped. "They froze to death."

Sammy stared at me. "Jesus." He paused a moment, then, "Well, I ain't goin' back. My dad says I don't have to."

I swiveled to look at him. "Really? He said that?"

He nodded. "Once I told him what's been going on there."

"What about your mom? What's she say?"

He shrugged. "We had a big fight about it. She says there'll be big trouble for the whole family, that they'll send the cops out. All that stuff." His voice was suddenly hatchet sharp. "But I don't give a damn. I ain't going back!"

I flinched at the sudden anger thrown in my direction. There was something about him I'd not seen before. A morose sullenness had replaced the playful boy I'd known in the past. The boarding-school system had claimed another young spirit.

I laid a comforting hand over his. "I know, Sammy. The whippings are bad, but you can't let them break your spirit."

Sammy snorted, "Whippin's are nothin'." A solitary tear rolled down his cheek and caught the moonlight like a fleck of ice. He quickly wiped it away. "Like I said, I ain't never going back." He sleeved away the tear and looked into the night. "That bastard won't ever touch me again."

A wave of embarrassment washed over me. It had never occurred to me that boys could also be molested.

We meandered back to the social in grim silence consumed with depressing memories. I shook them off. I had decided I wasn't going to think about St. Nic's over the summer. "You'll feel better when you get back to the drum,

Sammy," I managed. "Forget school. We're home and we're gonna have fun."

Ahead, we saw the glow of the campfire, heard laughing and talking and a few ragged drumbeats as the singers prepared for Forty-nine singing.

"It's about time," Sue snipped when she saw us. "Where'd you go?"

"None of your beeswax," I said.

Sammy took his seat at the drum. Some people set up folding chairs; others spread blankets on the ground. The teens settled at the opposite side of the drum, near the campfire, away from the adults. We laughed and sang along to *Lost My Gal in Oklahoma, Five Minutes More* and *One-Eyed Ford*.

I was surprised to see some of the kids passing beer around, and more of them were smoking since last year. I glanced worriedly at Sue, who was watching their activities with rapt attention. Fifteen-year-old Jeannette Boissonault, a second cousin, offered me a cigarette from a half-empty pack.

"No thanks," I said. I had tried a cigarette once and felt as if I'd sucked up half a campfire. Besides, Sue and her pal Mary, the two biggest *dedeens* at Loon Lake, had squeezed in next to her. Jeannette shrugged and lipped one from the pack, her mouth lipsticked deep red and looking like licked candy. Her boyfriend lit her cigarette, then his own.

> *"When the dance is over, Sweetheart*
> *I'll take you home in my one-eyed Ford . . ."*

When the song ended, I leaned over and whispered in Jeannette's ear, "Still going with Harley, huh?"

Jeannette grinned and nodded. "We're gonna get married."

I was taken aback. How'd I miss that piece of juicy gossip? "When?"

"This fall. When I turn sixteen."

"Your folks said okay?"

"*Eya.* Dad was against it, but my mom said I'd probably end up pregnant anyway." Jeannette shrugged and took a drag, tilted her head back and blew smoke. "She's probably glad to get me out of the house, what with four kids to feed."

I leaned around Jeannette and took in Harley with a new level of appraisal and curiosity. He grinned at me through a smoke ring.

The fire sizzled and spat.

"That's great, Jeannette. You won't have to go back to St. Paul's."

Jeannette winked. "You got it," she said, then elbowed me and whispered, "See Mae over there?"

I eyed fifteen year-old Mae Manchie necking with a boy I didn't know.

"She ain't going back neither. She's pregnant."

My mouth dropped open. "Who—"

Jeannette apparently expected my question. "She ain't talking, but there's rumors."

I had always hated Jeannette's habit of baiting a person. "What rumors?"

Jeannette forced a sigh. "Well, I guess you'll find out anyway. Rumor is it's your cousin, Earl. Guess he likes 'em old *and* young."

Chapter Thirty-Three

"Mom, you won't *bee-lieve* what I heard at the social," I blurted after Sue had begrudgingly gone to bed.

Sitting at the kitchen table, Mom thumbed through a six-month-old issue of *Life*.

I slid onto the chair next to her. "Mae Manchie's pregnant."

She continued reading. "Everybody already knew that, hon."

I felt a twinge of disappointment. "They do? And that the father is Cousin Earl?"

Mom's head snapped up. "Who said that?"

The sudden sharpness in her voice took me by surprise. "Jeannette—Jeannette Boissonault."

"Well, there you go," Mom snipped. "And you shouldn't be passing on such nasty rumors as that—about your own relations. I'm surprised at you!"

She marched out of the kitchen, leaving me puzzled. Her reaction was more like Gram's at such rumor passing. Mom always seemed to enjoy hearing good gossip. Gram forbade it. She had taught that gossiping was *manitouwaadizi,* that gossip could boomerang and foul your own nest. "A person should have better things to do than to speak badly of others" was what she said. But now I was really curious about Jeannette's comment.

Remembering I was to take some groceries to Gram, I

packed flour, a can of lard, sugar, powdered eggs, baking powder, macaroni and sundry other items into a pair of makeshift gunnysack saddlebags, then threw a saddle blanket on Star, the mare Gram had lent Sue and me for summer transportation. Star had been a gift from Dad, who worried about Gram walking and carrying things. I had named her for the almost perfect white star on her forehead. But Gram wasn't keen on horses, preferring her "own two feet."

Star nickered and nosed my arm in expectation of a ride. I caressed her soft nose and chin and shared a carrot. I tossed the gunnysacks over her neck, grabbed a handful of mane, swung up on her back, and trotted toward Gram's. It had been hot and dry the past several days, and we left a plume of dust lingering behind us.

Plum-colored clouds massed above. I could smell the teasing scent of a storm in the air. As I neared Gram's, the sky darkened into a thick cushion of charcoal gray, and soft thunder rumbled above like distant powwow drums. I heeled Star into a trot.

Gram's tarpaper house was in front of me when the first few raindrops pelted my head. As I tied Star to a tree, the front door swung open. "Don't tie her, Ruby," Gram called in Ojibwe. "There's a storm coming, maybe *wawasum, eya?*"

I hadn't thought about lightning.

"Let her loose. She'll be all right," Gram reassured me as she held the door open. *"Beendigin, beendigin."*

I grabbed the saddlebags, retrieved the saddle blanket and gave Star a gentle smack on her flank. She trotted hungrily toward the meadow. Gram, smelling of flour and garden herbs, gave me a quick hug as I ducked inside. A startling flash of stark light illuminated our surroundings like a photo negative, followed by a bone-jarring crack.

"Oooh," Gram exclaimed as she peered out at the sky.

"You got here just in time. *Mudji-keewis* is coming."

The one-room house was hot and smelled of freshly baked bread. I searched my mind as I started to unpack the groceries and arrange them neatly on the kitchen wall shelves.

"I remember that name, Gram, but I forget what it means."

Gram set aside her cornhusk broom and helped me with the groceries. "You forgot?" she *tsked,* her long gray braids swaying gently with her shaking head. "That's what happens when you trust too much in books. It makes your mind lazy. You don't remember things like you should."

I felt a lecture coming.

"In the old days we could hear a story once and we'd remember it. That was what was expected, *eya?* Weren't no books then." She tapped a finger on her forehead. "Everything was right here. Your elders expected it. You had to know your family history, tribe history, stories, everything. The only thing ever wrote down was the *wee'gwas* scrolls."

I brightened, eager to show off my knowledge. "Ah, the ones that had all our sacred ceremonies. And they hid them in a cave on the face of a high cliff so no one could steal them."

A wide smile broke across her lips as she reached over and patted my cheek. *"Eya!"*

Another lightning flash lit the room, followed by a chest-rumbling growl of thunder. Gram jumped, her hand flying to her heart as she looked uneasily toward the front door. "We were having a big storm one time, just like this, and I remember Grandma Wabunanung looking real worried. Then this big bolt of lightning struck a tree; split it right in half. Grandma, she ran out and kindled a fire in that old rusty potbelly stove we kept in a lean-to next to the house and threw in a handful of tobacco. I remember like it was yesterday." Gram held up beseeching arms toward the low log ceiling.

" '*K'mishomissinaun! K'okomissinaun!* Grandfathers, Grandmothers,' she cried at the sky. 'Don't be too angry at us. I didn't forget you. I was broke and didn't have no tobacco. But I got some now and keep it all the time and offer you some. I hope you're not too mad at us.' "

Gram pursed her lips in sober reflection. "And I'll tell you, I always made sure I had tobacco in my house and made my offerings."

"At school," I blurted, "they taught us that thunder and lightning are just hot air and cold air meeting each other up in the sky."

Gram stopped shelving, still holding a bag of sugar in her left hand, her right fist parked on her hip. "Is that so? And who do you think made the hot air and the cold air? Who do you think created the world and everything in it, *eya?* Never forget it." She finished shelving the last of the supplies. "All those priests know about the Great Spirit is only what they got wrote down in those books. They don't know what we know because they aren't Indian. They weren't taught the ways of the pipe, the ways of the *Midewiwin*. They don't even know the prophecies."

I saw this as a ripe opening and confessed, "That's why I don't want to go back to St. Nicholas, Gram. I can learn everything I need from you and Mr. White Bear and Grandmother Mink."

Gram smiled proudly at me as she fingered the tiny safety pin that served as the temporary top button of her faded dress, but then she turned pensive. "We live in a white world now. Learning is *onishishin*." The gleam returned to her eyes. "But you must still learn the old knowledge. The prophecies warn what will happen if a generation gives up our ways."

She pulled out a wooden chair Grandpa had made and bade me to sit. "It is a hard world out there, *Bineshee*

Ogichidaw, and it is important you know the truth. You remember the story about the trickster spider? The one that persuaded that bunch of ducks that if they would dance in a circle with their eyes closed, he would sing them beautiful songs? Those ducks, they fell into the spider's trap, *eya?*"

I grinned. It was a favored story from my childhood. "And as they danced the spider killed them, one by one."

Gram nodded. "Today, the government men are making us dance with our eyes shut and will take the rest of our land away unless we fight them with their own weapons. And they have a sharp weapon: book knowledge." Her hand balled into a bony fist. "So we must get this knowledge, too. Then we can fight and save what we have left." She got up and headed for the icebox.

Filled with wistfulness, I was still thinking about my great-grandmothers. Talk about government stuff bored me. Propping my elbows on the table, I rested my head in my hands. "I wish I could have met Great-Great Grandma Wabunanung," I mused. "Or Great Grandma Pitwoniquot. Sometimes I daydream about her, thinking about her telling me all the neat things about the old days—the hunts, the ceremonies, war dances, what it was like to live in a wigwam . . ."

Gram gave me one of her *oh-really?* looks as she placed a glass of powdered milk and a bowl brimming with fat, dewy strawberries in front of me. "And you think your grandmother knows nothing of those things?

Oops.

"Oh, no, Gram. I mean, what it would have been like to have met her and talked to her in person."

Gram looked into the distance. "They were strong, tough women. They had to be in them days." Her eyes smiled at me. "You have them in you." She sat back and lit her clay pipe. "I don't remember much about Grandmother Wabunanung.

She passed over when I was just a little girl. But I'll tell you, I loved being with my mother. I felt good when I was with her, like I was with Mother Earth herself, like I was with someone special that only belonged to me. She taught me about the ways of nature, about being *Anishinabe*—about myself. Taught me how to make pemmican, too, and how to dress hides, how to make moccasins."

"Just like you did with me," I said through a mouth stuffed full of succulent strawberries.

"Eya," Gram nodded and waved a finger in the air. "My first moccasins were a sight, but Grandmother, she praised them and told me they would get better as I practiced."

I grinned. "Did she always have a stash of goodies, like you? Huckleberries? Or a pie? Or little presents and stuff?" I wanted to know, thinking of Gram's little surprise gifts wrapped in tissue with string dyed red for lack of costly ribbon.

"Huckleberries, *eya,* and big fat strawberries, like those in your bowl, there during *Ode'imini-geezis*. She didn't make pies, but she made the best pemmican you ever tasted. And maple sugar candy, too." Gram wriggled her eyebrows and pushed herself up from the table. "How about some *bigiwizigan?* Thinking about all those sweets makes me hungry for some."

I nodded enthusiastically and Gram fetched the taffy. We chewed the treat in thoughtful silence, the taffy clinging to our teeth like rubber bands.

"Ahh." A gleam formed in Gram's eyes. "Whenever I have something sweet I think of the old days, of the old stories, and I think about your *biijiinag bakaanigeng oshkiniigikwe*. It is time for more of your training."

I was all ears. When around Gram or other elders, I felt like a sponge. I couldn't soak up enough.

"Well," Gram continued, "*Neebageesis,* you see, watches over you and me. She stands for womanhood and the cycle of *oon-da'dizoowin'*. *Gitche-Manitou* created woman to cast knowledge on man, just as *Neebageesis* casts her light on the Earth. Alone, Man is backward and clumsy, *eya?*" She winked. "He must have woman's light to make him whole."

I giggled, thoroughly enjoying Gram's gibe, then turned thoughtful. "I always loved how you said that *Gitche-Manitou* was the first thought and that He sent His thoughts out in every direction, but there was nothing to bounce them back, and the stars we see at night are the trails of His thoughts."

Gram smiled and nodded. "*Onishishin,* but you're interrupting your elder."

Too much time at St. Nicholas had caused me to forget my Indian manners.

By midafternoon slanting rays of sunlight poked through soupy clouds and into the open kitchen window. A breeze fluttered sun-faded cotton curtains. The air, rain-freshened and redolent with the smell of grass and wildflowers, mingled with the aroma of the fresh bread.

Gram took two reflective puffs on her pipe before continuing my lesson, then blew the smoke upward, toward the Creator. "Now, you remember that after *Gitche-Manitou* finished making the Earth and the sun and the moon, and all those other things, He gave us the seven grandfathers to watch over us. And the seven grandfathers gave seven important gifts to The People, *eya?*"

My mind reached back, trying to recall all seven gifts in case she asked me, but I could only think of three.

"These are the ways we are to behave as *Anishinabeg*. The first one is wisdom, because to love knowledge is to know wisdom. The next gift is love, because to know love is to know peace. The third is respect, to honor all that *Gitche-Manitou* has created. Respecting each of His creations for their place in the world, *eya?*" Gram took another bite of taffy and closed her eyes in concentration. "The fourth gift, you remember, is bravery, to face an enemy and keep your self-respect. The fifth, that one is honesty," she winked, "which needs no explanation. And the sixth is humility. A good Ojibwe is humble because he is but a small part of all the sacred things of the Creation."

I chimed in, "And the last one is truth—to know all these things as truths. I remember, Gram. You taught me those when I was little."

Gram puffed thoughtfully on her pipe. "Of course. You were raised right. But now, as you are to become a woman, it is time you think deeper about the seven gifts. Reflect on them as to what they really mean to you as a woman, as an *Anishinabe,* and about how you will pass them on to your children."

Gram rested her hand on mine. "You are Martin clan—a warrior. To be a warrior, you must especially use these gifts. Your grandpa, he was *benays* clan, the clan of the holy people, and by tradition became a holy man. You must follow the warrior's path, to be a fighter for your people, a defender of our ways."

I was starting to feel a weight of responsibility pressing down on me. "But Gram, I'm still a kid."

"Soon you will go through the *biijiinag bakaanigeng oshkiniigikwe,* and then you will be a woman." Gram's eyes sparkled with excitement. "A warrior, you see, does not always use a knife or a gun." She poked a finger against her temple. "A warrior uses his head. You are smart enough to take the useful things the Robes teach you and to wash out those that poison your spirit, your pride." She straightened in her chair and narrowed her eyes. "You will *waybeenun* those things that teach being Indian is bad, *eya?*" She gathered my hands into her own and squeezed. "Remember the gifts of bravery and truth. Those gifts have been given to you. No one can take them from you." She leaned forward, a strange smile upon her lips as she grasped my hands in hers. "You are *Anishinabe!*"

The rusty twang of the front screen door took us both by surprise, and Mom burst in. Perspiration dotted her forehead from the four-mile walk; her shoes muddy from the rain-soaked road. A lighted cigarette was clenched between two fingers. Her face was tense with agitation. "Ruby, get home! There's chores to be done."

I looked at Gram, who seemed perplexed, then back to Mom. "But Mom—"

"No buts! Do what you're told."

I stood to protest, but Gram, looking concerned, rested her hand on my shoulder. "Do like your mother says. We'll talk more later, *eya?*"

I trudged out the door, then circled around the tiny house and peeked in the kitchen window.

Mom glared at Gram, cocked her hip and blew out an angry stream of smoke. "I told you I didn't want Ruby confused with that old Indian stuff. She's bein' raised Catholic. I'm Catholic, Sue is Catholic, Jim is Catholic. You just gotta get used to it!"

Gram looked surprised and puzzled by the sudden storm.

Mom eyed Gram angrily. "Sue spilled the beans this morning. I know all about Ruby's period and about your plans for her. Jesus, Mom! This is 1957, not 1857. Them days are over, thank God. We're trying to be civilized Christian people and then—then you sneak around and do what I asked you not to."

Gram's face clouded as she pushed herself up from the

table. “Be careful, daughter! You forget you are talking to your mother. You were raised better than that. Is this what being Christian means—disrespecting your elders?”

Mom slapped at her dress. “That ain’t the point, Mom, and you know it. I can’t have you undermining me all the time. The girls have it tough enough without you trying to turn back the clock and make—make blanket Indians out of them.”

Gram stiffened. “The government gave us blankets to cover our shame after they took everything from us, but you never saw our family take any blankets. It’s pride I’m teaching them girls, how to hold up their heads and know who they are.”

Mom steadied herself on a chair back and massaged her forehead. “Oh, Mom.”

“Don’t ‘oh, Mom’ me. I taught you the same. It’s all right there,” she said, pointing an arthritic finger toward Mom’s heart, “if you’d only free your *Shinnob* spirit from that little box inside where you put it a long time ago, *eya?*”

Mom stubbed out her cigarette angrily. “Damn it, Mom, I don’t want to hear this again. It’s got nothing to do with the real world. Nobody cares about it any more except the old people, always crying about the old days. The rest of us want to move ahead.” Her voice and expression became almost pleading. “Don’t you want Ruby and Sue to get an education, to find decent men to marry and have nice homes? Why would you want them to repeat your life and have nothing?”

Mom’s face pinched up as if she instantly regretted her words. Gram, her hand tightly gripping her chair back, stood stone-like, her face expressionless save for an intermittent twitching at the corner of her mouth, a frightening expression I’d never seen before.

I couldn’t listen anymore. I wheeled and bolted, sprinted

down the puddled road, past the meadow of wildflowers sad from rain, mud sucking at my old hand-me-down shoes, blotching my legs and spattering my faded cotton dress.

How could Mom talk to Gram that way? How could she be so disrespectful, so mean? First she sent me to that hellhole St. Nicholas, and now she attacked the person I most adored, and I was the cause of it. It was obvious there would be no *biijiinag bakaanigeng oshkiniigikwe*. Maybe it was for the best. Adulthood had become frighteningly complex and far less liberating than I had anticipated. Suddenly, I wanted no part of it. Not if it would destroy the love between Mom and Gram.

Chapter Thirty-Four

Theresa glared at her mother. "I don't know why you're being so stubborn about this. I mean, after you saw that I wasn't interested in that Indian stuff, you'd think you would've given up. But no, you keep pushing." Her voice broke. "You're making me the bad guy all the time."

Cecelia's face darkened. She pointed to the chair across from hers. "Now you sit down and talk to me like a human being, with respect."

Despite her liberating feelings of defiance, Theresa found herself sinking into the chair. Still angry, she blurted, "And mothers should respect their daughters."

Cecelia sat, her eyes fixed on Theresa's. "You've always had my respect. You are my daughter and I love you. But when you do wrong I correct you, *eya?* You say I am trying to pull Sue and Ruby away from you. It hurts me that you think such a thing. A daughter's place is with her mother. Grandmothers teach and guide. That's my place."

Frustrated, Theresa felt the onset of tears, couldn't overcome the tremor in her voice. "Then do your job by supporting me. Things are hard enough." She slumped, her carefully worked-up bravado extinguished like a pinched match. Her head suddenly seemed too heavy to support itself. "It's so hard, Mom." She propped an elbow on the table, closed her eyes, and supported her head on splayed fingertips. "I'm tired, okay? I miss Jim. I need him. Sometimes I don't know what to do. There's never enough money for food, the house is falling apart, trying to find decent work, worrying about Sue being alone too much . . ." She trailed off, pulling a ball of tissue from her dress pocket and dabbing her eyes and nose. "I just want to get off this lousy reservation—live in a town, get away from the—the gossipers—from Loon Lake." She eyed her mother. "I'm sick of this place. Everybody knows everybody's business. I want to go where nobody knows my business or cares who I am."

"You cannot run from yourself, my daughter. That spirit is inside you wherever you go."

Theresa looked up. "Oh, yeah? What about Ted and Esther? They moved to Madison two years ago. Ted got a good factory job, and they got a nice apartment. And Mickey and Alvin are doing great in San Francisco."

Cecelia settled back in her chair. "And?"

"And what?"

"Ted ran off with a white girl, and your cousin Esther set to drinking. Their kids are in trouble all the time, so she's moving back here."

Theresa blinked in surprise. She hadn't heard about the move. "What? When did you hear that?" She narrowed her eyes. "I thought you don't believe in gossip."

"If you kept in contact with your relatives, you would know these things. Luther told me when I was at the tribal office. He had a letter from Esther."

It made sense, Theresa thought. Esther thought the world of Luther, her brother-in-law.

Adopting an expression of self-satisfaction, Cecelia settled her hands in her lap. "Now why do you suppose she's moving back here? Because her family is here. Because her spirit tells her she belongs here."

Theresa massaged her temples again. "Oh, please, Mom.

If her family lived in Timbuktu she'd be going there. What else can she do with no husband and no job and three kids? It's got nothing to do with her spirit or anything magic about Loon Lake."

A pause settled between them. Forest sounds floated through the open kitchen window—the rising and falling whir of insects. A crow cawed.

Cecelia breathed a long sigh. "Her kids, they had trouble there. One got beat up pretty bad, him. The white people, you know, they do got one good saying, about the grass is gree—"

Theresa sighed, "The grass is always greener on the other side. Yeah, Mom, I know."

Cecelia maintained her momentum. "There's been lots of our people try them cities, and they always come back, or something happens to them and their family never hears from them again."

Theresa sniffed and searched for a clean place on the hankie she'd found. "Millions of happy people live in towns and cities. You just use them bad examples over and over to try to scare everybody."

"You are talking about happy w*hite* people," Cecelia argued. "You are Indian people. Take my word for it. I been around longer than you, *Zeegwung Waabigwan*. We don't fit in there."

Theresa felt a prick of annoyance. Her mother had stopped using Theresa's Ojibwe name once Theresa graduated from St. Mark's and had made it clear she preferred her Anglo one. Now Cecelia used it when she was about to offer sage advice or deliver a thinly disguised I-told-you-so.

"No matter how much you try not to be, my daughter, you are Indian. It is in your blood, your skin, your bones. Only in your heart has it hidden away somewhere, hidden behind one of them priest's black robes. You are part of the Earth." She pointed to the floor. "Here, at Loon Lake. It flows in your veins. You can no more wish it away than you can wish away the color of your skin. Even if you go away, you cannot truly leave it, and you will become sick because of it."

Theresa tightened her jaw, closed her eyes.

"Close your ears if you will, *Zeegwung Waabigwan,* but think about it. Every person you know who left Loon Lake has had big trouble in their life—whiskey or trouble with their children, trouble with whites. Their spirits get sick. They are lonely for their land, their family. Most of them came back, *eya?*"

Theresa felt the fury returning. "Losers and quitters! They got too dependent on this place. It sucks out your guts, so all you want is to hide from the world! It's safe to be ignorant! Things get a little tough and they slink back to the rez like—like—"

Cecelia pushed herself up, eyes flashing, her face mottled with anger. "*Debise!* I will hear no more. You will leave my house until you have learned respect!"

"Fine!" Theresa snapped, startled. Her mother had never sent her from the house, even as a child. At a loss for words, she jumped up and walked out.

As she plodded down the road she was glad for the long walk home. It gave her time to sort out the blizzard of emotions whirling within her. In the end, she had wasted her breath. Why did she let herself get drawn into these worn-out arguments? She had come to make her point, to put Mom back in her place, but Cecelia had some mysterious power over her. Arguing with her was like fighting a flood with a mop.

Halfway home, Theresa considered that perhaps she'd overreacted a bit. But how else could she get it into Mom's head that she wanted something better for the girls? Hell—for herself. She and Mom would never agree on what was better.

God, she needed Jim, even though she was sick of his attitude. Lately, she was weary of feeling guilty about it, tired of it throbbing in her gut like a sore that wouldn't heal. She'd give anything if she knew where he was right now, when her anger provided a modicum of courage. She'd borrow the phone at the tribal office and give him hell for not being here for the girls. Even if he couldn't forgive her, he had no right to rob Sue and Ruby of a father. They were still married, damn it, still a family, and she needed his strength, his calmness, his steady compass.

But heartsickness bled away her courage, and her thoughts returned to her fight with her mother. Jim would know what to do, what to say, how to handle Mom and this whole Indian thing of hers. Jim was the key to getting off the reservation. If she could just patch things up between them, she could persuade him to move, maybe to Madison, maybe to Milwaukee. As her weather-beaten, one-room frame house came into view, Theresa pictured city lights, buildings, and bustling crowds of people—happy, white, and gratifyingly faceless.

Chapter Thirty-Five

The Alibi Lounge near North Branch, Minnesota, was one of Jim Loonfoot's favorite stopovers on the long trek home. Though it was in the seedier part of town, it offered a convenient on-off from I-35, making it easy to pull his rig into the parking lot without jockeying around. As usual, he'd stay the night; then it was only four hours to Loon Lake.

Compressed air whooshed as he set the brakes and switched off the ignition. He smiled as he spotted Harry Seymour's rig. Harry was married to Irma Loonfoot, Jim's favorite cousin, and they lived in a small frame house just off the rez. Harry was a kidder, always ready with a joke, most of them stale. Jim crunched across the graveled lot and entered the fire engine-red door. He paused a moment and let his eyes adjust from bright summer sunlight to dusky-lounge darkness. There were the familiar odors of stale beer, peanuts and cigarette smoke. A too-loud jukebox thumped out *Heartbreak Hotel*.

Harry spotted Jim first. "Hey, Loonfoot, over here!"

Jim squinted through the haze and spotted Harry sitting at the far end of the bar, waving like a drowning man.

"Hey, Harry. What's new?" Jim asked as he pulled up a stool and shook Harry's hand, his right arm instantly sticking to the Naugahyde bar edge.

The bartender materialized. "What'll ya have?"

Jim lifted a sticky arm. "Jesus, Hank, don't you guys

ever wipe this thing down?"

The stocky man, cigarette dangling from his lips, frowned at the bar edge. He gave it a quick wipe with a greasy-looking dishcloth. "You here to order or loiter?"

Jim ordered a Pabst.

Hank grunted and pushed off toward center bar.

Harry punched Jim playfully on the arm. "Hey, buddy. Long time no see. Christ, it must be—what, five, six months?"

Jim winced. Harry's voice still hurt his ears. Somebody had turned Harry's volume control to "blast" and never turned it back down. But, he was entertaining from time to time—and he was family.

"Well, I been busy," Jim replied.

The bartender plopped down a beer bottle and scuttled over to another customer.

As nonchalantly as possible, Jim stood and stretched while he toed his stool a couple more feet away from Harry, then straddled it and swiveled to face him. "So, you been home lately?" Jim asked, fishing for fresh news about Sue and Ruby. Harry was the traveling reporter of Loon Lake news and gossip.

"Yeah. Just coming back from there. I gotta pick up a load in St. Paul." His eyes lit up as he elbowed Jim. "Heyyy—saw Ruby and Sue the other day." He scooched his stool closer to Jim. "Prettiest girls at Loon Lake, I said to Irma. Ruby's already as pretty as her ma."

Jim felt a rush of pride and a twinge of guilt. It had been too long since he'd seen the girls. He suspected they'd be hurt, probably angry with him. He'd had a lot of time to think these past months, to put things into perspective. Theresa had been right. He was punishing the girls, and therefore himself, merely to maintain distance between himself and

Theresa. That was why he was on his way home.

"Hey, Jim. Get this." Harry tucked his hands into his armpits and flapped his elbows like wings. His mouth formed a nonsensical mimic of Red Skelton's pelican character. Harry started laughing at his own joke even before he started, then recovered. "Okay—Gertrude and Heathcliffe," he said, his wings flapping. "Hey, Gertrude. Did you see that funny-looking fish over there—"

"I saw that show, Harry," Jim interrupted. "It was a good one." Harry was about the only person Jim knew that he would rudely interrupt. He had learned long ago it was the only way to shorten Harry's broadcasts.

Harry deflated a bit and unfolded his wings. "Oh—yeah, it was, wasn't it?" He regained his composure. "That Skelton knocks me out."

"Yeah."

They sipped their beers. The jukebox switched to *The Great Pretender.*

"You on your way home?" Harry asked.

"Yep."

Harry's red face lit up. "Good, that's real good, Jim. It'll sure make those girls happy." He studied the label on his beer. "Theresa, too."

Jim said nothing.

Harry went on. "She looks tired. I think she really misses you."

"Yeah," Jim mumbled.

Harry leaned on his arms, absently twirled his beer bottle by the neck. "I know it ain't my business, Jim, but we all make mistakes. Theresa's a good girl, she—"

Jim shot Harry a warning glare. Everybody on the rez guessing the reason for their breakup was humiliating enough. The last thing he wanted was their pity or their judgmental stares. Though neither he nor Theresa had ever mentioned outside the house what had happened between her and Earl, there was no such thing as a secret at Loon Lake.

Harry pursed his lips and absently mopped at the bar with his cocktail napkin. "I gotta take a leak," he said and headed for the men's room.

Sometimes Jim thought maybe Theresa was right, that maybe they could make a fresh start somewhere else. All she could talk about was that damned Relocation Act and how the government would help them move to a big city like her cousin Minnie. But Jim's job allowed him to talk with Indians from all over. He knew many families had been tricked into relocating to big cities with the promise of jobs and assimilation into the great American dream. Poorly educated, unskilled, and hardly street-wise, they were the first to be laid off. Then they joined the growing pool of the inner-city hardcore unemployed and suffered increased poverty, alcoholism and family breakups. Besides, he hated the thought of leaving Loon Lake. Despite the current situation, he was at home there. It was comfortable, like a favorite easy chair.

As he thought about it, that was the way his love for Theresa had become. For him, their love never produced the hot flame he'd often heard about, with burning lust and all-consuming passion. They had met at the Shigwadja social eighteen years ago. She was skinny but cute and irresistibly shy. It was a love that had gently sprouted and gracefully matured over three seasons.

He didn't know if he wanted to keep the marriage going, his feelings about Theresa now a tangled skein. He sensed he still loved her, but those feelings lay submerged like a lost coin in Loon Lake. Yet he ached to see his girls.

He allowed himself a smile at the returning Harry. "Got Ruby and Sue some presents in Rapid City. And I got Sue a doll and Ruby a new Teddy bear. She gave hers to Sue a couple years ago. She still likes them on her bed when it's made up."

Harry reached out and clapped Jim on the shoulder. "That's real nice. The girls will appreciate that, yessir." Harry took another swig. " 'Course, Ruby might be getting too old for Teddy bears. Especially after her ceremony and all."

"What ceremony?"

"Oh," Harry said, "I figured you knew. I mean, ain't that the reason why you're headin' home?"

"Harry, I don't know what the hell you're talking about."

Harry looked contrite as he pushed up the brim of his pork pie hat. "The word is Cecelia and Granny Mink are plannin' a comin'-of-age ceremony for her."

Chapter Thirty-Six

"Damn it." I ducked my head and glanced over my shoulder, hoping Mom didn't hear me.

"Rubeee!" Sue exclaimed. "You better stop that cussin'."

My fingers groped at the bobby pins at the back of my head. "Oh, *bekayaan* and give me a hand. I can't tell if they're in right." Powwow day was finally here and my nerves were like coiled barbed wire.

Sue reached up, the rolled tin lids sewn to her jingle dress rustling softly, and adjusted the last pin in my braid. "There, perfect." She stood on tiptoes and checked her own mirror appearance. "We got plenty of time. Why you so nervous, anyway?"

I rolled my eyes at the mirror, then checked the positioning of my beaded barrette and the eagle plume jutting from behind it. The barrette felt precarious since my hair was still too short. I leaned closer to the mirror, bared my teeth and rubbed my finger across the front two. Huffing a sigh, I wished my teeth were whiter, straighter. Paula Gunhouse had perfect teeth. She had perfect everything—a nice house in Hayward, an A-student at the high school, cheerleader captain, homecoming queen, girlfriend of the quarterback. Her credentials went on and on. Worst of all, she knew it and flaunted it. It was enough to make a girl puke.

"Okay," I sighed. "Guess I'm ready as I'll ever be."

Sue stepped back and looked at me with awe. "You look

beautiful, Ruby. Now that I see the whole outfit and your hair done up and everything." She grinned. "You're gonna knock their socks off!"

I grinned back. "You don't look half bad yourself, brat." I strung my arm over Sue's shoulders and turned us so we faced the mirror. "Hey, when the Loonfoot sisters get dressed up, look out!"

Sue's smile faded slightly. "I wish Daddy could see us."

"What's taking you girls so long?" called Mom from the front room where Gram, Marvin Big Shield and several cousins were there waiting for us. "Eileen's got a camera."

"Coming," I yelled, and the Loonfoot sisters made their first grand entry of the day.

When we arrived at eleven o'clock, the powwow grounds were teeming with people. Dancers milled about, some already dressed in full regalia, others partially dressed and carrying dresses or valises packed with regalia. Singers toted their blanket-draped drums to the dance circle. There were people setting up crafts and food tables. Others were unloading blankets, tobacco-ties and sundry other gift items, laying them out on colorful quilts in preparation for "give-aways." Wiry Ed Greenfeather, the venerable *Wee-Gitche-Neme-Dim* emcee chattered away on the microphone, trying out a few of his time-tested powwow jokes on an audience of early-arrived elders and onlookers.

I paused and reveled in the sounds and smells of damp mown grass, fry bread, jingling ankle bells, the swish-rattle of jingle-dress lids, the soft clacking of deer hoof anklets. I could feel the excitement building within me. This one time a year, everyone seemed proud to be Indian. It was the time to show off new regalia, meticulously crafted over the long months since last year's dance. It was time to enjoy family, renew acquaintances, catch up on gossip, flirt, show off, sing, and dance.

We found choice seats under the pine-boughed arbor that ringed the dance circle. After Gram was settled in, Sue and I scampered off to the dancer registration table. I scanned the list of Senior Miss shawl dancers. Paula Gunhouse was number 15. "Gosh," I murmured to Sue with a twinge of worry. "There's twenty-four this year; some I don't even know."

Sue peered over my arm. "Wow. There was only eighteen last year." She looked down at the list of jingle dancers, her category. "I'm okay. There's eleven Junior Miss dancers. Same as last year."

We received our dancer numbers and pinned them on each other; they had to be in easy sight of the judges. I made a beeline for the drum area. There was room for four drum groups, two on either side of the emcee table. I spotted Sammy Brave Rock and his family setting up their drum.

"There's your boyfriend," Sue said, rolling her eyes.

"Keep your voice down," I hissed, then looked up and waved. "Hi, Sammy!"

Sammy waved as I made my way toward him, Sue swishing along behind.

"Why don't you go find your friends," I hinted.

She gave me one of her mischievous grins. "Nah, this'll be more interesting."

I sighed through my nose. "Just once I'd like some privacy." Two steps later I warned, "If you say anything stupid, I swear I'll brain you right in front of everybody."

Sue made a disgusting farting noise with her lips.

Sammy looked us over as we walked up. "Hey, you guys look sharp. A lot of new stuff since last year, *eya?*"

I beamed as I pulled my dress up slightly to show off my

knee-high moccasins, beaded with floral designs in orange and yellow against a white background. "Yeah. Gram beaded my mocs, and I made the dress and shawl."

Sue piped up, "My dress has 210 lids on it. My gram says I'll have all 365 when I get big enough."

"Man," Sammy chuckled, "you guys are definitely out for blood this year. Paula Gunhouse, watch out!"

I laughed, giddy from his compliment and delighted to see him in better spirits.

The P.A. crackled. "Fifteen minutes to grand entry. All dancers, report to the arena entrance. It's almost *powwow time!*" the voice announced, stretching out the last two words.

Chapter Thirty-Seven

Theresa helped her mother settle in by the arena, then wandered among the various craft tables set up about the grounds. There were fine quilts, beadwork, Indian jewelry, tanned hides, and the makings for traditional men's regalia: deer antlers and hoofs, turtle shells of all sizes, rattles, bells, feathers, painted shields. What a waste of their time, she thought, but she visited briefly with each vendor—all of whom she knew—enjoying, at least, the social aspects of the event.

She harbored mixed feelings about the girls' dancing. She'd rather they spent their time learning dances they could use in life: waltzes, foxtrots, maybe even that tango dance she'd seen one time in Milwaukee. They would surely grow out of this Indian stuff, but then they'd be behind the white girls when competing for the eye of a nice boy who might make something of himself.

Theresa had made up her mind. The only way for the girls to meet white boys was to move to a town, the farther from a reservation, the better. She often pictured the girls riding in flashy cars, visiting with friends at the malt shop, going to the movies. Sometimes the fantasy would go beyond that, picturing them married, living in nice homes, in nice neighborhoods, wearing the latest outfits. They looked so happy, so content. So prosperous. They'd have all the things Theresa never had. She'd carefully observed all this when she and Jim had visited various towns, watching the young people, how they looked, how they dressed, what music they listened to. And now, thank God, the government had handed them the opportunity—the Indian Reorganization Act. The government was actually helping Indians move to big cities!

But she knew Jim was content here, close to his family, his buddies. "Hon, I've been in towns all over this country," he had said. "There ain't a one of them where we'd feel welcome. Besides, they're cramped and noisy. This is where we belong."

Where we belong. She'd been hearing that phrase since childhood and she was sick of it. "Keep in your place," is what she eventually understood. You ain't good enough—ain't smart enough—to live with whites. Well, she was fed up with living with people who refused to change, who acted like whipped dogs, hiding on the reservation, satisfied with a subsistence living.

Sue broke her reverie. "Mom, can I have a quarter for some of Mrs. Shigwadja's fry bread? It's the best!"

Theresa gave her the quarter and watched her scamper off. Sue did look darling in her jingle dress, she had to admit. While part of her disliked watching the girls dance, something within her enjoyed it. As annoying as it was, she couldn't stem a begrudging feeling of pride.

Chapter Thirty-Eight

Back at the dancers entrance I spotted Paula Gunhouse, a sixteen-year-old quarter-blood with chestnut hair and a dainty nose. She had the deep blue eyes of her Norwegian mother and the high cheekbones and almond-shaped eyes of her half-Ojibwe father. Her skin was neither dark nor light, a permanent perfect tan. As usual, she was surrounded by a throng of admirers. She looked stunning in her silky red dress stitched with gold ribbon and layers of sparkling sequins. Her matching red-and-gold shawl was embroidered with awe-inspiring geometrics.

Our eyes met for a moment and Paula nodded, then turned her attention back to her fans. I had decided not to let her intimidate me this year. I felt the excitement building, goosebumps forming on my arms as the competition neared.

Dancers milled about, waiting to be placed in the grand entry lineup by Mr. Keeshig, the "head man dancer." I stepped back to allow the elder men dancers and veterans through. They would be first in, several carrying flags and eagle staves, the honor guard in their military fatigues and rifles.

How grand all the dancers looked—the traditional dancers bedecked in eagle-feather bustles, some with face paint; straight dancers with their fine head roaches made of deer and porcupine hair, their multicolored ribbon shirts, their intricate ribbon-worked sashes and belts. Next came the feather dancers, with their dual feather bustles strapped to their backs and shoulders, a dizzying palette of colorfully dyed feathers and fluffs. The grass dancers followed, with their bouncing, antennae-plumed roaches and long, flowing yarn outfits that moved and swayed like wind-swept prairie grass.

Behind them Mr. Keeshig placed the women's traditional dancers with their immaculate, brain-tanned buckskin dresses, beaded or porcupine-quilled in stunning detail, their body-length bone breastplates draping down their dress fronts. They held eagle or goose feather fans. Next came the shawl dancers in our gaily colored dresses and shawls, each one a work of art with its intricately stitched and ribbon-work designs. Then, the jingle-dress dancers, sunlight flashing from the polished surfaces of the hundreds of coned metal lids sewn to their bright-colored dresses. Last came a trailing hodgepodge of people in mixed regalia and civilian dress holding the hands of Tiny Tot competitors.

I laughed and chatted with the other female dancers—most of them cousins or friends—as we helped one another with final adjustments. I felt an inner glow, thinking how their appearance transformed them from rez-dreary to noble and striking. Each looked beautiful, proud and alluring. Their hair was perfectly arranged in plaits or pinned neatly up, their cheeks rosy with rouge, their lips lightly accented with lipstick. And the men—nothing is more impressive than warriors in regalia, some with intimidating face paint, their sculptured arms and chests adorned with silver armbands and bone breastplates, their heads crowned with fine porcupine roaches and eagle feathers.

"Al-l-l right then!" the emcee called over the speaker. "Head dancers, are you ready?"

Mr. Keeshig, the head man dancer, and Mrs. Acorn, the

head lady dancer, gave him the high sign.

"Ladies and gentlemen. Please stand and remove your hats." He looked to his left at one of the drum groups. "Bad River—when you're ready."

The Bad River lead singer brought down his beater with a *boom,* his voice singing out in a high falsetto, and the front dancers stepped off.

"Welcome friends and neighbors to the tenth annual *Wee-Gitche-Neme-Dim.* That's Ind'n for heap big dance in case you ain't in the know," chuckled the emcee, then he gave three loud whoops as the flags passed in front of the reviewing stand.

Though I was far back in line, waiting for the queue of dancers before me to start forward, my feet were already moving to the beat. Finally, the line snaked ahead and I was in the arena, the drum pounding through the P.A., surrounded by hundreds of rhythmic jingling bells, dancing feathers and waving eagle plumes. The men dancers whooped and yelled, moving the line forward, driving my pulse to match the drum's. It seemed to resonate in the earth beneath my feet, vibrate up my legs and throb in my chest.

I understood the sacredness of dance, but despite Gram's teachings and the personal and spiritual reasons one should have for dancing, my mind swirled with the pure pleasure of it—the movement, the steps, the appraising eyes of the audience.

I passed Mom and Gram, Gram's eyes filling with pride. Dancing around the circle, I looked skyward and thanked *Gitche-Manitou* for the blue sky, the warmth of the sun—and for a little help in the dance competition. I was careful to couch the prayer properly, asking for help to "dance my best" in deference to Gram's warnings about using prayer for material gain. "You don't pray for money or a better house or other selfish things," she always warned. I had become so used to this that I found myself ashamed when I lapsed. To be safe, I decided on a more communal prayer, for all the dancers.

The entry song ended and I stood in the now-silent circle of dancers in preparation for the flag song, squinting against the piercing sun. The flags popped and fluttered in the breeze. The song's plaintive words praised a warrior who fought for his people, never to return from the battlefield. I glanced to my right and watched Paula Gunhouse, who seemed more interested in adjusting her neckerchief than in standing still with respect for the solemn moment.

The song ended and the bearers posted the flags in front of the arbor. "Al-l-l right, ladies and gentlemen. Please keep your hats off for the veterans' dance. Calling all veterans into the arena. Don't matter if you're in regalia or not, we wanna see you and thank you for all you done for us. Our head veteran today is Luther White Bear." I spotted Sue and tried to catch her eye to tell her to stop picking her nose, but she was oblivious, intent upon whatever she sought within her nostril.

The drum started the veterans' song, and Mr. White Bear and the head dancers stepped off, followed by a small column of veterans, including the stooped figure of seventy-six-year-old Amos Brave, the only surviving Spanish-American War veteran. The audience applauded and whooped as the vets danced stately around the circle.

After the veterans' dance the arena emptied in preparation for the first of the competition dances. Chiding Sue about her nose picking caused me to almost run into Paula Gunhouse, who gave me one of her sly smiles. "So, Ruby, gonna try again, huh?"

"Oh, hi, Paula," I blurted, immediately wishing I'd said something witty.

Paula gave me a quick once-over, her lips pursed, her face revealing what she thought of my regalia. "Don't think it'll be this year." She forced a smile. "But good luck, anyway," and was gone.

I stood there and fumed. Why hadn't I come up with crafty repartee? Who the hell did she think she was, anyway? She was a nobody on the rez. The only time anyone saw her was at *Wee-Gitche-Neme-Dim*. She was just a powwow Indian.

Maybe there was something to the derogatory comments I heard about mixed-bloods. A lot of Indians felt they were more white than Indian, untrustworthy when the chips were down.

I reflected on this as I walked toward Mom and Gram, who had migrated to Mrs. LaFrambois's food table. I hadn't thought about it before, but all my friends were full bloods, or very near. At school it was the same. But then I thought of Rose Captain. She had turned into a loyal friend and was proud of her one-quarter Indian blood. I had even come to her defense against a couple of full-blood girls.

"Such a serious expression," Mom commented when I arrived.

"Oh, sorry. I was just thinking about something."

Gram grinned. "Paula Gunhouse, I suspect."

I chortled to myself. Gram always knew what was going on in my mind.

Gram winked. "I have a feeling this is your year. I felt it this morning. I saw the signs."

"You did? Like what?"

Gram shook her head. "A secret. Between me and the *bagojininiinsag*."

My eyes must've been big as gourd rattles. "You saw one? Really?" Then I suspected she was teasing. "Gram . . ."

Gram's eyebrows lifted in surprise. "You doubt your grandmother?"

"I saw one once," Sue piped up.

I looked at her disdainfully. She always had to be in on everything. "You did not."

Sue shot me a resentful look. "Did, too."

"When?" I challenged, my fists on my hips.

"Last summer. In Gram's field."

"How come you never said so?"

"I forgot, that's all," she replied.

"Sure," I snipped. "Like you'd forget something like that. What did it look like, huh?"

"Ruby," Gram interjected, "if *Nodinens* says she saw *bagojininiins,* I believe her." She winked at Sue. "You only see them if they want you to, and then you have to figure out why."

Sue flashed me a victory grin.

Mom sighed. "Honestly, Mom. I think the girls are getting too big for fairy tales."

Gram frowned. "*Gaawiin gwayak*. And they aren't tales. You'll know it when you see one yourself."

Mom rolled her eyes.

I wanted to believe in the little people and I wanted to take Gram's side, but I decided not to start an argument. Not today. Besides, I was working on not correcting my elders.

The P.A. interrupted. "Junior Miss jingle dancers! To the arena!"

"Gotta go," Sue said and bolted off, all of us calling good-lucks after her.

We slid into our seats. "I'm so excited for her," I said. "I think she's got a chance for second place this year." Grinning at Mom, I added, "Especially with that new dress you helped her make."

Mom made a wry half-smile. "It better. It took a carload of extra ironing to pay for it."

The drum started and all eyes focused on the dance circle as the young dancers strutted and bounced around it, left hands fisted and resting on their hips, right hands grasping their fans in a proudly cocked attitude. Like the other girls, Sue adopted a properly aloof expression, so mature and stately—a temporary suspension, I mused, of their true impishness.

The arena was filled with the swishing sound of hundreds of bouncing, curled tin lids. Careful not to rudely point, people gestured at various dancers with their eyes or heads, commenting on their favorites. For only her second year, Sue was holding her own against the more experienced girls.

The beat picked up in the second strain. Sue's face was a mask of studied concentration as she moved smartly around the circle, executing the steps and maintaining the right body position as I had taught her. Like her, I had started as a jingle dancer. I could hear the windup coming and hoped Sue was listening and counting. This song carried a five-beat ending.

I sucked in a breath as I watched her stop on the fourth beat. That misstep would cost her, but she had done herself proud.

The emcee boomed, "Let's hear it for these beautiful young ladies, folks!"

I jumped up and joined the enthusiastic applause. A dejected Sue soon joined us. "You were great, Sis."

She sagged into her chair. "I blew the last step."

"Don't worry about it. You was fab. You just watch when they announce the top three. You're gonna be in there."

The P.A. crackled. "S-e-e-nior Miss shawl dancers! You're up next."

A thousand grasshoppers jumped inside my stomach. "Well, this is it."

"Go get 'em, Ruby," Sue cheered.

Mom and Gram gave me hugs and I was off. The crowd chattered noisily as the shawl dancers found our way into the arena. Suddenly, all the other girls looked far older than me—taller, more experienced, prettier, with more stunning outfits. I swallowed, concentrated and waited for the drum. I heard the emcee say, "Brave Rock Singers, let'er rip," and with the first beat my body behaved instinctively. That beautiful blue ribbon and fifty-dollar cash prize floated before my eyes.

We spun and twirled around the arena, our shawls opening and closing like butterflies, our feet pointing, lifting, performing quick, intricate footwork like ballerinas. Everything felt right. I knew I was dancing like never before. Each movement felt perfect, my shawl movements strong and graceful, my head erect and proud, my feet lifting and floating, barely touching Mother Earth, emulating the feather-soft movements of a hovering butterfly.

Midway into the dance I filled with an inner glow. The crowd of faces became a blur as I twirled faster and faster around the arena. Somehow I knew my great-grandmothers were watching me and smiling. It was as if I was transported to yesteryear, to the dance circle in the old Ojibwe village by Gram's stream, filled with joyful dancing ancestors celebrating some wonderful event. I was there, dancing among them in the glow-shadow of the fire. Goosebumps sprouted on my arms and legs. Grandmother Pitwoniquot, with joyful tears in her eyes, was saying, "You've come home, granddaughter. You've come home."

Then I heard only the singers and the drum, each beat singular in its metronome-like regularity, and knew the song was nearing its end, my mind in perfect synchrony with it, preparing for that final beat when my feet would land flat, my arms thrusting outward in the final dramatic pose of the butterfly's open wings, my head thrown back. This was the unique ending I had worked out, a piece of high drama I hoped would be my edge against Paula. It was hardly traditional, but I wanted to win. I always did have a flare for the dramatic.

Suddenly, my left foot sank and twisted. Knife-like pain thrust into my ankle, shot up my leg, folding it under me—and I was on the ground. I lay in the dance circle, writhing in agony, frustration, and humiliation. No one ever fell during a dance except me, the club-footed idgit of Loon Lake—the loser, Ruby Loonfoot.

There was a lot of commotion around me as people crowded around. I heard Gram's voice, Mom's, then Sue's and Mr. Keeshig. But the strong hand that took mine belonged to someone I needed most right then. His gentle voice was in my ear: "Where're ya hurt, sweetheart? Don't worry, Daddy's here."

I looked up into his handsome and worried face. "Oh, Daddy," I blurted, and he slid his arms under me and carried me to our seats. It was as if he had never left. I was always a "daddy's girl," looking to him for succor and solace when I was hurt. While Gram was my spiritual rock, Dad had always been my anchor, my safety net against the potholes of life.

When I was ten I fell and broke my arm. Dad was driving for Schmidt Brothers, and when he got word, drove home two hundred miles in a blizzard to be with me. He could only stay for two hours, then had to go all the way back to finish his run. He almost lost his job over that.

"What happened to my favorite little dancer?" a woozy voice broke in. It was Cousin Earl, his craggy face pinched in an overly dramatic show of concern as he stumbled over to us. His breath left no doubt. He was drunk—drunk at a powwow. I couldn't think of a worse offense and shrank away from him.

I was hurting and just wanted my dad, wanted to be away from here with everyone staring, pitying the loser. And there was Paula Gunhouse's face in the crowd, staring at me, her expression almost thankful. Paula had done it again, and I had handed it to her.

"Go home, Earl," Daddy barked. "You're drunk."

Earl looked taken aback, then angry. "I'm family. I got a right—"

Daddy, his voice low and menacing, grabbed Earl's elbow and leaned in close to his ear. "You got no rights, here. You're embarrassing Ruby. Now take off!"

Earl yanked his arm away. "Who the hell you think you are? Some kinda big shot?" He made a sick laugh. "Some big shot," he said too loud.

Dad's face darkened. "I'm warning you, Earl."

Earl weaved on his feet. "Left your wife and kids—don't show Theresa no respect—"

Dad's fist came from nowhere and smashed into Earl's face. He stumbled backward and landed on his butt.

Mom looked stunned but said nothing.

I was too dumbfounded and in too much pain to say anything. This all wasn't happening, couldn't be happening. Then Mr. White Bear appeared. "*Howah!* That's enough!" He placed himself between Earl and Daddy. "Jim, I think you oughta take Ruby over to the clinic. I'll take care of Earl, here."

Dad stood there a moment, breathing hard, his eyes flitting between Earl and Luther. He didn't say anything; he just picked me up and headed for his truck, the rest of the family in tow.

At the clinic it was discovered I had a bad sprain, nothing broken. They wrapped my ankle and we headed home in a thick silence.

"I still think we should have Esa doctor her," Gram finally said, referring to a respected *nanaandawii'iwewinini,* one of our traditional doctors.

But no one answered.

Chapter Thirty-Nine

It wasn't until Cecelia had been dropped off and Jim had tucked the girls into bed that Theresa worked up enough courage to ask him, "Are you staying awhile?"

He was bent over, peering into the icebox. "No beer?"

"There ain't enough money for beer."

Jim turned and frowned.

She attempted to soften her tone. "I—I got some iced tea." She scurried to the icebox, reached around him and pulled out a tea-stained plastic pitcher. "Sit. I'll pour us some." She grabbed two plastic glasses and brought them to the table as Jim sat.

"Damn," he said. "I hated to see that look on Ruby's face when she knew she'd lost to Paula again."

Theresa's brow furrowed. "What about her ankle? That hurt a lot worse than losing a silly dance contest."

Jim looked at his wife and shook his head. "You don't know Ruby any better today than you did ten years ago, do you?"

Jim's hurtful remark took her by surprise, and she sat back in her chair as if shoved. "What do you mean? No one knows a daughter like her mother."

"That's just it, T. You don't. Losing to Paula hurt more than five sprained ankles."

Theresa sighed and studied her glass.

Jim tried to think of something more positive. "Hey,

though—how 'bout Sue taking second place? That was great, *eya?*"

Theresa nodded tiredly. Outside, darkness had brought no respite from the heat and humidity of the day. The yellowed curtains by the open kitchen window hung motionless. Theresa felt a trickle of sweat creep down her chest. "Lord, it's hot," she murmured.

Jim watched her a moment. She looked limp, drained. She had aged, too. He counted two new crows'-feet pulling at the corners of her wide dark eyes. But despite her frazzled appearance, she was still the handsome girl he had married. Suddenly he felt sorry for her, even a bit guilty. "I got some vacation coming. I thought I'd stay until Ruby goes back to school, then I'll drive her over in the rig. It's on my way."

Theresa's eyes remained glued to her glass. "Ruby'll like that."

Jim smiled, took a drink of tea, laid both hands on the table and drummed his fingers. "I guess we got a lot to talk about, don't we?"

Chapter Forty

Three days later Cecelia took little notice of her bursitis as she trudged the three miles to Nellie Mink's place. There wasn't a moment to lose in making preparations for Ruby's *biijiinag bakaanigeng oshkiniigikwe*. Ruby would return to school in less than two weeks. With Jim's return home, Cecelia figured he might be an ally in favor of the ceremony. If not an ally, he would be at least neutral and perhaps work on Theresa, using the what's-the-harm argument. After all, Jim wasn't a real Christian like Theresa, not a church-going Christian, anyway. Though he kept his religious thoughts to himself, Cecelia knew that deep down Jim Loonfoot respected the old ways. He knew a lot of the old songs and spoke good Ojibwe.

Cecelia also knew Jim's parents. Though they had Christianized on the outside, they had remained Ojibwes on the inside. Jim's father had been a respected flute man, a player of beautiful love songs, and had been a secret follower of the *Mide* lodge—secret because the Church forbade lodge meetings.

A stooped but smiling Nellie was waiting by her open door. *"Ahneen. Beendigin."* Cecelia chuckled, not surprised at Nellie's uncanny ability to foreknow things. "All is ready?"

Nellie Mink's aged eyes sparkled. "Of course."

Chapter Forty-One

"Wake up, sleepyhead. The fish are bitin'," Dad announced as he poked my ribs at five A.M. I sat up and gave him a sleepy hug. It was wonderful to feel his strong arms around me again, his manly smell.

"Shhh," he cautioned. "Don't wake your sister."

Sue hated to fish. She didn't like to touch anything slimy or fishy-smelling. This was our time together, like it used to be. I just wished it wasn't so darn early. We had a bowl of oatmeal together, then drove over to Loon Lake in his truck. Though I hated rising at dawn, I was always glad when I did, for it was a magical time when night and day mingled. Sunrise painted streaming lavenders and pinks across the eastern horizon, and a faded moon and a few stars were still visible.

"How's that ankle?" he asked, gently touching it.

"It still hurts," I moaned. "Now we can't go fishing."

"The heck we can't," he said, smiling confidently. "I'll carry you if I have to." He gently pinched my cheeks. "Just like when you was little, *eya?*"

In the early morning mist that shrouded the lake, the mewing call of catbirds played soprano to the bass ostinato of a hidden frog chorus. At our favorite place on the bank, we spotted an eagle circling above. Pickerelweed and arrowhead were in full blossom, and we listened to the haunting flute-like song of a nearby veery.

Dad said, "You hear him? He reminds me of my dad. He

was a flute man, you know."

"I think I remember. I was awfully little, but I remember hearing flute music."

Dad smiled as we baited our hooks. "He loved to play for you."

We fished awhile, not saying anything, enjoying the tranquility of the lake. Looking back, I realize that Dad and I never held many long conversations. We didn't need to. We just enjoyed each other's company. Having him there, close to me, was all I ever needed.

There was a sudden soft splash of two otters playing in the water. "Look," I said, and one stopped, floated on his back and stared at me. I laughed when his playmate nipped him from behind.

"Dad, are you home for good now?" I risked.

He cast his line. "I don't know yet, sweetheart. We'll see."

I swallowed, took a breath, and asked, "Dad, why did you leave?"

He gave me a quick look, a tinge of worry in his expression. "Well, that's kinda complicated. It's—something me and Mom have to work out."

I thought I felt a tug on my line and I waited for a second one, ready to set the hook, but the line lay still in the water. A green dragonfly hovered over it as if waiting to steal my catch.

"Is it something me or Sue did?"

Again, the look of concern. "No, no, it has nothing to do with you guys. It's just something your mom and I have to work out. Grown-up stuff."

I felt relief mixed with confusion. If it wasn't us, what was the cause of their split-up? "Is it about Cousin Earl?"

His expression darkened. "Where'd you get that idea?"

I felt myself cringing at his tone. "I dunno. I—I just asked because of what happened at the powwow, and because Earl hasn't been to the house in a long time, and . . ." I shrugged.

Dad's attention moved back to the lake. "You keep away from him, understand? Tell your sister, too."

Now I was dying to know what the problem with Earl was but dared not ask, not after seeing the look on Dad's face. It wasn't that I cared that much about Cousin Earl. I never had much of a relationship with him. But to shun a family member was strange.

We tried to concentrate on fishing for another hour, but there was no enthusiasm in it—for us or the fish.

"Looks like they ain't biting today," Dad said, pulling in his line.

We sat on the bank for a while, munching butter-and-jelly sandwiches and watching terns and strutting egrets. Cedar waxwings launched from the lacework of tree branches above, snatching their meals from the air.

It was now or never. Dad was relaxed; the mood was right. "Dad, Gram wants me to take the *biijiinag bakaanigeng oshkiniigikwe*."

His surprised face pinked slightly. He probably hadn't realized I had had my first period. "Yeah?" Then he looked at me with real interest. "And what do you think about it?"

"I want to do it—no—I *really* want to do it."

He sighed and stroked my hair. "My little girl is growing up too fast."

Suddenly, there was a nearby *cu, cu, cu*. Our heads swiveled back and forth like owls, trying to pinpoint the sound. This was a treat, for it was the sound of a cuckoo, seldom seen, and a renowned bearer of good news.

"There," Dad whispered, pointing to a bushy shrub between two trees. A thrill rushed through me as I spotted it, a black-billed cuckoo with its long brown-and-white tail.

"Cu, cu, cu," I called.

He answered me! Now I felt sure I had picked the right time to seek Dad's alliance. "Mom says no," I continued, "but I thought maybe you could work on her. Gram has fixed everything with Grandma Mink, and I only got ten days left before school."

Dad intently watched the cuckoo.

"Will you help me out?" I prodded.

He cleared his throat. "Well, you know your mom when it comes to Ind'n things. And with everything else that's going on now, maybe it ain't the best time."

I felt a flood of disappointment. "But you ain't against it, are you?"

"Me?" He smiled and shook his head. "No; it's good to keep some of the old ways. There's not that many kids your age who still do the *biijiinag bakaanigeng oshkiniigikwe*."

Elation replaced disappointment. "Then you'll do it? I mean, you'll convince Mom?"

He rubbed his chin, then gazed out over the lake. "We'll see, hon. Like I said, there's a lot going on right now, me just getting back and—"

I scooched closer to him, hugged his arm and batted my eyes. This usually proved *very* effective. "Please, Daddy. It's more important than anything. I need the *biijiinag bakaanigeng oshkiniigikwe* before I go back to St. Nicholas." I let go of his arm, my voice dropping. "I don't know if I can make it another year without it."

He gave me a surely-you-exaggerate look, then smiled. "We'll see."

I hated "we'll sees." They had a nasty habit of turning into "nos," and the thought that I'd be returning to St. Nic's in less than two weeks gripped me with dread. "Dad, please don't make me go back to St. Nic's. I can't stand it there. There's a lot of bad stuff going on, and the nuns—except for

Sister Steph and a couple others—are mean. And they never give us enough to eat. Can't I go to school in Hayward?"

He worked his jaw. "We got no relations in Hayward for you to stay with, Ruby. You got to have a Hayward address to go to school there." He cast out his line. "I'm sure St. Nic's ain't as bad as you think."

In frustration, it slipped out. "Dad, there's a priest there—Father Slater. He, well—he's—" God, it was hard to talk about such things to an adult, especially for a girl to her father.

Dad sighed. "Look, hon. We don't have much choice. The Church runs things around here, and your mom's big on you and Sue getting a Catholic education. So let's just go along with the program, okay? It might be a little tough now and then, but you're a tough kid. You'll be all right."

His expression brooked no argument. If there was no way to send me to the Hayward public school, I'd have no choice other than to attend an Indian school somewhere. The Church and the BIA would force it. But surely if he knew the truth about Father Slater, he'd find a way to pull me out of St. Nic's. If I had the guts to tell him.

Chapter Forty-Two

"Oh, Jim," Theresa said with frustration in her voice. "I was plannin' on fish for dinner. I don't have anything else."

Jim shrugged. "Just cook up some eggs and gravy. That's always good."

Theresa sighed. "We're tired of eggs and gravy. Be nice to have some meat on the table."

Jim grabbed an apple from the bowl on the kitchen table and straddled one of the chairs. He watched Theresa closely as she rummaged around the kitchen, making preparations for supper. "Ruby's sure growing up fast."

All the more reason you should be home, Theresa thought but didn't say. She took several eggs from the icebox and brought them to the stove. "Yes, but she's only thirteen. She still needs her daddy."

"That's just it, Theresa. Ruby ain't a little girl anymore."

Theresa gave him a puzzled look.

"You know, she's ready for the *biijiinag bakaanigeng oshkiniigikwe*."

Annoyed, Theresa barked, "I already said no." She was still hurt that Cecelia was the first to know about Ruby's period, and now Ruby had enlisted the aid of both Jim and Cecelia against her. Theresa flung the dishtowel into the sink, backed against it, and folded her arms in defiance.

Jim calmly lit a cigarette. He'd already worked out this conversation in his head. "Oh, c'mon, T. It don't hurt nothing. It don't make her less Catholic."

"She can't have it both ways. I haven't spent thirteen years of bringing her up right to throw it all away now."

Jim looked thoughtful as he flicked ashes into the ashtray. "It's real important to her, T." He took a slow drag and squinted through the smoke. "And she's scared to go back to school."

Theresa felt a new surge of frustration. "She's just softening you up like she always does when she wants you to change my mind." Theresa sighed and took a seat next to him. "I'm not so old I don't remember bein' thirteen. Everything's a big deal at that age. The world will come to an end when she don't get what she wants. It'll pass."

If you'd been home more, you'd know all this, is what she wanted to say. Theresa fixed him with an accusing glare. "Mom's behind all this, isn't she?"

He shrugged off her question. "Ruby is Ruby. You know your mom can't force it on her. A girl's gotta want to do it. Cecelia didn't force *you,* did she?"

There he went again, twisting things around, taking Mom's side. "Of course she didn't. I told her I was through with Ind'n stuff, that I was Catholic and that was that."

"Well, there you go," he said with that damned self-assuredness. "Look, T, Ruby ain't going to go heathen on you 'cause of one little ceremony. She just wants to feel grown-up. And if it'll help her back at school—in her mind—well, hell, what's the harm?" He reached across the table and touched her hand. "It means a lot to her. You remember what it's like at school, how homesick we got. And you told me about how some of them nuns got pretty mean. Hell, Ruby's got four years of Catholic schooling. She ain't going to forget all that."

He stoked the top of her hand with his thumb. She tingled

from his touch, felt a resurgence of hope that he still loved her, still wanted her. The issue of the ceremony dwarfed with the possibility of his forgiveness. She pulled his hand to her face, kissed it, then placed it against her cheek. “All right,” she breathed, her shoulders slumping, “but don’t ask me to go.”

Chapter Forty-Three

A week before school started I was suddenly filled with deep anxiety. Despite the excitement of my upcoming ceremony, thoughts of St. Nic's—carefully suppressed for the summer—began pulling me down like an undertow. And there was the irony that in a few days I would be deemed a woman, a full member of my nation, yet I would still be a kid with no say in her own future.

Sammy Brave Rock's words at his family social echoed in my mind: "I don't give a damn. I ain't going back!" But where could I run? All our relatives were on the rez and worse off than we were.

There was only one person I could talk to about St. Nic's, and that was Gram. Mom would never believe me, and I had been too embarrassed to talk to Dad. Maybe there was something Gram could do to get me out of St. Nic's. There had to be.

We'd had a severe drought for many months, and as I rode Star to Gram's I noticed that a few leaves had started to color. I had never seen leaves turn so early. Despite their beauty they added to my depression.

"And how is the *biijiinag bakaanigeng oshkiniigikwe* girl today?" Gram asked as I shuffled in the front door. My face must've mirrored how I felt because Gram's forehead became a sea of wrinkles.

I plopped down on her worn and springless sofa and shrugged.

"You don't look like a girl who is about to take her *biijiinag bakaanigeng oshkiniigikwe,*" she said, easing herself down beside me. I felt the gentleness of her hand as she combed sweaty hair from my face. "What is it, Little Warrior? Tell your old grandmother what troubles your heart."

I began to sob. Gram wrapped her arms around me and rocked gently back and forth. "What is it, little one, what is it?"

"It-it's about school, Gram. A-about St. Nic's."

Chapter Forty-Four

Cecelia marched the five miles to Marvin Big Shield's place in a cold rage, making it in half her usual time. She had decided to discuss Ruby's testimony with Marvin and Luther before attempting a conversation with Theresa. Time was of the essence and Luther was the only person on the rez who could do something.

Marvin's smile turned to concern when he saw Cecelia's troubled and perspiring face at his door. "What'd you do, run over here?"

Cecelia brushed past him and into the front room. "No time for that. We got trouble."

"Trouble?" he said as she whizzed past him.

"I'll get you a glass of water," he said and went to the kitchen area.

Cecelia was sitting stiffly in his favorite chair when he returned with the water. "What's the trouble?"

She took several long gulps. "It's that school Ruby goes to, that's what the trouble is. Them blackrobes are raping our children! They're starving them and they're beating them, *eya?* And I want to know what you and Luther are going to do about it!"

Marvin's eyes widened as he stood in the center of the room. He looked as if he was about to argue, then a wave of emotions transformed his face from shock to fear, then grief. His shoulders sagged and he dropped onto a chair.

Cecelia stared at him in disbelief. "You *knew.*"

Marvin's head drooped, his arms resting on his legs. "We'd heard stories over the years, you know, rumors and such. We just figured it was—well—blown out of proportion. Nobody *wants* to go to them schools. You know how tales get started, and . . ."

His words sounded hollow. Cecelia bored in. "You didn't want to believe them, *eya?*"

He looked at her for a moment, then looked away. "At first. But then there were stories from the other rez's." His voice dropped to where it was almost inaudible. "Too many stories."

"Well, know this, Marvin Big Shield," Cecelia said firmly. "It is the truth. Ruby came to me this morning, her spirit broken like a dry twig. She told me everything. Every day our children are raped and beaten. They beat my Ruby with a belt and a paddle."

Marvin's face pinched as if in pain.

Cecelia continued, "They put them kids in a dark basement for days. They don't feed them nothing. They scratch out words in their letters so they can't tell us anything." Her face twisted in bitter sorrow. "Two girls froze to death trying to run away. Two young Indian girls are *gone,* Marvin!"

Marvin covered his face with his hands. After a moment he looked up, his eyes glistening. "If we'd said the stories were true, we would've had to do something. But there was nothing we could do." His right eye twitched as it always did when he was emotional. "Because inside," he thumped his chest, "we knew we were no longer men. We are cattle kept by the government and the Church." He stood and shoved his hands in his back jeans pockets. "So we chose not to believe." He stared out the window.

Cecelia's jaw tensed and she shook her head. She wanted

to reach out and strike him. She felt betrayed. How many children had died or been ruined because of their leaders' conspiracy of silence? She wished she had never isolated herself from the rez gossips. Maybe she would've heard about this earlier, *acted* earlier.

She glowered at Marvin. "How could you—our leaders—let this go on for so long? How?"

Marvin hung his head.

Though Cecelia understood Marvin and the other men's feeling of helplessness, she was also sick of hearing about the all-powerful Church and the BIA. Enough was enough! She sighed and straightened in her chair. "Save your tears, Marvin. Now is the time to take back our pride, to take back our children. We're going to gather what elders we can and go to Luther. It is time we started our own school. It is time we put the Church out of business in *Anishinabe* country!"

Chapter Forty-Five

Cecelia and her posse of elders, who now sat around the council meeting table, focused on Luther White Bear. Thinking back, she realized there had not been such an assemblage since the Dawes Act crisis in 1887, when President Teddy Roosevelt and his congressional rough riders came up with his "mighty pulverizing engine to break up the tribal mass." The government had tried to force the Loon Lake Ojibwes, along with virtually every other Indian nation, to break up their reservations, allotting 160 acres to each tribal member. Remaining land was declared "surplus" and sold off. More than twelve million acres of Indian land was lost. But thanks to Loon Lake elders and leaders of a small consortium of other tribes, they fought hard, appealed the decision, and held on to their small reservation.

Luther pursed his lips. "Well, obviously, something is up and I guess it's pretty important."

Cecelia nudged Marvin.

He cleared his throat. "Luther, it's about these schools. We got to bring our children home. Right away."

Luther appeared puzzled, probably because Marvin did not begin the meeting with a prayer, then the usual chit-chat before settling into the business at hand. But this was not a normal meeting.

"Which schools?" Luther asked. "What do you mean exactly, Uncle?"

"All of them," Marvin said. "Church schools, BIA

schools. We want you to bring them home. We want you and the council to go to the Church or the BIA—whoever you got to go to—and tell them we want our children back. We will build our own school."

Now Luther looked dumbfounded. Considering Luther's fear of the iron-fisted Church-BIA authority over Indian country, it probably seemed inconceivable. Well, he'd get over it!

Luther tapped his fingers on the table, obviously weighing his response. "Okay . . . What's this all about, Uncle?"

Cecelia leaned forward in her chair. "Them robes are raping our children!" she said sharply in Ojibwe. "They're beating them and starving them, and we want you and the tribal council to do what's right. It's been going on too many years and it's got to stop here—today!"

"No disrespect, Cecelia," Luther replied, "but you know how those rumors get going. I understand your being worried about these stories, but—"

Rude or not, Cecelia interrupted him. "*Gaawesa.* Ruby told me everything." She recounted the incidents at St. Nicholas in full detail. When she finished she said, "So these rumors have been true all along and we have closed our ears to them. We have cowered in our houses and let our children be destroyed by these people!"

A full minute passed while Luther stared at her slack-jawed.

Marvin broke the heavy silence. "Some of us have suspected . . ." His voice dropped, "*known* about this for years. We—we just didn't know what to do about it."

Cecelia gave the elder men a hard stare, then turned to Luther. "So they hid from the truth. Convinced themselves it was gossip."

All eyes turned from Cecelia to Luther. "Christ," he whispered.

Marvin's face furrowed with bitter regret. "We are to blame, not you, Luther. Just as the Sixth Fire foretold of the loss of our children to them schools, the Seventh Fire foretold that a time would come when the elders would no longer provide guidance, that many of us would fall asleep, silent out of fear. This, too, has come to pass. Now we must take a stand. We must take back our ways, our culture. We have prayed on this. You are the man to do it, and we are here to help you."

Luther's hand shook slightly as he poured himself a glass of water from a pitcher on the table. "Look—Uncle. This is going to take some thinking. You know how it is with the Church and the BIA. They got us by the—. Well, you know."

Cecelia's eyes remained hard. "So let's think. But then we got to act, and fast."

Luther frowned. "Hold on, *Nokomis*. It's not going to be that easy. These are powerful people."

"And we are powerful, too," she said, gesturing to her fellow elders.

Still looking shaken, Luther ran his hand across his mouth. "All right. Here's what you're in for. The first thing that's going to happen is that the BIA won't believe us. The Church will deny it, and then I'll be shown the door. But that probably won't be the end of it. These people can get real nasty. They can withhold our money. They can do just about anything they want to us."

Jackson Mink stood. "You saying we got no rights at all? We're American citizens, ain't we? Many of us are veterans here."

Luther grunted. "We're citizens—or wards of the state—when the government wants to pass laws on us, but we're a sovereign nation when we insist on our rights. It boils down to this. The government pays us money they owe on our treaties with them. The BIA controls how that money is spent—"

he paused for effect "—or not spent. The BIA has complete power over us. They can override our decisions any time they want. As far as schools, the BIA controls them, too. And around here, the Church does that work for them. That makes it easy—and cheaper—for the government. One less headache for the BIA, *eya?* We're talking about the diocese, here. I don't need to tell you how much power they got."

Cecelia leaned forward. "We know all this, my nephew. They are the excuses we've hidden behind. But when it came to protecting our women and children, our ancestors fought much bloodier fights, them. Have we lost our pride, our will to survive? I say no—*debise!*"

She felt Luther's tense stare. "What do you wanna do, *Nokomis?* Declare war?"

Cecelia returned his glare. "We done it before."

Chapter Forty-Six

It was late afternoon when Theresa heard a car pull up in front of the house. She set down the iron and went to the front door. It was Luther's truck. She watched with growing puzzlement as he helped Cecelia out.

"Afternoon, Theresa," he called. "Just giving your mother a lift over."

"Hi, Luther. What's going on?"

Luther handed Cecelia her cane, then walked her up to the front stoop. "Oh, a little meeting we just had over to the office."

Luther seemed tense. Theresa's hand went immediately to her hair. I look a mess, she thought. "Won't you come inside for some lemonade?"

Luther shook his head. "No, thanks. You know what they say: a chief's work is never done." He made a weak attempt at a smile. "Well, guess you two have a lot to talk about. I'll just go on about my business." He nodded to Cecelia, got in his truck, and drove away.

Theresa looked at her mother. "What's going on?"

Cecelia said, "That's what I come about. Is Ruby home?"

"No. She and Sue went to Jeannette's house."

Cecelia nodded. "*Onishishin*. And Jim?"

"Back on the road," Theresa said sadly. "He'll be back for that—that ceremony you're doing for Ruby."

Cecelia opened the screen door. "*Beendigin*. We got a lot

to talk about." She plopped down on the frayed and sun-faded sofa. "You better sit down."

Theresa sighed. "Mom, I don't have time to argue with you today. I got a ton of ironing to get done for Mrs. Riley, and—"

Cecelia waved Theresa's protest aside. "I'm not here to argue with you. I'm here to tell you something about Ruby. Something real bad."

Theresa's mind slid from annoyance to concern. "Bad?"

Cecelia peered up at her from the couch. "You're giving me a crick in my neck standing there like that. Now sit down here next to me and I'll tell you."

Theresa sat and listened. Her mother's words fell on her like heavy stones: cruel nuns, beatings, molesting priests, the death of the two runaways. Her mind raced to grasp it all. Impossible. It wasn't true. This was some kind of horrible plot her mother had devised to defame the Church.

"Jesus, Mary, and Joseph!" Theresa blurted. She jumped to her feet and crossed herself. "How could you, Mom? How could you use Ruby like this?" She was shouting now. "You expected me to believe all this—about the Church, about nuns and good priests? Did you forget I went to a Catholic school?" Her mind raced. "And if Ruby did tell you some of this, she blew it all out of proportion because of the crap you feed her when she's at your place. You've got her brainwashed!" She tried to light a cigarette but her hand shook. After three matches failed to flare, she threw the cigarette and matchbook on the floor.

Cecelia's jaw tightened. "Did you tell *me* everything that happened to you at school?"

Theresa blinked.

Cecelia didn't wait for a response. "What I tell you is true—Ruby's own words to me. You know I don't lie, not to my children, not to anyone!"

Theresa felt a fresh wave of bitterness. "Even if it was true, why wouldn't Ruby tell her own mother such things before she went to you, huh? Tell me that."

"How can she tell her Catholic mother about such things, a mother who will never believe her, who might even punish her for such words, *eya?*"

Theresa waved her off. "Pshaw! It ain't going to work, Mom. Ruby's going back to school. She's going to be a good Catholic, and then she's going to get a job somewhere off this godforsaken reservation and make something of herself." She had never felt such outrage. She was sick of being pushed, of giving in, of feeling guilty, of being a nobody. Still, she was mentally reeling from Ruby's testimony. "I'll see to it! You ain't going to stop me, you hear? Nobody's going to stop me! Now get out! And take that flea-bitten horse you gave the girls. And leave Ruby alone!"

Cecelia pushed herself from the couch and stood erect. "My daughter's heart is dead. Now I must save my granddaughter's." She left, ignoring the horse she had given to Ruby and Sue—an animal too large to trust, let alone climb onto—and trudged the three miles home, alone with her thoughts. Twice she had dizzy spells and had to stop and rest in the shade until they passed.

Chapter Forty-Seven

It was finally the day of my *biijiinag bakaanigeng oshkiniigikwe.* The five days spent in seclusion with Grandmother Mink leading up to it had flashed by like an express train. It went quicker because Gram had taught me well over the years.

Dressed in my white buckskin dress, specially made for me by Gram, I passed through a bevy of smiling friends and well-wishers and entered the hot and smoky wigwam set up behind Grandmother Mink's house. Gram and Grandmother Mink, also dressed in white buckskin, sat by a small fire at the center. Through the smoky haze of wonderful-smelling sweet grass and hickory wood I saw the lodge was full of family members, except for Mom. Her absence left a dark hole. She should be here, standing beside me. But there was Dad, winking at me, wearing his ribbon shirt.

"*Beendigin,*" Gram said, and motioned for me to sit on a blanket next to Grandmother Mink. The wizened old woman said in Ojibwe, "Your grandmother has prepared you with the proper teachings. You have learned to make moccasins, to make a dress. You have learned of the seven prophecies and the ways of the pipe. You have learned your people's history and of the *wee'gwas* scrolls. And you have learned the language of your people. This is good, for everything said here today will be in our language, in the old way. Do you understand?"

I nodded. "Yes, Grandmother."

She closed her eyes a moment, then opened them, giving me a soul-penetrating stare. "Today you become a woman of the *Anishinabeg.* You will carry the weight and responsibilities of our nation within you. You must listen to the prayers and the teachings and hold them sacred, for they are the words of our grandmothers and our grandmothers' grandmothers. Words as old as time itself. Much of what happens here is never talked about until you have a daughter and she begins her own preparations. Do you understand, *Bineshee Ogichidaw?*"

I nodded, feeling the weight of my promise.

She smiled, and, holding a braid of burning sweet grass, she closed her eyes and prayed "Grandfather, *Gitche-Manitou,* I offer to You Your sacred herb. O Grandmother Earth, from whence we come, and Mother Earth, who bears much fruit, listen! I am going to make smoke, which will penetrate the heavens. It will spread over the universe, touching all things."

She placed the sweet grass on a hot coal, then blessed a pipe and several items she had laid out on a blanket. "All that will be done today will be accomplished with the aid of the powers of the universe. May they help us to purify and to make sacred this girl who is about to become a woman. I now fill this sacred pipe, placing within it the powers who help us here today."

Using the smoldering sweet grass and an eagle fan, she fanned its smoke over the three of us, then took a pinch of tobacco from a bowl on the blanket. Picking up the pipe, she prayed, "Grandfather, *Gitche-Manitou,* this is a special day, for we are about to purify this girl, *Bineshee Ogichidaw.* There is a place for all the powers of the universe in this pipe, and so have mercy upon us and accept our offering."

She looked westward. "O you where the sun goes down,

who guards the pipe, and who comes so terribly in order to purify the world and its people, we are about to offer this pipe to *Gitche-Manitou*. We need your help, especially with your cleansing waters, for we are about to purify and make sacred not only a young girl, but a whole generation. There is a place for you in the pipe!"

Grandmother Mink placed the pinch of tobacco into the pipe bowl, then held a fresh pinch toward the north. "O you, power of the north, who guards the health of the people with your winds, and who purifies the Earth by making it white, you are the one who watches that path upon which our people walk. Help us with your purifying influence, for we are about to make sacred a virgin, *Bineshee Ogichidaw,* from whom will come generations of our people."

She looked at me as she added another pinch. "I put now the power of the north into the pipe," then she looked eastward. "O you, the power of that place of the dawn and the light of *Gitche-Manitou*. O you, who are long-winded and who give knowledge to the people, give of your wisdom today to this virgin, *Bineshee Ogichidaw,* who is about to be purified. There is a place for you in the pipe!"

Again, she took a fresh pinch of tobacco. Facing south she prayed, "O you, power who controls the path of the generations and of all that moves, we are about to purify a virgin; that her generations to come may walk in a sacred manner upon that path which you control. There is a place for you in the pipe!"

She placed the power of the south into the pipe and held skyward another fresh pinch of tobacco. "O *Gitche-Manitou*—Grandfather—behold us! We are about to offer the pipe to You." She pointed the tobacco toward the earth. "O you, Grandmother, upon whom the generations have walked, may *Bineshee Ogichidaw* and her generations walk upon you in a sacred manner in the winters to come. O Mother Earth, who gives forth fruit and who is as a mother to the generations, this young virgin will be purified and made sacred. May she be like you and may her children and children's children walk the sacred path in a holy manner."

Holding the tobacco skyward she prayed, "O *Gitche-Manitou* and all the winged powers of the universe, behold us! This tobacco I offer to You, Chief of all powers, who is represented by the spotted eagle, who lives in the arches of the heavens and who guards all that is there. We are about to purify a young girl, who is soon to be a woman. May You guard those generations that will come forth from her."

Grandmother Mink then spokc to mc. "The pipe now contains the whole universe. I now lay it against this small rack, with its foot on the earth and its mouth pointing toward heaven." She gave a signal and everyone left the lodge except Gram and Dad. "The sacred ceremony that follows can be witnessed only by your closest relatives." She closed her eyes in prayer. "*Gitche-Manitou* has given to the people a fourfold relationship—with their grandfather, father, grandmother, and mother. These are always our closest relatives. Since all that is good is done in fours, the two-leggeds will walk through four ages, being relatives with all things."

After the secret part of the ceremony, Grandmother Mink bade me to stand and hold a bundle of sacred items above my head. "This, which is over your head, is like *Gitche-Manitou,* for when you stand you reach from Earth to heaven. Thus anything above you is like the Great Spirit. You are the tree of life. You will now be pure and holy, and may your generations to come be fruitful. Wherever your feet touch will be a sacred place, for now you will always carry with you a great influence. May the four powers of the universe help to purify you. As I mention the name of each power I shall rub this bundle down that side of you. May the cleansing waters from where the sun sets purify you. May you be as the purifying snow, which comes from the north. When the dawn of the day comes upon you, may you receive knowledge from the morning star. When darkness comes may you be filled with the light and the knowledge of *Neebageesis,* who guides all women.

"May you be made pure by the power of the place towards which we always face, and may those peoples who have walked this straight and good path help to purify you. May you be as the white swan, who lives at this place where you face, and may your children be as pure as the children of the swan."

We then sat while she told the ancient story of how the *biijiinag bakaanigeng oshkiniigikwe* was brought to a great holy man through a vision. It was a beautiful story, and as it unfolded I began to feel a strange warmth starting in my feet and moving up my legs. I closed my eyes and when the warmth reached my chest, I sucked in a breath at the power of it. My fingers and toes tingled. I felt suddenly older, wiser. I opened my eyes and saw my great-grandmothers sitting next to Gram. Their eyes sparkled with pride. And then Grandmother Mink chanted:

"These people are sacred;
From all over the universe they are coming to see it.
Bineshee Ogichidaw is sitting here in a sacred manner;
They are all coming to see her."

The chant finished, Grandmother Mink said, "*Bineshee Ogichidaw,* you have prayed to *Gitche-Manitou.* You will now go forth among your people in a holy manner, and you will be an example to them. You will cherish those things which are most sacred in the universe. You will be as Mother Earth—humble and fruitful. May your steps, and those of your children, be firm and sacred. As *Gitche-Manitou* has been merciful to you, so you must be merciful to others, especially to those children who are without parents. If such a child should come to your lodge, and if you should have but one piece of meat that you have already placed in your mouth, you should take it out and give it to her."

Grandmother Mink, looking very tired now, asked Dad to call everyone back inside, and I was once again surrounded by friends and family. Grandmother Mink took a piece of deer meat from the bowl and placed it in my mouth, and then a bowl of water and some cherries were passed around. She took up the pipe and held it stem upward while she prayed, "Hee-ay-hay-ee-ee, hee-ay-hay-ee-ee. Grandfather, behold them! These people and all the generations to come are Yours. Look upon this chaste woman, *Bineshee Ogichidaw,* who has been purified and honored this day. May Your light that never fails be upon her always and upon all her relatives. Grandmother and great Mother Earth, upon you the people will walk. May they follow the sacred path with light, not in the darkness of ignorance."

Gram took me by the shoulders. "*Bineshee Ogichidaw.* You now have the full power of the woman, the power of *Neebageesis*. Use it well; use it wisely, and she will protect you and guide you. Be just. Be kind." Her grip tightened and I looked into her eyes, seeing and feeling her strength, her love, her determination. "But most of all—be strong! You are *Anishinabe!* No one can take that from you." She closed her eyes and bowed her head, signaling she was finished.

Everyone said, *"Aho!"* Gram, holding a beaded bag, kissed me on both cheeks. Then she opened the bag and pulled out a stunning dentalium-shell necklace. I recognized it as the one she received from her mother at her own *biijiinag bakaanigeng oshkiniigikwe*.

She said, "These shells are a gift to the People from Otter. They represent the shell the Creator used to blow his breath of life into First Man." She draped the necklace over my head and onto my shoulders. "Your great-grandmothers—all your ancestors—are smiling today, *Bineshee Ogichidaw*. Go now and greet your people as an *Anishinabe* woman!"

I couldn't remember feeling more proud, more loved. Everyone rushed to hug me and congratulate me, and then we went outside to yelps and cheers. Sue gave me a playful poke and a wink. All kinds of food were spread out on blankets for our feast. On another blanket were small gifts Dad had bought to give away to our guests in my honor. The Brave Rock Singers, who had brought their drum, started a special song Sammy had composed in my honor:

"Bineshee Ogichidaw
She is coming
She is coming in a sacred manner
Look, she is a woman
Bineshee Ogichidaw"

Mr. White Bear gestured for me to lead off the honor dance. I gathered Gram and Daddy to my side and we stepped off. Everyone formed a line behind us and we danced around the drum. This time I wasn't a shawl dancer. Instead, I danced the slow and stately step of a woman traditional dancer, my long-fringed shawl folded carefully over my left arm so that the fringe swayed gracefully to and fro with the beat. I looked to my left and right and basked in the glowing pride in Dad's and Gram's faces. And as we snaked around the drum I saw the wonderful long line of people dancing behind me—all in my honor—and I recalled the daydream I had during the dance competition, of being transported back to the old village, to the old days. It had come true. I was being embraced by my nation.

I am *Anishinabe!*

I felt it surging through my body, visualized it pulsing through my veins. I wanted to shout it to the world—I am woman! I AM *ANISHINABE!*

PART III

St. Nic's

You can not destroy one who has dreamed a dream like mine

—Ojibwe adage

Chapter Forty-Eight

I stood in the dusk at the front steps of St. Nicholas, valise in hand, and watched Dad's rig clatter down the long drive, then turn onto the hard road and disappear. It felt like a ball of wet leather was caught in my throat. I wanted to sprint after him. I was thinking about how I might be able to catch up to the truck when I heard, "RUBEEEE!"

I turned in time to brace myself for Katie, who was sprinting down the stairs. She almost tackled me with a running hug. She looked wonderful, at least ten pounds heavier, the roundness returned to her face, her eyes glistening with excitement. She looked like a normal healthy girl again.

"Oh, Ruby, I missed you so much! Wait till I tell you about my summer at Rose's. I rode horses, and we went to town, and I met all her relatives, and we went to the fair, and—how was your summer? What happened at the powwow? Did you win? Gosh, there's so much to tell you about—"

"Whoa!" I said. "You're making me dizzy." I stepped back to take her in. "You look swell, brat. Looks like Mr. and Mrs. Captain fed you good."

"Mrs. Captain is a great cook, and we had candy bars—real ones—in town, and homemade ice cream, and—Ruby!" Her eyes were as big as muskmelons. "Real butter and eggs—and jelly, too!"

Jumping around and waving her arms, she had me laughing now—and such facial expressions. "Sounds like you had a swell time," I chuckled. I couldn't help but be drawn into her whirlwind of excitement. No one was more tickled that Katie had a wonderful summer, a million miles from St. Nic's—from *Kokoko*. "When did you and Rose get back?"

"About an hour ago," she said.

Rose appeared in the door and hustled down the stairs. We hugged. "Hey, Katie was telling me what a great time she had." I patted Katie's belly. "And how good you fed her."

Rose laughed. "She 'bout ate us out of house and home."

Katie looked concerned.

Rose chuckled and tussled Katie's hair. "Mom loved it. If you like her cooking, you're tops in her book."

Katie's grin reappeared.

"Did you have a good summer?" Rose wanted to know.

"Swell—well, almost swell. I lost out to Paula Gunhouse again." I didn't mention my other major disappointment: my still-separated parents.

Katie's face fell. "How?"

I didn't want to get into all that now. I was anxious to see Sister Steph again. "I'll give you the whole sad story later. Seen Sister Steph yet?"

Rose's brow furrowed. "Now that you mention it, it's funny she wasn't around in the rec room, greeting everybody like usual." She shrugged. "Maybe she ain't back from vacation yet."

Katie's face darkened. "But we saw Fatlips and *Kokoko*."

"Yeah," Rose said. "Looks like everybody's here 'cept Sister Steph. You don't think she'd come after dark, do you?"

I shrugged. "Maybe she's running late and she'll be back tomorrow."

Rose said, "C'mon. Get your stuff stowed. It's almost supper time."

We all looked at each other and moaned in unison, "Euuuu."

After dinner—the usual macaroni and cheese with the consistency of glue—we filed into the rec room for Fatlips' annual welcome speech, which, after the laundry list of rules were enumerated, made the overwhelmed new girls feel about as welcome as new inmates at the state pen.

The scene was all too familiar. The new girls, who had arrived early in the afternoon for orientation, delousing and hair-cutting, looked as if they had experienced the end of the world.

The little ones gathered around Father Sullivan, a young and flustered new teacher, like puppies, crying "Father, Father," and following him wherever he went. Their new oversized boots made their feet look clownish. For the first time in their lives they had no one in the world to look to, to touch, to hold on to. If they weren't huddled around Father's legs, they were hunched in their wretchedness and misery in a corner of the rec room. A couple of us brought rag dolls for them to play with, and they hugged them tight against their bodies.

After the formalities, we were taken to the basement to stow things in our trunks. I had only one thing to add this year—the delicate shell necklace Gram gave me. I fingered the petite shells, relishing their beauty, their meaning, feeling their cool smoothness before returning them to their beaded bag and laying it gently in the trunk.

We then had a brief free time in the rec room. Someone turned on the radio. The Platters crooned *My Prayer.* I was telling Rose and Katie about the dance competition fiasco, when I was interrupted.

"Well, if it ain't the three stooges, back again for another year at good ol' St. Nic's."

It was Agnes Knockwood, surrounded by her usual backup group. Darn, I'd almost forgotten about her.

I donned a mask of sarcastic disappointment. "Shoot, Agnes. I heard you got run over by a Mack truck and weren't coming back."

She scowled. "Keep it up, Loony butt, and this year you'll wish you was the one that got run over."

Rose sidled up to my side. "Oh yeah?"

Agnes gave Rose a once-over, then batted her eyes and feigned fear. "Oh, please, don't hurt me. I'm afraid of white girls. They got cooties." Agnes and her cohort laughed heartily.

Rose looked like she was about to strike when Sister Elizabeth entered the room and clapped her hands. "All right, ladies. Fifteen minutes to lights out."

Rose leaned closer to Agnes, and in a low voice said, "Don't push your luck, hatchet face."

Agnes twisted her lips. "You and whose army?"

Before Rose could answer, Agnes turned to me. "Oh, by the way, Loonbutt. Your dippy friend Sister Stephanie won't be comin' back this year. She's been canned!" With a hearty laugh, she turned and sashayed out of the room.

I stood there, stunned. Was Agnes lying, merely trying to get in a last dig? I looked at Rose and Katie. They were as clueless as me.

"She's full of it," Rose finally said. "They can't fire nuns."

A shadow of worry passed across Katie's face. "What if they can?"

Kokoko appeared as if from nowhere. "Welcome back, girls." His hand softly caressed Katie's head. "So good to see you back, Katie. I missed you."

* * * * *

At lights-out we lay stiffly in our beds, listening to the sobs of homesickness that cleaved the darkness. Moonlight streamed through the tall windows and illuminated the room in a ghostly light. Across the aisle I could see the little girl who had caught my attention earlier that afternoon, and I was struck with the sudden memory of Grandmother Mink's instructions at my ceremony: "If an orphan should come to your lodge, and if you should have but one piece of meat that you have already placed in your mouth, you should take it out and give it to her."

The night matron, on her first round, stepped inside the door. "Quiet!"

When her footsteps faded away I crept to the child's bed and held her hand. Moonlight played off big brown eyes brimmed with fear and misery.

"Shh, shh. It's all right," I said, and wiped away tears with my nightdress. "What's your name?"

"M-Minnie," she managed through raspy breaths.

"I'm Ruby. Where you from?"

She sniffled. "M-Mole Lake."

"I hear it's nice over there."

"I want my mommy."

I squeezed her tiny hand. "I know. I miss my mommy, too. But you'll feel better tomorrow; you'll see."

She blinked, her mouth forming a tiny pout. "The blackrobes scare me," she whispered in Ojibwe.

I nonchalantly waved my hand. "Oh, you'll get used to them. Most of them are okay. Just do what they say, and whatever you do don't get caught talking Ind'n."

Her other hand touched her head. "They cut off my hair. Why did they cut off my hair?"

Keys jingled from the stairwell. I gave Minnie's hand a last squeeze. "The matron's coming. Be a good girl now and go to sleep." I skittered to my bed and jumped under the covers just before the flashlight beam knifed across the room. Then I heard the matron's heavy step fade down the stairs. I lay awake for a while, misty-eyed and thinking about home and family. Muffled whimpers filled the room, and the memories of my own first days at St. Nic's floated into my mind:

That first morning the school people came to get me, Dad had tried to leave early so he wouldn't see them take me. But I awoke, heard him, and bolted into the front room. I was crying, and he said, "No, Ruby. You got to go to school."

"No," I sobbed. "I want to stay with you, Daddy. I want to stay with you." I wrapped myself around his leg. Each time he took a step he had to drag me along. Mom pried me off and sat me on the couch.

"You sit right there and don't you move till them people come." But she was teary-eyed, too. Then Sue woke up and came into the front room, rubbing her eyes. She was only three then. She started wailing. Dad just looked at Mom, then walked out, got in his truck and left.

When the big bus came I beelined for the back door. I had no idea where to go, only that I had to hide. But they chased me down and took me to the bus. I screamed and scratched at them. Then all the kids on the bus started to bawl because of my screaming and yelling. I reached out a window toward Mom. "Why are you mad at me, Momma? Why are you sending me away?"

A long, agonizing bus ride and then we arrived at St. Nic's. The towering, austere building loomed before us, staggering us with its enormity. I remember feeling as though it had swallowed us like a great whale. Everything about it was strange. The bathrooms were strange; the echoes in the arching stone hallways; the banging of heavy doors, the smells. Nuns, their flapping black dresses, their taut faces peering out of those tight head things—they looked so . . . white. Their long beads rattled ominously, and when they walked their tiny heels click-echoed on the linoleum floor.

"Get in line; get in line!"

Huddling together, we waited apprehensively in a line that snaked into the first-floor lavatory. Ahead were cries and whimpers and the ominous odors of turpentine and coal oil.

"Next!"

Then it was my turn. A nun bent my head over a galvanized washtub and poured the reeking concoction on my hair.

"Close your eyes and mouth," she said.

Some of it crept down the side of my face. I yelped and some seeped into my mouth.

The room resonated with bawling and moaning girls. The nun roughly rubbed my head with a towel. "Over there, dear," she said, pointing to a chair and another waiting nun. I walked through mounds of shorn black hair and sat, the nauseating taste of coal oil burning my mouth and throat.

"This won't take but a minute," the nun said. "Hold still, now."

Her scissors flashed as she grabbled handfuls of my long ebony hair. Snip, snip. I'll never forget that sound as I watched the chopped clumps drop to the floor, only to be swept away like yesterday's trash. I thought about how Gram loved my hair, how she used to brush it and braid it, and how Momma had put pretty barrettes in it. I wondered why I was being punished. What had I done?

No matter how many years I spent in boarding school, the first night back always brought heartbreaking homesickness. When the dorm floor finally quieted, I wept under my pillow as the warm memories of summer played across my mind, its sweetness soured by the fact that Dad and Mom remained separated. My dream that they would reunite over the summer died with the early falling leaves of the sugar maples.

After a while I sat up and looked across at Minnie. She was asleep, her tattered rag doll clutched against her chin. Now and then her face pinched up and her mouth pouted, and her free arm flailed at the fearsome things that chased her in her dreams.

Chapter Forty-Nine

Thirty minutes into my first class on Monday I was called down to Father Blewett's office. I was annoyed because for once my religion class was interesting. Sister Rose was talking about the lives of the saints, which included all kinds of gory details like torture, decapitations, burning at the stake and other weird stuff.

While I was a bit uneasy about being called to the office, I wasn't scared because I knew I hadn't done anything wrong. I hadn't had time. Also, I was worried that I might miss second period, which was English with Sister Steph.

In the alcove between Sister Margaret's and Father Blewett's offices I checked my appearance in the floor-length mirror. The sign above it said, "Neatness Counts!" Finding no obvious flaws, I knocked on the principal's door.

"Come in!" It was Fatlips' voice, her tone an angry command.

I opened the door. Father Blewett stood beside his desk. Fatlips was in one of the two wingback chairs.

"Sit!" she said, and pointed to the chair alongside hers.

I did as I was told. She thrust a three-page handwritten letter at me. "What do you know about this?"

I stared blankly at her a moment, then I took the letter and scanned the first few sentences. The letter was dated from last April. Then I recognized Sister Steph's graceful hand. "Dear Bishop Swazey." My heart pounded.

"You'd better read the whole thing before you speak," Father Blewett warned.

I fought a sudden sense of panic. My mind swam through crosscurrents of emotions while I tried to focus on her words. I was trying to think fast. What defense could I use? Could I feign ignorance? I could if she didn't mention my name in the letter. Surely she wouldn't . . . But on page two, there it was:

"A fine young student, Ruby Loonfoot, originally brought these matters to my attention. This brave young girl is to be commended . . ."

Oh, no. Sister Steph . . . Where was she? Why wasn't she here to help me?

"Well?" Fatlips insisted, her face pinched into a scowl.

"I—I—"

Fatlips stood and peered down at me. "I know your kind—arrogant in your misplaced Indian pride. You hate the Church, hate St. Nicholas. You're out to destroy this school." She leaned closer, emphasizing each word. "You would besmirch the name of a fine priest to do your dirty work. Do you have any idea what kind of humiliation and trouble you've brought upon Father Blewett and me?"

My mouth opened to say something—I'm not sure what—then closed. I hadn't a clue as to what besmirched meant.

"Well, do you?"

I summoned all my courage. There was only one defense: the truth. "I'm sorry, Sister Margaret, but I only told Sister Steph what I saw."

Fatlips slapped my face. "Liar!"

The slap startled me so that I jumped.

"What you saw was a way to get some kind of childish revenge," she said, almost shouting.

"All right, Sister," Blewett said, rounding his desk and holding up his hand. He glowered at me. "I don't know what your game is, young lady, but you've caused us a great deal of trouble. This is my last year at St. Nicholas, and I plan for it to be a quiet one. I've been more than patient with you over the years. I've even taken your side at times against Sister Margaret, silly me. Well, this time I won't stand in her way. We've got too much at stake here to put up with one child's malicious pranks." He looked at Sister Margaret. "I leave Miss Loonfoot to your care, Margaret." His eyes slid back to me. "Let's hope you will learn your lesson, make your apologies to Father Slater and the bishop and finish a quiet year."

Fatlips took me by the ear and yanked. "My office." Pain scorched through me as I struggled to stand and keep up with her. She marched me out the door, across the alcove and into her office, where Father Potts was waiting. When she let go of my ear, anger got the better of me. "Just ask Sister Steph!" I demanded, massaging my aching ear. "She'll tell you, she—" But before I could finish, Fatlips had her paddle. I glimpsed it too late and it smacked me on the left side.

"You're to be seen and not heard, child." Her eyes shot knives at me. "Thanks to you, Sister Stephanie is no longer with us." She looked at Potts. "All right, Father."

Father Potts grabbed my arm—hard—and we headed down the hall at a brisk pace. We rounded the corner, and Father Potts opened the door to the basement.

"Where—where are we going?" I asked. I don't know why I asked. I knew where we were going. I assumed I'd be locked in that dark basement storage room for a couple of days. The images of crawling things and total darkness flooded my mind.

We moved quickly down the long hallway of steam pipes and naked bulbs, then into the boiler room. Mr. Muller, the custodian, waited there, next to an odd-looking chair.

Father Potts asked him, "Ready, Jake?"

Mr. Muller eyed me, then scratched his head. He looked uneasy. "It'll work all right." He cleared his throat. " 'Course I ain't really tried it myself."

A brief look of concern passed across Sister Margaret's face. "You're sure it's safe, that nothing can go wrong?"

Muller said, "Oh, it's safe enough, Sister. Ain't hardly no amps in it. It can't do her any *real* harm, ya know." A nervous laugh. "It'll get her attention, though."

The back of my neck prickled. Something was very wrong here. "What's happening?" I asked.

Fatlips shot me a stern look, but I noticed a tremble in her hands, and she began to wring them. "Lord knows I've tried everything else on you with no effect. I hope this will do what I couldn't—snap you into a God-fearing young lady who knows her humble place in the world. I hope it shocks the deviousness out of you. It makes me even angrier that you've forced us to stoop to this."

Father Potts pulled me to the chair and sat me in it, then secured my arms and legs with the attached wrist and ankle straps. There were metal plates nailed to the arms, with wires running from them. The wires snaked across the floor, over to a small worktable near Mr. Muller, where they were attached to some car batteries. Now I was getting scared, really scared. Paddles, belts and dark confinement I knew and understood. This was something completely unknown.

"I want you to think of your Lord and Savior," Sister Margaret said. "Pray for His forgiveness and guidance." She looked at Father Potts. "We'll pray with you," then she nodded at Mr. Muller. He pushed a small lever.

What felt like a sledgehammer slammed into my arms and back. I convulsed and sucked in a breath as a thousand knives stabbed up my arms and through my body.

Fatlips threw a fearful glance at Mr. Muller.

"She's all right," he said, drawing on his cigarette. "Hardly no amps."

Father Potts made a short chuckle. Sister Margaret shot him a glare. He made a sheepish shrug. "Sorry, Sister—the way she jumped . . ."

Fatlips frowned, then looked back at me. "Let us pray, now." She and Father Potts bowed their heads and fingered their rosaries. "Hail Mary, full of grace. . . ."

I was still trying to catch my breath. My heart pounded in my chest, but I prayed along. Maybe it would help. Maybe Mary would hear and end my punishment quicker. "Hail Mary, fu-full of grace—"

Again the sledgehammer hit me. I yelped. My wrists and ankles throbbed. Fire raced up my arms and down my back.

"The Lord is with thee," they droned.

"Stop it!" I cried. "Please stop!"

The power surge hit me again.

"Blessed art thou among women."

Terrified, I was sobbing uncontrollably, struggling against the wrist and ankle straps. The more I struggled, the more they rubbed my skin raw. "Let me go! I didn't do anything!"

A short burst this time, like a warning. My heart slammed against my ribs. Panting, I blurted out, "Ble-blessed art thou among women!"

"And blessed is the fruit of thy womb, Jesus."

I was bawling and gasping so hard I couldn't talk.

Another hammer blow. My body jerked outward. My fingertips and toes felt as though they would burst. I wet myself.

"Oh, Jesus, help me!" I cried out. "I'm sorry, Sister, I'm sorry! Forgive me, Jesus; I'm sorry!" I'm going to die, I thought, here in this dank basement, hundreds of miles from Mom and Gram. I'll end up in the graveyard behind the school, and Mom, like a hundred other boarding-school mothers, would be told I died from the flu.

"Holy Mary, Mother of God," they droned.

Father Potts nodded to Mr. Muller again.

"Pray for us sinners."

I shouted, "PRAY FOR US SINNERS!" I felt suddenly faint.

Another jolt.

Bright lights swam before my eyes. The room spun, then—blackness.

I awoke in a basement storage room with a pounding headache just in time to watch Father Potts and Mr. Muller close the door behind them. My whole body ached. I raised myself up on my arms and looked around. I was on a musty mattress, covered with an old wool blanket. I'd been here before—the basement storage room. A small candleholder held a flickering candle. Next to it lay a box of matches and a bologna sandwich and an orange drink on a cafeteria tray. At the far end of the mattress sat a barely visible "night bucket" and a roll of toilet paper.

I felt a surge of panic, then spied the candle. I crawled over and inspected it, hoping they'd given me a fresh one. But no. It was about one-third used. I made a soft cry of frustration. I'd have to conserve if I wanted light to eat by and to use the bucket. Maybe Fatlips would send Mrs. Olsen, the cook, down to feed me. I might be able to wheedle candles from her. Please God, let it be Mrs. Olsen.

Based on the sandwich I decided it must be dinnertime. Father Potts and Fatlips had brought me down here around nine-thirty. It would be hours until supper. Suddenly famished, I sat next to the candle and gobbled the sandwich and the orange drink, then carefully moved the candle to my mattress and sat it next to me. Tucking the blanket tightly under my feet and legs, I pulled the rest of it up over my shoulders. Suddenly, I remembered what Fatlips said about Sister Steph: "Sister Stephanie is no longer with us, thanks to you." *Oh, God. What had I done?*

I started sobbing.

To add to the misery, the words to that stupid song they often made us sing started tapping at my mind like an unwelcome night visitor: "Our hearts were black and savage, until we opened them to the gift of our Lord, Jesus Christ. And now our hearts are red and bright, because we've seen the light. The darkness of our skin reminds us of our heathen past, but the acceptance of our Lord takes us to a place of light and love that will last . . ."

"No!" I screamed at the ceiling like a crazy person. "DO YOU HEAR ME? NO MORE!"

An idea sparked in my mind like the flare of a match in the dark, the kind of inspiration that sometimes comes with such a burst of cold anger and desperation. The idea would have to be crafted into a plan—a plan to get me home. But I would need to wait for the right moment. And I would need help.

I remembered the candle. I blew it out and yanked the blanket over my head. Cold blackness enveloped me with such suddenness that I got a sense of vertigo. It pressed down on me like a dead weight, and I felt the sudden need to urinate. I cringed and squeezed my legs together.

A damp cold draft seeped through my blanket. Pipes clanked and groaned. The boiler hissed and wheezed. Now the endless wait, the listening for rats.

Chapter Fifty

Luther and Cecelia pulled into the parking lot at the BIA regional office and found a space. Luther looked a bit pale as he sat there with the engine running. He stared blankly at the brick edifice, his lips moving unintelligibly. Cecelia guessed he was mentally practicing his *story*. He had told Cecelia that although he and Frank Zern had talked by phone a couple of times, Luther had never met the regional director in person. The word in Wisconsin Indian Country was that Zern was a tough customer. Luther had explained, "A typical BIA bureaucrat and a buddy of recently ousted Commissioner of Indian Affairs Dillon S. Myer, the man who had supervised the wartime internment and resettlement of Japanese Americans."

Zern always sent his secretary, Ida Miller, to Loon Lake tribal council meetings. Cecelia knew her well. Officious and efficient, she held powerful sway over the council. As far as they were concerned, Ida Miller *was* the BIA, and Luther had bent over backward to keep on her good side. *Too* far backward, in Cecelia's opinion, but she had held her tongue.

Now Cecelia sensed that the long drive had given Luther too much time to consider all this and that his courage was bleeding off like energy from a shorted battery.

"I got to consider the needs of the tribe on the whole, *Nokomis,*" Luther suddenly defended. "This talk with Zern, if it goes the wrong way, could affect the whole tribe."

"*Eya,* I know, Luther. You'll do fine."

Luther went on as if he didn't hear her. "I mean, there are a hundred priorities at Loon Lake. I can tell you that I've spent a few sleepless nights reprioritizing over and over, working toward that Yellow Hill water project." He looked at her with the face of a worried man.

Cecelia knew Luther had an aunt and several cousins living in Yellow Hill, and on every visit he was swept with guilt, helping them tote buckets of cold water into the house. And there was the fact that the water project was his key campaign promise, along with establishing an AA program and a small bus to transport diabetic elders and children to the health clinic for insulin shots.

Cecelia squeezed his arm. In Ojibwe she said, "Luther, the water thing has the importance of crow droppings compared to what our children are going through. What you are doing today is your most important work, and I am here as your witness, so don't worry about the council."

Luther twisted in his seat to face her. "I just want you to know the full story before we go in there, what we're risking. Tribes all over the country are still reeling from the double whammy of the Termination Act and Public Law 280. The hair on the back of my neck stands up when I think of our neighbors, the Menominees. Remember?" He snapped his fingers. "BAM, just like that—with the stroke of a pen—they were *terminated* as tribal entities. After centuries of existence, the United States government declares them *non-Indians* and buys their lands at bargain-basement prices, *eya?* And when they balked, the government threatened to withhold most of the money the Indian Claims Commission owed them! *That's* what we're facing in there."

Cecelia was aware of most of this, but she also remembered that Marvin had said this Public Law 280 violated tribal sovereignty by putting many tribes under state law.

Suddenly liable to taxation, many Indian families (including some of her relations) were now homeless and without a source of income, destitute. Their children had been placed in non-Indian foster homes, the parents forced to pay for their care from their own trust funds. So far, thank the Creator, Wisconsin had shown no interest in this new law, and Loon Lake had managed to avoid these catastrophes—except for the Relocation Act, which a few government-trusting families had participated in. Most of those folks now either languished penniless in big cities or barely managed to limp back to Loon Lake intact.

Cecelia squeezed his arm and donned a brave smile. "I have been praying on this the whole way, Nephew. Not to worry. *Gitche-Manitou* is on our side!"

Luther's eyes locked on hers for a long moment, then he sighed and switched off the ignition. "I hope you're right, Cecelia."

They got out and headed for the double glass doors, took the elevator to the fifth floor, and entered another glass door with the familiar Department of Interior seal. The floor was standard government-green linoleum. There was a reception desk and five polished oak chairs in a small waiting area. The receptionist, a moderately attractive young woman wearing a pink angora sweater over her shoulders smiled. "May I help you?"

Luther cleared his throat. "We're here to see Mr. Zern. I'm Chief White Bear and this is Cecelia Pitwoniquot, one of our elders."

She smiled at Cecelia, then looked Luther over admiringly before glancing down at a desk calendar. "You have an appointment?"

Luther nodded. "Yes, ma'am."

Save your bedroom eyes for your own kind, Cecelia thought.

The young receptionist's forehead creased. "I don't see anything here, Mr. Bear. What time was your appointment?"

He decided to ignore her misunderstanding of his last name and bent forward to view her calendar. "Ah, nine is what Mr. Zern said."

The young woman looked up. "Well, I don't see anything here. Maybe it was for tomorrow?" She started leafing through calendar pages.

Cecelia saw Luther's neck muscles tense. "No, I'm sure it was for this morning—nine this morning."

The girl looked sincerely puzzled. "I don't know what happened. Mr. Zern usually gets in around nine, but I think he has a meeting this morning down the hall." She looked down at the calendar again. "And he's booked the rest of the day."

Luther said, "We drove a long way. I'm sure it's a mistake. You say he's supposed to be here any time now?"

The girl glanced at the big wall clock. "Usually, yes, but like I said, he might just go straight to that other meeting down the ha—"

Her eyes jumped to the glass door. "Oh, here he is now."

They turned to see a tall, thin man in his late forties or early fifties entering the room. He wore a gray fedora and a tweed overcoat and puffed on a meerschaum pipe. "Morning, Darlene," he mumbled as he walked briskly by Cecelia and Luther toward his office.

Darlene called, "Oh, Mr. Zern. Chief Bear is here to see you."

Zern turned and frowned. "Bear?" He eyed Luther, then Cecelia.

"Yes, sir," Darlene went on. "From Loon Lake. He said he had a nine o'clock appointment. It wasn't on the calendar, and I was just telling him—"

Zern removed his pipe. He looked directly at Luther, then back to Darlene. "Oh—yes—White Bear. Give me a few minutes." He disappeared into his office and closed the door.

Darlene winked piquantly at Luther. "Looks like you're in luck. Just have a seat and he'll see you in a few minutes."

Cecelia and Luther took their seats. Cecelia didn't mind waiting as long as she knew Zern would see them.

"So . . ." Darlene said, "can I get you some coffee? It's government coffee, though. Pretty bad, I'm afraid." She batted her eyes at Luther.

Cecelia wished she had a willow switch.

"No, thanks," said Luther, who, disappointingly, looked intrigued with the hussy.

"You can call me Bunny, by the way," she said with a self-conscious laugh. "Everybody does." She grimaced and lowered her voice conspiratorially. "Except for Mr. Zern, of course." She fiddled with her hair.

"You call me Luther."

Her smile widened to the point Cecelia thought her face might break. "Nice name," she said. "Biblical, isn't it?"

Luther shrugged. "My mother never said."

Twenty minutes later they knew her life story, where she lived, her favorite color, and a number of other mundane facts. Finally, her intercom buzzed. A voice crackled, "You may send Mr. White Bear in, Darlene."

Darlene pressed a button. "Yes, sir." She winked again. "Well, time sure flies when you're having fun." A quick giggle. "First door on your left, Luther." She managed to put an enticing emphasis on "Luther."

They stood. Cecelia started toward Bunny, but Luther squeezed her arm and whispered in Ojibwe, "Remember your promise."

She did. Luther had asked her to let him do the talking,

whispering to him in Ojibwe if she wanted him to insert anything. So she held her tongue once again.

They walked to a rippled-glass door labeled "Regional Director." Luther stopped and turned back to the receptionist. "I thought you said your name is Bunny?"

She blushed. "Just to my friends."

Cecelia gave him a poke.

Luther knocked, then opened the director's door. A burr-headed Frank Zern, dressed in a gray herringbone three-piece suit, sat at a massive government-gray metal desk. On the wall behind him was a large Department of Interior seal and photos of President Eisenhower and two other officious-looking men in suits. To the left of the president's photo hung a large American flag on a lacquered flagpole. Zern removed his pipe with one hand, stood, and stretched his other hand across the desk. "Come in. Luther, isn't it?" he said with a stiff smile.

Luther shook Zern's hand. "Yes, sir, and this is Mrs. Cecelia Pitwoniquot, one of our elders."

Zern nodded at Cecelia, then gestured to two chairs facing his desk. "Have a seat. How's everything up at Loon Lake?"

They sat, Cecelia taking in the impressive brass nameplate on Zern's desk, flanked by miniature American and Wisconsin flags. "Fine," Luther said. "Thanks for asking."

Zern leaned back in his chair and puffed on his meerschaum. "Good, good. I plan to get up there one day and see you people." He glanced at his watch. "So, what can I do for you today? It must be important if you couldn't talk to Ida about it."

Luther shifted uneasily in his chair. "Ah, yes, sir. It is."

Zern leaned forward and retrieved a silver pipe lighter. He re-lit his pipe and referred to an open file folder on his desk. "I assume it's about that water project up there. No need to worry about that." His eyes flicked back and forth between Cecelia and Luther. "If you handle it right, I think you'll get that loan."

That was exciting news, though the phrase "if you handle it right" sounded typically double-edged.

Luther leaned forward. "No, Director, it's not about that."

Zern's eyebrows peaked. "No?"

"It's about—well—education programs." Luther cleared his throat. "As you know, we have a lot of kids going to boarding schools."

Cecelia watched Zern's face closely. It remained impassive.

Luther went on, "And their folks, you know, miss the kids and, well, with times changing like they are, we know a lot of tribes are sending their kids to public schools or even building their own."

Zern said, "That's correct. You can take advantage of that under the loan guarantees of the Indian Reorganization Act. Ida can walk you through all that."

There was caution in Luther's voice. "I'm glad you mentioned that, Director. This whole IRA thing has us a little confused."

Luther had told Cecelia on the way up that American Indian law, if it were a map boundary, would resemble the trail of a drunk. Also, thanks to her husband's experience on the tribal council, she knew that unlike most previous do-good government programs, the Indian Reorganization Act had brought welcome changes but had also created new problems. So far, with the exception of the section forcing tribes to elect tribal officials publicly, Loon Lake had managed to dodge these by lying low, a posture that, in the council's mind, had allowed them to avoid termination, the lethal weapon BIA wore threateningly on its hip. Consequently, Cecelia had only a hazy understanding of the act and its possible benefits.

Luther replied, "I intend to get with Ida and find out what we need to do on them loans. As far as the Hayward public schools, they say they won't take our kids unless they live in the district. They say they lose too much money on every Indian kid they take in. They say the government tells them to take in Indian kids, but then don't give them enough money to pay for them."

Luther paused, apparently for a reaction. Zern just puffed away.

Luther cleared his throat again. "So we kind of got a problem we have to deal with right away, here. And I was wondering if you might have another way for us to get our kids back home and into some kind of day school."

Zern checked his watch again and frowned. "I don't get it. What's the big problem with the boarding schools? The Catholics run a helluva fine educational system. Some say they're better than the public schools. I, myself, am a graduate of Xavier High in New York. I couldn't have asked for a better secondary education. In fact, I liked it so much I went on to Fordham."

Cecelia's spirits drooped. How could they now bring charges against the Church when this man Zern was one of them?

"I understand that, Director, and it ain't that we're not appreciative. It's just that it's hard on the families, what with their kids sent away for so long. We'd just like to be like everybody else and send our kids to day school." Luther gestured to a small desk photo of Zern and two young boys holding up sizable trout. "As a parent, I'm sure you understand."

Zern sighed. "Well, if you people up at Loon Lake would

get out of the dark ages, you could probably get an IRA capital loan to build a small day school. Trouble is, I doubt you could also get your water project done, too."

Fuming, Cecelia pulled at Luther's shirtsleeve and whispered in Ojibwe, "Ask this *chimook* what he means by dark ages!"

Zern looked expectantly at Cecelia. "I'm sorry, I didn't catch that."

"Oh, it's nothing, Mr. Zern. You see, Cecelia doesn't speak English all that well. She was just admiring your picture of President Eisenhower."

Zern eyed Cecelia skeptically, then stood and moved toward his coat tree. "Tell you what. I'll use my influence to get you a loan for that water project." He donned his hat and started to put on his coat. "Right now you have the best of both worlds: free first-rate schools, and loan money to modernize your reservation. Like I told the other tribal chairmen, you have to learn how to operate like the president of a company. You can't let the criers and complainers get in the way of what's best for them in the long run."

Luther and Cecelia stood.

Zern said, "I know it isn't easy, Luther, trying to keep up with a fast-moving world, but that's your job. You'll always have your nay-sayers and those old-timers who fight you every inch of the way, but you have to be tough, because you and I know what's best." He winked and stretched out his hand. "Keep moving, keep pushing ahead. That's the name of game. They'll thank you for it in the end." He quickly shook Cecelia's hand, then checked his watch. "Unfortunately, I have another meeting," he said, ushering them into the waiting area. "I'd like to spend more time with you, but I've got a busy schedule. See if Ida can see you today to explain more about that loan process, huh?" And then he was out the door and gone.

Cecelia and Luther stared at the closed door for a second, then went to the coat tree to retrieve their coats.

"Mrs. Miller is using one of her sick days today, Luther," Bunny said behind him. She cupped her hand as if to whisper. "Actually, she's throwing a baby shower for her daughter." She cocked her head and smiled. "I overheard what you were talking about. I can give you an information packet about the loan program if you'd like."

"Thanks," Luther said, and accepted the thick manila envelope from her.

Back in the truck, Luther sat quietly, staring out the windshield. Cecelia could guess what he was thinking. He could return home feeling comfortable that he had at least tried to do the elders' bidding. That although he was unable to bring the kids home immediately, he hadn't left the BIA office empty-handed. He could probably say the water project was a sure thing.

Gram reached into her basket purse, pulled out Ruby's photo and showed it to Luther. "Remember what she is going through." From her sweater pocket she fished out a business card, took Luther's hand and pushed the card into his palm. Written on it was the local address of the Catholic diocese. *"Ombay!"*

Chapter Fifty-One

After three days and nights in the basement I emerged something of a hero in the eyes of my classmates, even with the girls who had never liked me. Somehow the rumor mill had churned out that I had endured some horrible punishment and a record stay in the dungeon. This fit perfectly into my plan, and over the next two weeks I made sure I told everyone I knew about Father Potts's electric chair.

"Holy . . ." Alice Nadjiwon gasped as I filled in another small group of girls in the lavatory two days later. All hands flew to their mouths, their eyes wide with fear and awe. I leaned in, brimming with intensity. "And I'm telling you guys, either we stick together and stop them, or every one of you could end up in that chair sooner or later."

Norma Red Sky straightened. "Not me. I'm a good student. They've never sent me to the dungeon. You're just a troublemaker, Ruby Loonfoot. Now you want the rest of us to get into trouble, too."

I hated to do this, but I was desperate. I gave her a hard stare. "You think you never been punished, Norma? Think back. It wasn't that long ago you were one of Father Slater's girls, was it?"

Norma shrank back, her face turning crimson. "You shut up! You don't know what you're talking about!"

The other girls eyed her knowingly.

"Don't I?" I pressed on, scanning their faces. "I bet I can't talk to any ten girls in the school without one being messed with by Slater, and you know it!"

Silence.

"That's right," Rose, my ally for the group meetings, interjected in a mocking tone. "Keep quiet about it. Don't say nothing. Watch out for yourself and too bad about everybody else, right? We're just dumb Indian kids that don't deserve no better, huh?"

They looked at each other, then studied the floor. Each group's reaction had been almost identical. First, looks of horror, then denial, then stark fear when they realized what I was asking of them.

"Look," I said. "Either we stick together on this thing, or all this crap just goes on and on. I don't know about you but I'm sick of it! I wanna go home; I wanna get out of this hellhole, don't you?"

Alice shot me an angry glare. "You're crazy, Ruby! You'll get us all in trouble and sent to the dungeon. I'm outta here," and she headed for the door.

Rose grabbed her arm. "So you want to wait until it's your turn in the chair? You want to chicken out and let the rest of us fight for you?"

Alice yanked her arm away. "Leave me alone!" She looked at the group of uneasy girls. "If you guys know what's best for you, you'll get out of here and stay away from these two."

She started to leave, but I headed her off, my voice low and forbidding. "You keep your flap shut, Alice. I ain't kidding."

Her face filled with fear; then she sped out the door.

There was an awkward silence; then, with downcast eyes, the others milled out. Norma turned to me with contrite eyes. "Sorry," and went out the door.

Rose frowned and fell back against the tiled wall in frustration, her arms crossed. "Damn it! They're just too chicken.

They'd rather get messed with by Slater, starve to death, and go to the chair than have the guts to do something about it."

Rose had come a long way in a short time. She was tough. Besides Katie, she had turned into my most loyal friend. I had come to rely on and trust her completely. I had confided to her my plan to get us home, and she supported me all the way. We were partners in crime.

She looked at the small rippled-glass window high above the stalls. "Maybe they don't deserve no better."

"Hey. Now you sound like Fatlips," I said testily. "Don't start going sour on me. If I don't have you with me, I don't know what I'll do."

Rose sighed, "I know, I know. But now they got you on every dirty chore list. You hardly got time to pee. They watch you like hawks." She loosed another noisy sigh. "And trying to hide all this from Agnes and her bunch is gonna be impossible."

I clasped her shoulder. "There's enough girls who hate Agnes. And I'm the new hero around here, remember? They'll keep quiet. And don't worry about me. I'll find the time." I shrugged. "When I can't, you'll do the talking for us. We'll keep working on them. They'll come around." I found myself slumping against the wall next to her. "They got to."

Chapter Fifty-Two

The diocesan office was housed in a stately Victorian home on Ash Street. A sign just under the beveled stained-glass window in the front door read, "Please ring bell and come in." Luther twisted a quaint wingnut doorbell, and with Cecelia he entered the foyer. An oriental rug covered a long, dimly lit hallway. The floors and walls were made of rich, dark wood, as was the wide, stained-oak stairway in front of them that led upstairs. On the walls to the left and right were religious paintings: the Sacred heart, various saints, Jesus surrounded by adoring children.

"In here," a pleasant voice called from an opening in the hallway just ahead and to their left.

Luther removed his porkpie cap, and they stepped softly down the hall to where a spacious side room opened to their left. A smiling elderly woman wearing glasses with a thin, silver neck strap looked at them expectantly. She sat behind a wooden desk laden with files, knickknacks, and a typewriter.

"May I help you?" she asked.

Luther moved a little closer, hat in hand. "Ah—yes. We'd like to see the bishop, please."

She squinted at him. "I see. Do you have an appointment, Mr. . . . ?"

Luther said, "White Bear—ah—Chief White Bear. And this is Mrs. Pitwoniquot. We're from the Loon Lake Reservation."

She nodded at Cecelia, then looked thoughtful. "Loon Lake?"

Luther chuckled self-effacingly. "I forget that people down here haven't always heard of us, being way up near the border. It's a Chippewa reservation."

"Oh." She smiled and laid down her typewriter eraser. "A chief, you say?"

"Yes, ma'am."

"Well," she chuckled, "we don't get too many chiefs in here."

Luther smiled. "No, ma'am."

"And may I ask what this is concerning?"

The room was overheated and Cecelia and Luther still wore their coats and gloves. The woman didn't offer to take their coats. "Well, it's—kind of confidential."

The woman frowned, more a puzzled look than one of disfavor. "I see." She shifted in her chair and scanned something on her desk. "Bishop Swazey is a very busy man, you know. People make appointments to see him way in advance."

Luther put on his most winning smile. "I'm sure . . ." He looked at her nameplate. ". . . Mrs. Elliot, but we've come a long way and have something very important to talk to him about. It's about St. Nicholas School."

Her eyebrows arched. "St. Nicholas?"

"Yes, ma'am."

She looked concerned. "Perhaps I could help you. I'm in charge of our school records. Is it about a student?"

Luther unbuttoned his coat and removed his gloves. If he was half as hot as Cecelia, he was burning up. "No, not about a particular student. It's—well, I really have to talk to the bishop about it, and I gotta be getting back on the road in an hour. Is there any way I could see him?"

She sighed and chewed at her lip as she studied him.

Finally, she rose. "Please, take off your wraps and have a seat. I'll see what I can do."

They shed their coats and sat in antique chairs in front of the bookcases. Mrs. Elliot walked across the room, slid open double sliding wooden doors and closed them behind her. Cecelia scanned the ornately decorated room. There was a massive fireplace to the left of her desk, but it was unused, the hearth covered by a metal enclosure to keep out drafts. Over the fireplace hung a large painting of the Last Supper. A large, elaborately carved crucifix adorned the opposite wall. The room contained several antique tables and lamps, accompanied by varying styles of wooden chairs with finely upholstered seats. Three of the walls contained floor-to-ceiling shelves packed tightly with books. Cecelia gaped at the opulence of it all. She'd never seen such a house.

The double doors slid open and Mrs. Elliot and a squat rotund man in priest's garb entered the room. "I'm Bishop Swazey," the priest said, stretching out his plump, stubby-fingered hand.

Luther took his hand, then Cecelia. She sensed not friendliness but all business.

Swazey gestured toward the open double doors. "If you'll follow me to my office, I have a few minutes for you."

Mrs. Elliot closed the doors behind them, and they found themselves in a spacious and handsomely appointed office. The bishop pointed to two chairs in front of his desk. "Have a seat." He then moved around his desk and sat in a high-backed brown leather chair, the size and richness of which Cecelia had never seen. The short cleric was dwarfed by its size. A doilied table next to Cecelia's chair held a silver tea service that looked like something from a storybook.

The bishop leaned forward and smiled at them. "Are you Catholics?"

"Ah—no, sir, I'm afraid not."

The bishop's smile faded. "I see." He sat back. "It's Luther isn't it?"

"Yes, sir."

"You're rather young to be a chief."

"Yes, sir. Tribal chairman, actually."

The bishop nodded. "Well, you say you came to talk about St. Nicholas? Is there a problem I should know about?"

Luther glanced sidelong at Cecelia, then swallowed. "I'm afraid there is. I don't know of a good way to tell you all this, but I've been hearing some troubling things about St. Nicholas—about all the schools, actually."

The bishop frowned. "Troubling things?"

Luther fiddled with his hat, his coat still held in his lap. "I'm hearing that a lot of the kids are being whipped and that they ain't getting enough to eat."

Cecelia was puzzled when she saw what looked like relief in Swazey's expression.

Swazey smiled. "I understand your concern, Luther, but we've been running Indian schools for almost eighty years. We know how to handle our children. Unfortunately, a few have behavior problems and, as you know, have to be punished to get them back on the straight and narrow. As far as food is concerned, it's only natural for children to complain about such things. Were you in the service, Luther?"

Luther was puzzled. "Ah—yes, sir. Korea."

Swazey sat back and clasped his fingers over his protruding belly. "Well, then, you know how soldiers constantly complain about the food. It's only natural. We do our best with what we have." He made a snorting sound akin to a chuckle, something he was obviously unaccustomed to. "I can assure you that none of our students ever starved."

Luther studied his hat.

"Was there something else, son?"

Luther looked up. "Indian kids don't need to be whipped like dogs, Bishop. We don't raise 'em that way. I mean, there are other ways of correcting them, eh? Whipping a kid breaks his spirit, that's the way we look at it."

Swazey's smile tightened. "I've heard that old argument from you people before. I'm afraid it doesn't work. It's the same kind of nonsense Dr. Spock put out." He leaned forward. "Look, son. We have a responsibility to prepare these children for the real world, the white world, if you will, and that world is a disciplined world, a world with rules and expectations. If Indian children are going to be given an education and prepared for a job, they need a strong, guiding hand. To be frank with you, many of these children just can't follow rules, so they have to be punished—to toe the line. It's all in their best interest. As I said, we've been at this for a long time."

Luther said nothing.

Cecelia boiled.

Swazey looked uncomfortable with the silence and cleared his throat. "Tell you what. I'll make some inquiries. If there are any irregularities going on concerning punishments, I'll see to it personally. How would that be?"

Again, Luther said nothing.

Swazey went on. "And I'll look into the food complaint as well." He looked at his watch, then at Luther with a sly smile. "Of course, we could arrange for you to visit St. Nicholas at your convenience. See how things are for yourself."

Luther knew such prearranged tours were put-up affairs, where the dirt was swept under the carpet for a day while tribal chairmen or government inspectors were escorted around the school. Government men might be fooled by the smiling, singing children and the bountiful feast laid out in the dining room, but Indian people were not. A surprise visit, Luther mused, might be more interesting.

Swazey frowned. "Is there something else?"

"I'm afraid so, Bishop. You see, there's other things going on at the schools that worry us." Luther paused to gather his thoughts. "We're—" He fiddled with his cap. "We're hearing a lot of talk about people—well, messing—with our kids. Too much talk, if you know what I mean, to be just rumors. We're real protective over our kids. So, our people, they want their kids brought home. We're planning to build our own school one day, and—"

At first Swazey's paunchy face reflected confusion, then it reddened. "Now hold on, son. Let's not let this get out of hand. If you're talking about what I think you are, you're making a very dangerous accusation, here. You can't just waltz in and casually accuse my staff of molesting children. Do you realize the gravity of such a statement? Good Lord! This is the Holy Church. Our teachers are priests and nuns!" He opened his mouth, then closed it. There was an uncomfortable pause, then, biting his lower lip, the bishop sat back with the look of a man who was suddenly impressed with his own insight. "Look—Luther—I understand your position. Your people pressured you and you had to come down here and at least make an effort to look into their complaints. I understand that, I do. But you and I—as chiefs of our flocks—are required to be above all that. We chiefs have to separate the wheat from the chaff, as they say."

Swazey cleared his throat. "Now just because one very crafty student manages to fool one very young and impressionable nun, doesn't mean we chiefs should be misled and run around in a panic. That's for the braves and the squaws to do, right? You and I, we have to maintain reality. Do you see the analogy here?"

This was too much. *"Gaawesa!"* Cecelia blurted.

Swazey gave her an icy glare. Luther held up a hand, and leaned over to whisper in Cecelia's ear. "I think the bishop just let the cat out of the bag. I think he's referring to Sister Stephanie's letter Ruby mentioned. Let me play this hunch."

Cecelia gave him the nod.

Luther straightened in his chair. "Bishop, Ruby Loonfoot ain't the kind of kid who lies to her grandmother, here. We believe her, and we believe the other kids, too. I've talked to people all over our reservation. There's been talk about this stuff for generations. I'm asking you—as a wise chief—to investigate it and put a stop to it."

Swazey popped from his chair with the alacrity of a man half his age and weight. "That's enough! I'll not listen to such vicious and unfounded accusations!"

"So you did get a letter from a nun at St. Nicholas—about her own investigation?" Luther asked.

Swazey had moved to the side of his desk, but now halted with a startled look. Then fresh anger replaced it. "That's ridiculous! There's no need for any investigation!" He glowered down at Luther. "You're on very dangerous ground, Mr. White Bear. Very dangerous. I don't know what your angle is, but I can assure you I will discuss this with Frank Zern and anyone else at BIA I can get to!"

Cecelia knew they'd hit home. The bishop definitely knew about Sister Stephanie's letter, of that she now felt sure.

Luther looked angry as he stood, Cecelia following suit. "I came here with respect, Bishop. I didn't come in shouting or calling you names. I was raised with holy men who listen and who seek truth. I expected the same from you. I guess I was wrong."

Swazey's face was a mask of anger, his right hand trembling. "This conversation is ended." He lumbered to the sliding doors and flung them open. Miss Elliot, who had turned to see what the noise was about, jumped.

"Joan, show this man out."

Cecelia started out, then turned back to face Swazey. "Shame on you! You are no holy man."

Back in the truck, Luther slammed the door and pounded the dashboard. "Sonofabitch! The bastard is covering it all up!" He sat there a moment, his heart pounding, his breath fogging the windows. "I've failed you, *Nokomis*. First with Zern, now with Swazey. Worse, I've failed the children. Now the tribe will likely pay a bitter price." His shoulders slumped. "Maybe a smarter tribal chairman would have handled this whole thing better."

Cecelia said, "*Gaawiin gwayak.* You did good, Luther White Bear. Now let them fret about what we might do."

Luther gave her an incredulous look, then shook his head. He started the engine and headed down Ash Street. When they turned onto the highway, Luther grabbed a roll of Tums and thumbed a couple into his mouth, then offered some to Cecelia.

"I don't need them things," she said. "That big holy man might, though. I ain't done with him yet."

Chapter Fifty-Three

Ten days after Cecelia and Luther's trip to the BIA, Theresa worried that she hadn't seen her mother since then. They had never gone more than two or three days without contact; it gnawed at her conscience. She cringed at the memory of her own angry words: "You ain't going to stop me, you hear? Nobody's going to stop me! Now get out!" And then her mother's unforgettable words: "My daughter's heart is dead."

She hadn't changed her mind, however, about getting the girls off the rez. She'd had a brainstorm soon after the row with her mother and had zipped off a letter to her cousin Mickey in San Francisco. Mickey and her husband, Alvin, had relocated under the IRA a year ago and seemed to be making it in the big city. They weren't able to have children, and Mickey had always doted on the girls. Sure enough, Mickey wrote back that she would be more than happy to house the girls for a few months until Theresa and Jim could join them.

She had yet to discuss her plan with Jim. In fact, she hadn't a clue how she was going to not only repair her marriage but persuade her rez-bound husband to move a couple of thousand miles away to California. One thing she could use was Mickey's testimony that there were other Indian families in their apartment complex, a couple of whom were Ojibwes. Also, Mickey said that the schools were within walking distance!

Donning her worn wool coat and gloves, Theresa thought again about her mother. It was way past time to check on her. And maybe it was time for a confession.

Along the lonely road to the Yellow Hill district an early October ice storm had crusted the trees, and the branches sagged tiredly under the weight of it. Theresa's forehead ached from the wind, so she kept her head down, watching each footfall as it crunched against ice-encrusted snow. She shivered. The sound reminded her of chalk squeaking against a blackboard.

Twice along the way she almost turned back. She dreaded this meeting and its unpredictable outcome. Not only would she have to grovel, but she planned to admit to Cecelia that at St. Mary's School twenty-four years ago, Theresa had been molested. In her case it wasn't a priest but the visiting doctor. It had eaten at her insides all these years, and she blamed it for her problems with men. But only recently—perhaps spurred by their fight and the realization that some of the things her mother said about the schools were true—did Theresa feel a yearning to confide this. It was an old ache that only a mother could soothe.

Ten minutes later she was knocking on Cecelia's front door.

No answer.

She knocked again, harder.

Still no answer.

Concerned, she entered the tiny house. "Mom? Mom, it's me."

Silence hung in the air with her frozen breath. The house was ice cold. Theresa felt a surge of panic. She was heading for the propane furnace control when she noticed the pile of blankets on the couch. "Mom?"

She pulled the blankets down and looked into her mother's peaceful but slack, gray face. Her lips were dark blue. Theresa gently shook Cecelia's shoulder. "Mom! Wake up, Mom! It's Theresa!" She groped under the blankets and found her mother's hand. It was ice cold, stiff as a frozen branch.

"Oh, God! No, Momma, NO!"

Chapter Fifty-Four

It was the end of another exhausting day of kitchen duty—pots and pans all week. Next week I would get lav duty—again. Restricted to the dorm floor when not in class or doing chores, I was effectively kept out of circulation. The rec room was off limits for me, part of my continuing punishment. This made it nearly impossible for me to hold any more group meetings, so I had to rely on Rose for that. She reported her progress nightly—who we could add to our supporters and who needed to be worked on. That was my job, and I sneaked around after lights-out, recruiting and cajoling. This risky activity was intense and tiring, and lack of sleep was starting to wear me down.

There were three hundred of us at St. Nic's. I figured I needed at least a hundred to pull off my plan, though I'd feel more confident with a hundred and fifty. The best time to do anything as a group was just before or after Mass, when everyone was together.

"Hey, Rube," Rose called as she entered the dorm.

"How'd you do today?" I asked.

She winced and rocked her hand back and forth. "So-so. "We got Jennie, Eileen, and Mary, but I'm having a really tough time with the twelfth-graders. They figure they're almost outta here. They ain't gonna rock the boat."

"Yeah, I was worried about that. Let's just work on the seventh-through-eleventh-graders."

Rose chewed the inside of her cheek. "You sure that'll do it?"

"If we get enough of them. I been thinking that maybe a lot more might join us on the spur of the moment, you know, when they see all the excitement going on and how many of us there are. You said just the other night that the whole school is scared ever since they heard about the chair."

Rose made a rueful smile. "You mean you hope they'll join us." She sighed and plopped down on my bed. "What we need is a divirgin."

"A what?"

"Something I saw in this war movie when I was home. This sergeant, see, he was trying to attack this German ammo dump, but he didn't have enough guys, so he said what they needed was a divirgin."

"Yeah?" I prodded, wondering what in the world she was talking about.

"So, they had one of their guys plant some kind of bomb on the other side of this ammo dump, and when all the Germans ran over there to see what happened, our guys attacked."

She had my interest. Then her mouth twisted into a but-then-again expression. "But we ain't got no bombs."

"Ha," I snorted. "Don't worry. The Robes will give us our bomb."

The following morning Sister Francine droned on in history class: "And so we see how the courageous Pilgrims survived that first winter and invited the starving Indians to share their bounty."

This lesson had been halfway interesting, since Indians were involved. We seldom heard about Indians in our history classes unless it was to mention massacres or torture. It helped immeasurably in further lowering our self-esteem. The only positive thing we heard about our ancestors was in this Pilgrim story, where Indians were friendly and brought the Pilgrims corn. It wasn't until college that I learned the truth. It was the Indians who saved the poor starving Pilgrims.

The door opened, and Sister Margaret and Father Potts entered the room. "Excuse me, Sister Francine," Fatlips said. "I need Miss Loonfoot down in my office."

We walked to the office in silence. They never pulled you out of class unless it was something bad. I was wondering what new dirty chore they had come up with. And if they headed toward the basement, I had already decided to run for it.

Fatlips opened her office door. "You have a phone call from your mother. You can take it in my office." She pointed to the phone receiver lying on her desk, then backed out and closed the door. A chill ran up my spine. Phone calls also carried bad news. I swallowed hard and picked up the phone. "Mom?"

"Ruby? Is that you? I can barely hear you?"

I cleared my throat and spoke louder. "Yeah, Mom, it's me. What's wrong?"

Silence. For a moment I thought we'd been disconnected, then, "Honey, I'm afraid I got some bad news."

Here it comes.

"It's Gram, honey. She—" Her voice broke. "Honey, Gram passed over yesterday."

I stopped breathing. My throat constricted. "No, Momma, *no*."

"Everything was fine when I left," I blurted.

Mom said, "Her little furnace broke down, and—well—she didn't have no pain, honey."

What did she mean? Some kind of gas leak? Oh, God, don't tell me she froze. "But—"

"Everything's taken care of. I'm sorry to do this on the phone, but I couldn't get ahold of a car. But don't you worry. She's gonna have a nice funeral. They're taking up a collection right now."

My mind swam in a sea of grief and shock. I *had* to get home. I had to bc sure Gram was . . . I couldn't bear to think the word. "But, Mom. I—somebody has to come get me. I have to come home. Please, Mom, I have to come home."

"Ruby, the funeral is the day after tomorrow and I got no way to get you here. I don't even have money for the bus," she cried. "Look, don't worry. I'll take good care of Gram, you know that. Father O'Connor from Hayward is going to do the funeral. I know you're upset about this, but I was thinking that maybe it's for the best that your last memories of her will be when she was alive. You know how hard it is to see someone you love that way."

"But—"

"Honey, I have to get off the phone. I'm at the tribal office and, you know, the phone charges. I'll take care of everything. Pray for Gram and think of all those good memories of her. That's what she would want. I'll send you a letter right after the funeral and tell you about it. Good-bye, honey. I love you."

I blubbered into the phone, "But, Mom! Mr. Big Shield has got to do the ceremony—" I heard a click. "Mom? MOM?"

The dial tone. I was almost hysterical now. It was too much, too sudden. Fatlips swished back into the room. She looked properly remorseful. "I'm sorry about your grandmother, Miss Loonfoot."

I was still holding the phone. "We've got to call her back!

The funeral, it's all wrong!" Mom's words echoed in my mind. *Father O'Connor!* What about Mr. Big Shield? What about the *pagidaendijigewin,* the Ceremony for the Dead? Gram's spirit couldn't rest without it.

Fatlips tried to take the receiver from my hand, but I held it in a death grip. The room spun—the electric chair, the constant harassment, the sleepless nights, the secret planning, and now Gram.

God, I was only thirteen.

"Miss Loonfoot?"

I released the receiver and she replaced it. Then I felt her hesitant hand touch my shoulder. "Loss is always hard," she said softly. "But it's God's way, this circle of life. Think of your grandmother now standing next to Jesus, smiling and waving, happy to be in the arms of her savior. She's safe now and will have eternal happiness—" Her face suddenly took on a worried expression. "She was Catholic, wasn't she?"

The day of Gram's funeral was the loneliest and bitterest of my life. I was given the afternoon off to pray in the chapel, but that was the last place I wanted to be. The prayers I needed to say must be done in God's true house, outdoors. I had to be among the trees, standing on Mother Earth, with the sky above me. After Fatlips escorted me to the chapel, I waited there a few minutes, then sneaked outside through the sacristy door.

There was a chill in the air. Ponderous gray clouds scudded across the sky. The old maple tree I loved so much stood patiently waiting, sad with its falling leaves. I wished I had some sweet grass to burn. I walked up to the tree, spoke the proper greeting, and pressed my hand against its powerful trunk. I looked skyward. "I miss you Gram. I need you."

I had seen a lot of death on the reservation, but never for

someone as close to me as Gram. I had never even thought of her passing, let alone having it happen so suddenly and with me not there. It wasn't real.

I thought of one of her favorite old Ojibwe songs, a love song that always made her think of Grandpa. I chanted softly to myself:

> *Kego kishkaendigaen.*
> *Kego muwihkaen.*
> *K'gah abi naunin.*
> Do not be sad.
> Do not cry.
> I will come for you.
>
> *Tibishko peedauniquok, w'gee abi-izhauh*
> *Tibishko waebauniquok, aubidji-maudjauh*
> Like a cloud has he come and gone
> Like a cloud, gone forever
>
> *K'weedjeewin*
> *Tibishko mong punae cheega/eehn*
> I am by your side
> Like a loon, always nearby

I thought of Mr. Big Shield. This day would be a very sad one for him as well. He and Gram and Grandpa grew up together, and now he would not even be allowed to conduct the Ceremony of the Dead for her. I pulled out the scissors from my pocket and snipped off a piece of my already school-shorn hair. Imagining him saying the words, I chanted,

> *"Our sister, you leave us.*
> *Our sister, you are leaving.*

Our sister, your spirit.
Our sister, four days on the Path of Souls.
Our sister, to the Land of Souls you are bound."

Then the air suddenly filled with the scents of sweet grass and fresh-baked bread. Gram was *here*. She was all around me, her love, and I decided that Mr. Big Shield would perform the ceremony in secret and that Gram's spirit would soon be on its way to the Land of the Souls.

Chapter Fifty-Five

UNITED STATES DEPARTMENT OF THE INTERIOR

Bureau of Indian Affairs
North Central Region
Finance and Audit Division

DATE: October 8, 1958

TO: Luther White Bear, Tribal Chairman,
Loon Lake Tribe of Ojibwe Indians

FR: Delbert Norberry, North Central Finance Division

SUBJ: Special Field Audit

Chairman White Bear:

Based upon your annual October audit, two irregularities have surfaced that require immediate attention. Standard procedure under "BIA Audit Policies 27-5, para. 47" requires a special field audit by a BIA field auditor. This letter is to notify you that Field Auditor Perry Weeks will arrive at your office one week from today to conduct said audit. As usual, we expect your complete cooperation. Please have all tribal financial records in good order and available to Mr. Weeks upon his arrival.

We recognize Loon Lake's superior financial record to date under your leadership. There is every possibility that the audit will resolve these irregularities without prejudice.

Sincerely,
D. W. Norberry
Branch Chief

Cc: Regional Director Frank S. Zern

Chapter Fifty-Six

It was Friday, two weeks after Gram's funeral, and I sat with Rose and Katie in the cafeteria, eating my meager supper. They'd been doing their best to cheer me since Gram's passing, but I was too heartsick.

"Ruby, what about our plan?" Rose whispered impatiently. "Kids have been asking me and I don't know what to tell them."

I shrugged and nursed my milk. Lately, my mind seemed to be stuck in a listless neutral. Gram had been my rudder. I drifted through each day in a haze.

Katie's face scrunched in worry. "Ruby, you got to eat." She looked to Rose for support.

Rose frowned. "You gotta snap out of this, kid. You started something and now you gotta finish it." She eyed Sister Greta moving nearby, then leaned close to my ear. "We're gonna lose these fence-sitters if we wait much longer."

The bell rang. The cafeteria exploded in the usual din of scraping chairs and clanking metal trays. As we stood in line waiting our turn to pass our trays through the dishwashing window, Father Slater sauntered up.

"Ah, Katie. Glad I found you. I need to see you in my office."

Katie's face turned white, her eyes widened with terror. She glanced at me, then back to Slater. Her mouth moved but no words came out.

"She can't," I said automatically, remembering Sister Steph's directive. "She's supposed to see Sister Stephanie after supper."

He looked sharply at me. "As if you weren't in enough trouble, Miss Loonfoot, now you're becoming a comedian."

I suddenly realized my goof. "I—I meant Sister Elizabeth."

His eyes flashed back to Katie. "Is that right?"

Katie nodded.

"All right," he said, grabbing her hand and pulling her toward him. "We'll go see Sister Elizabeth." He eyed me threateningly. "This better be the truth or you'll be visiting Sister Margaret in her office."

Rose squeezed my arm. "Now!" she whispered in my ear. I stood there, frozen, and watched *Kokoko* march Katie out of the cafeteria. I knew I should do something, shout the code word "Strike!" but I didn't. I just stood there, feeling completely disconnected, impotent. I glanced at Rose. Disappointment was written all over her face. She turned away to drop off her tray and left. I stood there as other girls brushed past me with looks of confused expectation.

"Get moving, Miss Loonfoot," snapped Sister Greta as she moved up the queue. "You're holding up the line."

I knew I should be scared of what would happen when *Kokoko* discovered I had lied, but I merely felt numb, detached. They had done everything to me they could do, and Gram was gone. I just didn't care anymore.

Then I remembered today was Trunk Day. I wanted to hold Gram's dentalium necklace again. Besides my dance barrette, it was all I had of hers. I felt that if I held it when I prayed for her, like an Indian rosary, I would be able to feel her presence again, like back at the tree. "These shells are a gift to the People from the otter spirit," she had said. "And they carry the spirit of your great-grandmother."

We lined up by class down the hall in front of the basement doors, then filed down the stairs to the trunk room, passing the first groups now on their way to the chapel to wait for us. With 300 girls sent down in groups of thirty, that usually took over an hour. Friday-night Vespers would start when everyone had finished with their trunks.

"Ten minutes, ladies," Sister E called out. The musty room filled with the scraping and clicking of trunk lids, the low buzz of chitchat. I opened my trunk and found the red felt pouch Gram had sewn to hold the necklace. I carefully pulled it out and immediately felt the magic of the cool, smooth shells. I held them to my cheek and prayed silently, oblivious of what was going on around me.

"Time's up, ladies."

I was still in a kind of trance when I donned the necklace, closed the trunk and joined the line. In the chapel I sat next to Rose. Katie was sitting behind us. Her face was pale. She was trembling. I always knew when she had been with *Kokoko*.

During Mass I fingered the necklace and thought of Gram. I didn't hear one word of the service, nor do I remember kneeling and standing, or reciting prayers or hymns. I was at Gram's house, talking, laughing, helping her make *manomen*.

Rose's poking elbow brought me back to the present. Mass was over and everyone was heading toward the chapel doors. "Ruby! What's wrong with you?" she whispered. "You were in dream land. I've been poking you forever." She pointed at my neck. "You got your necklace on!"

We reached the hallway, crammed with students. Sister Margaret was waiting for us. "Miss Loonfoot!" She took two long strides to reach me, grabbed my necklace and yanked.

The soft sinew stretched, then snapped, showering the linoleum floor with the tiny delicate shells. "Such trinkets do not belong in God's house!"

Something in my mind snapped along with the necklace. A raging fire pulsed through me, rage like I had never known. "STRIKE!" I shouted at the top of my lungs. I gave Fatlips an angry push. "STRIKE!"

Rose, looking astonished, blinked at me, then joined in. "STRIKE! STRIKE!"

Katie rushed to retrieve my shells. A chorus of voices around me started to chant, "Strike, strike, strike," hesitantly at first, then the volume grew as more and more voices joined them. "STRIKE! STRIKE! STRIKE! STRIKE!"

"SIT DOWN!" Rose shouted. She crouched and gestured with her hands. "EVERYBODY SIT DOWN!"

Chapter Fifty-Seven

Nuns came flapping from all directions. Fathers Slater and Potts rushed from the chapel, still in their vestments.

I shot them a murderous look. "TOUCH ANY OF US AND WE'LL BURN THIS CRAP HOLE DOWN, I SWEAR IT."

Rose started a new chant, "NO MORE! NO MORE! NO MORE!" The hallway echoed with a hundred shouting voices: "NO MORE! NO MORE!"

Agnes Knockwood pushed her way through the crowd, her hands covering her ears. "You're crazy, Loonfoot! Stop it!"

Rose and two other girls stood, pushed her back. "Shut up Knockwurst, or we'll punch your lights out!" Rose snapped.

Fatlips was trying to shout over us. "Stop this! Stop it this instant!" but she was drowned out. She yelled across us to the two priests. "DO SOMETHING!"

Father Potts reached down and grabbed one of the girls. He tried to pull her up, but she was dead weight. "GET UP! ALL OF YOU, GET UP AND GO TO YOUR FLOORS."

The chant continued, "NO MORE, NO MORE, NO MORE." The hall was bedlam, packed with sitting, shouting girls and frantic faculty.

Many students cowered against the walls, watching with fearful eyes. I had expected that. As long as they didn't try to interfere, they could cower all they wanted. Sitting girls grabbed at the bystanders' hands, prodding them to sit and join us. A few did, but most yanked their hands away and tried to melt into the walls.

"I AM WARNING YOU." Fatlips whirled around and around like a crazy woman, waving her paddle ominously. "ALL OF YOU."

"NO MORE. NO MORE."

Father Blewett came running, his face red, eyeglasses askew. "Mother of God! What's going on here?" he shouted at Fatlips.

She glowered at him, trembling with frustration.

Father Slater shouted, "WE DON'T KNOW."

Father Potts' face was twisted in contempt. "I KNOW HOW I'D HANDLE IT."

Father Blewett shot him a hostile glare. "WELL, YOU'RE NOT HANDLING IT." His eyes shifted to Fatlips. "Sister Margaret! I want order here! Get these students quiet and up to their floors!"

The din was incredible. Fatlips covered her ears with her hands and grimaced at the noise.

Then the fire alarm blared. I looked around. Sure enough Katie was missing. She had done her job!

"GOOD LORD!" Father Blewett cried, looking like a man teetering on the edge of a cliff. "IS THAT REAL?" Fatlips' flabbergasted expression provided no answer. Father Blewett looked at Fathers Potts and Slater. "CHECK THE BUILDING. GET THESE GIRLS OUTSIDE."

The standing girls rushed toward the main entrance. Father Slater turned just in time to see the horde hurtling toward him. "WALK, DON'T RUN," he screamed, but it was too late and he was knocked down by the panicked girls. Father Potts escaped the rush and ran around the corner, apparently in compliance with Father Blewett's orders.

Father Blewett cupped his hands and screamed, "GET UP, GET UP. CAN'T YOU HEAR THE FIRE ALARM?"

But we knew there was no fire. "NO MORE, NO MORE, NO MORE!"

Fatlips picked her way through the sitting girls and up to me. "THIS IS YOUR DOING. CALL IT OFF—NOW."

I glared up at her and kept up my chant.

Her eyes crackling with rage, she raised her paddle. As it swished downward, I ducked sideways, but several pairs of hands reached up and grabbed it, stopping it midair. Fatlips grunted and pulled back, but she couldn't overcome four pulling, screaming girls. She lost the tug-of-war and fell backward, but was saved by a flock of jutting hands from the sitting girls. She regained her balance and picked her way back to the safety of the wall.

The stalemate continued for several minutes, the kids chanting, the faculty shouting. Then we heard the sirens.

Two police officers and a bevy of firemen with rubber coats, boots and fire helmets rushed down the hall. "CLEAR THE HALLS. EVERYONE OUTSIDE." They stopped short when we remained seated and kept chanting. "NO MORE, NO MORE."

One of the cops shouted at Father Blewett: "WHAT'S GOING ON HERE? GET THESE KIDS OUTSIDE."

Father Blewett's jaw tightened. "THEY WON'T MOVE."

I stood, followed by Rose. The chanting died down, then stopped. "There ain't no fire," I said. "We want to talk to you, and we ain't moving until we do."

The cop looked both annoyed and perplexed. "What?" His glare shifted to Father Blewett. "What is this?"

Father Blewett eyed the cop nervously. "We've got some troublemakers, that's all, Officer. We'll get to the bottom of it, you can be sure of that."

The cop looked accusingly at me. "Who pulled that alarm?"

I ignored his question. "We ain't moving until we talk to you."

Sister Margaret butted in. "That's ridiculous! If you have a problem, you see me!"

I sat back down and shouted, "NO MORE, NO MORE."

The chant cranked up again.

"Good grief!" the cop yelled. He looked at Fatlips, then Father Blewett, then back at me. "ALL RIGHT! WE'LL TALK."

I stood and signaled the crowd. The chanting died away.

Fatlips scowled at the cop. "We can't give in to them just because they throw a tantrum. If you'll just help us return some order here, we'll take care of this."

The cop turned to one of the firemen. "False alarm, Bill. You guys can go home." He turned to Fatlips. "What would you like us to do, Sister? Wade into them with billy clubs?" He looked at me. "All right. You've got five minutes to explain yourself, young lady." He held up his hand and spread his fingers. "Five minutes."

We led him into the chapel—Rose, Katie, who had returned from her mission, me, and three other girls who had helped organize the strike. This was the riskiest part of our plan, because if the police sided with the school . . . I didn't want to think about it. But I was banking on sympathy—that soft spot that men had for little girls in distress.

We entered the chapel. The cop closed the door behind us. He looked us over with an expression of suspicious impatience and folded his arms. "I'm Officer Burton. This better be good, ladies, or you're in big trouble. You can go to jail for pulling false alarms."

Despite Burton's imposing size he had kind eyes. And there was something about his use of "ladies" that made me feel he might actually see us as something other than a bunch of dumb Indian kids. I took a deep breath and began, "Officer Burton, we want this place closed down."

Another girl piped up, "And we wanna go home."

Burton cocked his head and tented his eyebrows. "Oh, you do?"

"We have good reasons," I said hurriedly.

Burton switched his gaze to me.

"Officer Burton, what we're gonna tell you—well—it's gonna take longer than five minutes, because you ain't gonna believe us at first. But on the graves of my grandmother and all my ancestors, what we're gonna tell you is the God's honest truth, and we'll swear it on a stack of Bibles." Anxious he might cut me off at any moment, I pointed toward the altar. "Over there—under the crucifix, if that's what you want."

His expression changed to guarded interest. "Go ahead, I'm waiting."

I licked my dust-dry lips and took Katie's hand. It was ice-cold. Her lower lip was already trembling. I hadn't wanted to start with Katie, for her sake, but with Burton's time pressure I felt we needed to startle him enough to make him listen to our full story. I glanced at the altar, for a moment, and at the eight-foot crucifix that hung behind it. It seemed the right place for our testimony.

"This is Katie Red Star," I began. "She's ten years old." I squeezed her hand in assurance. "She was raped by Father Slater."

Five minutes stretched to forty before we emerged from the chapel. We had held nothing back—the molestations, the lack of food, the electric chair. Officer Burton, cynical at first, then astonished, proved to be a good listener. For us, it was as if a great dam had broken, a dam of shame, sorrow and pain. There had been a lot of tears.

Burton leveled his eyes at Father Blewett. "I want to take a look in your basement, Father. Then I want to talk to you and a Father Slater—" He scanned the standing faculty. "Which one of you is Father Slater?"

Blewett gestured nervously toward a very pale *Kokoko.* "This is Father Slater."

Burton nodded, then narrowed his eyes at Slater. "I want to see you and Father Blewett in his office when I come back."

Kokoko's normally confident face blanched.

Burton looked back at Blewett. "But first, I'd like you or Sister Margaret to accompany Ruby and me to the basement."

Blewett's Adam's apple bobbed like a cork in water. He looked puzzled. "The basement?"

"That's right."

Blewett glanced at Fatlips. "Sister Margaret, would you escort Officer Burton to the basement? Father Slater and I will return to the office."

Fatlips shot Father Potts a worried look. Potts stammered, "This is a waste of time. We could use your help instead, getting these girls back upstairs."

Officer Burton looked annoyed. His voice was low, his words measured. "Like I said. I want to see the basement."

I said to the crowd of sitting girls. "Okay, guys. The strike's over—for now. Great job." A noisy cheer went up.

Officer Burton said, "All right, Ruby. Show me the chair."

A tight-lipped Fatlips led us down the hall and through the doors leading to the basement.

* * * * *

John Vincent was only slightly worried as Father Blewett closed his office door, pulled out a handkerchief from his back pocket and mopped his brow. "What in God's name is going on?" he muttered. He straightened and looked at John Vincent. "We've got a riot going on here, that's what it is, a riot." He fell into his chair like an exhausted man, then reached for the phone. "Have to call the bishop . . ."

John Vincent cleared his throat. "You really want to do that? My cousin won't react well to the news."

Blewett's hand hesitated an inch above the receiver.

John Vincent went on, "He'll be disappointed if we can't handle our own problems, especially if we cause him embarrassment."

Blewett slumped back in his seat and dabbed at his upper lip with the handkerchief. "But the fire alarm, the police—there'll be reports . . ."

John Vincent was one step ahead of him. The possible ramifications of all this had already clicked off in his mind. "Don't forget our excellent relationship with the town fathers. We're a Catholic school, after all. I think we can work with the police to—well—quash this thing. We can assure them we have the situation back in control. It was a freak incident, after all, incited by a couple of troublemakers."

Blewett seemed to consider this a moment, then, "You've got to find out who the ringleaders are on this. We've got to separate them from the others somehow." His face turned sour. "That Loonfoot girl. She's the main one. Always been a troublemaker."

"Margaret can handle her."

Blewett said nothing, his face lined with worry. "Why do you think that policeman wants to see the basement? What's that all about?"

"I haven't the slightest," John Vincent lied. "He'll be back up here in a couple of minutes, mad as the devil at the Loonfoot girl for taking him on some wild-goose chase. Then he'll see this for what it is."

Blewett grunted, drummed the desk with his fingers. "I hope you're right."

When we reached the chair room, Officer Burton stared at Mr. Muller's device with an expression of bewilderment. "What's the purpose of this thing?" he demanded of Sister Margaret. Father Potts and Mr. Muller stood next to her. Fatlips wrung her hands. Potts looked calm as Loon Lake on a summer day. Muller shifted back and forth on his feet and sucked on his cigarette.

Burton's eyes flashed to Potts. "Well?"

"It's for our incorrigibles."

Burton removed his cap. His voice was low and menacing. "You mean you strap kids into that and turn on the juice? You admit to that?"

Mr. Muller spoke up. "It don't hurt 'em none. Hardly no amps in it."

Burton eyed the three with increasing incredulity. "Jesus Christ! Who came up with this?"

Potts said, "Muller, here, put it together. It's harmless, really."

Burton shot Potts a piercing stare. His voice was almost a whisper. "Harmless."

Fatlips spoke up. "Believe me, officer, I wouldn't allow its use until I was completely convinced it couldn't really injure the girls. You see, we have a difficult job here. These girls—well—" She shot me a menacing glance. "Some of them are still fresh from the reservations, if you know what I mean." Her speech seemed rushed now, as if she feared Burton might suddenly cut her off. "Like Miss Loonfoot here, some don't respond to the usual punishments. We had to come up with something that would be effective in correcting bad behavior, yet could do no real harm."

Burton shook his head in disbelief. "I never would've believed it. Nuns and priests . . ." His voice trailed off. He glanced at me, rested his hand on my shoulder, and spoke very softly. "How many times did they put you in that, Ruby?"

"Once," I said. "And I ain't the only one. If you leave us here, they'll try to put me in it again, for sure."

He squeezed my shoulders. "Oh, no, they won't." He leveled reproachful eyes at Fatlips and Muller. "You two follow me up to Father Blewett's office—now." He looked back at me, his voice softening. "Come along, Ruby. Something tells me these *grownups* might be a bit more truthful with you around."

Chapter Fifty-Eight

Officer Burton closed the office door and turned to face Fathers Blewett, Potts, Slater and Sister Margaret. He ran his hand through thick, curly brown hair, then replaced his cap. When he spoke, his voice was taut as stretched wire. "You know, I have a little girl maybe two years younger than Ruby." He made a rueful smile. "That little girl is my whole world. All she has to do is give me that smile of hers and she's got me." He tilted back his cap and perched his hands on his hips. "Now what do you suppose I'd do—as her father—if some son of a b—" He glanced at me, then went on, "molested or tortured her?" He hesitated only a moment, then, "But you people don't know anything about that, do you? You never had your own kids." Now he waited, but the only sound was the tick of the second hand on the wall clock.

He shook his head. "I don't know what happened to you people. You're supposed to be representatives of God. Like good shepherds over your flock. Instead, you turned this place into some kind of house of horrors."

Homing in on me with her evil eye, Fatlips interrupted. "Miss Loonfoot, return to your floor at once!"

Officer Burton frowned at her. "She stays here. She's my B.S. detector." He smiled at me. "Aren't you, Ruby?"

I didn't know what to say. As much as I wanted to hear all this, I felt like bolting.

Her chin quivering the way it does when she's fuming,

Fatlips retorted, "Surely you can't believe everything you hear from a bunch of Indian girls. You've only spoken with the wild hares—the troublemakers. Most of our girls are happy here." She stiffened. "And I resent your remarks about a house of horrors. Really!"

Father Blewett jumped in. "Exactly. We've been educating Indian girls since 1880. Our reputation is unquestioned."

I almost choked on that one.

Burton eyed Blewett. "Too bad you weren't wired for electricity until 1900, eh, Father? You lost a good twenty years of serviceable use out of that electric chair."

Blewett's brow furrowed in bewilderment. "What? What are you talking about?"

Burton shot him a sarcastic expression.

Blewett's eyes flitted to Margaret. "What's he talking about?"

Burton answered for her. "So you ain't in on all the dirty little secrets around here? It seems that good Father Potts here, in his love and concern for his students, had the janitor build a real slick little electric chair so's you can strap little girls into it and watch them squirm when the juice is cranked on."

"I was just following orders," Potts interjected confidently.

Fatlips eyed him angrily. "No one told you to build that thing."

Potts looked mildly surprised. "I remember very clearly. You told me to come up with something to control the troublemakers. So I did."

Fatlips huffed in frustration.

So that's the story! I thought.

Tiny blisters of perspiration dotted Father Blewett's brow

and upper lip. He gave Fatlips a withering scowl, then looked at Burton. "I can assure you, officer, that I'll get to the bottom of this and that disciplinary action will be taken. I knew nothing about this electric chair. I would never approve of such tactics. It's outrageous!" He scanned his staff. "God forgive them."

Burton looked at me. With head and eye movements I let him know that I thought Blewett was probably being truthful.

Burton rested his hands on his hips. "If that's the case, Father, you've been asleep at the switch. Who's running this place? You or these three . . . ?" He seemed at a loss for the appropriate pejorative.

Fatlips' face puffed up like a red balloon. "Now, see here, officer."

Burton raised his hand to silence her. "You'll have your chance to tell your stories to Chief Mason and the town attorney. We can do this quietly or I can arrest all of you, put you in handcuffs and run you in. Which will it be?"

"This is insane!" Blewett protested. "Do you realize what you're doing?"

Burton eyed him contemptuously. "Which will it be, Father?" He pulled out his handcuffs and dangled them at his side.

Slater looked petrified.

"He wouldn't dare," Potts snapped defiantly to Blewett.

Blewett slammed his fist on his desk. "Father Potts, shut up!"

Potts, Slater and Fatlips—*and me*—gaped at Father Blewett.

Blewett's shoulders slumped. "Only one more month to retirement," he muttered to his desk, then looked with defeat at the policeman. "Very well, we'll accompany you to town—quietly," he emphasized, "and iron all this out."

Burton put away his cuffs. "For now, this school is temporarily closed. You'll need to make the necessary calls to get these kids home."

Father Blewett looked panic-stricken. "You said we could do this quietly. I'd have to call the bishop for that."

Burton shook his head. "Not my problem, Father. Just get it done." He glowered at Slater. "Actually, that little chair is the least of your problems."

Father Blewett's shoulders sagged further. "Oh, Lord," he mumbled. "What next?"

Burton continued, "You've got an accused child molester here."

Chapter Fifty-Nine

UNITED STATES DEPARTMENT OF THE INTERIOR

Bureau of Indian Affairs
North Central Region
Director's Office

DATE: 14 October, 1958

TO: Luther White Bear, Tribal Chairman,
Loon Lake Tribe of Ojibwe Indians

FROM: F. S. Zern

SUBJ: Audit Irregularities

Chairman White Bear:

Your audit of 4 October revealed several irregularities. You must contact my office within three (3) days of receiving this letter to schedule an appointment with the audit committee. Failure to comply will result in the immediate suspension of your elected tribal position and a federal investigation.

Respectfully,
Frank S. Zern
Regional Director

Cc: Deputy Director, Washington, D. C.

Chapter Sixty

When Mom arrived at school to pick me up, she looked taken aback. "Honey, you haven't been eating." She stepped back and held my face in her hands. "And it looks like you haven't been sleeping good, either. What's wrong, sweetheart?"

I was dumbfounded. Here she was, picking me up at school in the middle of October along with dozens of other confused-looking parents. "Mom!" I moaned, frustrated. "What do you mean, 'What's wrong?' "

Again she looked befuddled. It was obvious she hadn't a clue.

"Mom? Didn't they tell you why you're picking me up?"

"About the boiler? Yes—"

"The boiler!"

Her brow furrowed. "That's right. About the boiler breaking."

I pulled back in frustration. "Mom, the boiler ain't broken. It's got nothing to do with the damned boiler."

"You watch your mouth, girl."

I slapped my hand on the pickup's hood. "Jeez!"

Mom stood there a moment, staring at me in total confusion. "What's the matter with you? You get to come home for a week, and you act like you're sore about it."

I folded my arms, set my jaw. The school lied, and I was once again stuck with telling my mother the impossible. Well, not this time. I grabbed her hand and pulled. "C'mon,

Mom. I'll show you *the boiler.*"

We made our way through the crowd of parents and students and found Rose and Katie, coming up from the basement with Rose's trunk. "Rose, Katie. I need you for a minute."

We wended our way down the stairs, fighting the upstream current of girls struggling with trunks, then down the dimly lit hallway.

"Ruby," Mom said. "This is silly. I don't need to see an old boiler."

I pulled her down the passageway, then finally to the last door on the left, where I stopped short. The door had been recently fitted with a padlock. "Damn it!"

"Ruby!" Mom exclaimed.

"That wasn't there before," Rose said, glaring at the lock.

"Wait here," I told Mom.

She turned as I stalked back down the hall. "Ruby!"

I turned the corner and opened Mr. Muller's office door. Luckily, he wasn't there. I quickly scanned the small, cluttered room, eyeing the tools hanging from a pegboard. Then I spied what I wanted—a small sledgehammer standing on its head on the floor next to Muller's beat-up desk. I grabbed it, gratified by its heft, and headed back to Mom. "Stand back," I said as I approached the padlocked door.

Mom saw the hammer. "Ruby, what on Earth—"

Using both hands, I swung the hammer as hard as I could. The noise was amplified by the brick-and-concrete passageway. Splinters flew and the hasp holding the lock bent and was partially pulled from the wooden door. Mom jumped. "Ruby Loonfoot!" She reached for my arm.

I turned on her like a cornered badger. "Watch out!"

She hesitated, and I took another swing at the lock. This time the hasp tore loose from the door, leaving it and the padlock dangling from an eyebolt in the doorframe. I swung open the door. "There's your boiler, Mom!" I shouted, pointing to Mr. Muller's invention. I turned to look at Rose. "Tell her what it is, Rose! Tell her!"

The long ride home was mostly silent. Mom chain-smoked while she white-knuckled the steering wheel. Everything she believed had been suddenly defiled. I could guess the torrent of emotions boiling within her. Her eyes never left the road when she finally said, "You ain't going back there."

Jim Loonfoot was livid. "They did what?" He had driven all night to get home after he got Theresa's call through his dispatcher. "They put my little girl in a electric chair?"

Theresa sat on the sofa, her head hanging. Jim watched her a moment. "How long have you known about all this?" he asked accusingly.

She shook her head. "About the chair, just yesterday. The other stuff she tried to tell me last year, but I wouldn't hear it. I thought she was exaggerating, you know, the way kids do, to get out of school." She looked up at him, her eyes puffy. "How could I believe it—about the Church . . ." Her voice trailed off.

Strange. The bitterness he had carried in his heart against his wife seemed to wither away. After what had happened to Ruby, their own troubles seemed dwarfed, even selfish. What was important now were Ruby and Sue, their safety, their happiness, their education.

Jim took her hand, gently opened it to remove her handkerchief, then wiped away her tears. "Ruby needs us now, T. Sue, too. We gotta get them into public school." A shadow of sadness passed across his eyes. "We'll move to Hayward as soon as I can find a place."

"Oh, Jim," she said as he took her into his arms.

Chapter Sixty-One

Two days after my return home, Mr. Big Shield accompanied us to Gram's grave site at the reservation cemetery. It was a crisp fall day, the trees aflame with fiery reds, pumpkin oranges, and maize yellows. A few wispy clouds floated in a sky the color of a robin's egg.

Mr. Big Shield chanted the death song. We said several Ojibwe prayers. Then the Brave Rock Singers, who had come to honor Gram and our family, sang an honor song they had composed for her. The song would forever belong to our family. The sad thing was that Sammy wasn't with them. Mr. Brave Rock said he had run away from St. Paul's a month ago and no one had heard from him.

While Mom and Dad looked on, I laid a bunch of freshly cut fall flowers from Gram's garden on her grave. I asked Mr. White Bear in Ojibwe, "She has now taken her *babamadiziwin, eya?*"

Mr. White Bear smiled and clasped my shoulder. "All is *onishishin* now."

Once again, the air around me filled with the aromas of fresh-baked bread and sweet grass. In the past I had always been alone when the smells came. I turned quickly to my parents. "Do you smell that?"

Mom was teary-eyed, her hand covering her mouth in awe. "Yes, sweetheart, I do, I do smell it."

Sue was grinning and nodding like a jack-in-the-box.

"I smell it, I smell it."

We laughed and cried at the same time. Then I said, "Everybody, I found a special poem for Gram. I don't remember the poet, but I want to read it now while she's here."

I pulled the folded paper from my dress pocket. It's called *Her Passing*. I took a big breath and began:

"A last sigh on her lips,
her spirit released,
the world becomes blurred, unreal

"There's Grandfather smiling,
extending his hand,
knowing they would meet

"Now they are flying,
above the clouds,
the assurance of her grasp

"Up, up they fly
toward the brilliant light
Sparkles and shimmers,
spirits dance into sight

"Closer, closer
the spirits transform
People—HER people
as many as stars

"Red people,
the first people,
dance and sing,
their voices rise anew

"They're the old ones,
the chaste ones,
unspoiled by whites
Their shadowy whispers
heard only at night

"Ojibwe and Cherokee
Choctaw and Cree,
Apache and Micmac,
Kiowa and Creek

"Oh, how they dance,
five hundred drums
Heartbeats of nations,
beating as one.

"Grandmother dances
with beauty and grace
Like fronds in a current,
shawl swaying in space

"Moving so stately
she bows her head,
lifting her eagle fan
to each honor beat

"Grandfather is singing,
he leads the drum
His resonant voice
soars to new heights

"Now they beckon
with faces of light

They are her relations
who fought the good fight

"Grandfathers, uncles,
cousins and aunts,
freed from the fetters
of earthly life.

"Then countless others
she knows are her flesh,
tied by a sacred cord
to First Man and First Woman,
the sacred womb.
They show her the crimson road.

"Now they embrace her,
such rapture and peace
It's the end of her journey,
sacred circle complete

"She turns now to face us,
and speaks with her eyes

"Oh, what radiant feelings of love."

Epilogue

The BIA and the Church got their pound of flesh—Luther's. To stir things up on the rez, BIA Regional Director Zern had leaked the "accounting irregularities" information to the tribal council. Folks took sides. People Luther had known all his life turned on him. Earl Loonfoot called for his prosecution. Imagine that. Earl Loonfoot, a drunk and a man who bragged about having illegitimate kids on four different reservations. For Luther, it was either resign or face prosecution.

But Marvin Big Shield stood by his nephew. He told Luther that he knew "the 'blanket chiefs' cooked all this up just to make us start fighting each other again." He was right when he said the government liked to "keep the *Shinnobs* fighting among themselves so they forget about how the government's screwing them."

A week later the BIA named an interim tribal chairman. The announcement left us stupefied. It was Cousin Earl. We stood with the crowd as Zern shook Earl's hand and announced that Earl had successfully negotiated the grant for the Yellow Hill water project. Only Earl's immediate family and pals cheered. The rest of us looked on sullenly. I was sickened by the whole affair. I thought the world of Luther White Bear. As far as I was concerned, he was the best chairman we'd ever have.

Shortly thereafter Marvin called a meeting of the elders. They agreed to forgo the Yellow Hill water project for a school using the old tribal fire station as the structure. I asked Mr. Big Shield about the need for running water for the Yellow Hill people. He just smiled. "We can wait a while longer," he told me. "We're old and used to hard times, *eya?* The children, you are our future."

Unsurprisingly, by the way, after Luther quit we heard not another word about the so-called accounting irregularities.

The next day we moved to an apartment in Hayward, and Sue and I were enrolled in public school. Mr. White Bear left the following day to look for a job somewhere in California. He comes back from time to time to visit family.

Three weeks after I left St. Nicholas, it reopened. Harriet Sigwadja, who returned to St. Nic's, sent me a newspaper clipping from Doanville, the town near the school. The headline read: "St. Nicholas reopened after boiler troubles." Harriet said Father Blewett had retired, and Father Potts and *Kokoko* were transferred to other boarding schools, where they could "continue God's work." Sister Margaret remained as assistant principal.

Not long after, I received a letter from Rose Captain. She wasn't going back to St. Nicholas but instead was going to attend a BIA school. The exciting thing was that accompanying her would be her newly adopted sister—Katie Red Star Captain. Katie had donned lipstick so she could plant a kiss on the bottom of the letter.

Eleven months later we returned to Loon Lake for a very special ceremony, the opening of the Cecelia Pitwoniquot School. As we walked through the newly renovated firehouse, Marvin Big Shield leaned down and whispered. "Ruby, we got a special surprise," and he opened a door that read "Principal."

I almost fainted. Grinning at me from behind her desk and dressed in a very smart suit, was Miss Stephanie McMahon, once known as Sister Stephanie. Mr. White Bear had tracked her down and offered her the job before he left. During our joyful reunion I learned she had written Luther about the things that had happened to me at St. Nic's, and she told him that she was leaving the sisterhood. He had kept her letter and address.

Though we lived in Hayward, we often visited friends and family on the rez, attended socials and, of course, the annual Big Dance. In fact, the summer after we moved to Hayward I once again entered the *Wee-Gitche-Neme-Dim* shawl dance competition. I took great pleasure in Paula Gunhouse's pained expression as she watched me pick up first prize.

After graduating from the University of Wisconsin, I moved back to the rez. Now married—and yes, he's Ojibwe—with a son and daughter of my own, I teach English and music at the school named for my grandmother. Today, we even have our own community college and vocational school. As this book is completed, Loon Lake has produced a medical doctor, three nurses, a couple of lawyers, and an engineer.

After Dad retired, Mom got her wish and they moved closer to Milwaukee—near the new mall. But I'll never leave Loon Lake. It is part of me. Like Gram said, if I was gone too long I would "get sick or end up in trouble." She was right, of course. One cannot be too long away from the land that cradles the bones of her ancestors.

Glossary

Ahneen - greetings
Aho! - a pan-Indian interjection roughly meaning *It is good!*
Anama'ewikweg - nuns
Anishinabe - Ojibwe/Ojibway/Chippewa (Anishinabeg, plural)

Babamadiziwin - journey
Bagojininiinsag - legendary "little people" with mysterious powers who live near waterways
Bawajigaywin - vision quest
Beendigin - come in
Bekayaan! - hush!
Benays - thunderbird
BIA - Bureau of Indian Affairs (U. S. Department of the Interior)
Bigiwizigan - maple taffy
Biijiinag bakaanigeng oshkiniigikwe - girl's puberty ceremony
Bineshee Ogichidaw - Little Warrior
Boozh' - hello (short for boozhoo)

Chimook - a white person

Daga - please
Debise - enough!
Dedeens - blue jay (a gossiper)

Eya - yes

Fires, the Seven - see wee-gwas scrolls

Gaawesa! - no way!
Gaawiin gwayak! - Nonsense!
Geesis - the sun
Geget - true
Gikinoo - school
Gitche-Manitou - Great Mystery, Great Spirit (God)

Howah! - all right!

K'mishomissinaun - grandfathers
Kokoko - a mythical monster often used to frighten children into behaving correctly
K'okomissinaun - grandmothers

LCO - Lac Courte Oreilles reservation, northern Wisconsin
Little People - see Bagojininiinsag

Manitou-min-esag - beads used for decorative beading
Maengun - The Wolf
Makade majii-manitou - black devil
Manitouog - spirits
Manitouwaadizi - evil
Manomen - a wild rice dish
Meememgwe - butterfly
Midewiwin - society of holy men (often referred to as the Mide Lodge)
Misko-binesheenh - red bird (cardinal)
Mudji-keewis - a frightening storm being

Naagaj apee - see you later
Nagamoon—traditional prayers
Nanaandawii'iwewinini—one who practices traditional medicine
Neebageesis - the moon
Nimisenh - cousin
Nindaan - my daughter
Nisheeme - little sister
Nodinens - Little Wind
Nokomis - grandmother
Noozis - grandchild

Ode'imini-geezis - June (heart berry month)
Odo-iday-miwan - the clan system
Ogichidaw - warrior
Ojibwe tea - herbal tea believed to have healing powers. It has been found effective as a treatment for cancer, lupus, chronic fatigue syndrome, arthritis, diabetes, and many other illnesses. Also, part of a ritual intended to restore strength and balance
Ombay! - let's go!
Onishishin - good
Oon-da'dizoowin' - birth
Opwagun - pipe

Pagidaendijigewin - funeral ceremony
People, the - reference to Indian people or Ojibwe people

Roach - A head ornament worn by men and typically constructed of porcupine guard hair (not quills) and hair from the tail of the white-tail deer

Shinnob - Indian

Shkonigun - left over

Wabizhashti - martin - the bird or the clan
Waeginaen baebau-nindoyaek - what do you want?
Wawasum - lightning
Waybeenun - throw away
Wee-Gitche-Neme-Dim - big dance
Wee'gwas scrolls - sacred scrolls from ancient times that spell out seven prophecies (fires) concerning life stages that will confront the Ojibwe people
Wewaagijeezid - banana
Wisikodewinini - half-breeds

Zeegwung Waabigwan - Spring Flower

About the Author

Paxton Riddle lives in Connecticut. He holds a degree in American history. He serves as the Eastern Regional Director on the National Caucus of the Wordcraft Circle of Native Writers & Storytellers and is a member of the Western Writers of America.

Mr. Riddle's first novel, *Lost River*, published by Berkley (Penguin/Putnam), was a Western Writers of America double Spur Award finalist in 1999.

Lost River is a historical novel based on Riddle's cousin by marriage, Toby Winema Riddle, a Modoc Indian woman who distinguished herself as a liaison between the U.S. Army and her cousin, the war chief known as Captain Jack, in 1873.

The employees of Five Star hope you have enjoyed this book. All our books are made to last. Other Five Star books are available at your library, through selected bookstores, or directly from us.

For information about titles, please call:

(800) 223-1244

or visit our Web site at:

www.gale.com/fivestar

To share your comments, please write:

Publisher
Five Star
295 Kennedy Memorial Drive
Waterville, ME 04901